Devonmere

*To John
With my very best wishes*

Jacqueline Armitage

This is a work of fiction. Names, characters, places, and incidents either are the product of the author's imagination or are used fictitiously. Any resemblance to actual persons, living or dead, events, or locales is entirely coincidental.

Copyright © 2021 by Jacqueline Armitage

All rights reserved. No part of this book may be reproduced or used in any manner without written permission of the copyright owner except for the use of quotations in a book review. For more information, address: info@Jacqueline-Armitage.co.uk

First paperback edition 2021

Book design by Publishing Push
Cover Designed by Amy Corbin

ISBNs:
Paperback: 978-1-80227-328-1
eBook: 978-1-80227-329-8

www.jacqueline-armitage.co.uk

Table of Contents

Dedication..iv

Foreword...v

Chapter One 7

Chapter Two...51

Chapter Three..84

Chapter Four...120

Chapter Five..159

Chapter Six..188

Chapter Seven..213

Chapter Eight..227

Chapter Nine...242

Chapter Ten...257

Chapter Eleven...294

Chapter Twelve..305

Chapter Thirteen..335

Chapter Fourteen...342

Chapter Fifteen..366

Chapter Sixteen...376

Chapter Seventeen..402

Chapter Eighteen...411

Character Map...418

Bibliography..420

Dedication

For my dear friend Edward, who would have made a fantastic Duke Morgan Bodine. Taken far too soon from us all, and never allowed to reach his full potential on screen. Sorely missed and thought about every single day.

For Wendy, for her honesty and feedback; for pushing and bullying me to 'go for it'. Thank you, my dearest friend.

For Andy, my husband; who suffered my typing long into the night, and my 'weird' telephone calls to Wendy, about the project.

And finally, for my other friends who have supported me; Sarah, Dave and Kathy, who said they wanted a copy without even having a clue about what the story was about—apart from the fact that it was set in medieval times.

Thank you!

Foreword

God created man in his own image; they were one with the earth, the sea, and the air; and they flourished, although life was hard.

Then a faction grew that did not want the hard life, so they turned to stealing and taking what they wanted, and because of this, they lost their affinity with the elements. Over time, two separate races developed, the Kadeau and the humans.

The Kadeau stayed with the elements and were despised by the humans, for they had magic. Every year, their crops and animals flourished because they watched and listened to nature. Feeling they had suffered enough persecution from the humans, a few Kadeau rose up, and, using their magic, did some terrible things, but the humans retaliated and almost wiped them out.

Eventually, an uneasy truce arose; the Kadeau hid their powers, fearful of further persecution. The church tried to have any they found burned at the stake, but the rise of the Cantrell royal family stopped that from happening and they began to have Kadeau as royal protectors for the princes and kings.

Now finding favour, the Kadeau started to secretly infiltrate the church and began to grow in strength again, with some having titles bestowed upon them.

Our story is based several generations down the line. Stuart Cantrell is King of Devonmere and has a young son. His wife, Alexandra, hates the Kadeau and does not trust Morgan Bodine, the Duke of Rossmere, who is the King's Champion, General of the Armies and, of course, Kadeau, although he actually rarely uses his powers as much as he ought to.

Foreword

Unrest is growing. Nigel McDowell, the Duke of Cottesmere, has ambitions to rise above his station and is looking to overthrow Stuart Cantrell to claim the throne for himself; but to do this, he requires a substantial army and needs to weaken Stuart's supporters. One of his neighbours, Richard Coltrane, the Duke of Invermere, has a daughter who Nigel plans on marrying, but the King is against it and so is the daughter. Should the Duke of Cottesmere succeed, he will obtain a substantial army and put a stranglehold on the Duke of Rossmere—his neighbour to the south—further weakening Stuart's position as his general fights a war in his own Duchy.

Then he hears disturbing news; Bronwyn Coltrane, the Duchess of Invermere, is finally with child again, and it is rumoured to be a boy. The Duke of Cottesmere realises he has to act now, before the child is born. So, our story starts with Inver Castle under siege by a supposedly unknown force…

1

Chapter One

"Your duty, John, no matter what else happens this night, is to ensure Colwyn reaches Ellesmere and the protection of the king."

"But, your Grace—"

"Promise me, John!"

"I swear, on my vows as a knight and a loyal supporter of this family, that I will deliver her safely into the protection of King Stuart."

"Thank you, my friend. Take whatever route necessary to get her there; she must not fall into the hands of Nigel McDowell. Our attackers bear no herald, but I suspect he is behind this evil plot." Duke Richard Coltrane lowered his voice to a mere whisper. "We both know the situation, John. All I can say to you, my friend, is to thank you with all of my heart for your loyalty over the years. We've seen many a campaign together. It would have greatly honoured me to have you by my side now, but there is no one I trust more to take care of my daughter. Now, are you prepared for the journey?"

"Yes, Your Grace. The horses and supplies stand ready at the north-east exit, but I have grave reservations. Weather conditions are appalling—the mountain pass is blocked; we will have to cross the River Wyvern and travel along the High Hills, as I believe the low road will be under surveillance by McDowell's men. It will take us almost three weeks to reach Ellesmere in these freezing conditions. Your Grace, with the current weather conditions, I will not return for four, even six weeks, whereas if we went to the east, to Strathmere, it would take half the time and—"

"The old Duke of Strathmere does not have the strength of numbers to assist; it is too small a Duchy, and he has seen the last of his fighting days. I know young Giles would help, but he is still to be knighted and he is not yet the duke."

"Then let us try for Rossmere."

"No, Duke Bodine is not in residence, but carrying out the King's business far to the east. It must be Ellesmere. You must go now, John, before we are overrun."

"Father?" Colwyn lifted her riding skirt slightly and ran down the stairs towards them. "Father, I can't leave you... and what about Mother?"

"Daughter, you must leave. Your safety and well-being are of paramount importance to the stability of the Kingdom. Nigel McDowell wants you so he can claim this Duchy. Should he succeed, that will put a stranglehold on the Duchy of Rossmere and Duke Bodine will be facing a war on two borders, weakening the King's position. Your mother is too far advanced with child to travel; we will hold out under siege until help arrives from Ellesmere. Go now, Colwyn. God bless you and keep you safe. And... if anything should happen, then turn to the King for guidance. Sir John," Coltrane turned his attention back to his Master-at-Arms. "Take this and make sure it is delivered into the King's hand personally." He handed him a sealed scroll, which MacKenzie placed inside his aketon.

"Yes, Your Grace..." He faltered, knowing with dreaded certainty that he would never see his Lord and Lady again; that these unmarked assailants would gain access to the castle, murder the duke, the duchess and the unborn child, and seize Colwyn to deliver her to McDowell, where she would be forcibly wed to the ambitious duke. The situation had been brewing for

Chapter One

years, but the announcement that the Duchess Bronwyn was with child—a possible son and heir to Invermere—had, at last, he believed, spurred McDowell into action.

Bodine of Rossmere was the King's closest friend, King's Champion and General of his Armies. He was also the most feared man in the Kingdom, as he was a Kadeau with magical powers. It was said he could read minds and cast spells, although no one, apart from his closest friends and family, could say with certainty that they had actually ever seen him do any of these things. Without him, the Kingdom of Devonmere would be thrown into war. Even if Colwyn had liked McDowell, there would still have been no hope of a union between the two Duchies, for McDowell was rumoured to want to usurp King Stuart Cantrell. Obtaining Invermere would start him on his path. Colwyn, too, knew this. She hated the Cottesmere Lord and always did her utmost to avoid him at social functions. At home, when he visited, time after time, to request her hand in marriage, she feigned illness. Although McDowell was an attractive man physically, tall, dark-haired and brown-eyed, his aura and air made her exceedingly uneasy, for she sensed an evil within him.

Now the castle was under siege by an unknown enemy, but everything pointed to McDowell of Cottesmere.

Duke Richard Coltrane sensed MacKenzie's turmoil and surrendered to the moment, hugging the ageing knight fiercely. "My friend, take care of yourself, and my daughter." He released him and stepped back. "Now go!"

The Duchess Bronwyn, though heavily pregnant, still managed to walk with an air of grace. Her mahogany hair was plaited and pinned up; her hazel eyes almost sorrowful in her slightly heart-shaped face as she approached with Sarah, Colwyn's handmaiden.

"Mother!" Colwyn threw herself into Bronwyn's arms.

"Go, child; do as your father bids. Time is against us. Quickly now." She kissed her daughter's cheek. "Remember all that you have been taught and know that whatever happens, we love you."

"Colwyn, daughter." The duke opened his arms and she returned to him. "Be brave; be resilient. You will need all your wits about you. Go now." He too kissed her cheek and pressed something into the palm of her hand before he released her and indicated for MacKenzie to take her.

Colwyn looked down and found herself staring at the duke's ring—the seal of Invermere. Colwyn's eyes widened in horror and she looked back at her father in anguish. His handing to her of the ring meant only one thing; that he assumed he was to die. She stared at him as if to ingrain the memory of his features in her mind. His short brown hair, greying slightly at the temples; his kind, brown eyes, in a ruggedly handsome, square-jawed, clean-shaven face; the regal air. He may have given the impression of being almost easy-going, but he had seen many a battle with the young king's father and—to a lesser extent—with the younger King Stuart, and was one of the most trusted dukes in Devonmere.

Richard gave her that look, the one that indicated for her to behave as a Duchess, to hold her head high; be proud and show no emotion. Colwyn nodded imperceptibly, swallowed slowly and took a deep breath to regain her composure.

Sarah placed a warm, hooded black woollen cloak around her shoulders, fastening it as her lady stood, numb with the nightmare that was unfolding all around her.

The sounds of battle were growing ever nearer and at last, MacKenzie, began to move, taking Colwyn's elbow. "Come, my Lady," he urged and began to lead her towards the library and the secret passage, with Sarah following on their heels, carrying two oilskin saddle bags, that contained a change of clothing.

Chapter One

Colwyn still hoped that it would all turn out to be some terrible nightmare, but it was not so. She knew, as they crept from the castle via the secret exit with their small escort, that unless help arrived soon, all would be lost and it was this thought that kept her going. They had to reach Ellesmere! The Rossmere capital of Belvoir was closer, but with Bodine away on the far side of the Kingdom, help from that quarter was out of the question.

They were travelling light, with saddlebags containing clothing and one pack horse carrying food and supplies for twenty days. MacKenzie had decided to head for the cover of the woods and then turn north to the River Wyvern. The route was a hard one; trying on both man, woman and beast. The temperature was far below freezing and driving snow was falling, nearly blinding them. The only consolation was that the amount of snow falling was likely to cover their tracks within an hour.

He knew Colwyn was strong; he had seen to that. As a child, much to her father's horror, she had joined the young pages in the Pell who were training for knighthood. Yet Colwyn had enjoyed it so much that MacKenzie had continued to teach her in secret. She was a quick learner, graceful, supple and wielded a sword as well as any young squire of similar age. He had strapped her sword to her saddle, so it was close at hand, should she have need of it.

She was alone now and MacKenzie knew she had to be strong in both mind and body if she were to serve her people in a fair and just way. The Duke and Duchess of Invermere had been remarkable people. As the only heir, they had ensured that Colwyn had been taught to read and write and been given schooling in mathematics and in politics, sitting with her father when he held court. In her thirst for knowledge, Colwyn had even gone out to the people to learn about them, of their needs and way of life and about the land and its care. On the gentle side associated with her sex, her mother had taught her the needlework skills long-associated with Invermere and

Colwyn, in turn, had taught her people, holding classes for gifted childrenremarkable achievements considering she had not long turned sixteen.

In return, the people loved her. Something about her made them warm to her, but no one knew why. Perhaps it was purely her genuine concern for those around her and her willingness to help. Those who attempted to take advantage of her only tried the once. The red chestnut hair was a warning that Colwyn also possessed a fiery temper and a sharp tongue. It did not surface very often, but when it did, those who had displeased her were left in no doubt of their mistake.

MacKenzie smiled to himself, thinking back to how she had given the heir of Strathmere, the young Squire Giles Dernley, the sword-fight of his life because he had made an un-knightly remark about 'girls and swords'. From that moment on, that young squire had been devoted to her, much to her embarrassment.

Now he was here, in the special escort, attentive to her every need; keeping his horse close to hers in case of danger. If all went well, Giles Dernley would be knighted in June by King Stuart.

With the appalling weather conditions, it took the best part of two days to travel through the woods. They had taken the smaller, less-used track, rather than the road. The wood was thicker on this route, which actually made it more difficult to ambush anyone, because of the closeness of the trees and the dense, heavy undergrowth of dead leaves, twigs and other decaying matter, currently frozen in the cold conditions, but there was also less light to see by, despite the lack of foliage on the trees, which leant an ominous and menacing gloom to their surroundings. They travelled for five hours at a time, resting for one and then were permitted a rest for three hours in the thickest part, where the trees had offered some semblance of shelter from the driving wind and snow, but it was cold, wet and miserable, with no fire to

Chapter One

even provide an illusion of warmth. MacKenzie did not want to stay in one place for too long in case they were being pursued and also to prevent lethargy from setting in because of the freezing conditions. He looked around at the group. Sarah was sitting huddled with Colwyn, and Dernley was hovering close by. He had wrapped a blanket around both of them to help keep them sheltered. Four knights were standing guard and the other four were attempting to get some rest.

The next stage of the journey would be one of the most dangerous—the crossing of the River Wyvern. Most of the year, the river was wide but shallow. MacKenzie was hoping that the low temperatures would mean any excess water would be frozen in the High Hills and mountains beyond, and the level would still be relatively low, but it had been a long, wet winter. They would have to wait until they got there to see what the situation was. So, they had set off again in their pattern of travel.

Finally emerging from the thinning trees of the woods, they battled through the deep snow, eventually re-joining the main thoroughfare and moved north, towards the river. On either side of the road, there were open fields bordered by high bushes, which effectively marked the route. The snow had been blown into drifts against the bushes resulting in it only being about a foot deep on the trail, but several feet deep where it had been swept against the vegetation. It was eerily quiet; wildlife was sheltering below ground or deep within the woods, and the usual smells of the trees and fields were strangely absent. Even though the snow seemed to deaden any noise, the sound of a flowing river gradually became louder as they approached it, and finally, they reached the banks of the Wyvern. MacKenzie sat astride his horse, contemplating the scene before him. The level was higher than he would have liked and the water was flowing fast.

"What do you think, Sir John?" Dernley asked him.

MacKenzie sighed before answering. "It's higher than I expected, but we have no choice. McDowell must be following; he probably also has some men ahead."

"Won't he think we'll go by the Low Road? That has more shelter. Surely, he wouldn't think we'd take the High Hills, because of the women."

"That's what I'm hoping; plus, this snow has covered our earlier tracks, but we can't be certain of anything, especially anything to do with Nigel McDowell. We can't go further east to cross; the river banks will be too steep for the horses, especially in this weather, and we can't go west to the shallow crossing as it's too close to where the Cottesmere army may be." He indicated for the first two guards to attempt the crossing. If they made it, then they would all follow.

Nerves were taut as the two knights encouraged their horses to enter. Ears pricked, the destriers stepped uneasily into the freezing water. Their heads jerked up at the cold, but they were well trained and slowly continued. They stumbled a number of times due to the unevenness of the rocky bottom beneath their hooves but never lost their footing, and, minutes later, they were heaving themselves up the opposite bank.

That was good enough for MacKenzie. "Take it slowly; the current is fast and footing for the horses uneven." He looked at the women, suddenly wishing he'd made them dress differently; perhaps even disguised them in men's clothing; concerned their dresses could hamper them during the crossing, as the water level was higher than he'd anticipated. The two palfreys they were riding were smaller and much lighter in build than the knights' stallions and were likely to have problems, what with the water currently being the depth it was, so he made the decision to sandwich each of them between two knights, with another knight taking the lead and another bringing up the rear. Instructions issued, the first knight led the way with Colwyn and her two knights following.

Chapter One

Colwyn gasped in shock as the freezing water touched her booted feet and crept up her legs. She had never encountered anything so cold and found herself unable to control her shivering. Within a minute, she had lost all feeling in her legs.

Dernley glanced at her, concerned. A woman of gentle breeding should not have to suffer so—and they had at least ten more days of this journey to endure.

Behind her, Sarah's horse panicked and leapt forward, catching the knight's horse in front, which, in turn, leapt forward, barging into Colwyn's mount. The palfrey stumbled and lost its balance. Wildly, it thrashed around trying to regain its footing whilst Colwyn grimly hung on as tightly as she could, gasping as the freezing water totally drenched her.

"My Lady!" Sarah screamed as she watched both horse and rider disappear for a moment or two before the palfrey struggled up again.

Dernley reached out and managed to grab Colwyn round the waist and pull her off the frightened horse. Grimly, he held her tightly against him as he urged his mount forward, reaching the other side. He continued up the bank to safe ground where the first two knights were waiting. One quickly dismounted and took Colwyn from him, holding her as her numb limbs refused to support her. Behind them, the remaining riders reached shallow water and Colwyn's horse finally regained its footing and trotted up the bank.

"My Lady?" Dernley asked in a worried tone, dismounting. Colwyn was soaked to the skin and shivering violently.

"I-I'm al-all r-right, Giles," she stammered and gave him a feeble smile which was gone in an instant as her shivering took over. "I-I just c-can't feel m-my legs, they're s-so c-cold. I'll b-be all right in a m-minute."

"We need to find shelter, to get you warm," he stated.

"T-there's n-no t-time; w-we must c-continue."

"No. We must at least get you dry; in this chilling wind you will freeze to death," he insisted.

Colwyn shook her head. "J-just help me mount my horse," she said firmly. "Sarah," she turned her head to look at her handmaiden. "Are you a-all right?"

"Y-yes, my Lady."

"Then we shall keep going. Sir J-John," she called, "l-lead on."

MacKenzie admired her spirit but Dernley was right; they had to find shelter, so he despatched two knights ahead to see what they could find; a barn, a cottage; anything.

In the meantime, he indicated for four other knights to use their blankets to create a screen around her so that Sarah could assist her to change her clothes. The knights stood, arms outstretched, backs turned inwards to form a square. Sarah quickly obtained a change of clothes and within the screened-off square, assisted Colwyn to change. It was a difficult task because the clothes were so wet and beginning to freeze on her body, but eventually, the task was done. Dernley assisted Colwyn to remount her horse. A thick blanket was wrapped around her in an attempt to keep the chill wind at bay before they set off at a brisk pace to get the horses warm again. They were their most important asset and had to be cared for. Without them, they would all surely die.

They made reasonable headway for the next few hours. Their next obstacle would be the narrow pass at the High Hills, approximately a day or so ahead. It was the perfect place for an ambush, for it consisted of a sheer cliff on one side, a ledge, just wide enough for wagons to pass one another, and a sheer drop down to the River Elles below, which, at this time of year, if it wasn't frozen, would be a raging torrent with small cascades and rocky outcrops, and MacKenzie was very uneasy. He wanted to get through there as soon as possible.

Chapter One

The two knights returned just before nightfall and reported no sign of any habitat. MacKenzie was worried about his charge. Yes, they had all received a soaking crossing the river, but the men were used to such hardships. Women were not. He sat quietly on his destrier, frowning hard, deep in thought. Everyone watched as he tapped his gloved fist against his chin as if trying to loosen a memory deep within his mind. He was sure there was some form of shelter… and then, he remembered. His eyes suddenly lit up and they knew he had thought of something. The caves! On the other side of the narrow pass at the base of the High Hills. They could take shelter in the caves and even light a fire.

With renewed spirits, he urged them on through the night at a brisk walk. The horses could keep going for hours at this speed and it would be dangerous to attempt a faster gait. Overnight, they walked for six hours and stopped for one before journeying on again.

As the sun rose on the fifth day of their journey, MacKenzie could not help but notice the depression surrounding him. Warmth and hot food would do wonders for their spirits. The snow had stopped falling and the wind had died, making it feel a little warmer, but everyone knew it was still very, very cold. With the improved visibility, he stepped up the pace a little, wanting to get through the pass and to the caves before nightfall.

The sheer walls on either side of the pass caused an echoing effect, making it sound as if there was a large army travelling through it, with the sound of the hooves and the jangle of metal of armour and the horses' livery. The rear guard kept glancing behind them, just to make sure there was nothing following them, and they also kept looking up at the cliffs, constantly on the lookout for heavy overhanging snow; nervous that the noise could trigger an avalanche.

A few hours passed when suddenly, the sound of many hoofbeats approaching brought them to a halt. Everyone glanced back and saw a group of knights heading towards them, swords drawn.

"Women to the back!" MacKenzie ordered as the escort whirled as one, drew their weapons and stood ready. The battle was brief but vicious; the small group had been outnumbered three to one, but fortunately, most of Colwyn's guard were hardened veterans of war, with plenty of experience. Two of her knights were cut down in the ensuing battle. One had been slain and fallen from his horse to slither down the steep bank into the raging river below; the other lay against the steep cliff, dead, where he had fallen. It had been a close call, but what had won them the battle was Colwyn unsheathing the sword strapped to her saddle and killing one of the un-heralded attackers who had attempted to grab her horse's reins and make a run for it.

Calmly, she had cleaned the sword and re-sheathed it whilst her maid and the majority of the remaining escort looked at her in a mixture of amazement, disbelief and horror. Dernley looked at her in awe. Practising in the Pell did not prepare anyone—especially a woman—for the act of actually killing someone. MacKenzie was proud of her, for she had proved herself in battle, but he knew the realisation of what she had done would hit her hard. Consequently, he drove them on through the pass towards the relative safety of the caves.

The knights silently mourned the death of their fallen comrades; there had been no time to bury them; the threat of another attack was too high. Weather permitting, they would recover one body and search for the other when the current risk was past and Colwyn had been safely delivered to the King at Ellesmere.

They continued to pick their way carefully along the narrow pass, struggling through the occasional deeper drift of snow, their progress slow.

Chapter One

Night was falling when they arrived at their destination, every single one of them, tired, weary to the bone and thoroughly miserable. The caves went deep into a high limestone escarpment, and there were several entrances of different sizes, most of which were obscured by trees, bushes and other greenery during the summer, but at this time of year, with no leaves, they were reasonably visible. One of the entrances was large enough to get the horses through, so MacKenzie led the way on foot, leading his mount. Dernley followed, still mounted, ducking his head to avoid the low roof, leading Colwyn's mount. One by one, the others followed. The passageway led to a large higher-roofed chamber, large enough to accommodate them all, and they stood here, looking around, standing in near darkness.

The caves smelt damp but they were infinitely better than being exposed to the elements outside, especially on a bitter winter night.

Using flint and some fine grass that had been safely wrapped in oiled skin to keep it dry, MacKenzie lit a fire. A couple of the guards quickly scanned the entrance to the cave looking for suitable kindling and returned with a few meagre pieces of wood that would at least tease the fire into a small blaze and keep it going until they gathered more.

In the subdued light, it could be seen that a number of passages led off from the chamber they were in. Making torches from some wood and strips of cloth, the knights explored the immediate passages. One led to a chamber large enough to put the horses in, and Dernley found a smaller one the women could use as a private enclosure.

Quickly, he grabbed a blanket from his saddle, went into the smaller cave and spread it out on the floor, then he went back to the main chamber and assisted Colwyn from her horse. She was very quiet and listless and he was worried, fearful that she may have caught a chill. Sitting her down on the blanket, he rounded up another couple and placed them around her, before assisting Sarah down, bidding her join her Lady to keep each other warm.

Leaving them to the privacy of their little alcove, he set about finding more wood to get a good fire going so that the women could be warmed and they could all, at last, have something hot to eat.

MacKenzie supervised the escort, organising them into settling the horses down, collecting more wood and preparing food. They melted snow in a small container over the fire and added some salted meat, spices and potatoes, and let that boil until it was piping hot.

The smell of the spiced meal wafted through to the small alcove and Sarah left her mistress to find out if it was ready. Seeing one of the escort placing food on small plates, she quickly returned to Colwyn and bade her come through, but Colwyn shook her head and huddled further into the blankets.

Worried, Sarah returned to speak to MacKenzie. He stopped what he was doing immediately and went to the alcove. Moments later, he returned with Colwyn in his arms and placed her down near the roaring fire, hoping the heat would revive her. He motioned to Dernley to bring a plate of food and instructed the young squire that he was to force-feed his charge if she refused to eat anything.

Dernley immediately sat down by her side and whispered to her, "Please, my Lady, you must eat something to keep your strength and to help fight off any illness."

"I can't eat anything, Giles. I have no appetite."

"I will be in grave trouble if you do not eat something," the young squire pleaded. "Sir John is threatening me with all sorts. Surely you wouldn't want anything horrible to happen to me, after all the years we have known each other. Since you were the little girl who gave me the fight of my life?"

She smiled at him then, noting his light brown hair was once again falling over his forehead, now it was free of the coif. "You insulted me, sir."

Chapter One

"I did not! I simply said it was no place for a girl," he retorted, his brown eyes twinkling; his full lips forming a slight smile.

"I lost my temper then, didn't I?"

"Most certainly. You know, Sir John didn't scold me at all; he was too proud seeing that his secret pupil was doing so well."

"Father was furious when he found out."

"I know; we heard his voice from the other side of the castle," Giles joked. "But that didn't stop you from carrying on, though, did it?"

"H-how did you know?" Colwyn gasped.

"The way you wielded that sword earlier. You would have been far too out of practice to have fended off that fiend. Sir John is very proud; you have proved yourself in battle and worthy to wear the sword."

"To kill is against God's law."

"But the knight is sworn to uphold good and defeat evil on behalf of the Lord and his King. To defend the weak and be righteous in all things. You defeated evil this day; a noble act. Now, eat this; it will help warm you."

Dernley's words had eased her mind a little, and gallantly, she did as he asked, finding that it did in fact make her feel warmer and a lot better.

"I will light another fire in the alcove so you may have warmth and privacy this night. If you wish it, I shall stand guard over you," Dernley stated after she had finished her meal.

"The fire would be most welcome, but you will not stand guard, Giles Dernley. You will get some sleep, and that is my command."

He grinned boyishly at her as he rose to carry out his task, taking a burning branch from the existing fire to start the other. Colwyn knew that he cared a great deal for her; perhaps even loved her, but to her, he could be no more than the brother she had longed for and now, with the probable death of her parents, would never have.

Her heart suddenly grew very heavy and she felt the need for some privacy. Rising, she went to the alcove to see how the young squire had fared. The fire was burning brightly and would soon be hot enough to start heating the area. Quietly she thanked him and bade him join his companions. Sarah appeared, but Colwyn motioned her away. Only in private would she shed tears and allow some grief to come through.

In the end, she cried herself to sleep and was not aware when Sarah returned to check on her mistress. She saw the moistness on her Lady's cheeks and felt her own eyes suddenly start to sting with tears. She quickly retrieved Colwyn's wet clothes from the saddle bag and lay them out near the fire, hoping it would help them dry overnight. Task done, she quietly lay down beside her mistress and snuggled close to share body warmth.

The following morning, a little before dawn, Dernley crept into the alcove to awaken the women, but found Sarah already awake and gathering their few belongings together. Kneeling down beside Colwyn, he noticed her flushed features and the rasping sound of her breathing. He gently laid a hand on her forehead and was shocked by the heat that he felt there.

The coolness of his hand woke Colwyn, but she could barely open her eyes.

"My Lady is ill," he told her softly.

Gallantly, Colwyn pulled herself together, feigning cheerfulness. "Nonsense, I'm just tired, like everyone else. Are we preparing to leave?"

"Colwyn," Dernley insisted, not caring that he was not addressing her as etiquette dictated.

"I am fine, Giles, just give me a few moments." Her tone was firm—albeit a little shaky. "You will say nothing to anyone, is that clear?"

Dernley nodded slowly as she leant back and allowed her eyes to close again, but he had no intention of following her wishes. They were about to embark on the trail through the High Hills. This was their last chance to

Chapter One

make a change of direction to another destination. If Colwyn collapsed up in the High Hills, she would surely die. Making a decision, he nodded to her and left her and Sarah to prepare for the journey. In the main cavern, he cornered John MacKenzie.

"Sir John, I am gravely concerned about Colwyn. She is seriously ill and I fear she will not survive the journey to Ellesmere. We need to find a closer safe haven."

"When I last spoke to our Lady, she insisted she could go on."

"'Tis but an act, Sir John. Go see for yourself, whilst she is in an unguarded moment."

MacKenzie knew that Giles was very protective towards the young Duchess, but he also knew he possessed great integrity, despite his youthful years. Quietly, he approached the two women. Sarah did not look too well herself, but it was Colwyn who suddenly gave him grave concern.

She was obviously suffering from a fever for her features were flushed and she was shivering. Seeing her in such an unguarded moment, MacKenzie realised that she had managed to successfully deceive him for the past few days, for it was now clear that she was extremely ill and needed urgent medical attention.

He knelt down by her side and placed a hand on her forehead. The heat she was generating alarmed him.

Colwyn opened her eyes and looked up at him.

"Sir John?" she asked breathlessly, her eyes sparkling far too brightly.

"My Lady, why did you not tell me you were unwell?"

"I-I'm fine, Sir John, just very tired."

"No, Colwyn, you are ill."

Tears appeared in the over-bright eyes. "I have failed you, Sir John. I have let you down."

"Never, Colwyn. It is I who have failed you, but I will see you into safe hands, you have my word." He turned to Sarah and beckoned her closer. "And how do you feel, Sarah?"

"I fare better than my Lady, Sir John."

"Then take care of her."

MacKenzie took his leave of them and returned to where he had left Dernley.

"You are right; we will not reach Ellesmere," he said softly. "Our closest safe haven is Belvoir. The duke is not currently in residence, but I hope we will still be safe there. If we leave now, with luck, we can be there by tomorrow night."

The young squire nodded his acquiescence.

ප ඉ ප ඉ

Dernley rode close to Colwyn for the entire journey. MacKenzie kept up the gruelling pace, now very concerned at how ill Colwyn was. He knew she was strong, but the soaking in the river, the attack and just the shock of the events over the past number of days had finally taken their toll. By the time they reached Belvoir, night had just fallen and she was barely conscious, now cradled in the arms of the squire on his powerful stallion.

Bone-weary, they rode into Castle Belvoir, Ducal home of Morgan Bodine, King's Champion and General of the King's armies. The duke was not currently in residence, but elsewhere in the Kingdom on official business, however, MacKenzie was confident they would be safe, at least for a short while.

They were escorted to guest quarters; Dernley carried the unconscious Colwyn to her allocated room and a physician was summoned. The squire was dubious about his skills, but held his tongue. However, he became more

Chapter One

concerned at the statement that blood-letting was required to remove the bad humours.

"We need to get word to the King," MacKenzie whispered to Dernley as the physician carried out his work. "But I am loath to lose any of our escort with the duke away. I fear McDowell may have the nerve to come here—once he learns of our whereabouts—and try to take her from the castle."

"Then he will have to get past me," Giles stated grimly, his hand moving to the hilt of his sword.

"You, my young squire, will be a fine knight," MacKenzie replied patting his shoulder. "I think I will arrange for word to be sent to the King via one of Bodine's men. Keep watch."

"Yes, Sir John."

03 80 03 80

Duke Morgan Bodine reined in his powerful black stallion, bringing his guard to a halt. Something was not right, he was sure of it; he had an uneasy feeling in the pit of his stomach, and the hairs on the back of his neck were suddenly standing on end.

"Morgan?" Monsignor Colin McLeod, the duke's cousin questioned.

"There's something wrong," he replied, frowning.

"Up ahead?"

"No, at Belvoir. I've just got.... oh, call it intuition." He looked up at the night sky as if contemplating his next decision. "I was going to camp, but I think we'll press on. If we keep up a fair pace, we should be home by morning."

Decisively, he urged his stallion into a slow canter and the guard followed on behind.

As predicted, they arrived back at Belvoir just after dawn. Morgan's steward, Edward, warned of his impending arrival by a herald, was standing at the base of the steps to greet him.

"Your Grace, I wasn't expecting you back until sometime this evening, or tomorrow," he said, his face wearing a rather worried look, but slowly starting to relax now that his master was safely back; he had a feeling that things were going to get rather hectic.

"What's happened, Edward?"

"My Lord never ceases to amaze me with his intuition," Edward replied as he followed his duke up the stone steps. "The Lady Colwyn and her guard arrived late last night from Inver."

"Not a social visit, I take it?"

"No, my Lord. Sir John MacKenzie has stated the castle has been attacked by unidentified forces, but he believes it may be Nigel McDowell's doing. The castle was under siege when they left eight days ago, but he fears the duke and duchess have been murdered. Lady Colwyn is probably now the new duchess, but she is gravely ill. It does not bode well."

Bodine stopped in his tracks. The Coltrane's had been his second family; taking him in when he had been orphaned at a very young age, treating him openly with affection until the King had taken him into his service, starting as a page at the age of seven, then all the way through to knighthood and his current position: King's Champion and General of the King's Armies. Whenever he had returned to Inver for a visit, he had continued to receive that love; something that rarely happened elsewhere, due to him being a Kadeau with magical powers. During his formative years at Ellesmere, the former King's protector—also a Kadeau—had taught him how to use his powers and hone his skills, preparing him to take over the position when he was ready. Realising the youngster was truly gifted, his Aunt Mereli had also

Chapter One

trained him on the more complicated aspects of being a Kadeau and all that it meant.

The last time he had seen Colwyn nearly five years ago, she had developed a severe crush on the duke, which had increased his feelings for the family tenfold.

"I assume Colwyn is in the guest quarters?"

"Yes, Your Grace."

Bodine called back over his shoulder. "Andrew, Colin, with me, quickly! Edward, I need to despatch a messenger to Ellesmere immediately to inform the King of the situation, and please arrange some food; we're starving!"

"A messenger has already left for Ellesmere, Your Grace. I will arrange for food to be taken to the guest quarters for you," Edward said bowing, and he ran off to carry out his task.

Bodine nodded, then bounded up the rest of the stairs two at a time, Andrew and Colin on his heels, and strode briskly along the corridors and other stairs that led to the guest quarters.

A guard opened the door to the outer chamber for him as he approached and he walked in to find Sir John MacKenzie, eight knights and a squire standing nervously, guarding the door to the bed-chamber at the other end of the room.

"Sir John," Bodine said approaching the knight, hand outstretched.

"Your Grace!" MacKenzie looked and sounded surprised to see him. He took the offered hand gratefully, bowing respectfully. Now he had an ally to share his burden.

"My steward has briefed me on the situation and I have been told a messenger has already been despatched to Ellesmere to inform the King. What is the latest on.... the Duchess?"

MacKenzie shook his head. "It does not look good, my Lord. There is a physician with her now."

"Andrew," Morgan indicated for his battle surgeon to precede him through to the inner bed-chamber, McLeod still following on behind. He immediately noticed an older woman crying silently as she sat by the huge bed and recognised her to be Colwyn's handmaiden; he also saw the physician laying out his tools. The latter looked up as the three of them entered and paled considerably as he recognised the duke.

"Your Grace." He bowed nervously.

Bodine ignored him and indicated for Andrew to examine the Duchess.

"I-I was about to bleed the patient again," the physician explained.

"She's too weak for that," Andrew countered.

"You, sir, are a battle surgeon. I am the physician."

"I don't care what you are, you're wrong. My Lord," Andrew pleaded, turning to face Bodine. "Send the physician away, he will surely kill her if he bleeds her again."

That was good enough for Bodine. "You may go, physician," he ordered.

"But, Your Grace—"

"Out!" he said firmly and the physician grabbed his tools and fled, terrified at the expression that had appeared on the duke's face.

Bodine approached the bed and stood transfixed. Colwyn had changed considerably since he had last seen her. He had known that she would grow to be a beautiful woman but realised he'd underestimated how much, and felt a jolt of something shoot through him as he surveyed her finely chiselled features; the high cheekbones and full lips. It took him a few moments to pull himself together, then he watched as Andrew examined his patient.

Colwyn's pale, yet flushed features were covered in a sheen of perspiration that had also soaked her beautiful chestnut hair, turning it several shades darker. Her breathing was laboured and harsh and her body shivered in its fever.

Chapter One

Gently, Andrew placed a hand on her forehead and frowned deeply. "She is burning up. We need to get her temperature down quickly." He placed an ear to her breast. "There is fluid on her lungs." Andrew straightened up. "This is very serious, Morgan. We will need all the help we can get if we are to succeed in this." The battle surgeon gave him a knowing look.

Bodine nodded gravely. He moved to the older, fair-haired woman. "You are the Lady Colwyn's handmaiden... Sarah?"

"Y-yes, Your Grace, that is correct."

"Sarah, I need you to regain your composure, for there is much to do and quickly. Bathe your mistress with cold water to try and keep her temperature from rising further. Do you understand me?"

"Yes, Milord." She wiped her eyes and got to her feet, moving to a small table that held a basin of water and a cloth.

Bodine pulled Andrew aside. "Tell me what you need."

"The best thing we can do is place her in cold water to get her temperature down. I know it's rather unorthodox, but we haven't a lot of time. This is a desperate measure, but we have no other choice. I will also prepare a powder for her. Monsignor," he turned to Bodine's cousin. "I think we could do with all the help God has to offer as well."

McLeod nodded grimly, his blue eyes full of concern. "If you need me to do anything more practical, just let me know." He knelt down by the bed at Colwyn's head and bowed his head in prayer.

Bodine nodded, turned and returned to the outer room. John MacKenzie strode across to him.

"What news, Your Grace?"

"The situation is grave, Sir John, but all is not lost, yet. My battle surgeon has a plan of action."

"This is my fault. His Grace trusted me to deliver his daughter to the safety of the King, and I have killed her! May God forgive me!"

"It isn't your fault, Sir John. It's Nigel McDowell's. Colwyn is not dead yet. She has spirit, she's young and she's strong. Do not give up on her so easily. Now, I must arrange for a bath and water to be delivered here. It is a drastic measure, but one that Master Andrew believes is most likely to succeed to bring down her temperature."

"My escort can help."

"Leave them be, Sir John. You have had a hard journey. Rest. You will need it before you embark on the return journey. I will despatch my Captain, with a detail, at noon, to Invermere."

"Thank you, Your Grace."

There were several pages lurking in the corridor and Bodine issued various orders - one to arrange for the bath and water, another to locate the Captain of the Guard, and a third to make his steward aware that they may get an unexpected visit from Nigel McDowell.

That done, he returned to the bed-chamber to assist Andrew in any way he could. Bodine was determined that they would win the forthcoming battle; he could not bear to lose Colwyn. Sarah, he noticed, was bathing her mistress with a cloth dipped in cold water, dabbing at her face and neck.

His Captain of the Guard was the first to arrive. Bodine left the inner bed-chamber and issued orders that he should take a detail of men and head for Invermere at noon. A larger force would follow as soon as possible, but the captain was to despatch a messenger back with news of what they found.

No sooner had he left the room, when Bodine's steward arrived, breathless and agitated.

"Your Grace, the Duke of Cottesmere has arrived and is insistent that he see you."

Bodine closed his eyes briefly and took a deep breath. This he could do without, he thought, as he opened his eyes and noticed how Colwyn's

Chapter One

personal guard immediately got to their feet; their hands moving to the hilts of their swords.

"Did the duke happen to mention why we have this honour of this visit?"

"He says he is here for the duchess, and that it was her father's dying wish that she be looked after by him."

"He lies!" Sir John MacKenzie spat venomously. "I have written instructions on me that say Colwyn is to be delivered to the safety of the King!"

Bodine held up a hand to pacify the ageing knight.

"Have no fear, Sir John. He will be leaving empty-handed. I'd also be interested to know how the duke knew that Inver had been attacked, but that will have to wait. We need to get rid of him quickly; so we will extend him the courtesy of seeing for himself that the Duchess is in no fit state to go anywhere and, in fact, is not expected to last the day."

The guards looked horrified until Bodine added his final sentence.

"However, I may, of course, be exaggerating somewhat." A tiny smirk caught the corner of his mouth. "Very well, Edward. Escort McDowell up here. We'll let him see how ill the Duchess is."

"Yes, my Lord."

As Edward left, the wooden bath arrived.

"Hide that. We want McDowell to think there is no hope," Bodine ordered. The pages moved the bath to a corner of the room and threw several blankets over it to disguise what it was. "And hold the water until McDowell has left."

"Yes, my Lord."

Bodine turned to Colwyn's guard. "I ask that you remain calm. I assure you, McDowell will leave here alone. Please trust me." With that, he turned and went back into the inner bed-chamber.

Everyone looked up as he came in.

"We have an uninvited guest. McDowell is here. Colin, I need you to start administering the last rights. We need to get rid of McDowell as fast as possible."

McLeod nodded.

"Everyone else, look like this is the end for the Duchess."

His words must have carried to the outer room, for when he returned, he found most of Colwyn's guards kneeling on the floor praying quietly.

Several minutes passed and then heavy footsteps were heard approaching. The door opened and Edward announced: "His Grace, the Duke of Cottesmere."

Nigel McDowell swept into the room, spurs clanking on the stone floor, with two aides behind him.

"Bodine."

"McDowell."

There was clearly no love lost between the two men.

"To what do I owe the honour of this visit?"

"I was unfortunate to arrive too late at Inver to save the duke and duchess, but with his dying words, the duke begged me to take care of his daughter so, using my best men, I tracked her to this location. I am here to collect the Duchess Colwyn. Is she ready to leave?"

Both men ignored the fact that the Invermere Guard had stopped praying, got to their feet and placed their hands on the hilts of their swords.

"I'm afraid not."

"Then you will make her ready."

"I can't do that, McDowell."

The duke's dark eyes flashed with anger. "You are disobeying the last wishes of her father?"

"Yes, I am."

"By what right?" McDowell stepped forward.

Chapter One

"By the fact that the Duchess is gravely ill and is not fit to travel anywhere."

"You lie!"

Bodine ignored the insult and, instead, gestured towards the bedroom with his left hand. "You may summon your battle surgeon if you wish the facts to be verified."

McDowell, his face but a scowl, brushed past Bodine and entered the bedroom, leaving him to follow on behind.

The Duke of Cottesmere strode to the bed, pushing Sarah roughly out of the way as he did so. He eyed the praying McLeod suspiciously, before leaning over Colwyn's prone form. One look at her should have been enough to convince him, but McDowell didn't want to believe what he saw. He was convinced she was pretending; fevers could be faked, but he grudgingly realised that the sound of her breathing was real. It was rasping and bubbling in her lungs, the fluid building up in them, slowly drowning her.

He grasped her shoulders and pulled her up, feeling the fevered heat of her body under his hands. Limp as a rag doll, he found no resistance and realised what Bodine had said was indeed true.

Colwyn Coltrane was very near death. He let her drop back onto the pillows and stepped back, anger evident on his face that his plans had been thwarted.

Master Andrew pushed past him to make sure Colwyn was as comfortable as she could be.

"You are welcome to stay to the end if you wish," Bodine said softly, crossing his fingers that McDowell would not take him up on the offer.

"No. I have matters to attend to." He glared again at Bodine and stormed out, slamming the door behind him.

McLeod let go of the breath he had been holding and gave his cousin a look that implied he'd been lucky.

"We must act now, Morgan. She is deteriorating fast," Andrew whispered.

Everyone flew into action. The bath was brought in and many buckets of cold water poured into it. Andrew did his best to get the powder, now dissolved in wine, past her lips. It was a mixture of honey and many types of herbs and berries, known to have strong healing powers, but with Colwyn unconscious, it was proving extremely difficult.

"If only we could get her conscious, even for a minute, to get her to swallow this," he muttered.

"I'll see what I can do," Bodine whispered back. "I can't lose her, Andrew. I suspect she is the only member of the Coltrane family left… I won't lose her!"

McLeod ushered everyone out, save Andrew, and closed the door. It could be said that what Bodine was about to attempt went against the teachings of the church. However, McLeod felt that if he could help a young woman to live, God would not be angry. "You're clear to go ahead."

Bodine sat down on the bed and flexed his fingers. The procedure he was about to perform was risky at the best of times. With Colwyn in her fevered state, it could all go horribly wrong.

"Colin, stand by to pull me out just in case."

His cousin nodded and waited quietly. Master Andrew stood to one side, holding the potion, and watched the scene unfold as his duke prepared himself for what he was about to attempt.

Carefully, Bodine positioned his fingers at specific points on Colwyn's face. His thumbs rested just under her ears, the index fingers at her temples and second fingers on her eyebrows. The remaining fingers steepled together on the top of her head. Checking once more that he was positioned correctly, Bodine closed his eyes and let his mind go blank, using his powers of

Chapter One

concentration to slow his heart right down, and enabling him to reach out a gossamer tendril of thought towards his patient.

The strength and power of what he encountered turned out to be far stronger than he anticipated. Colwyn's fevered mind was living a nightmare of jumbled images and wild imagination. As the wave slammed into Bodine's mind, the duke visibly reacted as if he'd been struck and gave a gasp of shock. The images were flooding through his mind faster than he could take them in and seemed to be spiralling out of control; his handsome features contorted in pain.

Morgan? McLeod's concerned voice broke through on a lower level.

I'm all right, he threw back and gritted his teeth in a determined effort to take control of the situation.

In his mind, he called out to Colwyn, trying to get her to respond, but she didn't seem to be listening or able to hear him. It took him several attempts and then with one final monumental effort he blazed into her mind. *Colwyn!*

As one, their eyes shot open and Bodine gasped as he met the fevered gaze in Colwyn's. Their green colour was so bright, it almost blinded him in its intensity, but she appeared to be conscious.

"Andrew, hurry…. I can't hold her here long…"

Andrew stepped forward and deftly managed to get the potion down her. "Done," he said triumphantly and watched as Bodine withdrew, bowing his head to recover himself as he broke contact.

"Are you all right, Morgan?" McLeod asked anxiously.

The duke took a huge breath, held it and then slowly let it go. "That was…different," he finally managed to say. "The power of her mind was truly amazing."

"That was the fever, I assume, or are you trying to tell me something else?"

"No, it was the fever. I didn't detect anything else if that's what you're asking. No magical Kadeau blood in there; no tell-tale sign or anything."

"A pity, really," McLeod said. He was also a Kadeau, but that was a secret never to be revealed, outside of a few friends and the King, as Kadeau were not allowed to be in the church.

Bodine shrugged his shoulders. He was feeling a little 'odd'. That was the only way he could describe it, but he put it down to what he had just experienced. Already, his subconscious was beginning to sort out the jumble of images that had assaulted his mind. Later, in the privacy of his own rooms, he would analyse and try to make sense of what he had seen. The one thing that still did burn in his mind was the memory of Colwyn's fevered green eyes, staring—albeit unseeing—into his. It had shaken him to the core, but he had no understanding of why. This too he would ponder, but for now, they still had a life to save.

Standing, he quickly removed his sword belt, surcoat belt, surcoat, cuirass and hauberk, letting them drop to the floor. He pulled back the covers on the bed and lifted Colwyn into his arms. The heat of her body was incredible as he held her limp form close to his. He turned and walked to the bath of cold water and carefully lowered her into it, watching as she responded in her unconsciousness to the shock of the cold water.

The fine silk of her chemise turned almost transparent in the water and Bodine felt his body respond to the sight of her breasts and the hardened nipples under the near-translucent material.

She was beautiful, he could not deny the evidence, and his body honoured her with its response, but now was neither the time nor the place, and he clamped down on his emotions, desperately trying to get himself back under control before his cousin or Andrew noticed something was wrong.

His reaction shocked him. Never had he responded to a woman in such a way and he wondered why it had occurred with Colwyn, but all he could

Chapter One

do was make conjecture. It could be nothing more than the fact that the Coltrane family had shown him nothing but affection all his life, which he had gratefully accepted and returned, or... it could be something more. He shied away from the intimate thoughts, not ready to contemplate those. Instead, he turned to Andrew.

"How long must she stay in here?"

"To be honest, I'm not sure. Let's see how it goes."

There was a respectful knock on the door.

"Come."

A page appeared at the threshold. "There is food and wine, Your Grace, as you requested."

"Thank you, Toby. We'll be there shortly."

The young page nodded respectfully and exited, closing the door behind him.

Bodine turned to his two companions. "Well, I don't know about you two, but I'm starving. Go and get something to eat. I'll stay with Colwyn until you come back."

The other two nodded and did as he suggested.

Thirty minutes later, everyone, including Colwyn's personal guard, had eaten their fill.

Andrew checked on Colwyn; she was looking less flushed. "I believe she has been in a sufficient amount of time."

Bodine lifted her from the water, Andrew and McLeod immediately wrapping her in blankets to dry her off and Bodine averted his eyes respectfully whilst her sodden clothing was removed and a fresh garment put on. When he, at last, dared to look again, Colwyn was safely tucked up in bed.

"What happens now?" he asked of Andrew.

"We wait," came the simple reply.

Bodine nodded thoughtfully. " Let me get out of the rest of my armour and I'll take the first watch. Why don't you two get some sleep? We were up all night, and this is going to be a very long day. If I need you, I'll send one of the pages to fetch you."

"If it's all the same to you, Morgan, I'd like to stay close by. Things are going to get worse before they get better," Andrew said quietly.

"Why not take the next guest room then? You'll not be disturbed by Colwyn's guard and you're close enough if I need to call you."

Andrew nodded.

"Would you mind some company, Master Andrew?" Colin asked. "I, too, feel I should be close at hand."

"Of course."

Bodine saw them out of the inner chamber and went to speak briefly to Sir John.

"I have been informed that the situation is likely to become worse before it gets better. My surgeon is only next door, but he has already been awake for over thirty hours. He needs to rest if he is to be of use in the darkest hours. We will take turns on watch. Get as much sleep as you can. I will summon you if necessary."

"Surely, my Lord, you too have been up that length of time?"

"True, but I can last long enough to give you all a few hours' sleep." Bodine returned to the inner chamber and began to remove the rest of his armour. The spurs, chausses, and finally the padded aketon, leaving him in boots, leather breeches and silk shirt with his tailored jerkin over the top. Now feeling several pounds lighter having removed all that metal from his body, he once again sat down by Colwyn. Not really sure whether to keep quiet or not, he began to talk softly to her, retelling stories of old that he thought would interest her, whilst continuing to bathe her face and neck with a cool wet cloth.

Chapter One

She had changed a great deal since he had last seen her almost five years ago. Several inches taller, her girlish body had blossomed into that of a young woman and her features were more beautiful than Bodine could have imagined. The man who finally claimed her hand in marriage would indeed be blessed—if she survived.

His thoughts drifted back to the final visit he had made to Inver five years ago. At that time, he had recently won the title of King's Champion and was going to be made General of the King's Armies once they returned to Ellesmere.

They had arrived at Inver amid a great deal of pomp and circumstance. Numerous colourful banners of the attending Duchies were flying, with the King's rampant red lion leading the procession, and his own golden dragon following close behind. Flags and pennants adorned the ramparts of Castle Inver in welcome, and the duke and duchess were standing at the foot of the steps to the main keep to greet their royal guests.

Bodine was riding the young, now almost fully trained black stallion that the King had presented to him on his fifteenth birthday. The stallion was black as the darkest night, and Bodine had chosen to dress in dark, sombre colours. Most people feared him, even though he was just seventeen, because of what he was, and he had decided to cultivate that air of fear in the way he dressed. Even the golden dragon of Rossmere was on black. He was a serious young man who seldom laughed or smiled; his eyes were usually a steely grey, giving nothing away in their expression, and were often piercing, conveying the impression that he was reading the minds and souls of those who fell under that gaze.

He noted his 'sister' was not in the welcoming committee, and his thoughts turned to her, wondering what she looked like now, after his five-year absence, and whether she would still welcome him as a brother.

Dismounting, he handed the reins of his horse to one of the appointed pages and waited for his Liege.

Richard and Bronwyn Coltrane bowed and curtsied as the King and Queen reached them, then the duke shook hands with his sovereign, and then it was his turn. Coltrane shook his hand warmly, clasping his hand with both of his; then Bronwyn had hugged him and kissed his cheek, whispering words of welcome in his ear, which had made him smile at her before he once again donned his usual, serious expression.

He felt a sudden urge to look up to where he knew Colwyn's rooms were situated and did so. Even at this distance, he could almost see the joyful expression on her face, and he could most definitely feel the warmth of love flowing from her. Their eyes locked and Bodine gave her the slightest of nods in acknowledgement, smiling inwardly as she had clasped her hands in delight and inclined her head, before returning his attention to the matters at hand.

That evening, he had presented her with a collection of silk threads and had been almost overcome by her outpouring of love for him, along with Bronwyn's comment that she was proud to consider him her son. It had actually been a visit that he had never forgotten; not because of the overwhelming feelings of affection his adopted family had continued to bestow upon him, but because of the event that had occurred in the hidden room behind the library, when he and Colwyn had taken refuge from the Duke of Cottesmere, and she had asked him to teach her some magic.

It was also at that visit, that he had become aware of the Duke of Cottesmere's interest in his 'sister' and had his first sword fight with the man who was eight years his senior. Although Bodine was the King's Champion, no one expected him to win against Nigel McDowell, but he had, much to the duke's anger, for his record had been broken by the young upstart, and the seed of animosity and hatred between the two dukes had been sown.

Chapter One

The hours passed and Colwyn's breathing became more ragged and harsh as she fought for every breath. Concerned, Bodine leant over her, thinking desperately what he could do. Then he remembered Andrew's words - *Her lungs are filling with fluid.* He frowned in thought, then moved to place his arms around her and pulled her into a sitting position. After just a few seconds, her breathing improved slightly. Sitting her upright appeared to let her breathe a little more easily. Bodine hoped this would buy her more healing time as the potion Andrew had given her got to work.

He had been sitting with her in this position for another hour or so, when Andrew appeared, carrying another potion.

"It's easier for her to breathe sitting up," Bodine replied seeing him frowning.

Andrew nodded in understanding. "I will make a physician of you yet!" he teased. "Let's see if we can get this down her. It's rather stronger than I would usually make, but I'm hoping it will work faster."

Colwyn's head was cradled into Bodine's shoulder. Gently, he eased it around and Andrew tried a few drops at a time, finally managing to get her to take the whole dose.

"Do you want me to take over?"

"No. Go get some more sleep, I really want to stay until I know for definite that she's over the worst of it."

"It could take a while, Morgan."

"I know, but I have to stay. I promised Bronwyn I would look after her daughter." Unconsciously, he brushed a stray lock of hair away from her eye, and kissed the top of her head.

Andrew nodded, and left quietly.

More time passed and Colwyn began to shiver, even though she felt very hot. A small moan escaped her lips and she huddled closer to Bodine, as if seeking warmth. Gently, he reached forwards towards the end of the bed and managed to grab a couple of blankets that had been draped on the edge, then he carefully wrapped them around her. Colwyn snuggled into them, her right hand clutching tightly to Bodine's jerkin.

Sir John appeared in the doorway. "My Lord, is there anything I can do?"

"Yes, get some more blankets. We'll keep piling them on until she stops shivering… this may be the turning point of the fever."

They kept adding blankets until Colwyn had nearly disappeared under them. By rights, she should have been roasting hot, but she still shivered. Her low cries of despair tore at Bodine's heart as he watched her struggle for her life. Regular doses of the potion were given and then, on the dawn two days later, she finally gave one last jagged breath and it suddenly went very quiet.

Bodine, who had been on the brink of dozing off, having exhausted himself using magic to keep himself alert, suddenly jerked awake; the silence deafening. Suddenly fearful, he threw the blankets back, shouting for Andrew at the same time, and moved so that he could face her. Colwyn's flushed face seemed at peace; the bedclothes underneath her were sodden where she had sweated in fever. Andrew came rushing in, felt for a pulse and, after what seemed like an eternity, let go of the breath he had been holding.

"The fever has broken. She's sleeping."

Bodine bowed his head and offered a prayer of thanks to the Lord for sparing her life. Suddenly, he realised that he could not have stood the heartache of losing Colwyn, the last of the Coltrane Duchy.

"Now, I insist you go and get some real sleep," Andrew told Bodine. "You're all in, and you've got to be ready to ride in a day. The King should be arriving shortly. Colin, Sarah and I will take care of Colwyn."

"Oh, Lord, yes." He took a deep breath. "If I'm needed, I'll be in my private rooms."

Sir John met him at the doorway of Colwyn's room. "Your Grace?"

Chapter One

"The fever has broken, Sir John. Colwyn is sleeping."

"Praise be to the Lord," MacKenzie said emotionally as he turned and smiled at the rest of the guard, his eyes resting on Giles Dernley's face. The young squire seemed to have aged years in a few days, but suddenly, at the joyous news, he was miraculously young again.

"Thank you, Duke," Dernley said emotionally.

"No, don't thank me, thank Master Andrew. It was his potions that did the work. Now excuse me, gentlemen. I must get some real sleep. The King should be arriving shortly and we have a hard journey ahead of us."

He left Master Andrew, Colin and Sarah to take care of Colwyn and headed to his rooms, carrying his armour over his left arm.

Bodine was exhausted and tired beyond measure. The long ride back from the Marches, nursing Colwyn and using his considerable powers to bring her back from the brink had taken their toll, both physically and mentally. He so wanted to take the time to analyse the kaleidoscope of images that had bombarded his mind when he had touched Colwyn, but the King would be arriving in a few hours, and he would be required to ride with him to Invermere. Unless they had been granted a miracle, the duke and duchess were probably already dead, along with Colwyn's unborn brother. His tiredness proved too much and he fell instantly into a deep sleep.

○₃ ₰ ○₃ ₰

It was early evening when the herald alerted Belvoir Castle to the arrival of King Stuart Cantrell. He had brought a considerable force with him, and was also accompanied by his brother, Prince Michael.

Edward made his way to the duke's rooms to inform him of the King's impending arrival, but the herald had already woken Bodine, and he had dressed and was just fastening his sword belt when Edward knocked on his door and entered.

"Thank you, Edward," he said before his steward had even uttered a word. "I heard the herald." He smiled slightly as the man promptly shut his open mouth.

"Your Grace, I sometimes wonder if you really do need me at all!"

"Oh rest assured, I most certainly do. There is no other I would trust with my estate in my absence."

Edward's chest swelled with pride at the compliment. "Shall I bring the King to the guest quarters, my Lord?"

"Yes, please, Edward. I will meet you there."

"I shall also see that food and wine are prepared in the hall," Edward added as he bowed slightly and left.

Fifteen minutes later, the door to the guest quarters where Colwyn and her guard were staying was opened.

"His Majesty, King Stuart and His Royal Highness, Prince Michael," Edward announced formally.

Everyone knelt respectfully. Bodine stepped forward to kneel at his King's feet and kissed the ring on the sovereign hand.

"My Liege, welcome to Belvoir."

"Thank you, Morgan. Please." He indicated for everyone to stand. "Tell me, what is the current situation?"

"The Lady Colwyn rests easily now; her fever broke this night gone. Master Andrew believes she will recover. As yet, I have had no word back from my scouts, but I fear the worst for the Duke and Duchess of Invermere. Quite soon after Lady Colwyn and her guard arrived, McDowell paid us a visit and attempted to take her, saying it was her parent's dying wish that he look after her. He was persuaded to leave. Sir John has documents he has been instructed to deliver into your hands alone."

Stuart nodded and motioned John MacKenzie to join them.

"My Liege."

Chapter One

"Sir John." Stuart held out his hand to shake the elder man's warmly. "I am sorrowed that we should meet in such harrowed circumstances. I believe you have something for me?"

"Yes, Sire." MacKenzie reached into his aketon and retrieved the document, carefully unwrapping it from its oilskin covering before placing it in the King's hand.

Stuart glanced at the Invermere seal before firmly breaking it and unrolling the scroll.

My Liege

I have asked Sir John MacKenzie to deliver this communication personally into your hand as there is no other—apart from the Duke of Rossmere—that I trust. You have been a wise and true King and I have deemed it an honour to serve you these past years. Now I ask you as my sovereign and friend to assign your protection to my daughter, the Lady Colwyn.

The Castle Inver is under siege by assailants unknown; they bear no arms or identification, but we both know the most likely suspect. The Duke of Cottesmere has long cast envious eyes on the Duchy of Invermere and has been attempting to gain the hand of Colwyn in marriage. This would be an extremely dangerous and unwise liaison, for McDowell has great ambitions. The stranglehold that such a union would inflict on Rossmere would leave the rest of the Kingdom vulnerable to attack from two fronts and throw you into a war that would be long and bloody, undoing all the good you have achieved.

With a possible son and heir to the Invermere Duchy soon to be born, McDowell has had no alternative but to act now to ensure that the only kin is a woman, whose lands will go to the man she weds.

Both the Duchess Bronwyn and I would wish that Colwyn could have, perhaps, another two years or so before a husband is chosen for her. We trust your judgement in this matter and Colwyn has been instructed in the correct etiquette. Her future I place in your hands.

I hope that I may be allowed to be forward at this dark time, to call you friend. May God be always with you and the Cantrell family.

Your humble and obedient servant
Richard Coltrane
Duke of Invermere.

Chapter One

There had been a grim silence whilst the King had read the document. The only sign of emotion had been the hardening of Stuart's mouth and a slight muscle twitch in his jaw. He looked up, carefully rerolled the letter and placed it within his own aketon.

"My Liege, food and refreshment will be ready shortly in the hall," Bodine stated softly.

"Good. We will leave at dawn tomorrow morning and make all haste to Inver Castle."

"Yes, Sire." Bodine nodded to Edward, who left immediately.

"May I see Colwyn?" Stuart asked.

"Of course, Sire, although I believe she still sleeps." Bodine indicated the inner door towards the bed-chamber.

As the doors opened to admit the King, both Andrew and Sarah, respectfully, got to their feet to bow and curtsey.

"Master Andrew, how fares the Lady Colwyn?"

"Sire, I am hopeful the Duchess will recover, though I cannot, at this stage, say how much. Her fever was great and prolonged; there may be some damage to her…faculties."

Bodine looked at him sharply. Andrew hadn't mentioned this possibility before.

"Then I shall offer a prayer on her behalf," said Stuart, approaching Colwyn's bedside. He looked down at her pale and somewhat gaunt features before carefully taking one of her small, delicate hands in his and bowing his head. No one could hear the words he uttered apart from the Amen; then he released her hand and crossed himself. "She must make a full recovery," he stated and left the room, Bodine and MacKenzie on his heels. "Do we have any idea of McDowell's whereabouts?"

"No, Sire, although I have despatched a number of scouts who have orders to get news back to me, should there be any sighting of him."

"Excellent, Morgan. I want to know what McDowell is up to."

"Yes, Sire. However, there is one thing that concerns me greatly; how did McDowell know that Inver was being attacked unless he organised the attack in the first place?"

Stuart looked at him, a thoughtful expression on his face.

Whilst they supped in the hall, plans were finalised. "We shall leave at dawn tomorrow. Sir John, I ask that you ride with us. However, the rest of your guard will stay here with the Duchess. Should she recover enough before we return, I would like her to be escorted to Ellesmere. The Queen will be anxious to receive the Lady Colwyn into her care. I will also leave a small detachment of my men as additional protection."

"As you command, my Liege. Please excuse me whilst I issue instructions to the guard." MacKenzie bowed and left the head table to go to where the Invermere guard sat.

Giles Dernley looked up as his mentor approached.

"You are all to stay with the Lady Colwyn. The King is also leaving a small detachment. If Colwyn is fit enough to travel before we return, you are ordered to go to Ellesmere, where the Queen will be waiting for your arrival. It is her wish that Colwyn be delivered safely into her hands as soon as possible. I am returning to Invermere with the King and Duke Bodine. We will be leaving at dawn tomorrow, so, I shall wish you all a safe journey to Ellesmere." The guard nodded and wished him well. "Giles, a word if I may."

The young squire left his seat and walked with Sir John.

"I know I have no need to say this, but I am leaving Colwyn's well-being entirely in your hands. I know you have a fondness for her and will look after

Chapter One

her, but do not let her bully you. Delay not a moment. As soon as she is well enough to travel, leave for Ellesmere."

"Very well, Sir John, you can rely on me."

"I know, lad. I think it best that Colwyn will have the support of the Queen when we return and confirm the worst. We both know that the duke and duchess are dead, but I believe Colwyn still holds onto that last thread of hope. If we are going to break it, then she should have comfort from her fellow women, not us rough knights."

"Yes, Sir John. A safe journey. I hope the news will not be as bad as I fear but…" Dernley's voice trailed off. He didn't want to finish the sentence.

MacKenzie placed a hand on his shoulder and gave it a gentle squeeze of reassurance.

Guest quarters were assigned to the King and Prince, and the rest of the army bedded down for the night. Before retiring, Bodine instructed Master Andrew to stay and care for the Duchess. It would be he who would advise when she would be ready to travel to Ellesmere, as it was feared Colwyn might play on her illness to stay until they returned. Bodine issued various instructions to his steward before turning to have a word with Giles Dernley.

"The Coltrane family have been very kind to me over the years. I am putting my trust in you to see that Colwyn is safely delivered to Ellesmere. I know you will guard her with your life. Perhaps, when we return, I will be able to speak to you further. I understand you are to be knighted this midsummer?"

"Yes, Duke. I will not let you down, for I care for Colwyn a great deal."

Bodine nodded and looked at him contemplatively before retiring for the night.

Everyone was up well before dawn to eat and prepare for departure. It took a while to put on all the layers associated with wearing armour, and

Bodine had quickly paid a final visit to Colwyn to check on her before putting his on. He sat on the edge of the bed and spoke softly.

"We leave for Inver shortly, Colwyn. I am praying, but I fear we are far too late. I promised your mother I would take care of you, and I shall." He leant down and placed a soft kiss on her forehead. "When you are well, you will be delivered to Ellesmere for your safety. McDowell has started his war, and you are in danger. I will return to you as soon as I am able." He gently stroked her hair, then stood up and went to dress for travel.

Dernley and McLeod were waiting at the bottom of the steps as the King, the Prince, Bodine and MacKenzie came down them.

"Giles, ensure Colwyn reaches Ellesmere safely," Bodine said quietly. "McDowell has effectively declared war on the Kingdom and Colwyn is a vital key in his plan."

"She will get there safely, Duke. I give you my word."

Bodine nodded. McLeod came forward and shook his cousin's hand.

"God's speed, Morgan. I will pray for you all."

"Thank you, Colin. I ask that you also watch over Colwyn; she may need comfort when she learns she is not returning to Inver."

"I will be there, ready."

Bodine nodded and turned to mount his horse.

"God's speed!" several cried as the King led the way from the castle.

2

Chapter Two

Colwyn drifted in and out of consciousness for a number of days after the army had departed, and it was on a freezing, mid-February morning that her eyes finally opened. Her mind was a jumble of confused images and especially of a pair of grey-blue eyes, looking at her intently. She felt tired; exhausted, but at least she was warm and comfortable in the bed. The surroundings were unfamiliar; had they reached Ellesmere after all? If the truth be known, she had not been aware of anything since they had left the cave.

She turned her head to see Sarah looking worn and haggard, even in sleep, a frown deeply etched on her face. Why was she not sleeping on a cot or in a bed instead of looking so uncomfortable in that chair? Colwyn attempted to move but was shocked to find she did not have the strength and moaned in frustration.

Sarah jerked awake from her sleep and saw that her mistress was at last conscious. "Oh, oh my Lady Colwyn!" she wept and threw herself down from the chair to hug her mistress. "Praise be to God!" She sobbed loudly causing the door to open and a stranger to peer in.

"Sarah?" the man asked.

"Oh, Master Andrew, 'tis my Lady, returned from the dead!"

Colwyn tried to register what had been said. *Master Andrew? Returned from the dead?*

"Where…?" she whispered hoarsely.

Sarah straightened up as Andrew came to examine her mistress.

"Hello, my Lady; welcome back to the land of the living. You have been seriously ill this past week. I am Master Andrew, the Duke of Rossmere's battle surgeon; we last met a few years ago. You are safe here at Belvoir Castle."

Belvoir? Then they had failed to reach Ellesmere. Her face became stricken. "The Duke…"

"Is not here, my Lady. He left with the King and the King's army for Invermere several days ago."

"What news?"

"None, I'm afraid, my Lady. His Grace dispatched a guard immediately, but he will intercept them on route before they return here. I'm sorry. I wish I had some news to give you, but I have none. Now, we need to get you well again. The Queen awaits your arrival at Ellesmere."

"No, I'm not going. I will get well and return to Inver Castle; my people will need me."

Andrew said nothing. He decided it was better not to argue with her at this time. Her thinking she would return home would give her the incentive to get well, but when the time came, she would be forcibly moved to Ellesmere.

"I will arrange some food for you." Andrew bowed and went to the door where he was met by Giles Dernley.

"Master Andrew?"

"She is awake."

Dernley's face lit up and he smiled for the first time since they had arrived at Belvoir. "May I see her?"

Chapter Two

"For a little while. She is under the assumption that when she gets well, she will be returning to Inver Castle. Do not say otherwise at this time. This will give her the incentive to get well."

"I understand. Thank you, Master Andrew." Gently, he knocked at the door before opening it to see Colwyn propped up in bed. "May I approach?" he asked.

Colwyn nodded, already too tired to speak much.

Eagerly, Dernley approached her bedside, pulling a chair close so he could sit down. "I am so relieved to see you awake. You gave us much concern."

She smiled weakly at him. "Poor Giles," she whispered so softly he had difficulty hearing her. "I'm sorry you were worried." Her eyes began to close again.

"I will leave you to rest. Get well soon, my Lady." He took hold of her nearest hand and lifted it briefly to his lips, before rising and leaving the room.

Colwyn's recovery was slow. She was so weak she hardly had the strength to eat and had to be force-fed at first. Master Andrew made up several potions designed to provide her with nourishment that she could sip through the day, and rich broth and soup containing blood and finely diced meat were also regularly fed.

Dernley was desperate to get her to Ellesmere. He was concerned that the scouts would be returning any day—unless they had joined the King's forces—and he didn't want her to receive any news until she was safely delivered to the Queen. He feared that the news the scout would bring would cause her a severe relapse in her recovery. So, each day, he questioned Andrew. The battle surgeon understood his eagerness to depart, but would not be rushed. As it was, any journey Colwyn took would have to be by carriage as she would not be fit to ride a horse for several weeks. Even the carriage would tax her strength and he began arrangements to make the carriage as comfortable as possible, altering the interior so she could lie down, rather than sit.

It was ten days before Colwyn could leave her bed and even then she could only walk a few steps before becoming exhausted. Andrew finally decided to take a chance and risk a journey starting on the 1st of March.

The scouts had not returned to Belvoir, so Dernley assumed they had intercepted the King's forces and stayed with them as they were now overdue.

The carriage had been piled with soft cushions and blankets to ensure the Duchess had as comfortable a journey as possible. He arranged for oiled skins to cover the wooden roof and sides of the carriage to keep water out, and for heavy oiled skins to cover the windows when necessary to keep the wind and rain out as well.

The journey had been carefully planned so that the entourage would shelter at houses or inns along the way, as Colwyn was not fit enough to spend any time outside at night.

Finally, the day dawned. Colwyn was still half asleep when Dernley lifted her from her bed and carried her downstairs to the carriage. Master Andrew had prepared some draughts to keep her partially sedated so that she would not realise they were travelling in the opposite direction until it was too late.

Along with the few knights who were left over from Colwyn's guard, McLeod, and Master Andrew, King Stuart had assigned a sizeable escort to the party to ensure they got to their destination. This guard contained some of his best and most trusted men.

It was a bright but cold morning, and Sarah was glad of the huge pile of cushions and blankets for her mistress and herself. The movement of the carriage seemed to lull Colwyn to sleep and it was well after midday before she stirred.

"Sarah, where are we?" Colwyn asked sleepily.

Chapter Two

"I'm not sure, my Lady. Rest, we have a long way to go."

"I can't believe they're taking us back to Inver."

Sarah averted her eyes. "They did not want to distress you," she said simply, neither denying nor confirming their destination. "Now keep wrapped up warm, my Lady, it is extremely cold and we don't want you becoming ill again."

As they were moving at a slow but steady pace, they only stopped briefly to allow the horses some water and a slight breather before continuing on to reach their destination for that night. Dernley knew that it might well be then that Colwyn would realise she had been deceived and that they were actually heading towards Ellesmere and not back towards Inver.

Andrew gave her another powder to keep her drowsy and they safely reached their first stop without her knowing the direction of travel. Dernley carried her into the inn and up the stairs to the small room, where he gently laid her on the bed. A cot had been provided for Sarah. Two guards were posted outside her door. Half the remainder of the guard stayed downstairs, and the rest were in the barn keeping watch on the horses. The innkeeper's wife and daughter brought them all food and wine.

Master Andrew checked on his patient, who was just beginning to stir again. He left her in the care of Sarah and stopped the innkeeper's daughter before she went in. "If the lady asks you where we are, say nothing. Just go in, put the food and wine down, and leave," he ordered.

"Yes, sir." The young woman curtsied and entered the room with her tray of food and goblets of wine, placed it on the small table, then turned to leave.

"Thank you," Colwyn said weakly. "Pray tell me, where is this place?"

The young woman turned back to face her, shook her head and ran from the room.

Colwyn frowned, suddenly suspicious.

"Where are we, Sarah?"

"I am not sure, my Lady. I, too, was dozing in the carriage. Come, you must eat if you are to regain your strength, and…return to Inver."

"Fetch Giles Dernley. I will know where we are, now."

Sarah looked worried but opened the door. The guards turned to face her.

"My Lady wants to speak to Giles Dernley," she said.

"He's downstairs with Master Andrew and Monsignor McLeod."

Sarah quickly descended the stairs and spied them near the roaring fire. Master Andrew looked up as she approached, and they all stood as he saw the worried expression on her face.

"Please, I don't know what to do. My Lady is demanding to see Giles. I think she wants you to tell her where we are. She is very suspicious of our direction."

"I will handle this," said Andrew. "It is the will of her King, and she will obey the order to go to Ellesmere." He took a deep breath and ascended the stairs. Knocking quietly, he opened the door and entered Colwyn's room.

"Master Andrew. We're not going to Inver, are we?" Colwyn said to him.

"No, your Grace. We are on our way to Ellesmere."

"I told you I was to go to Inver. We will start there tomorrow morning," she ordered.

"No, your Grace. I am following the orders of His Majesty. He has decreed you are to be delivered to Ellesmere, and I obey my King, as you should do."

He could tell by the widening of her eyes, the sharp intake of breath, and the tightening of her lips to stop them from trembling that she was stricken at hearing this news; however, she held herself together and turned her head away from him, but not before he saw the glistening of tears.

Chapter Two

"I'm sorry, your Grace, but you must obey your King, and you are not well enough to withstand the journey back to Inver. If you were able to walk out of this room, down the stairs and across to the stable, then maybe, but you are not. Now eat, and sleep." Andrew bowed respectfully and left the room.

Colwyn stared at the closed door. So, Master Andrew was offering her a challenge, was he? She'd show him! Stubborn determination took over and she managed to get to her feet. The room was small, so she had no doubt she could reach the door. Five shaky steps later, she pulled it open. Her two guards looked round at her. Holding her head high, she stepped out onto the landing, holding onto the rail to help her keep upright. She eyed the stairs before her, and her resolve wavered slightly, but her face took on a look of determination and she started down, one step at a time.

Sarah gave a gasp, and Dernley looked up and stiffened in alarm. Unconsciously, he rose from the chair and went to the base of the stairs, ready to spring into action, should he be needed. Colwyn had managed four out of the thirteen steps and was beginning to realise the foolishness of her actions as her legs started to tremble with the effort. Dernley started to make his way up towards her, as he saw a flash of fear in her eyes before she slipped and started to fall. He sprinted up the last few steps and caught her before she did any damage, holding her tightly in his arms as she clung desperately to him, burying her head in his shoulder with shame at having failed.

"Colwyn," he said softly, as he swept her up into his arms and climbed back up the stairs and deposited her back on the bed in her room.

"Leave me," she commanded softly.

"Colwyn," he began again.

"Get out!" she said, her voice sounding desperate.

He bowed and backed out of the room, closing the door behind him. He turned to find Sarah standing there, and shook his head. "Not yet," he said to her. "She needs some time alone." He indicated for her to go back downstairs, at least for a little while.

Alone in the room, Colwyn's body shook as tears crept down her face. She was ashamed of her weakness and her failure to complete the challenge that Master Andrew had thrown at her feet.

When Sarah quietly entered the room an hour later, she found Colwyn had fallen asleep, tears now dried on her cheeks, and the food had not been touched.

CR ED CR ED

The sound of many hooves approaching the main street of the city of Inver resulted in a few brave souls opening their doors to investigate. As the riders came into sight, the banners of the King, Prince Michael and the Duke of Rossmere became visible, and the people started shouting.

"It's the King, the Prince and the Duke of Rossmere! The King!"

More people started to emerge from their homes as the column came closer and started up the main street towards the castle.

"God save the King!" voices were heard to shout.

The column slowed to a walk as they went along the main street, and the people bowed and curtsied their respect as the King, his general, and the Prince drew level with them. Stuart acknowledged them as he rode by and on towards the castle, leading a huge detachment of men behind him.

The King's party rode across the drawbridge, under the barbican and into the lower bailey of Inver Castle. It was obvious to everyone that a fierce battle had taken place; there were overturned grain barrels; doors were broken and hung off their hinges; splintered wood and twisted metal lay scattered everywhere. All was silent and eerily devoid of life, littered with snow-covered bodies from both sides. Stuart's face was grim as he led the way through the gatehouse and into the main bailey where there were more

Chapter Two

bodies, again covered in snow. It was fortunate that the temperature had been consistently below zero for the past two weeks, or the stench of decaying flesh would have been overpowering.

They dismounted at the bottom of the steps leading to the keep. Stuart issued orders to his men, and they split up in small groups to carry out a systematic search of the castle. Bodine wondered where he would find the Coltranes. He hoped that Richard would have insisted on hiding Bronwyn, perhaps in the room behind the library, where Colwyn and himself had hidden one time during a banquet to avoid McDowell. He ran up the steps, remembering the way, MacKenzie on his heels. On reaching the library, he stepped over the books that had been thrown from the shelves onto the floor and reached the shelf on the back wall where he pressed the secret combination. The shelf and wall clicked open, enough for him to get through. It was dark and cold inside. Using a flint, MacKenzie lit a candle and they surveyed the room. Bodine's heart fell; it was empty. No one had taken refuge here.

"Where do you think they could be, Sir John?" Bodine asked quietly.

"We could try the chapel," came the equally subdued response.

They retraced their steps back along the corridor, down the stairs and along more corridors to the chapel. Bodine paused at the side door, swallowed slowly, took a deep breath to prepare himself and opened it. Steeling himself, he stepped through, MacKenzie on his heels, and went to the altar.

He stopped and closed his eyes briefly. Lying on the altar steps were the Duke and Duchess of Invermere, with the bodies of the Elite Guard at their feet. They had obviously put up a brave but futile defence, being overpowered by the sheer numbers of attackers, but had managed to dispatch quite a few of them before being overrun. Grief washed over Bodine at the sight, especially of Bronwyn, whose body had been mutilated, the unborn child, cut from her womb, lying at her side. He pulled the cloth from the altar and draped it over the three bodies before kneeling, head bowed. MacKenzie knelt by his side, almost grief-stricken at the loss of his Lord and Lady. He had been in service to them most of his adult life, and to the duke's father before him; it was as if he had lost his family.

For Bodine, it was like losing his parents all over again. The Coltranes had welcomed him into their family and had shown affection, love and trust as soon as he had arrived to stay, and at every visit, despite his Kadeau heritage. Desperately, he fought to maintain emotional control, but in addition to the grief, he felt his anger rising at those who had done this terrible thing.

☙ ❧ ☙ ❧

Sarah had been instructed to wake her mistress and get her to eat, but Colwyn was refusing any food. She was on her feet again, eyes blazing and about to give Sarah a piece of her mind, telling her to leave her alone, when the most horrific vision flashed before her eyes; the sense of grief almost overwhelming; but it wasn't hers—at least not yet. She gasped, taking a sharp intake of breath, but had trouble getting any air into her lungs as the vision unfolded before her of her parents' dead bodies on the altar steps. The mutilation of her mother's body and her dead brother was as sharp an image as if she were actually there. She started to tremble violently, seeing but not seeing.

"My Lady?" Sarah asked, concerned.

But Colwyn just stood, a look of pure horror on her face. "N-n-no!" she screamed, sending chills through her handmaiden, and the door burst open to admit the two guards, as all the colour left her and she crumpled to the floor, unconscious.

Chapter Two

Below, McLeod suddenly put a hand to his head and gave a sharp intake of breath as the same feeling of grief hit him.

"Monsignor?" Dernley questioned, but got no further, as the scream from Colwyn reached their ears.

Recovering himself, McLeod gained his feet and ran up the stairs, Master Andrew and Dernley right behind him.

They burst into the room.

"What's happened?" Andrew asked Sarah, as he knelt down beside the duchess.

"I don't know. My Lady stood up, and then a…a look of horror came over her face as if she were looking at something terrible. All the colour drained from her and she screamed and fainted."

Andrew gently turned her over and cradled her in his arms, concerned at her lack of colour. He indicated for Dernley to pass him his medical bag, and retrieved the salts. The sharp aroma was unmistakable as he un-stoppered the small bottle and wafted it under her nose.

The response was immediate and her hands came up blindly trying to push the pungent odour away. Her eyes flew open and Andrew saw the look of absolute horror in them as she started trembling again. Realising she was going into shock, he quickly lifted her and moved to the bed.

"Quickly now, we must keep her warm. She is in shock," he said, and Sarah reached for more blankets from the base of the bed.

"Master Andrew, what is wrong with her?"

"I have no idea," he answered truthfully. "But it's as if she has seen something terrible. Can you pour some wine? Let's see if she will take something."

"She has indeed seen something terrible," McLeod whispered quietly to himself.

Sarah did as he asked and handed him the goblet.

"Come Colwyn, drink," he instructed, holding the goblet to her lips. A few sips were successfully taken, but she was not mentally with them in the room, but elsewhere. "My Lady, what's the matter, what have you seen?" he asked gently.

Her bottom lip trembled but her eyes remained unfocused as she tentatively replied, "Th-they're dead…a h-horrible death," she whispered.

"Who?"

"M-my fam-family."

"You can't know that for certain," Dernley said, sitting down on the bed and reaching for her hand.

"Yes, I can," she replied quietly.

Andrew frowned. Something was not right, but he still did not have the knowledge to understand what. Although he had been in service to the Duke of Rossmere since learning his skills as a surgeon, he still did not gauge fully the extent of Bodine's power and all that it involved. He looked at Monsignor McLeod for an explanation. The priest shook his head subtly, indicating he would explain, but not here and now. Andrew rose from the bed and mixed a strong powder in the goblet of wine.

"Drink this, Lady Colwyn," he said, handing her the goblet.

With shaking hands, she took the goblet from him and did as she was told. Dernley took it from her and settled her back down on the pillows before pulling the blankets up around her, and they all watched as the drug took hold and she succumbed to sleep.

Leaving her in the care of her handmaiden, they descended the stairs and went to sit by the fire again. Andrew looked at McLeod.

"Have you an explanation for what just occurred?" he asked him.

"I'm not sure, but I believe there may be a residual link between Morgan and Colwyn, following his attempts to revive her so you could administer the powder that night, at Belvoir," McLeod replied softly.

Chapter Two

"A link?" Dernley asked.

"It was a desperate measure the duke took to save her life," McLeod answered, still keeping his voice low. "She was dying. Master Andrew needed to get the potion into her, so Morgan attempted to bring her to consciousness so it could be achieved. I remember he flinched quite violently as he attempted it. Colwyn may well have held onto a tenuous link at the contact, in her fevered state." He paused before continuing.

"Will it harm her?" Dernley asked.

"No, it shouldn't. But in times of severe stress, they may feel what the other is feeling. I … I too witnessed what Colwyn has seen. The vision has come from Morgan… he has witnessed the sight of the duke and duchess that has deeply affected him, and this has been passed onto Colwyn and myself. I am sorry to inform you all that the Duke and Duchess of Invermere are indeed dead."

Dernley closed his eyes in grief. Deep down, he had known it would be so, but it still hurt very much to have it voiced by another.

"I will attempt to contact Morgan… Please excuse me."

McLeod left them, picked up his cloak and went outside, looking for a quiet, deserted spot. He found such a place behind the stable. Clasping his hands together, he closed his eyes, cleared his mind and slowed his breathing to bring on a feeling of total calm. This achieved, he reached out gently to his cousin.

Morgan… Morgan, are you there?

He waited, patiently, but no reply was forthcoming; in fact, he couldn't even detect his cousin, which meant one of two things; he had either erected a wall to block all thought, or he was dead. McLeod assumed the former. For the barrier to be this solid, he realised that his cousin was attempting to shield him, and had, indeed, seen something to deeply upset him.

McLeod brought himself back to the present, opened his eyes and sighed heavily at the loss that must surely have occurred.

※ ※ ※ ※

The main doors to the chapel were thrown open to admit Stuart, Michael and Stephen, the King's battle surgeon. They spied Bodine and MacKenzie on their knees, heads bowed, and moved swiftly towards them. As they approached, they saw that the altar cloth had been placed over some bodies, and Bodine was holding a hand that was protruding from under the cloth.

"Morgan," Stuart said softly. He watched, concerned, as his General took a shuddering breath, put down the hand he had been holding, and stood up with his back to his king.

Finally gaining control of his emotions, he turned to face Stuart, his expression set in stone, the steely grey eyes cold. Fists clenched, knuckles white, he met his gaze. The only sign of emotion was the twitch of a muscle in his jaw.

"Morgan, I'm so sorry," the King said quietly. "The Kingdom has lost a loyal family, and I have lost a good friend." He placed a brotherly hand briefly on his shoulder.

John MacKenzie got to his feet and also turned to face his king.

"Sir John, there is nothing I can say that will ease the pain, except to say that their deaths will be avenged."

"Your Majesty," MacKenzie replied tightly.

Bodine still didn't trust himself enough to speak.

Stephen moved to the altar cloth and lifted it slightly. "Oh God," he said, replacing it, then crossing himself.

Just then, footsteps were heard, and several monks appeared through the main gateway, the Bishop of Inver close behind them.

Chapter Two

Stuart turned and watched them approach. "Bishop," he started, "I have to ask, why are the duke and duchess still lying here where they were slain? Why have you not started preparations for their state funeral? You will take care of this immediately."

"Sire, I beg forgiveness; we have been dealing with the wounded and trying to keep order."

"I see; very well. You will now carry out your civil duty to the duke and duchess. My guards will assist you."

"Sire, I am going to take a look at the bodies of the attackers, see if anything can be gleaned about them," Bodine finally said. He bowed and made his exit, needing to get out and be alone to work through his grief.

The King ordered mass graves to be dug for the dead, whilst the bishop and the monks started work on preparations for the Coltrane family. Bodine examined many of the dead attackers to see what information—if any—he could obtain from them that would provide testimony that it was McDowell, but he was drawing a blank until he delved a little deeper and looked at the aketons they were wearing. They were of Cottesmere issue. He stripped a dozen soldiers of their padded protection as evidence to take back to Stuart, but it still probably wasn't enough proof. McDowell could claim a supply had been stolen. They needed more, and Bodine found it frustrating.

Stuart was pleased with his discovery but agreed that it was insufficient proof. They had now done everything they could do for the present. The snow still made it impossible to do any tracking, but he asked Bodine to stay in Inver and govern the duchy, appoint new officers and then return to Ellesmere, and to be back by the second week in April. This would give the duke a month to get everything sorted. He asked that John MacKenzie stay also, as he had been close to the Coltrane family and would have valuable information and advice to offer. As yet, they had not managed to find the Coltranes' steward, Markus.

The duke, duchess and the baby boy were laid to rest in the crypt in Inver cathedral. The King risked a glance at his General during the ceremony and saw his features were carved in stone; his body rigidly at attention throughout.

Stuart permitted the people to pay their last respects, and many came, laying their hands upon the tombs that held all three bodies, their heads bowed in prayer for a few moments before they crossed themselves and left the cathedral. Stonemasons were yet to create the effigies that would sit atop the tombs, but they had been ordered to work carefully and create accurate likenesses of the duke and duchess.

Gradually, the cathedral emptied, until only Stuart, Michael, MacKenzie and Bodine remained. Each of them paid their final respects, but Bodine stayed, and the King indicated for them to leave the General alone in the cathedral, sensing his need to stay longer.

He stood, head bowed, hands resting on the tomb, seemingly lost in a world of his own. The bishop watched from a distance, not realising that the young General was fondly reliving happier memories of his time at Inver with the Duke and Duchess of Invermere…

Bodine had been around nine months old when he arrived at Inver, with his wet nurse, following the death of his mother. She had never really recovered her health after giving birth to him, and had fallen again when he had been five months old, but lost the child. She had developed puerperal fever, which had led to sepsis, and, in the end, she lost her battle for life. At least, that was the story that had been circulated; however, it was not true. What had really happened was that his wet nurse had been slowly poisoning both his mother and him. It had been discovered, but not in time to save her; just the infant. He vaguely remembered a beautiful, fair-headed young woman—perhaps too young to have been burdened with childbirth, now that he thought back on it.

Chapter Two

His father he could hardly remember at all; he had been absent a lot of the time, but Bodine had one memory of him; of sitting with the duke astride his destrier one time. The smell of horse, leather, and oiled chainmail was ingrained in his mind, but he could not for the life of him recall his father's features—there was not even a portrait of him back at Rossmere, as he had never had the time to get one done because he had been away for such long periods.

Then suddenly, Bodine had found himself in a strange place, with people he did not know, and it had all been so upsetting for the infant. He was convinced he had been a problem child in the early days; but throughout that, he remembered Bronwyn, smiling kindly at him, holding him in her arms rather than leaving him with his new wet nurse; offering comfort and warmth and, most importantly of all, unconditional love. He distinctly remembered touching her face and sensing the intense feelings that had flowed from her to him. She had loved him as if he had been her own son, and gradually, he had responded. The oh-so-serious child, who never smiled, suddenly, one day had given her a radiant expression that lit up his entire face, and Bronwyn had wept with joy and given him a hug that had almost suffocated him. Then she had succumbed and behaved in a very un-duchess-like fashion and tickled him and he had giggled happily.

He had her undivided attention for the next few years, along with her husband, Richard, who had taken him all over the Duchy, educating him in his role as a duke of his own Duchy when he would finally come of age and, from the moment he could walk, had him training for his duties as a future knight and protector of the throne, and of the young Prince Stuart. Richard soon recognised his ability with the sword and ensured he received the best tuition.

At no time did his Kadeau pedigree alarm or scare his guardians, and they also invited his aunt to stay, to gauge his abilities in that area. She had imparted all the knowledge his serious, yet tender mind could absorb.

Then he remembered the day Bronwyn had taken him aside and told him he was to have a baby brother or sister; that he would still continue to be loved; but he had to understand that because babies were so helpless and vulnerable, they needed a lot of looking after.

"I will help you look after the baby," he had told Bronwyn solemnly, his pale eyes huge.

"I will need all the help I can get, Morgan," she had responded, "and I will most certainly take you up on your offer; bless you." She had hugged him and then kissed his cheek.

The pregnancy had not been an easy one; Bronwyn had suffered severe morning sickness and spent a great deal of time resting in her rooms. Bodine had visited her whenever he could, and he told her about what he had done that day, what he had learnt and seen. No matter how poorly she felt, she always responded to his stories with enthusiasm. He felt it was his duty to cheer her up and always tried to tell her an amusing story to lift her spirits. One time, he became very concerned as she had pulled a face.

"What's wrong, Aunt Bronwyn?" he had asked.

She smiled at him. "The baby is kicking. We are getting close."

"Why is the baby kicking you? That's not a very nice thing to do."

"Ah, my pet, the baby is telling me it is almost ready to make an appearance and is running out of room to grow much more. Oh! That was a hefty kick, it must surely be a boy." She studied Bodine's frowning features. "Give me your hand," she said to him, and he obeyed willingly. Bronwyn placed his hand on her swollen abdomen and held it there.

Chapter Two

"Oh!" he suddenly said as he felt a sharp kick under his hand, an expression of awe on his face, and continued to hold his hand in the same place, feeling more blows. "Does it hurt?" he asked.

"No, my darling; but I will confess it can be a little uncomfortable. Now, off you go; it's time for your supper."

Bronwyn had fought hard not to go into the birthing chamber a month before she was due to deliver, as protocol dictated, as she felt Bodine would think she was deserting him, and so, although Richard was forbidden entry, she insisted the child be allowed to visit. She also insisted on there being more light in the room. Usually, it would have been kept dimly lit, with cheerful tapestries covering the majority of the windows, and only one being allowed to let the light and fresh air in.

She kissed his cheek, and then he had left, but when he came back to say goodnight, he was refused entry.

The duke took him aside. "I'm sorry, Morgan, you cannot go in. Bronwyn is in labour; the baby is coming."

"How long will it take?" he asked, then gave a gasp of anguish as a cry of pain was heard from behind the solid door. "It hurts?" he questioned.

"Come, Morgan," Richard insisted, taking his hand and leading him away.

"But I want to help!" he protested, dragging his heels.

"This is women's work, son. We must leave them to do what must be done; the midwives are with her, and it's time you were in bed."

In the end, Richard had to pick him up and carry him to his room, as the child had protested vehemently, stating he had promised Bronwyn he would help her, but the duke kept going, and eventually managed to settle him down for the night. He had gone to his own room for a brief respite before returning to pace the corridors outside Bronwyn's rooms.

Sleep did not come for Bodine. He lay in the darkness, chewing his lip with worry, scared that Bronwyn would not survive. He had been told about his mother; that she had been too young to be with child. Bronwyn was a grown woman, but it still scared him. He tossed and turned in his bed, then stopped and suddenly lay very still, concentrating. Closing his eyes and breathing slowly and deeply, he reached out with his mind, searching for the woman who, to him, was now to all intent and purpose, his mother.

In the darkness, he frowned deeply, his mind searching, practising the techniques his aunt had started to teach him. Bronwyn was not Kadeau, but Aunt Meleri had told him that it was possible to reach out to the human mind, providing he concentrated hard enough, and for the fleetest of moments, he managed the barest of touches; but all he felt was pain that made him cry out, and he withdrew, tears in his eyes.

He was not allowed to visit Bronwyn at all, so he went in search of Richard, who he found pacing the main hall.

"Uncle Richard?" he had asked.

The duke had stopped his pacing and turned to face him, seeing his own worry reflected in the young child's eyes.

"Is…is Bronwyn going to be all right?"

Richard knelt down to be at his height. "I hope so. We are all praying that she comes through the ordeal safely, but it is hard for her."

"I don't want her to die."

"We are in the hands of God, child. What He decrees will be. Come, will you pray with me?"

They made their way to the chapel and spent the next hour in their own thoughts and praying that Bronwyn would survive.

It was there that a page found them.

"Your Grace! Your Grace! Sir, you have a daughter!"

Chapter Two

Bodine watched as Richard closed his eyes, briefly. "And the Duchess?" he finally dared ask.

"She is exhausted, but appears to be well."

For the first time since the labour had begun, Richard smiled in relief and looked down at the young boy.

"You have a little sister," he told him.

"I was sure it was to be a brother!" Bodine almost complained. "It kicked like a boy would."

Richard gave a hearty laugh, took his hand, and led him to Bronwyn's chambers.

The moment Bodine had set eyes on the baby, he was lost. She had a mass of red chestnut hair, and a hearty set of lungs on her and he vowed to protect her always, with the last breath of his body.

At the age of seven, he reluctantly had said goodbye to Colwyn, as he left Inver to begin his service to Prince Stuart at Ellesmere. In the eighteen months or so they had spent together, he had carried her around, looked after her, told her stories; he had even taken her riding, holding her tightly as they rode around on his pony. Just before he left, he told her he would come and visit her as often as he could. Little did he know, his visits would be very few and far between; but she had looked at him with such love in her emerald green eyes, he just knew she would never forget him.

At Ellesmere, the current King's champion and protector took the young duke-in-waiting under his wing, and, in earnest, began to train him in preparation for his future role. His training in the use of the sword continued, and in other weapons began, and the King ensured he was taught politics, manners and diplomacy.

Prince Stuart had immediately warmed to the youngster; seeing the hidden pain in his eyes, and knowing the amount of sorrow he had already suffered in his life, he was determined to make his time at Ellesmere as pleasant and rewarding as he was able.

On his tenth birthday, he came of age and was recognised as the new Duke of Rossmere. He left his ancestral home shortly after and travelled on to Inver with the recently crowned King Stuart and his new bride, Alexandra, who did not like the Kadeau. In her ancestry, many of her family had been killed by the rising Kadeau order of the time, so her hatred was inbred, despite Stuart's attempts to change her attitude towards his young page. Regardless of her hatred of him, Bodine bore her no ill-feeling. He showed a wisdom far beyond his youth and understood her reasoning; determined never to provide her with any evidence that what she felt was true in any way.

The visit to Inver was brief; Alexandra had fallen in love with the four-year-old Colwyn, suddenly wishing for a daughter of her own, and bestowed favours upon her. Bodine renewed his acquaintance with his 'sister', who had insisted on following him around everywhere, much to Alexandra's alarm and annoyance, but, as a guest within the castle, she dared not say anything. She observed the love and care that Bodine gave freely to the young girl, and how the child appeared to return those feelings without reservation; her complete trust in the Kadeau was there for all to see.

All too soon, the party had left. Colwyn had tried so hard to be brave, but Bodine had seen her bottom lip quiver as she fought to hold back the tears, and it warmed him to know how much his adopted family loved him. He returned to visit two years later, but it would then be another five years before they managed to visit again…

Stuart stood just inside the cathedral door and looked down the length of the aisle to where his champion and general was still standing, head bowed. He hated to disturb him, but the preparations for the journey back were completed, and he needed to depart and return to Ellesmere. Taking a breath, he started to walk down the aisle.

Chapter Two

Bodine heard the approaching footsteps; straightened up and walked up the aisle to greet him.

"My King," he said softly.

"I'm sorry, Morgan, we need to start on our return journey. I'm leaving you in control here. Do you think you can get the Duchy under some semblance of control in the next month or so? I'd like you back in Ellesmere by mid-April."

Bodine nodded slowly. "I will have John MacKenzie to help me, Sire. The Duchy will be under control by the time I head back."

"I know I can rely on you." He wanted to say more, but it was deemed not the thing to do by a King, especially in so public a place, so he simply shook the duke's hand.

"A safe journey back, my Liege."

"Thank you."

Then Stuart left with Prince Michael and his army and headed back to Ellesmere, leaving his trusted general to pick up the pieces.

Bodine threw himself into the task and set up camp within the castle walls, his guards occupying rooms, rather than the normal quarters. They went hunting in the nearby fields and forest for game and returned with fresh meat. Staff, who had escaped the attack, returned and were interviewed by him and MacKenzie, then set to work to clean the castle up, get the fireplaces lit, do the cooking, and all the normal things that they had done before. Ioan, Bodine's personal steward, went searching for bedding and other items to make the bedrooms more habitable and, at last, the duke got to sleep in his own bed and was comfortable for the first time in nearly three weeks.

Armour and padding removed, he lay on the bed, head resting on a pillow, closed his eyes and breathed deeply, concentrating on emptying his mind. He could not afford to allow the grief he felt to overwhelm him, so instead, realising this was the first time since the nightmare had started, he now had the time to analyse the images that had flashed into his mind when he had brought Colwyn to temporary consciousness so Andrew could administer the medicine to her.

He worked at slowing the images down so he could make sense of them. He saw the last image of the duke and duchess that Colwyn had seen, a flash of the journey through the forest, the incident at the river, the fight. He shook his head and his eyes flew open at Colwyn killing one of the attackers, and the grief and shame nearly overwhelmed him. Bodine grimaced as a pain shot through his head. All he could see were those bright, fevered green eyes. The pain centred itself at his temples forcing a groan past his lips, and then suddenly it was gone, leaving him breathing heavily.

૭ ৪ ૭ ৪

The powder Master Andrew had administered enabled Colwyn to have a peaceful night, but the following morning, she only picked at her breakfast. She was still upset at her failure of the night before to prove her fitness to return to Inver, and the horrific image of what she had seen yesterday was still vivid in her mind. No amount of cajoling could encourage her to eat more that morning, so they were forced to leave, but took extra provisions in case she became hungry on the journey.

Andrew was worried. All the fight seemed to have left her; she was subdued and lethargic, and simply lay in the carriage, not moving, not talking. Sarah tried on several occasions to get her to eat something, but she simply turned her back on her maid and closed her eyes.

He voiced his concerns to Monsignor McLeod.

"If the situation does not improve, do you want me to speak with her? Perhaps a man of the church may be more persuasive."

"That would be most appreciated, Colin," Andrew replied. "Let us see what the next day brings."

Chapter Two

As it was, Dernley beat the Monsignor to it. At their next stop, Giles carried her to her room and placed her on the bed. She turned away from him and simply lay there.

"Colwyn, you must eat to recover," he told her.

"Go away, Giles. Leave me alone."

"I can't; not until you eat something. Is this how you serve your Duchy? By deserting them, starving yourself to death and leaving them without a leader? Your parents raised you better than that! You must do your duty, no matter what the circumstances. Right now, your duty is to get well, so that you can return to rule Invermere, or do you want Nigel McDowell to take the Duchy and throw the whole of Devonmere into war? That's not a good way to serve your King."

Dernley watched as her left hand gripped the pillow tightly until her knuckles went white. Maybe he was starting to get through. He took a deep breath, moved around the bed, pulled her upright and shook her.

"Are you listening to me? Do you understand what I'm saying? If you don't pull yourself together, you could plunge the Kingdom into a bloody war!"

She looked at him then. Duty; it's what her father had trained her for, what he would expect her to do, but she couldn't do it alone. He hadn't prepared her for that. She looked at her right hand, to the seal of the duchy on her middle finger. Her father had given her the ring. She was the leader now.

"I-I'm sorry," she whispered and buried her head in his shoulder.

"It's all right. I'm sorry I spoke to you like that, but I had to get through to you. Now, I want you to eat properly. You need to get well if you are to serve your people. We shall be in Ellesmere in two days; you need to be fit enough to meet the queen."

Colwyn started eating again, and continued to improve, although she built a barrier within her mind, awaiting news from Invermere.

Both Andrew and McLeod breathed a sigh of relief. Whatever conversation Dernley had had with her, it appeared to have done the trick.

An hour after sunrise three days later, Castle Ellesmere appeared on the horizon, high on a hill, looking small and insignificant; but MacKenzie knew that was not so; it was purely because they were still a long distance away from it. He estimated it would take them at least half a day's travelling. The sight of it, however, despite its distance, lifted all their spirits, and they picked up the pace slightly.

Slowly, as they drew ever closer, the castle gradually grew in size and magnificence. It was the largest and most grand citadel in Devonmere, as befitting the residence of a King; a powerful symbol of government. Standing atop the hill made it appear even more imposing. The walls were tall, thick and of a hard, dolomite limestone, its battlements having crenels, with eight towers supporting them. These towers enabled the guard to have a three-hundred-and-sixty-degree view of the surrounding countryside and, being high on the hill, offered a far view of the land, allowing them to see an enemy coming from many miles away, giving them plenty of time to prepare for battle.

Outside the high walls, halfway down the side of the hill, a wide ditch had been dug as a form of defence, with a wall on the castle side, that also possessed a crenelled battlement, and there were two drawbridges across, both with barbicans, on opposite sides of the castle. At the bottom of the hill was the moat, which had been created by diverting the nearby river into a huge ditch, traversed by another two drawbridges.

Colwyn had never been to the castle before. She had thought her home was impressive, but it almost shrank into insignificance compared to

Chapter Two

Ellesmere, and her eyes slowly widened as they grew ever closer and its sheer size began to register.

They travelled through the main street of the city below, which sprawled alongside the river. People were going about their daily business but stopped to stare as they recognised the livery of the King, curiously wondering who was in the carriage and frowning, not recognising the features of the young woman who was staring almost in awe at the castle above them. Neither could they identify the livery of Invermere, then an old man whispered something to his neighbour, and the word began to spread. They watched as the small entourage went by, crossed the bridge over the moat and followed the zig-zag trail up the hill, crossing the next bridge over the ditch, passing under the barbican before travelling the rest of the trail up to the castle itself.

The sound of a herald was heard as they approached the main barbican and went through into the lower bailey, before continuing through the gatehouse into the main bailey where the keep and other buildings were.

Queen Alexandra was notified of their arrival and was waiting in the throne room. Dernley carried Colwyn all the way there. She attempted to take note of her surroundings; how they differed compared to her own home; even to begin remembering the layout of the part of the castle as they traversed the corridors, but she was having problems concentrating and keeping her eyes open. As they approached the doors, she managed to rouse herself sufficiently and insisted Dernley put her down on her feet just before they entered. The doors were opened, and they were announced into the room.

"The Lady Colwyn Coltrane of Invermere."

Colwyn walked slowly down the length of the throne room, followed by Dernley, Master Andrew, McLeod and Sarah. Above the throne hung the bannered arms of the Cantrells; the rampant gules (red) lion of Devonmere, on a vert (green) saltire with a tincture of or (gold); to its right was the or rampant guardant dragon of Rossmere on a sable (black) tincture, bordered by an or double tressel trefoil; and to the left was the argent (silver) rampant unicorn of Prince Michael on a gules fess cotsied with an azure (blue) tincture.

Along both side walls were the pennants of the various Duchies and knights currently in service to the King, proudly jutting out on their poles, all edged with a gold fringe. Her own arms, a sable salient Pegasus on gules chevronels with an argent tincture, hung at the far end of the throne room, first in line after the main three, indicating the loyalty and favour of Invermere. On a normal day, the sight would have been uplifting, with the room ablaze with colour, but Colwyn's heart was heavy, and, at that precise moment, she wished Bodine was with her; for he was the only family she had left now.

On reaching the base of the stairs, she dropped into a deep curtsey. "Your Majesty," she said softly, and then, to her horror and embarrassment, found she did not have the strength to rise.

Dernley walked forward, bowed respectfully, and assisted Colwyn to her feet. Alexandra rose from her chair and came down the steps.

"My dear Colwyn," she took her hands, seeing the lack of colour and the gaunt features. "Come, we have prepared rooms for you."

"Majesty, please, has there been any news?"

"None, child. Come, rest. As soon as word arrives, you will be sent for."

Colwyn nodded and swooned against Giles, exhausted. The squire lifted her effortlessly into his arms.

"Follow me," the Queen said, and he did as he was told, with Andrew, McLeod and Sarah following on. Any staff they encountered on their journey to the duchess's appointed rooms, bowed and curtsied respectfully.

Chapter Two

Once safely in the room, Sarah quickly pulled the bed covers back and Giles set her down gently. Andrew moved forward to remove her slippers and check her condition.

"And you are?" the Queen asked.

"Majesty, I am Master Andrew, battle surgeon to his Grace, the Duke of Rossmere. I have been treating her Grace since she arrived at Belvoir Castle, seriously ill. She has made some recovery but has a way to go. We almost lost her."

The Queen looked at him sharply. "Very well; continue." She stood by as Andrew mixed another potion in some wine, and gently lifted Colwyn's head to place the goblet against her lips.

"Come, your Grace, drink this, and rest."

Colwyn opened her eyes and did as she was told, before closing them again, and relaxing into sleep.

"She will be asleep for the rest of the day," Andrew said, pulling the covers up over her slender form.

"Very well. You must tell me the whole story so I am prepared. Come, you must be hungry and thirsty after your journey. Food should be arriving here shortly for you, Sarah."

"Thank you, Your Majesty." Sarah curtsied as the Queen swept by.

Over their meal, Dernley, McLeod and Andrew told the Queen all that had happened, starting with the escape from Inver, right up to their arrival at Ellesmere.

"Weather conditions were appalling, Your Majesty. I believe it was the harshest February we have had in many years; driving wind and snow; drifts; freezing temperatures; we had no choice but to make the journey, to prevent Duchess Colwyn from being captured and taken by the attackers," MacKenzie told the regent, who was listening quietly, making no comment as she absorbed the information.

"We had no option but to cross the River Wyvern. We hoped the amount of snow falling would cover our tracks, to throw off any pursuers off our trail; and we assumed the freezing conditions would result in the level of the river being low," Dernley added.

"Unfortunately, as you know, it's been a long, wet winter. It was higher than we expected; the horses stumbled during the crossing and unfortunately, the Duchess was soaked through."

"In the river?" the Queen queried.

"Yes, Your Majesty. Her maid assisted in changing her clothes, but as you can imagine, conditions were so bad, and I believe that is when she became ill. We searched urgently for shelter, but before we managed to find any, we had to repel a small force that attacked us. We lost two of our guard during the skirmish.

"We finally took shelter in the caves at the cliffs and managed to light a couple of fires and prepare some hot food. Lady Colwyn did her best to hide how ill she was, but thankfully, young Giles here saw through her deception. It was then we realised we wouldn't be able to make it to Ellesmere and diverted to Belvoir instead. If it hadn't been for Master Andrew, Colwyn would have died."

The Queen looked at the battle surgeon. "Were no physicians available?" she questioned.

"There was one with her when I arrived, but I doubted his actions. He wanted to bleed her again to dispel the bad humours, but she was far too weak to have withstood that, so I asked Duke Morgan to dismiss him. Thankfully, he did, and allowed me to treat her. It was touch and go for a while. His Grace refused to leave until we had a result—one way or another."

"Bodine stayed with her the whole time?"

"Yes, Your Majesty. He also managed to get rid of the Duke of Cottesmere, who arrived and tried to remove the Duchess from Belvoir."

Chapter Two

"I see."

"Finally, her fever broke. We had won the battle. Only then did the duke go and get some rest. The King arrived shortly after, and they all left for Inver first thing the next morning, and we were given orders by His Majesty to deliver her Grace into your hands as soon as she was well enough to travel; and now we are here."

"I thank you for briefing me. Colwyn will require time to mourn. I will ensure she gets the opportunity and space to do this. Please, all of you, rest now, and thank you for delivering her safely to me."

Alexandra rose from her chair, and all the men stood and bowed respectfully as she swept past them and left the room.

They had purposely left out the details of any Kadeau magic and other 'suspicious' occurrences, knowing how much the Queen hated Bodine.

Colwyn gradually improved over the next few days, but progress was slow. She desperately needed news about the situation in Inver to know if her vision was true, but that was still days away.

McLeod tried on several occasions to get Colwyn to talk to him, even to confess to her killing of an attacker, but she remained silent and reserved, merely thanking him for his concern. As it was, he still had not been able to make contact with Bodine and grew increasingly concerned at the lack of communication from his cousin.

King Stuart and his army arrived back at Ellesmere twelve days later. Colwyn watched them arrive from a vantage point and was concerned that Bodine was not with him. She wondered when it would be appropriate for her to see her King to obtain any news. In fact, she did not have long to wait. Knowing that Colwyn was desperate for information, he immediately came to her chambers, still dressed in full armour, spurs clanking on the stone floor, accompanied by the Queen.

There was a respectful knock on the door, and Sarah opened it to admit them; she immediately dropped into a curtsey, and Colwyn followed suit.

"Your Majesty," she said, bowing her head as the king approached. She kissed the ring on the sovereign hand, and Stuart assisted her to her feet.

"Colwyn," he said softly. "Please sit." He indicated a chair by a small table and knelt down in front of her. She fixed her gaze on his eyes, seeing the sadness in them. "I am pleased to see that you are recovering from your illness. You had us all very worried. As you may have realised, I have returned from Inver and… regret to inform you that I have sad news." He paused as he saw her bottom lip tremble, and watched as she clamped them together. "The duke and duchess are dead. We have laid them to rest in the crypt. You are now recognised as the Duchess of Invermere, my dear."

Her eyes were bright, but no tears fell. "I-I knew they were dead, Sire. W-what of my people? I need to return to govern."

"I have left the Duke of Rossmere, along with Sir John MacKenzie, to govern temporarily. They will appoint staff to run the Duchy until you are well, and it is safe enough to travel. We still need to catch the perpetrators of this terrible deed. I expect the duke to return by mid-April and he will deliver his report then."

"T-thank you, Sire. I am grateful for what you have tried to do."

"Is there anything we can do for you now, at this moment?"

"No, Sire. If you please, I would like to be left alone. I must gather my thoughts and start planning for the future."

"Colwyn, you have time; don't rush. The Duke of Rossmere will ensure that all is in order before he leaves, and you still need to recover from your illness."

"Yes, Your Majesty."

Chapter Two

Stuart stood up and Colwyn immediately left her chair and dropped into a deep curtsey. The king bent down and lifted her to her feet and kissed her forehead.

"My child, we are here for you when you need us." He released her and turned to leave.

The Queen then went to Colwyn and hugged her. "I am here for you also, my child."

Colwyn nodded, unable to speak.

"Rest awhile." The Queen motioned for Sarah to take charge and then left.

Colwyn waited until the door had shut behind them, and then her legs refused to hold her any longer. She dropped to the floor and just sat staring blankly ahead.

Sarah rushed to her side and knelt down. "Oh, my Lady!" Sarah pulled her into her arms and started to rock her back and forth, trying to soothe her.

No tears were forthcoming, for Colwyn had erected a stone wall to shield herself from her emotions. They stayed where they were for half an hour before either of them moved, then Sarah helped her mistress up and made her lie down on her bed for a while.

And as she lay there, her mind wandered back to a much happier time…

೧೮ ೧೮

Chapter Three

Colwyn let her mind drift back to the event that had probably planted the initial seed for the uprising.

It had been so exciting. King Stuart Cantrell, his Queen, Alexandra, and heir, Prince Llywelyn, were visiting Inver, and, in celebration, there was to be a holiday for all the people, along with feasting and competitions that were to include swordsmanship and jousting. They had visited once before when she had been very young, four or five years of age, and the Queen had fallen in love with the red-headed, green-eyed little girl, making her yearn for a daughter of her own.

Out of courtesy, an invitation had been extended to the neighbouring Duchies. Morgan Bodine, Duke of Rossmere, would be present as he held the immediate, neighbouring Duchy; additionally, he was the new King's Champion and had been adopted by the Duke and Duchess of Invermere on the death of his parents when he was very young, so was considered part of the family. Also in attendance would be Kenneth Dernley, the old Duke of Strathmere and Nigel McDowell, Duke of Cottesmere. Colwyn had only ever met McDowell once when she had been much younger and hadn't liked him at all. Now, it seemed, she was to meet him again. This celebration was to be her first 'official' engagement.

Chapter Three

Her father had decided that as she was of marriageable age, she should begin to be seen at official engagements. Not that he was looking to marry off his little girl. He wanted her to have a full and happy childhood and then, eventually, when she was ready, to hopefully choose a husband for herself. However, if necessary, he—or the King—would make the decision for her, for the stability of the Kingdom.

The castle was a hive of activity as preparations were made. There were rooms to clean and dress for guests, food to cook, the jousting arena to check and the banqueting hall to be made ready. As host, her family had the honour of sitting with the King and his entourage on the head table. Somehow, in all of this, Colwyn had been given a place next to the King's Champion, the man she had always considered to be her older brother. She was so excited at the thought of seeing him again and being allowed on the top table, she had almost made herself ill.

At around midday, castle lookouts announced the approach of the royal party with a herald.

Colwyn was not to be at the first meeting, as, after a brief welcome and lunch, there would be business to discuss. However, this did not stop her from watching the approach and all the pomp and circumstance it involved.

From her vantage point, Colwyn was able to see everything. The rampant red lion of Devonmere led the procession, followed by the golden dragon of Rossmere, with the other Duchies mingled in along the column, resplendent with colour.

She watched as the King rode into the courtyard. An imposing figure of a man, dressed in riding leathers and a fine mail, covered by his surcoat, he was tall, with shoulder-length black hair, beard and hazel eyes, but it was Bodine who took her attention. He was just seventeen, slightly taller than the King, with burnished gold hair that reflected the sun, tied back in a ponytail. He possessed the beginnings of a beard; Colwyn wasn't sure whether he just needed a shave or if he was attempting to grow one, but she didn't care. She was going instantly into her first crush at his handsome features, and with him being dressed in black riding leathers, fine mail and riding a huge black stallion, this simply added to his air of mystery and wonder.

Unable to take her eyes off him, she watched as he easily dismounted his horse and handed the reins to an awaiting page, before turning to await his King.

Her mother and father were standing at the bottom of the steps waiting to greet the royal entourage and she watched as her mother curtsied and her father bowed as the King and Queen approached. Their polite exchange faded away as Colwyn continued to stare at her new hero, as her mother kissed Bodine on the cheek. If he looked up and saw her, she would die, she just knew she would.

Then, as if he had read her thoughts, Morgan Bodine did glance up to where Colwyn was standing. He inclined his head slightly and the mere hint of a smile touched his lips, but it was enough for Colwyn to clasp her hands together in delight and beam back at him in a most un-ladylike fashion.

"Colwyn! What are you doing?" It was Sarah, her handmaiden.

Colwyn jumped, looked around guiltily, then glanced back, regained her composure and inclined her head slightly as etiquette dictated, before slowly backing away, all the while attempting to keep Bodine in her sights until the last possible moment.

It seemed to take forever for the evening to arrive and Colwyn was getting very impatient. Sarah had never seen her in such a state and was concerned that her young charge would be ill. But eventually, time moved on and Colwyn was summoned to attend the great hall for the banquet. Needing no second reminder, she left her rooms in a sedate manner but when she was sure no one was around, ran down the rest of the corridor, down the stairs

Chapter Three

of the south turret and skidded to a halt on the ground floor, panting for breath. She paused to get her breathing under control, then looking around to make sure no one was there, ran the length of the corridor to the antechamber, slowing once again to a more lady-like pace as she approached it.

A guard shook his head in a kindly fashion, indicating that he had heard her headlong dash, smiled and then winked at her. Her secret would be safe. Smiling her sweetest smile that usually managed to wrap anyone around her little finger, she bobbed him a little curtsy and walked through into the antechamber, along the side wall and into the small room on the side of the great hall where her parents, the King and the rest of his royal party were waiting.

Duke Richard Coltrane turned as his daughter entered and bade her approach. Remembering her manners, she dropped into a low curtsy in front of the King and Queen, bowing her head. The young prince, aged only five, was up in their rooms, being looked after by his nurse.

"My goodness, this is Colwyn?" Stuart asked Richard.

"Yes, my Liege."

"How she's grown! Colwyn, my dear." The King indicated for her to rise. "What a beautiful young lady you are turning into. I fear you will break many a young man's heart."

"Your Majesty is most kind," she whispered quietly, unused to such comments, but thrilled at his words. She curtsied to the Queen, who took her hands and bade her rise.

"Colwyn, you are a true beauty." The Queen had a very soft spot for the child. She longed for a daughter of her own, but as yet had not fallen, so doted on Colwyn whenever she saw her.

Colwyn found it impossible to hide her excitement as she was introduced to the rest of the party. Next was the Duke of Strathmere—Uncle Kenneth, as she called him—who had once again brought her a small gift, as he always did on his visits. He knelt down to receive a hug and kiss from her. Colwyn was beaming from ear to ear at this point, but it faded abruptly as she came face to face with the Duke of Cottesmere, Nigel McDowell.

"My dear, you are looking positively exquisite tonight," McDowell complimented her. Colwyn minded her manners and gave thanks, not liking the way he was contemplating her, as if scheming something. She let go of his hand as quickly as etiquette dictated was suitable.

She was under the impression that no one seemed to notice her discomfort in the presence of this man until she looked to her left and saw the Duke of Rossmere looking down at her; his usually steely grey eyes, soft and understanding. He had known Colwyn most of his life, but the last time they had met was when he had been a newly appointed squire to the King on their previous visit. Prior to that, he had been taken care of by the Coltranes' on the death of his parents, until he had entered the service of the King. Bodine gave her a very subtle encouraging smile and indicated, with an almost imperceptible nod of his head, for her to come closer.

"Duke Morgan," she bobbed a curtsy at her hero, her face once again radiant.

"Colwyn, I hardly recognised you. How you've grown, and into such a beautiful young woman," Morgan Bodine stated, as he leant down and kissed her cheek; for it was true. The last time he had seen her, she had been but a child, but now she was at the brink of womanhood, approaching her twelfth birthday, and she was going to be an extraordinarily beautiful young woman, especially with that long chestnut hair and those amazing emerald green eyes.

"My Lord is very gracious and kind," she responded in almost a whisper. Hearing such compliments from her hero was awe-inspiring. "You too have changed, matured and are most handsome." She wasn't sure whether she should have said that, but it was too late; it was said.

Chapter Three

"I too have brought you a present. I'm afraid it's not a toy, though, it's something rather more practical."

Colwyn was beside herself, as Bodine handed her a slightly larger package than Kenneth had done. Gleefully, she looked around for somewhere to sit and open them. Morgan gestured to two chairs near the fireplace and escorted her there.

"Would you mind if I sat with you?" he asked.

"Not at all, Duke. I would be honoured."

So, they sat and Bodine looked on indulgently as Colwyn opened Kenneth's present first. A small wooden jointed horse, exquisitely carved. The workmanship was outstanding.

"May I?" Bodine asked.

Colwyn handed it to him, as she concentrated on opening his present.

"This is an amazing piece of work. What will you do with it?"

"I'm going to stain it black," Colwyn replied without hesitation. *Black like your stallion*, she whispered in her mind. "What is your horse's name?"

"Banner. He's a young horse, and still learning, Bodine replied smiling, his eyes alight with mischief as if he had heard her unspoken thoughts, but he was prevented from saying anything further, as she gasped in delight at the present he had given her; a box of the most delicate silk threads for embroidery, every colour of the rainbow.

"Oh…. Oh, Duke…. they are beautiful! How did you know?"

"Your mother remarked that you had the gift for embroidery and needlework, so I thought as I was passing through Applegarth, I would purchase a selection of their finest threads for you. I take it you are pleased?"

"Oh, more than pleased. Thank you so much!" She got up from her chair then, gave him a huge hug and kissed his cheek. Bodine was almost overwhelmed by the intensity of the love that seemed to flow from her to him. "I shall use these for my best work."

Just then, her mother arrived. Colwyn reluctantly let go of the duke, who swiftly got to his feet, his manners impeccable as ever.

"Oh Mother, look what the Duke has brought me! Applegarth silks! Aren't they beautiful? And Uncle Kenneth has brought me a wooden horse."

"Morgan, you shouldn't have gone to all that trouble to seek out a gift for Colwyn."

"You always make me feel most welcome whenever I'm here, so it was for that reason that I did this. You have been like a family to me since I lost my parents. On every visit, I receive love and affection from you, so I felt it was the least I could do."

"Bless you. If I were to have a son, I would wish he were exactly like you." She leant forward and kissed his cheek. "You are the son I have not had."

Bodine blushed at the compliment. He was a Kadeau, with supposedly magical powers. Friends and affection such as this were rare and he treasured it beyond measure.

It was then announced that the banquet was ready. Bodine offered Colwyn his arm which she eagerly accepted and they walked into the banquet hall to take their place at the head table. The King and Queen took centre stage, with Bronwyn next to the King, then Bodine and Colwyn on one side and Richard seated next to the Queen, then Dernley and McDowell. Other local dignitaries and their wives were seated at the tables below the main one.

There were generous quantities of food for the banquet and wine flowed freely. Even Colwyn was allowed to drink a little, interspersed with water. She spoke to Bodine, whilst Bronwyn spoke in turn to both the King and Bodine.

Bodine asked Colwyn what she had been up to recently.

"Father has had me sitting in court, to learn how the duchy operates," she replied seriously. "I have also been out, meeting the people. Do you

Chapter Three

know, we have some very gifted women and children in our duchy? I am hoping to be able to help them."

"Oh, in what way?" the King asked, eavesdropping on the conversation.

"Sire, I hope to be able to teach them our special embroidery and lace techniques, to help them earn a living."

"My, but that's an ambitious project for one so young," he replied, smiling kindly, looking thoughtfully at her. It was a shame she was older than the young prince, as he believed she would have made a fine wife and future queen, and he knew that Alexandra was very fond of her as well; but by the time the prince was old enough to marry, Colwyn would be at least twenty, and the prince needed to marry a woman younger than himself. However, he would not dismiss the possibility entirely, yet.

"I want our people to flourish and prosper."

"That is a fine aspiration, Colwyn," Bodine said, amazed at the maturity she was exhibiting at her tender age.

"Thank you, Duke."

The banquet continued with entertainment, and then the musicians moved to set up for the dancing that was to follow. The King invited Bronwyn to dance, whilst Richard invited the Queen, and Colwyn looked on enviously as they moved around the hall to a farandole, tapping her foot to the beat of the music.

Bodine suddenly sensed her stiffen in fear and looked up to see Nigel McDowell approaching. He did not particularly like the duke either, but he was curious to know what it was about him that made Colwyn react so. How McDowell could not sense her unease, he did not know; it was so tangible—or was this, once again, his Kadeau magic making him far more sensitive to her feelings because he cared about her?

If McDowell noticed, he made no comment, which implied there were underlying motives. The duke was ambitious, Bodine knew that. Could it be he was looking to make a match with the young Lady Colwyn? As the only heir, she would be an exceedingly wealthy woman when her parents died, and a liaison between the two Duchies would actually put Bodine in a rather dangerous situation. His eyes narrowed as he realised this could be McDowell's ploy. The match would not be in the interests of the Kingdom, of that he was certain.

Coming to a very abrupt decision, he turned to Colwyn and asked quietly, "Colwyn, would you do me the honour of granting me the next dance?"

"Oh yes!" came the nearly desperate reply. She didn't even wait for him to help her from her chair, but stood up and literally forced her hand into his.

McDowell stopped abruptly and glared at Bodine, then kept on walking towards them.

"My dear," he said, ignoring his adversary. "I believe this is our dance?"

"You are mistaken, Duke. I promised this dance to the Duke of Rossmere. Perhaps later." She curtsied and carried on quickly. "I'm sorry, Duke," she said to Bodine making sure they were out of earshot of McDowell. "I know you don't really like dancing and it was very kind of you to offer, but I believe Duke Nigel is watching. If we don't dance, then—"

"I understand perfectly," Bodine replied.

They joined a circle of dancers for a carola and moved around the floor gracefully, also singing in a round. Colwyn was so pleased that her mother had taught her how to dance for the occasion, and Bodine was such a handsome partner, she glowed with the pleasure. They stayed on the floor for another dance; this time the sarabande, but towards the end of this one, Bodine noticed McDowell trying to casually make his way over.

"Colwyn, do you trust me?"

"Sir?" she questioned.

Chapter Three

"Do you trust me?"

"With my life," she answered unhesitatingly. "Why?"

"I take it you do not want McDowell near you, correct?"

She suddenly looked alarmed.

"Very well, just follow my moves." With that, as they swept around the room once more, Bodine used a small crowd of guests to make his escape, pulling Colwyn with him, out of the room and into the corridor. Knowing he was far more familiar with the castle layout than McDowell, Bodine moved swiftly along the corridor causing Colwyn to have to make little running steps to keep up with him. He kept going at this pace until they had turned a corner, gone down another corridor, up one flight of stairs, and along to the library, which he knew would be deserted at this time.

The room was in total darkness. Colwyn felt Bodine let go of her hand and chant something and suddenly, there was a blue-white flame, dancing on his right hand, that allowed them to find their way around the huge room.

"Where do you think would be a good place to hide for a little while?" Bodine asked.

Colwyn didn't answer him immediately; she was fascinated by his open display of magic. "May I?" she asked, tentatively holding out her hand.

Bodine smiled at her. "If you like." Carefully, he transferred the light across into her hand. "Hold your palm out straight and flat, that's right, now you can lead on."

"It's cold," she whispered in awe, staring mesmerised at the flickering flame. "Is it possible to teach me to do it?"

Bodine blinked. It was the last thing he'd expected her to ask. "I don't know," he finally answered, truthfully. "No one has ever asked me before, so I've never tried."

"Would you…would you try though, please?"

"Very well."

She smiled up at him and led the way across the library. "There's a secret room over here. If Duke Nigel does perchance find his way here, he'll never find that room. Father doesn't know that I know about it, but I don't think he'd be very cross. I'd have to know about it eventually, wouldn't I?" Colwyn stopped at a huge section of shelves studying the titles on a row that was too tall for her to reach. "See that big thick red book on the sixth shelf—the one entitled *Tales from the Eastern Desert*? If you pull it out, you should just about be able to feel three small knots in the wood on the back, in a row? Using your three middle fingers, press the knots simultaneously and then push the middle knot again on its own, then put the book back."

No sooner had Bodine done this than a panel to the left of the shelf sprung open. Using her left hand, Colwyn felt one of the stones that seemingly made up a solid wall, and suddenly part of it slid back enough for them to creep through one at a time, closing behind them once again as Colwyn touched another stone inside the secret room.

Seeing some candles, Bodine used the flint lying near them to light them, and then turned to Colwyn. "Hold your right hand thus," he instructed holding it flat and palm down. "Make a circular movement like this, starting at the wrist, then wipe it across the palm of your right hand."

She did as he instructed, and her blue-white flame vanished.

"That's the more flamboyant way of extinguishing the flame. The usual way is to just clench your fist." He looked around. "Come, sit over here, and let's begin your first lesson."

They spent a couple of hours practising until finally, Colwyn managed a tiny little flicker. Bodine was full of praise, but Colwyn was not impressed.

"It's not very bright, is it?" she said dolefully. "That won't allow me to see where I'm going."

Bodine laughed kindly. "To have conjured it up at all, is most impressive, Colwyn. You simply need to practice more; you are showing that you have

Chapter Three

begun to focus your mind correctly. As you learn to do this more effectively, your flame will become stronger and brighter. It's like everything; the more you practice, the better you become; like playing a musical instrument, or riding a horse. You're not perfect after the first lesson now, are you?"

"No, no, you're not." She frowned in concentration and quietly whispered the chant again. This time, her flame was a little larger and brighter. Her eyes lit up.

"See, you're getting better already. The keyword is focus. Focus the mind on what you want to achieve. You can apply that principle to anything. Now, I know I don't need to say this, but I will anyway. Be careful where you do this. Very few people are tolerant of Kadeau magic."

"I understand you, sir."

"Why so formal? You used to call me Morgan."

"Mother said I had to use the correct etiquette this evening, as the King and Queen were present."

"Oh, I see, but I don't think that refers to me; I'm your brother." He watched her as she tried a few more times, then decided to ask the question on his mind. "Why don't you like McDowell?"

Her flame disappeared with a pop and she looked up at him, feeling suddenly uneasy, but decided to answer his question without any pomp and circumstance. "He's evil."

"Would you care to elaborate on that?"

"There's something about him. I don't trust him. He makes me feel ill whenever he's near me; I can't explain it. He scares me too, and…." She swallowed suddenly feeling tears welling in her eyes. "I know I'm of marriageable age now and…I'm terrified that I might be forced to… to marry him. I won't do it, I won't. I'll… I'll kill myself first."

Bodine saw her bottom lip quivering and the tears in her eyes.

"It's childish, isn't it?" she stated, but then the tears began to flow.

"Oh, my pet, I didn't mean to upset you with that question. We've had such a wonderful evening, and now I've gone and spoilt it for you; forgive me." Bodine held out his arms and Colwyn collapsed into them.

"No, it's not your fault," she mumbled into his shoulder. "I-I didn't think anyone noticed how I felt about him."

"Have you spoken to your mother?"

"I've told no one. I thought they'd notice, but.... Only you seem to have picked up on it. And I'd feel foolish telling Mother or Father; they'd think I was being childish, and I don't want them to think I'm being petulant or anything."

"How about if I do some delving for you? Your mother treats me like her own son, so she may well confide if your father has any plans yet."

"Would you? Really?" Colwyn drew back and stared into his eyes, her own full of hope.

"Yes. Your mother considers me one of the family, so let me take this opportunity to be an older brother to you and see what I can find out."

"Oh, thank you, Morgan." Colwyn hugged him again.

"Now, I think perhaps it may be time for you to go to bed. It's rather late, and there's a big day ahead tomorrow and the day after, with the tournament and everything else that's going on. As King's Champion, I also have some fierce competition to overcome. I shall need all the help I can get."

Colwyn studied him thoughtfully for a moment, then reached into one of the sleeves of her dress and drew out a delicate handkerchief with her initials sewn into one corner. "Then take this favour, sir, as a token of my support for you tomorrow."

Morgan accepted the gift and placed it inside his jacket. "Thank you, my Lady." He kissed her hand then helped her to her feet. "I will escort you safely to your rooms."

Chapter Three

They carefully retraced their steps and Bodine, as good as his word, saw her safely to the care of her handmaiden, before returning to the great hall to inform her mother where she was.

"Thank you, Morgan. You have been so good to her this evening, I'm sure she's enjoyed your company very much, especially as you have treated her like an adult."

"Well, she is now of marriageable age, so, by rights, she is now an adult."

Bronwyn sighed heavily. "She may be considered adult, but as yet, she is not a woman in the true sense of the word. Both Richard and I are planning to allow her to enjoy her childhood a while longer before we consider any marriage. Life is short enough as it is. I don't want her married off straight away, and with child; it's too dangerous for one so young."

"I believe Duke Nigel McDowell is interested in approaching you regarding marriage. His interest has been obvious, especially this evening."

Bronwyn frowned. "I don't think he would be right for her, or the Kingdom. I realise the possible danger of that liaison, as does my husband. Besides, although Colwyn has said nothing, I know she does not like the duke. I'm not particularly fond of him either. I would dearly love to see her marry someone who she cares deeply about, but we shall see. It could be the King already has plans for her."

"None that I am aware of, my Lady," Bodine replied. "As you say, there is no hurry."

"Morgan," Bronwyn placed a hand on his arm. "You will watch over her, won't you? I know she is very fond of you."

"Like an older brother, my Lady."

"God bless you and keep you." She leant forward and gently kissed his cheek.

Bodine bowed deeply and took his leave, wanting to get a decent night's sleep before tomorrow's competition.

However, sleep evaded him for a while, as his mind reviewed the conversations he had had with Bronwyn. Colwyn would be happier once he told her that her mother was aware of her feelings about McDowell and that there were certainly no marriage plans in that—or, for that matter—any other direction at present. His mind then turned to the time he had spent with Colwyn in the hidden room. For her to have managed to conjure the fire-light at all was indeed a remarkable accomplishment, and he began to wonder more about her pedigree. Was there Kadeau somewhere in there? As far as he knew, there wasn't, yet for her to have mastered fire-light was an indication that there was Kadeau blood somewhere in her past, or that she had an exceptionally sharp and focused mind. He pondered a while longer, but slowly he began to relax and he finally fell into a deep dreamless sleep.

The following morning dawned bright and promised to be pleasantly warm. The castle was a hive of activity as the final last-minute preparations were finished off. The day of celebrations was to be formally opened after breakfast and events were to be both serious and for amusement. In addition to the formal tournament, which was to include swordsmanship and skill with the bow and arrow, there was to be a demonstration by the young squires and pages to show how their skills were developing both in horsemanship and with weapons. The following day was the joust, and, to end the tournament, there was to be a pillow fight on horseback.

Colwyn had been awake over two hours before normal; her excitement was getting the better of her. She had gulped down her breakfast and gone running off to see how everything was progressing. She also wanted to see Bodine before the events started, to wish him luck and tell him she would be supporting him to the bitter end.

Chapter Three

She found him warming up in a practice ring. Seeing her approach, he stopped and went to the fence.

"Colwyn, you're up early," he told her.

"I've been up for over two hours, I'm so excited! I just wanted to see you before all the activities started to wish you luck and tell you I will be supporting you all the way."

"Thank you, my pet." He pulled her handkerchief from under his sleeve. "See, I have your favour safely on me as good luck as well."

She smiled a radiant smile as he tucked it safely away again.

"Regarding our other conversation last night, about McDowell; I spoke to your mother and you need not fear. She is aware you do not like him, and there are no plans to marry you off. *Now* are you happy?"

"Oh yes! Thank you so much, Morgan."

He knelt down as she ducked under the fence rail so she could give him a hug, and then boldly kissed his cheek, which surprised and pleased him.

"I love you, so much!" she said, letting go of him. "Now I'd better get back so I can watch you fight." She was gone before he could say anything.

Bodine stood up and smiled to himself. He always received love and affection when he came to Invermere, and Colwyn, like her mother, thought the world of him. He turned round and spotted McDowell in the distance, staring at him and he suddenly had the urge to upset the duke as much as he could during the tournament. It was an illogical feeling, but he just felt he had to make sure that McDowell knew that he was the favoured one at Invermere, although he suspected that McDowell might already know that.

It was a well-known fact that Bodine had never been beaten in a sword fight since the age of fourteen, thus it was no surprise that he should reach the final of the swordplay. However, it was another fact that Nigel McDowell had also never been beaten since coming of age and had also reached the final. In addition, he was also eight years Bodine's senior and thus in theory, stronger and more experienced. The fight had drawn a large crowd, as many also knew the two men had little affection for one another, and as much as many feared Bodine, they liked the Duke of Cottesmere even less; his cruelty and selfish ambition were known throughout the Kingdom. McDowell resented the open show of warmth that the Coltranes bestowed upon the Kadeau Duke, so if there was an opportunity that he could defeat the young whippersnapper in front of them, he was going to grab it with open arms. This would be the first time the two would meet in any kind of battle.

Aware of the animosity they felt towards each other, everyone was eagerly looking forward to the forthcoming match and wagers on the outcome were flying around.

"So, Richard," the King began, "what do you wager on the outcome?"

"Strictly speaking, my Liege, McDowell's more experienced and has seen more action, so that speaks in his favour; however," Coltrane quickly continued seeing the King about to try and persuade him to wager something foolish, "Bodine is fitter, and more level-headed. It is a difficult decision."

"Father!" Colwyn chastised. "Morgan will win," she said confidently.

"And pray tell, young Colwyn, why this will be the outcome?" the King asked, an amused expression on his face.

"Because I want him to win."

The King laughed delightedly. "See, Richard, 'tis nothing to do with skill and experience, but what a woman wants!" He laughed again, clearly enjoying the day.

"Your Majesty," Colwyn said gravely. "Morgan is the best!"

He held out his arms to her. "Come, child, sit with me and let us see if you are right."

"Richard," Bronwyn whispered quietly to her husband, "do you think it wise that Colwyn watches this? It is likely to be a rather… heated fight, knowing how these two men feel towards each other."

Chapter Three

"It is best she learns here of war; in play—rough though it might be—than to see the real thing first hand. Let her be."

A herald announced the arrival of the two opponents who walked into the arena and up to where the King and Queen's party were sitting. A great hush came over the audience as the two men bowed respectfully to their King, and then less amicably to one another. Each then made some final adjustments to their armour and it was at this time that Bodine made a great flourish of showing the fact that he possessed a lady's favour and bowed once again toward the royal entourage. The watching crowd murmured amongst themselves.

Curious as to who it could be, Bronwyn glanced along the line of ladies, then turned her head in the opposite direction, just in time to see her daughter's face light up with pure delight, incline her head slightly and give the most perfect of royal waves with her right hand.

"Methinks your daughter is growing up too fast," Coltrane murmured in his wife's general direction, making her smile. Whenever Colwyn did something 'unusual', she was always her mother's daughter, rather than her father's.

The King eyed Colwyn thoughtfully and contemplated a possible future for her.

And the whole show that Bodine put on had the desired effect on McDowell, who openly scowled at his opponent.

"Your Champion is playing with fire, Majesty," Coltrane stated quietly.

"We shall see." The King indicated with his right hand that he was ready for the final contest to begin.

Bodine and McDowell turned to face one another. The Kadeau Lord smiled amicably at his opponent, further fuelling the resentment.

"I shall wipe that smile off your face, Bodine, make no mistake," McDowell hissed.

"Sounds more to me like an old cockerel making a lot of noise to cover the fact he's no longer functioning as he should," Bodine retorted and smiled even more.

As the two men walked round in a large circle, sizing one another up, everyone was wondering who was going to land the first strike. McDowell attacked first, but Bodine lithely side-stepped and struck the first blow, as his sword made contact with his opponent's armour, knocking him sideward. The duke parried and responded, the sword glancing off Morgan's shield. The swords continued to clash against each other, sparks flying, their movement almost a blur as they moved around the ring; the battle was fierce, for both men were very evenly matched. It looked like it was going to be decided by whichever one of them had the stamina to continue at such a pace for any length of time.

Colwyn was doing her utmost not to fidget too much as she sat on the King's lap watching the heated battle continue. It was the first time she had ever witnessed a real sword fight. The crowd were gasping, cheering and making other sounds of approval at the skill of both swordsmen.

Bodine was still smiling, even though he was concentrating on how McDowell moved and handled his weapon and shield. He was learning a lot about his opponent who, it appeared, was not a particularly patient man when things were not going his way. Impatience usually led to mistakes, and this time was no exception, as he foolishly lunged at Bodine, who was effectively waiting for him to make such a move, and he countered with a heavy blow that sent the Cottesmere Duke flying past him to land on his face on the grass.

This did nothing to calm McDowell, especially when a loud cheer went up at his fall. Bodine gallantly allowed the duke to regain his feet, and saw the fury appear on his face. Up on the royal dais, Colwyn clapped delightedly.

Chapter Three

The duke initiated a compound attack against Bodine, delivering a deluge of blows, driving him back, until he managed successive parries, and launched his own riposte. It became evident to the spectators that McDowell was losing both his patience and temper with the youthful Bodine, who was still lithely moving around the enclosure, launching his compound attack which drove McDowell back against the rail with nowhere to go.

Seeing that he was about to lose, McDowell resorted to some unknightly tactics; he lifted a mailed foot and kicked out at Bodine, catching him at the hip and sending him staggering backwards.

"Foul!" Colwyn shouted, for she knew all the rules of engagement. "Foul, sir! Shame on you!"

The King glanced at her in amazement, wondering how she could possibly know of such things, but it immediately went out of his mind as the Duke of Cottesmere immediately followed up with a barrage of blows that Bodine parried from the ground.

Colwyn could not prevent a shriek as McDowell suddenly raised his sword to plunge it down into Bodine's chest. The cuirass was designed to stop the tip from piercing through his mail, but if severe enough, could result in severe bruising or even a serious wound, despite the padded aketon underneath. Somehow, Bodine managed to use his shield to deflect it, and it caught his side instead. Bodine grimaced as the blade sliced through one of the leather straps, punctured through the mail and the padded aketon underneath and McDowell, seeing he had wounded his opponent, tried to press on his attack, but the Rossmere Lord was far from finished and used his shield to knock his opponent off his feet.

With surprising agility, despite the wound he had received, Bodine gained his feet, knocked McDowell's shield from his hand, trod on the wrist of his sword arm, forcing him to let go of his weapon, and placed his own sword at his throat. The battle was over.

Forgetting all etiquette and manners, Colwyn leapt from the King's lap and stood up, clapping and cheering.

"Do you yield, McDowell?" Bodine asked. He was breathing heavily but looking pleased that he had scored a victory over his opponent to remain unbeaten in battle.

McDowell lay there, wincing at the amount of force Bodine was exerting on his wrist, and knew it was over. "I yield," he spat at the Kadeau Duke, and Bodine removed his foot. McDowell rubbed his wrist and looked at Bodine with hate in his eyes before gaining his feet.

Bodine nodded and walked away to stand directly below the dais where the King was now standing. McDowell went to stand next to him. They turned and saluted each other before turning, saluting the king, and sheathing their swords.

"Our champion of the sword; Morgan Bodine, Duke of Rossmere!" proclaimed King Stuart. Everyone cheered, and then the King motioned for him to ascend the dais to receive his crown.

Bodine knelt in front of his King, who handed the gold band to Colwyn and indicated for her to proceed. In awe and wonderment, she placed the gold band upon the duke's head and another cheer went up. Gaining his feet, Bodine turned and acknowledged the crowd, then graciously bent over and kissed Colwyn's hand. He would now be able to rest, for the jousting was to take place the following day, which was just as well, as his side was feeling rather sore.

He was suddenly aware of Colwyn frowning at him, and he looked down at his right side. Suddenly suspicious, he placed his fingers on his surcoat, where McDowell's sword had penetrated, drew them back and saw the blood.

"Morgan!" Colwyn whispered.

Chapter Three

"It's nothing; just a scratch," he assured her. "I will get my battle surgeon to check it. Do not worry."

"Make sure he does," the King said. "You have the jousting tomorrow. I expect my champion to win!"

"Yes, Sire." He bowed and left the dais to go and find his battle surgeon.

Colwyn, concerned that her champion was hurt, curtsied to the King and Queen and ran after him.

Bodine went to his rooms and found Master Andrew reading a book he had borrowed from the library. He stood up as Bodine entered.

"Congratulations, Morgan. You won then," Andrew said, noting the gold band on his head.

"Yes."

"Your record continues. I assume you sent McDowell packing with his tail between his legs."

"Yes, but it's not over yet, there is the jousting tomorrow." Bodine dropped his gauntlets onto the table and looked around for his personal steward. "Where is Ioan?"

"I'm sorry, Morgan, I let him go and watch the activities. I wasn't expecting you to return so soon. Let me help you instead." Andrew unbuckled the sword belt and surcoat belt, and Bodine pulled the surcoat over his head, wincing slightly as he did so. It was as Andrew was undoing the buckles on the right side of the cuirass that he found the severed leather, and spied the blood. With a sense of urgency, he started to undo the other buckles, just as there was a knock on the door.

"Enter!" shouted Bodine and Colwyn came in. "Colwyn, you should not be here."

"You are my champion this weekend; I need to make sure you are all right." She walked up to him and started undoing the buckles on the left side of the cuirass.

Andrew looked at Bodine, who inclined his head, and they carried on. Andrew removed the cuirass and inspected the mail before lifting it over his head. "This will need repairing, Morgan," he said. Bodine did his best not to grimace as he lifted his right arm, so Andrew could pull the hauberk off.

Bodine looked down and saw the blood on his aketon. He undid the lacings and eased out of it, then out of his silk shirt. Now bare-chested, Andrew leant over and inspected the wound, which still bled. Colwyn stood quietly, looking on. As yet, she was still too young to appreciate the athletic build of her hero, or any sexual feeling of attraction. Bodine was broad-shouldered, with narrow hips; a slight dusting of hair on his chest. The skin was lightly bronzed and tight over the muscles. He had a small scar on his right arm from an old wound he had suffered in the past.

"Do you require a basin of water, Master Andrew?" Colwyn asked.

"Yes, Lady Colwyn, I do."

She immediately went to the dressing table and poured some water into a small basin and took it to Andrew, who had retrieved a pouch from his medical supplies and poured some powder from it into the water. Using a strip of cloth, again retrieved from his supplies, he dipped it in the bowl and wiped the wound clean. Bodine grimaced, for whatever was in the powder stung quite badly.

"This will stop any infection, Morgan," Andrew said as he then sprinkled another powder directly onto the wound to stop the bleeding.

Seeing that the wound wasn't too serious, Colwyn inspected the damage on the aketon and the surcoat. "I will get this cleaned and repaired in time for tomorrow, Morgan, if you will permit me."

"Colwyn, you don't need to do that."

"Yes, I do. I will return this by first thing in the morning. It's a good thing you bought me those silks." She also grabbed his silk shirt, turned on a heel and left.

Chapter Three

Andrew watched her go, then returned his attention to treating the wound. "She loves you very much," he said to Bodine.

"Sisterly love," Bodine replied.

"At the moment, yes, but that may change when she's older. Right, I want you to relax for a couple of hours; longer if you are able. It's stopped bleeding. I'll take your hauberk and cuirass to the blacksmith and get them repaired for tomorrow."

"Thank you, Andrew," Bodine replied, moving to the huge four-poster bed and lying down. He was feeling a little sore, so he decided to follow Andrew's advice and closed his eyes, breathing slowly and deeply, mulling over what Andrew had said about Colwyn.

Colwyn ran to her rooms to retrieve her needlework box.

"Colwyn, what are you doing here?" Sarah asked. "Shouldn't you be downstairs?"

"Sarah, would you try and get the blood out of this aketon, please, whilst I start work on the surcoat?"

Sarah looked at the coat of arms on the surcoat. The rampant dragon clearly indicated that it belonged to the Duke of Rossmere.

"What are you doing with this?" she asked.

"I'm repairing it."

"You should be with the Duke and Duchess, my Lady."

"Morgan is my champion for this tournament, I must see that his attire is fit to wear. Now please, do as you are told." Colwyn sat at her little work table and inspected the surcoat. To her relief, she realised she could get away with sewing it, rather than darning, which would be a lot quicker, and set to work. The tear was only as wide as the sword that had done the damage and she had completed the repair quickly. It was the same for his black silk shirt and that was also repaired by the time Sarah came back with the now-clean aketon.

The aketon was a more difficult challenge, with four layers to repair, but she diligently worked on it, and after a couple of hours, it was done. She gave the repair a tug or two and was pleased that the stitching held. Satisfied with her work, she spot-cleaned the surcoat and the shirt and then took the items back to Bodine's rooms. She knocked quietly but there was no reply, so she carefully opened the door and entered. The antechamber was empty, so she assumed he was either out or in the bedchamber. Knowing he would need the items, she quietly entered his bedroom and saw him lying on the huge bed, apparently asleep.

Carefully, she laid the repaired items over a chair, then went to stand by the bed, and looked down at him. Something stirred within her; something new and strange that she didn't understand. Quietly, she reached for a blanket at the bottom of the bed and started to draw it up over him. She'd got as far as his hips when he suddenly stirred, and, with lightning speed, he had retrieved a dagger from under his pillow and it stopped, mere millimetres from her throat.

Colwyn froze but made no sound. There was no fear in her eyes, just complete trust. "You have nothing to fear from me, Morgan," she said softly.

He gasped in shock at what he had nearly done, and slowly lowered the dagger. "Colwyn!" His voice shook as he surveyed the expression on her face. No one had ever looked at him the way she was looking at him now. "I-I could have killed you! W-what are you doing here?"

"No, you wouldn't, Morgan. You could never harm me. The damage to your aketon, surcoat and shirt was not as bad as I thought. I have repaired them." She dropped the blanket and indicated the chair the items were draped over. "I thought you looked cold, so I was just covering you with a blanket."

"Oh, my pet, I'm sorry, I'm just not used to all this affection." He put the dagger down and held his arms open.

Chapter Three

Colwyn surrendered herself to him, wrapping her arms around him and hugging him tightly as her head nestled into his shoulder. "I could stay here forever," she whispered. "But I know I can't." She drew back slightly. "Will I see you at supper tonight, or are you dining here in your room?"

"You will see me tonight, Colwyn."

"In that case, I shall leave you to rest and recover. My champion has to win the jousting tomorrow." She looked down at his right side. "Does it hurt much?"

"No; a little sore. It's just a scratch."

"I wish I could make it better."

"Oh, Colwyn, your affection for me more than helps. Now, hadn't you better get back? I'm surprised no one has sent out a search party for you."

She giggled, then leant forward and kissed his lips. "I love you, Morgan Bodine," she whispered innocently, and then she was gone.

Bodine smiled and shook his head. It felt good to be loved.

Bronwyn decided to go in search of her daughter, and found her in her room.

"And where have you been, young lady? I started to get worried."

"Mother, I had to take care of some repair work for my champion," Colwyn replied seriously.

"You didn't have to do that; one of the maids could have done it just as easily."

"But not as well," she replied. It was not a vain or boastful comment, but just a statement of fact, for Colwyn had a very rare talent in regard to anything associated with needlework.

"You are fond of Morgan, aren't you?" her mother asked.

"I love him with all of my heart," she answered seriously.

"And I am sure Morgan appreciates that greatly. He has not known a lot of love in his life. Now, are you changing for supper?"

"Yes, Mother."

"Very well; we shall see you downstairs shortly."

Sarah helped her young charge prepare for the evening and watched her skip out of her room.

In the King and Queen's chamber, Stuart was still thinking about Colwyn.

"Husband, what troubles you?" Alexandra asked.

"I was thinking about Colwyn. She would make a fine queen for our son, but her age is against her."

"She will only be twenty when Llywelyn is ready to marry; that is still young enough to provide an heir; that is, if you think she would be right for him?"

"I think she would be, but we still have a few years, and, at the moment, she seems rather taken with Morgan Bodine."

"She is not right for him," Alexandra replied quickly; too quickly.

"Why do you hate my Champion so much?" he asked her.

"He is Kadeau. That is reason enough."

"But the Cantrell family has always had Kadeau in their service and for protection. Morgan has more than proved his loyalty. There isn't a finer knight in the Kingdom. He is honourable; he excels in his duties, Llywelyn thinks the world of him, and so do I."

"I don't like him being near our son or this family, and I definitely do not like him being near Colwyn."

"Don't let her hear you say that; he is currently her hero, and she has given him a favour for this tournament."

"Yes, I saw that. I will speak to Bronwyn about having Colwyn at court so I can keep an eye on her, train her, and seek out a suitable husband, if it turns out not to be our son."

Chapter Three

"Whomever is chosen, it needs to be for the good of the Kingdom. Invermere and Rossmere would make an excellent match."

"I don't want to argue about it now. We are guests here. And, as you say, there is time."

Stuart kissed his wife and they went down to dine.

The seating arrangements were the same as the previous night, and, once again, food and wine flowed. Bodine was dancing with the duchess after dinner and made polite conversation.

"Bronwyn, Colwyn is truly gifted with regard to her needle skills," Bodine told her.

"She told me she had made the repairs to your attire herself. She would trust no one else with the job, because quite frankly, she is the best in the duchy, even at her tender years."

"I can't even see where the repairs were made, they were so well done."

Bronwyn lowered her voice. "Morgan, you must tell me if she is making a nuisance of herself. She appears to have grown rather fond of you."

"Never a nuisance, Bronwyn. I love her very much, like my sister, and I believe she loves me like a brother."

Bronwyn considered his words for a few moments before whispering, "And what if that changes to another kind of love down the line?"

"That would be a few years from now; things may change."

"Perhaps, but at the moment she is fond of you; and I have no objections, Morgan, whatever happens. Now, or going forward."

Bodine found himself colouring slightly.

"We would be honoured to have you in our family, one way or another."

"I-I don't know what to say."

"Then say nothing." She smiled at him.

McDowell decided to approach Colwyn and she started looking for a way to escape. The King just happened to glance in her direction, and noticed her expression, as the Duke of Cottesmere approached.

"Colwyn, my dear," the King said. "I apologise. I believe this is our dance, is it not?"

"Yes, Your Majesty, it is," she confirmed, amazed that her sovereign had come to her rescue.

Bodine had noticed the situation and breathed a sigh of relief as Stuart came to Colwyn's rescue, but the King could not dance with her all evening. Sooner or later, McDowell was going to get his way and dance with the Duchess-in-Waiting.

In the end, he was unable to save her, as the King had made the Queen dance with him. He could feel her dislike through the entire dance, politely saying nothing, but Alexandra felt him stiffen as McDowell at last cornered Colwyn and she was left with no option or avenue of escape.

"You do not like Duke McDowell being near the Lady Colwyn?" the Queen said to him.

"My Queen, Colwyn is scared of the duke, and I made a promise to the Duchess Bronwyn that I would keep her daughter safe."

"Are you sure you do not have designs on her yourself?"

"Your Majesty, Colwyn is still a child, and I love her like my sister. This family has been so kind to me since I lost my parents. I now think of them as my family."

"She is of marriageable age, Duke."

"True, but she is still a child, and any marriage must be for the good of the Kingdom."

The dance ended and Bodine escorted Alexandra back to her chair, bowing respectfully, before he turned and saw Colwyn still with McDowell and he frowned, concerned.

Chapter Three

Colwyn had erected a stone wall in her mind and was not letting McDowell get close to her thoughts. He was known to dabble in the black arts, and she was not about to let him try anything on her.

"My dear," McDowell said conversationally, "You are again looking beautiful tonight."

Colwyn said nothing.

"I was thinking, perhaps when the tournament is over, you and I could get to know one another better. We have had so little time with each other."

"Why?" Colwyn asked rudely.

"You have been avoiding me, and I believe a man and a woman should get to know each other before they are wed."

It was no good. Colwyn stopped dancing at that instant and jerked her hands free of him.

"Know this, Duke, I will never marry you!" she hissed quietly.

"You will do what your father tells you to do, and one day, in the very near future, you will be mine," he whispered in reply, reaching for her.

She stepped back away from him and clasped her hands behind her so McDowell couldn't grab them as he continued to step forward. Suddenly, she reversed into an immovable object. Looking up and behind, her eyes closed briefly in relief. It was Bodine. He bent down and lifted her into his arms and she grabbed him around the neck, burying her head in his shoulder.

Even with all the finery of their clothing, he could feel her heart racing with fear, thudding against his chest. Bodine glared at McDowell, his grey eyes cold as he surveyed his adversary.

McDowell stepped forward. "Hang onto her whilst you can, Bodine. She will be mine," he whispered, before turning and leaving the room.

Bodine took a deep breath, and let it out slowly. "I will avenge you tomorrow, my pet, in the joust," he whispered into her ear. He looked up to see Bronwyn's worried face, as she started towards them. Anxious to avoid a scene, he walked towards her, still carrying Colwyn.

"Morgan, what's happened?" Bronwyn asked, worried.

Bodine shook his head, indicating this was not the place for a conversation. She nodded, immediately understanding and turned to the King and Queen.

"My daughter is overtired. Forgive us, Your Majesties, as we put her to bed."

"Of course," Stuart said, but studied Morgan and Colwyn thoughtfully; he had witnessed the entire scene from across the hall.

Curtsying and bowing, they made their exit, leaving Richard Coltrane to look after their guests. Nothing was said all the way to Colwyn's rooms, and she was very reluctant to let go of the duke once they were there, until her mother reminded her that her champion had a jousting tournament tomorrow and needed to rest.

"Thank you, Morgan," Colwyn whispered, and kissed his cheek before he set her down on the ground.

"Do not worry, my pet. You will be safe, now."

"Sarah, please put my daughter to bed," Bronwyn instructed. "Goodnight, my darling." Bronwyn bent down and kissed her daughter before exiting with Bodine. Outside, Bronwyn asked, "So what was all that about?"

Bodine sighed. "McDowell wants her for his wife."

"Oh, dear God. He didn't actually say that in front of her, did he?"

"Yes."

Bronwyn was horrified. "She must have been terrified. Oh, Morgan, I'm so glad you were there. Richard and I will need to think very carefully now, about her future. We will keep her safe until she is older, and then we must think what we can do to stop McDowell getting his hands on her."

Chapter Three

Bodine nodded but said nothing. He was currently the King's Champion, and was due to become General of his armies shortly. He needed to concentrate on that, and consequently, there was no time to divert to other activities. It would be unknightly to offer to step in as a prospective husband, as that could upset the Cottesmere Duke further, and lead to even more unpleasantness.

"Somehow, we will keep her safe," he finally answered. "If you will excuse me, Bronwyn, I need to get some rest for tomorrow. I will probably be up against McDowell again."

"Of course, Morgan. We will all see you tomorrow, and be cheering for you." She kissed his cheek and left for her rooms.

Bodine went to his own chambers, stripped off and got comfortable in the huge four-poster bed. Sleep took a little while to claim him, as his mind was filled with ways to keep Colwyn safe from the clutches of McDowell.

The following morning, after breakfast, everyone gathered at the jousting ring for the main event of the day. There was a lot of pageantry associated with this event, with all the flags flying and tents just outside. It was a very colourful sight, and a gentle breeze accentuated this as the flags fluttered under its caress. The weather was good again, and the ground firm beneath the horses' feet.

Colwyn had wanted to go and wish Bodine luck, but the events of the previous night had knocked her confidence and she was subdued; unsure about wandering about her home on her own with McDowell present. The King immediately noticed this and tried to cheer her up by again having her sit on his lap and ask her opinion of the opponents.

Bodine made it easily through the various rounds, and Colwyn finally started to relax again; however, when McDowell appeared, she was deathly silent. Stuart whispered softly in her ear, "You have nothing to fear from McDowell; I will not allow him to harm you."

Colwyn smiled tentatively at him. "Thank you, Your Majesty," she said in a whisper.

"Now come, cheer; here is our champion," Stuart said, as Bodine again entered the jousting arena, and once again dispatched his opponent on the first run to reach the quarter-final.

Bodine glanced up at the royal enclosure as he cantered out of the arena. He could see that Colwyn still wasn't particularly happy. Whatever happened, he had to make sure McDowell hit the ground to avenge her.

It took two lances to take down his next opponent in the quarter-final, and another two to dispatch his opponent in the semi. Now it was the final and again, he was facing McDowell. The sword was Bodine's primary weapon of choice, but he had been practising hard with the lance, which in all tournaments was the top award to win.

The duke's young stallion, Banner, seemed to know they had reached the final and was prancing with anticipation, making it difficult for Ioan, Bodine's personal steward, to hand him his lance. Bodine spoke to his spirited black steed, and the horse stood still long enough for him to take it from Ioan.

The two opponents lined up at either end of the run, then kicked their horses into a canter. Lances were lined up and splintered as they hit each other's shields. A roar went up from the crowd. They cantered back past each other to pick up a replacement lance and lined up again. The flag went down, and they charged at each other again. Up on the dais, Colwyn was clutching the King's hand, willing Bodine to knock McDowell off his horse, but it was not to be. McDowell deliberately aimed for Bodine's right side, where he had injured him the day before. It did not work as well as he wanted, and both riders sustained severe blows. McDowell was almost unseated but managed to hold on. Bodine was winded, even through all the padding of his aketon under the mail, and they returned for the third lance.

Chapter Three

"My Lord, are you all right?" Ioan asked Bodine as he took hold of the lance. The duke nodded, although he thought his wound from yesterday had started bleeding again.

At the other end of the run, McDowell had felt a rib crack under the last onslaught and was furious that Bodine had managed to inflict an injury on him.

Once again they charged at each other. Bodine now thought he had seen a way through McDowell's defence, and this third run was to be the final confirmation. Again, damage was inflicted on both sides; Bodine felt himself leaning forward clutching his right side. He could probably manage a fourth lance but after that, he wasn't sure he would be able to withstand any more. He grimaced underneath his helm as he took the fourth lance, and he was breathing heavily, but looking down the other end of the arena, he was pleased to see that McDowell wasn't fairing much better. Bodine's stallion picked up his unease and started prancing again, jarring his injury. He squeezed his legs against the horse's flanks and it leapt forward. He sighted his lance, and then, at the last second, shifted it slightly to the left so it slid, scraping the side of the shield by the barest of measurements and struck McDowell's body. The force knocked him from the saddle to hit the ground, but also travelled up Bodine's lance and through his arm, and caused him to drop it. He collapsed forward on the saddle but managed not to fall.

Up from their vantage point, Colwyn cheered, but then the King heard her agonised, "Morgan!" as he collapsed forward in the saddle, but managed to stay mounted. His squire ran into the arena, ready to hold Bodine's stallion when it reached the base of the steps to the dais. The duke cantered back past McDowell, who was still on the floor, his steward at his side, and pulled up by Ioan, who grabbed the reins. Bodine dropped his shield on the ground and dismounted with a little difficulty. He pulled off his helm, dropped that and pushed the mail coif off his head. Wearily, he ascended the stairs towards his Liege.

Once again, Colwyn was standing next to the King. Bodine bowed with some difficulty and straightened up again.

"Sire," he whispered.

"Our tournament champion!" Stuart announced to everyone present. "Morgan Bodine, Duke of Rossmere!" Again a large cheer ran out. "Colwyn, my dear, would you again do the honours?" He handed her a more ornate band. Bodine knelt before her, and she placed the band on his bowed head. "Arise, champion," said Stuart.

Bodine grimaced as he got to his feet, but raised his hand and turned to the crowd, who cheered. The King's Champion was unbeaten and had proved once again why he held the position.

"Well done, Morgan," Stuart whispered. "Now go, see your battle surgeon and get that injury seen to." He looked down at Colwyn. "My dear, accompany your champion."

Colwyn curtsied and led the way down the dais to the arena. She glanced across to see that McDowell was just getting to his feet and was glad he'd been hurt, then paused to pat Bodine's stallion, who snorted at her. Ioan led the horse away, the duke's shield now hooked on the saddle, and the squire was carrying the helm. Bodine and Colwyn headed for the castle and his rooms.

Andrew was waiting for him. He had watched the proceedings and knew that Ioan would be seeing to the horse, so had returned to Bodine's rooms to help him out of his armour and examine his wounds.

With Colwyn's help, they removed the many layers that made up the armour and padding, until he was, again, sitting shirtless on the bed. Colwyn fetched a basin of water for Andrew to start his ministrations. The wound

Chapter Three

had reopened and was now accompanied by bruising, but apart from that and some general aches and pains, Bodine was unharmed.

"Would you like me to arrange a bath for you, Morgan?" Colwyn asked him. "I can arrange it for a few hours' time so you can rest a while, then get freshened up for the final banquet."

"Thank you, Colwyn. Morgan would greatly appreciate that," Andrew answered for him.

"Very well; I will sort it out."

"Thank you, Colwyn," said Morgan, and he kissed her hand. He found it hard to believe that she was only coming up to twelve years of age, for she acted far older, but then he remembered Bronwyn saying something about girls maturing much faster than boys.

"Okay, Morgan, lie down and get some rest," Andrew ordered, and the duke did as he was told, easing himself back against the pillows and mattress, relaxing with a heavy sigh.

"Thank you for avenging me," Colwyn whispered to him as Andrew busied himself tidying his tools and bandages away. "But I'm sorry you got hurt."

"It's nothing, my pet," Bodine replied softly.

"I'll leave you to rest," she said, and leant over and kissed him.

Bodine sighed and smiled; his eyes closed, his chest rising and falling slowly as he relaxed.

Colwyn sighed as she came back to the present. Yes, that had been a weekend to remember. It was the birth of McDowell's burning ambition to rule the Kingdom, and the confirmation for Colwyn that the sisterly affection she had held for the Duke of Rossmere had changed to another kind of love.

༄ ༅ ༄ ༅

4

Chapter Four

Every day, Colwyn accompanied the Queen, along with the other ladies-in-waiting. The Queen was more than capable of conducting court whilst the King was absent, and Colwyn learnt a lot from her. When she was not ruling the Kingdom, they spent the majority of their time in the Queen's rooms, sewing and playing various games. Colwyn found it rather boring, compared to what she was used to doing back at Inver; she had taken to always being seated by the window as it provided better light to work by, but also enabled her to keep an eye on the courtyard, and an ear out for any herald that would signal the approach of the Duke of Rossmere. He was due back from Inver any day now, and she desperately needed news of the situation.

It was a bright but breezy mid-April morning and Colwyn was once again in the company of her Majesty, Queen Alexandra, in her private ante-chambers, along with the rest of the ladies-in-waiting. As usual, she was seated in her favourite place, overlooking the main courtyard, working half-heartedly on the delicate lace that was famous throughout the Duchy of Invermere. It was an edging for a veil for the Queen—although Alexandra did not know this—and Colwyn had worked long and hard on a special design for her.

Chapter Four

The reason for her distraction was the rumour currently circulating; that He was on his way. The mere mention of his name had a devastating effect on everyone and Colwyn was filled with curiosity. She had known the duke all her life, but the last time she had seen him, she had been but a child, almost twelve years of age, and he barely a man. That had been nearly five years ago, and she remembered she had grown very close to the Kadeau Duke. In her near-death experience on her harrowing journey to safety just a couple of months previously, she had been told that he had nursed her and brought her back from the brink of death, but she had no recollection of this, apart from the memory of a pair of intense grey-blue eyes, which she now realised had been his, and thus, was looking forward to the opportunity of thanking him for his kindness. Hence, she had one eye on the courtyard and the other on her lace.

Time seemed to drag. Noon approached and there was still no sign. Colwyn was just about to give up hope of his arriving before lunch, when Lady Constance burst into the room in a most undignified fashion, breathless and flushed.

"Oh, oh, he's coming! He's coming! He's on the final approach!" she stammered breathlessly, her rather plump figure quivering in a mixture of excitement and fear. "The Duke of Rossmere!"

And as if to confirm this, the sound of a herald wafted through the air.

Colwyn glanced at the Queen in time to notice her features harden. Was it with displeasure at Lady Constance, or was it something more than that?

"Lady Constance, please conduct yourself accordingly, I have a severe headache today," Alexandra stated sharply, putting her own needlework aside. "In fact, it is so bad, I shall retire to my bed-chamber. You may all leave me now." She rose abruptly and the ladies present followed her lead to curtsy as the Queen left.

Colwyn's gaze shifted once more to the courtyard. If he was on the final approach, she would have enough time to get down to the antechamber preceding the Great Hall and obtain a good vantage point. Trying to appear casual, she moved swiftly along to the antechamber to await his arrival.

The news had spread throughout the castle, for already the room was crowded. Although all afraid of him, they were there to get a glimpse of the dreaded Kadeau Lord, Duke of Rossmere, King's Champion and General of the Armies; the most feared man in the Kingdom of Devonmere. Personally, she was at a loss to understand it. The King trusted Morgan Bodine implicitly and the King was a good man. There was no evil in him, therefore, there could be no evil in Bodine—yet almost everyone feared him. The exceptions were those who had known him all his life: his cousin, Colin McLeod, Llywelyn, the young prince (after all, children were very astute); James Douglas, the Bishop of Ellesmere and King's confessor; and of course, King Stuart Cantrell.

On thinking further, it was not really the man they feared, but what he was; a Kadeau, with magical powers; powers which he rarely used, and when he did, had only been used for good. He would not be able to deceive so many good and powerful men. Furthermore, he had shown Colwyn nothing but kindness and affection. Therefore, until he showed this so-called evil to her, she would show him all the respect and courtesy such a man deserved.

It was said that Bodine had been riding hard from Invermere, having finished arranging the temporary governing of the Duchy. If this were true, then he would be tired, dirty, and no doubt irritable. A friendly face in the hostile crowd would perhaps make him feel a little better.

Colwyn positioned herself at the top end of the antechamber near the double doors to the Great Hall. There were steps here, and she stood level with the front line of the crowd. From this vantage point, she would be able

Chapter Four

to observe Bodine's entrance and his entire journey along the length of the antechamber. Her heart almost missed a beat at the thought.

Suddenly, the doors to the antechamber were thrown open and an incredible hush descended upon the room as the Kadeau Lord walked in, followed by Bishop James Douglas.

Colwyn had not been sure what to expect on seeing him after all this time and she had deliberately tried to stop her imagination from getting the better of her with regard to his possible appearance now, to go along with some of the things she had heard about him. On seeing the real object, she came to the conclusion that she was still very much in love with the duke.

Five years older, now twenty-two, she noted he still dressed totally in black, including the rich cloak that hung from his shoulders. Even his sword possessed a black hilt, and, hidden within a black scabbard, was almost invisible against the rest of his clothing.

He was an imposing figure, very tall, slim, yet powerfully built, with broad shoulders; his hair was the colour of burnished gold and that beautiful now fully bearded face still possessed those steely grey eyes. The added years had given more character to his features, and, if it was at all possible, Colwyn thought him more handsome than ever. Even in his dusty and rather unkempt state, he emitted an aura and the look on his face challenged everyone as those eyes swept the room.

Slowly and purposefully, he began to walk along the length of the antechamber, a hand resting on the hilt of his sword, his spurs clanking on the stone floor and catching the light that streamed through the long windows. Onlookers drew back uneasily and in fear as his gaze fell upon them, and they dropped their eyes, unable to meet the intense stare, frightened that he would read their very souls.

All around her, Colwyn felt the people step back, leaving her to stand forward of them all. Confidently and proudly, she met that gaze and held it as he drew abreast of her. Abruptly, he stopped, one foot on the steps leading to the Great Hall, to brush the dust off his clothes.

In this brief moment, Colwyn had time to notice the grime on his face, the mud spattered on his long boots and the unkempt appearance of a man badly in need of a good, hot bath, before he straightened and looked again at this young woman who was not afraid to meet his gaze. A surge of—he wasn't sure what—went through him as she dropped slowly and deliberately into a long, graceful curtsy, to the horror of the onlookers.

Bodine pulled off his gauntlets as he walked towards her, extended a hand, took hers in his and placed it to his lips.

"My Lady Colwyn," he said softly as he drew her to her feet. "I am pleased to see you well again."

"Welcome, my Lord," she replied softly, lowering her eyelashes briefly before meeting his gaze once more, and green eyes locked onto intense grey-blue. "Your absence has been sorely felt." She wanted to say more, but here, in front of all these people was neither the time nor the place.

He smiled warmly at her before giving her an almost imperceptible nod. Then he released her hand and her gaze and continued his journey through into the Great Hall and the King's Chamber. Behind him, Bishop Douglas nodded what looked like his approval, before following.

The moment the doors closed behind them, noise erupted around Colwyn. Many stared at her as if she were mad; others crossed themselves reverently. She held herself proudly, even though her heart was thudding almost painfully in her chest, and glided out, enjoying being the centre of attention for once. That would certainly give them all something to think about!

Meanwhile, in the King's Chamber, just off the Great Hall, the noise penetrated for a minute or so before fading away. King Stuart Cantrell

Chapter Four

vacated his seat of state and came down the steps towards the man he fondly thought of as his brother.

"Now what have you been up to?" he asked in mock indignation, preventing Bodine from dropping to one knee, as etiquette required, by giving him a fierce hug of welcome.

"Not I, for once, my King," Bodine replied smiling and returning the embrace.

"Indeed. Methinks General Bodine has an admirer outside," James Douglas chipped in, bowing gracefully.

Stuart Cantrell straightened abruptly and held Bodine at arm's length. "Morgan! You mean there was someone out there who did not cower from your steely gaze?"

"Alas, Sire, 'tis true –"

"—and furthermore, she curtsied most prettily and welcomed him back!"

"James, please shut up!"

"A woman! And Morgan, you not looking your best! Surely, in full splendour, she would swoon at your feet!" Stuart was enjoying teasing his woman-shy friend. "So, who was she?"

"It was the Lady Colwyn, my Liege."

"Aha! Colwyn! I might have guessed," the King stated triumphantly. "But come," Stuart continued, placing a brotherly arm around Bodine and leading him towards some well-padded chairs in front of a huge log fire. "Let us at least be comfortable. Give me a brief rundown on the situation in Inver and we'll talk in depth tomorrow. I want to make sure you get some rest; I've laid on a small banquet in celebration of your return."

CB ED CB ED

Having had something to eat, Colwyn went for a walk and stumbled across the stables. The castle was so large that she was still trying to get used to its layout. Curious, she went and explored, and saw Dernley feeling the front legs of his destrier.

"Giles, what's wrong?" Colwyn asked as she approached.

"I think Archer is limping, but it's very slight."

"Bring him out; let's look more closely," Colwyn said.

Dernley did as she asked, and walked him past her.

"Front left," she said before Dernley even had a chance to move him properly.

"How can you possibly know that?"

"I can hear it." She knelt down and placed a hand on Archer's fetlock and gently felt around the area and then compared it with the other. "The left one is warmer than the right, and there is just a slight swelling in the area. I suggest no exercise; confine him to his stall, get a cold compress on it, and then bandage to offer support, but don't make it too tight. Let me try something I saw one of our old ostlers do. Bring him back to his stall."

Dernley lead him back into his stall and Colwyn gently began to massage the area. Archer tossed his head and she spoke quietly to him. "Shush now, Archer. I know it hurts, but let's try this, shall we?" She carried on for around ten minutes, then soaked a cloth in some cold water and applied it, pouring more cold water over it for a few minutes. Dernley left her whilst she did this and went looking for cloth that could be used as a bandage. He returned after a little while.

Colwyn carefully wrapped the fetlock and leg, and, after tying it off, stood up.

"I will return and treat him every day," she said to Dernley. "Let's see if we can make him better."

"You don't have to do this," Dernley said to her.

"But I want to, Giles," she replied, stroking Archer, who was nuzzling her. "Now, Archer, you be a good boy; no prancing about, just stand quietly

Chapter Four

and let your leg heal. Giles, you will have to find an alternate mount for the next few weeks or so."

"Weeks!"

"Yes, I think he has damaged a tendon."

"If that is true, he will have to be destroyed."

"No! Let me try this first, please! There … there has been enough death already this year," she finished in a whisper, suddenly feeling emotional. "Excuse me," she added and quickly left, to return to her rooms to collect her lace before going to hide in the rose garden.

☙ ❧ ☙ ❧

Following his reasonably brief meeting with the King, Bodine decided he needed some fresh air to help him unwind before retiring for a few hours, and thus he made his way into the walled garden. Douglas had arranged for a page to sort out a bath and Bodine's personal steward was sorting out a change of clothes for him for the evening's festivities.

The Kadeau Lord wandered along to the rose garden where there were several secluded spots for him to take refuge in, and he could let go and unwind without being seen. He knew he was over-tense, as if waiting for something to happen.

His senses alerted him to a presence ahead in a rose-strewn alcove. Cautiously, he approached, hand on the hilt of his sword.

"Now this is the last morsel for today," a soft voice was saying.

Bodine peered around curiously. It was Colwyn, and she was feeding a red squirrel that was sitting on her knee, busily chewing its titbit.

"There, all gone, and so should you be! I've got some lace to finish and it must be perfect. Go on, off you go!"

Bodine stepped around into full view, and the squirrel ran for its life. Colwyn looked up sharply and seeing who it was, rose briefly to her feet before dropping into a curtsy.

"Duke Morgan."

"You do not need to drop into a curtsy every time I appear, Duchess Colwyn," Bodine said kindly as he once again took her hand, brought it to his lips and then pulled her to her feet. "And why address me in such a manner? We are family; you and I are equals; there is no need for such formality between us."

"No, my Lord, not at this time. I have no control over my lands; the Duchy is in ruins. What good is a title without the land it belongs to?"

"They will be returned to you, I give you my word; and once I have finished talking with the King, I promise I shall give you an update." Still holding her hand, he led her back to the seat. "Please, sit with me awhile; we cannot be observed from here."

She frowned at him as she did as he asked.

Bodine explained as he sat down beside her. "Have you so quickly forgotten? A lady of breeding alone with a dreaded Kadeau? Come now, you must have heard the talk, especially around this castle."

"I have heard; one cannot help but do so and, from what I have observed so far, my Lord, you yourself do little to discourage it. Dressing in black, phrasing things in a way that makes people think you have read their minds… shall I go on?"

Bodine studied her profile, then fixed his silvery gaze on her green eyes as she finally looked back at him. "So, why are you not afraid of me, like everyone else?"

Colwyn found she could not break away from his gaze, but it didn't matter because she wanted to admire those grey eyes. She was also finding it

Chapter Four

difficult to breathe as they stared intently at one another and once again, her heart was pounding. After a few moments, she managed to speak.

"You know that I have never been afraid of you. What have you done, that I should be afraid, my Lord? His Majesty, the King trusts you implicitly; you are his Champion and General of his Armies, a position of the highest responsibility. The young Prince speaks fondly of you. My mother thought the world of you. We spent time alone together on your last visit to Inver Castle. You cannot, therefore, be evil."

"Why do others not think as you do?"

"Because, as I said, you do nothing to discourage it; the people are ignorant and they are afraid of what they do not understand."

"So, you understand?"

"I'd like to think I understand you more than most, and I do have an open mind, whereas theirs are closed. You cannot blame them entirely, for in our history, some Kadeau—albeit a minority—did the most terrible things. But that was long ago."

Bodine broke eye contact and nodded. "I will admit your welcome earlier was most appreciated."

"I wished you to know that not all around you are potential enemies."

"You must be careful though, or you will be shunned by all who fear the Kadeau."

"I thank you for your concern, but it was the least I could do; you are the only family I have left and I wanted to… for the man who, I understand, saved my life."

"It wasn't only me," Bodine stated quickly. "My battle surgeon had a lot to do with it as well."

"Then I must give thanks to him also. But I do thank you. I have been told it was… very close."

Bodine nodded gravely. "My sister gave me some considerable concern. But I am pleased to see that you have made a complete recovery. You have grown up so much since I last saw you at Inver Castle."

He smiled openly at her then before unconsciously placing a thumb and forefinger on the bridge of his nose, as if to brush away the fatigue he was feeling.

"Forgive me, my Lord, you must be exhausted after your ride back from Inver; although I am desperate to hear your news, you should rest. I have waited this long, I can wait a little longer."

"I will confess to feeling somewhat tired."

"Then I shall leave." She made to rise.

"Please, wait." He grabbed her hand, amazed at himself. This was the first time they had met as adults and been able to converse and Bodine decided he wanted to get to know her more. It was so refreshing to speak with someone who was not afraid of him or of what he was. He had made an abrupt decision that he still liked her—even more so now that she was truly grown. Her eyes were her most striking feature, followed by her wonderful hair. She was pretty, but it was her aura that attracted Bodine; it was like a soothing balm on an open wound, and his subtle attempt at reading her mind had revealed no malice or deviousness within. "His Majesty has laid on a banquet this evening in honour of my return."

"Yes, I have heard."

"Will I see you there this evening?"

"If my Lord wishes it, I shall attend."

"I wish it, Colwyn."

"Then I shall wear something special for you, my Lord."

"You used to call me Morgan."

"Morgan," she repeated softly and looked up at him from under long sweeping lashes.

Chapter Four

He stared deep into her emerald eyes and gradually became aware of a rising need within him. Desperately, he fought for control, shocked at himself for almost surrendering to such a weakness. He forced himself to stand and took a deep breath to recover his composure. To Colwyn, it sounded like a heavy sigh.

Suddenly curious, Bodine looked around. It was totally deserted. "Tell me, Colwyn, can you still make the fire-light?" he asked her quietly.

"You remember?"

"It is not something I can easily forget; you asking me to teach you."

She smiled shyly, opened her left hand, palm up and concentrated. "*Ignite lumine ignis*," she whispered, and the blue fire-light appeared on her hand, burning brightly.

Bodine was impressed. "You have most certainly mastered that now," he told her, returning her smile.

"*Eatenus exstinxisti*," she continued and clenched her fist. The light vanished. "I would think so, after five years! Now that you are here, what else can you teach me?" she asked.

"We will have to experiment, if you so wish, but for now, we both need time to prepare for this evening, and I, for one, would like to get in a couple of hours sleep beforehand."

"But of course, Morgan."

"Allow me to escort you to your rooms." He offered his arm, which Colwyn gracefully accepted.

Above them, in Stuart's private chambers, the King and James Douglas were mulling over the information that Bodine had provided them with, the complications of the situation nearer to home and the happenings that had occurred in the antechamber.

"Of course, Sire, you know perfectly well it was Nigel McDowell behind the attack on Inver. His interest in the Duchy has been going on for years,"

James Douglas was saying. He had observed the young Duchess of Invermere, walking earlier in the rose garden below. "It could place the whole of Devonmere in an unstable and dangerous position if he were to take control of the Duchy by marrying Colwyn. It would place a stranglehold on Rossmere, which, in turn, would jeopardise your own position. You could very well find yourself fighting a war on two fronts."

"Colwyn hates McDowell," Stuart stated matter-of-factly. "There is no danger from that quarter; she will never marry him; I will not allow it."

"I advise you to at least be conscious of her whereabouts. If she were to be kidnapped and—"

"From within the castle?!" Stuart swung round. "James, do you know what you are saying?"

"I'm merely being cautious. McDowell has a great deal to lose if a union could be made between Invermere and some other Duchy…like Rossmere…" He let his voice trail off as he observed Bodine entering the rose garden. The movement was natural; there was no planned rendezvous.

Stuart snorted loudly, diverting Douglas's attention.

"The mere mention of Bodine's name makes every woman in Devonmere shrink and shrivel!"

"Not every woman, Sire." Douglas looked back down into the garden to continue his observations, but Bodine had disappeared. *Damn!* "Our young Colwyn bade him welcome earlier today." He turned to face the King.

Stuart's face took on a thoughtful look.

"Colwyn is a different matter altogether, James. Let us face facts. Morgan Bodine, King's Champion, General of the Armies and… bachelor; a highly desirable catch. Handsome, impeccable manners, powerful; but a Kadeau, therefore feared and rejected by all, save those who know him. Devonmere requires a Kadeau to protect the throne and the young prince. Colwyn, of marriageable age, rich, with valuable lands which are currently in ruins. She

Chapter Four

needs a husband. I had been considering her as a wife for Llywelyn; however, a union between Morgan and Colwyn… if this could be—"

"But what of your promise to her father?" Douglas broke in, feeling honour bound to mention the matter.

"From what you have described of the happenings earlier today, my promise may well be safe; and there has always been some form of affection between the two. However, I see no harm in… how shall we say… helping things along?"

"A wise precaution, my Liege." Douglas returned his attention to the garden. "Well, well, Sire, you may find this worthy of your attention."

Stuart cocked his head on one side. Filled with curiosity, he moved to where the bishop was standing and followed his gaze out of the window. Down below, Bodine and the Lady Colwyn were walking arm-in-arm.

"A good start to the proceedings, James," Stuart said softly, afraid his voice would carry to the two below. "Ensure the Lady Colwyn attends tonight and is seated next to my Champion."

"The Queen will not be pleased, Sire. She favours the Duchess."

"I shall take care of my Queen, James. This romance must be encouraged if Devonmere is to remain stable; even Alexandra must understand that."

"It will be done, Sire. After all, McDowell may even have the audacity to approach the throne and ask for Colwyn's hand. What a blow would be delivered if it could be stated he is too late!"

"Exactly, James, exactly!"

ଔ ଥ ଔ ଥ

Colwyn's handmaiden was waiting for her when she entered her rooms. "There is colour in your cheeks, young lady," Sarah scolded. "I have heard all about the episode in the antechamber."

"How can you talk like that when we were given shelter there after fleeing Invermere and after he saved my life?"

"I am not speaking against him, I am merely not condoning your actions. It has been put to me that you should stay in your rooms tonight, and I agree."

"Oh! But I can't. I have been specifically requested to attend the banquet tonight."

"By whom?"

"By the Duke of Rossmere."

Sarah's face lost all colour, but before she could reply to this horrifying news, there was a respectful knock at the door which she moved to open. She was confronted by one of Stuart's young pages who had an official royal summons for Colwyn to attend the banquet.

"There is a conspiracy going on here!" Sarah stated as she closed the door after giving her thanks for the message and turned to watch Colwyn inspecting her wardrobe.

"Nonsense! I am probably required to be the buffer between the Queen and Morgan. You know they don't get on at all," Colwyn replied innocently.

"Morgan? You've seen the man once and already you are on first name terms!"

Colwyn swung round angrily in his defence. Why did everyone hate him so?

"Sarah, please remember who you are! You're not my mother, you're my maid. Besides which, we are equals and I have known him all my life."

The sharp retort stopped Sarah in her tracks. Never had her Lady spoken like that to her, and she was forced to re-appraise the situation. Colwyn was no longer a child to be scolded; she was a woman with a mind of her own, the ruler of a Duchy, and more than ready for marriage. It was a wonder she

Chapter Four

had not already been betrothed, but the King seemed intent on honouring the wishes of her father.

"I'm sorry, my Lady. I forgot myself for a moment. It won't happen again."

Colwyn sighed. "I'm sorry too. I shouldn't have snapped at you like that, but I get so angry when people just follow each other blindly on the words of hearsay. What has the Duke of Rossmere ever done to us that we should fear him? I grew up with him, for goodness' sake, and he has never, ever done anything to warrant your feelings of distrust. Sarah, I owe the man my life!"

"I apologise, my Lady. I will be more open-minded in future. Now, what will you wear this evening?"

Colwyn chose a simple gown in rich emerald green velvet, decorated in a most tasteful fashion around the neck, hem and cuffs with gold thread in an intricate design. Around her waist, she wore a simple gold chain. Sarah then made her sit down so that she could brush and set the beautiful long chestnut hair.

ଊ ଅ ଊ ଅ

Bodine closed his eyes and sat back, allowing the hot water to wash over his tired limbs and soothe away the aching caused by remaining too long in the saddle without rest.

His mind drifted to Colwyn. He thought her beautiful, with full lips and high cheekbones. Of course, she did possess those wonderful dark green eyes that Bodine had never seen in a human—or Kadeau, for that matter—in his entire life. They were truly outstanding. However, more important than external features was the life within, and in his latest brief meeting with Colwyn, he had liked what he had seen and sensed. He had always liked her; he considered her his sister; but now she was a woman, he suddenly realised he liked her even more—and perhaps not in the way a brother should. In the five years since he had last talked with her, she had matured in many ways beyond measure.

Colwyn had a sharp and quick mind, filled with relevant and important details—not the usual contents of a woman's head. She was curious and willing to add to her knowledge. Most importantly though, she was still not the slightest bit afraid of him.

Bodine admitted this unnerved him slightly. It hadn't concerned him much whilst she had been an innocent child, but now, she was a woman. He had been careful to cultivate a specific aura of mystery and wonder, tinged with a hint of darkness. Purposefully, he dressed in sombre colours—usually black—and although he actually rarely used those Kadeau powers, by careful use of words and phrasing, he often gave the impression that he was reading the minds of all those around him. Women usually grew pale at his approach, which, up until now, had suited him very well. He was not looking for any entanglement anyway and none were likely to be interested when he frightened them all… except Colwyn. She had critically assessed him and seen through the façade, although he noted that she had not asked the question in her mind. Tactful, thoughtful and perhaps caring for his feelings as a man.

But what if she had asked, would his manly pride have denied it? Not certain, he decided to ask the question himself.

*All right, Bodine, what **are** you afraid of?*

He analysed the question from all angles. Tangent answers came to mind, but they were not the correct solutions to this particular query.

Betrayal? Fear that if he let his guard down or relaxed for an instant, someone would find a flaw; a weakness that could be used to destroy him because of what he was: a dreaded Kadeau with magical powers. That was the true answer, wasn't it? Afraid of being found humanly vulnerable; hence this great façade. Born of others' ignorance, it would have to continue for

Chapter Four

the sake of his life. But it was hard; it tired him and he yearned to be able to relax once in a while. Those times were rare; only in the seclusion of his rooms in the tower at Belvoir, or in the hidden cove on the coast, north of the city, could he truly be himself. His role as King's Champion and General of the Armies kept him away from home longer than he really liked, although he was proud of his responsibilities to the King and of his friendship. Now and again, he wished he had someone with whom he could share the burden; share his fears; his life; someone who was equal to him and not his liege. Was that person possibly Colwyn? Dare he inflict his heritage on her, if she really was the one?

ଓ ଘ ଓ ଘ

Despite her severe reservations, Sarah had taken extra care with her Lady's preparations and was stunned by the final result. She had to admit, her Lady Colwyn was no longer a little girl, but a beautiful young woman. The emerald velvet dress clung to Colwyn's youthful body, its colour perfectly offsetting the vibrant chestnut hair and fair complexion. Her hair had been carefully braided and tied with gold ribbon. Around her throat, she wore a simple gold necklace with a green crystal resting just at the top of the cleft of her breasts, and another gold chain encircled her waist, enhancing the curves of her body.

Sarah had sprinkled fresh rose water in her hair and dabbed it behind her ears and on her wrists. The redness of her lips had been accentuated using the juice of seasonal red berries.

"You are so beautiful, my Lady," Sarah whispered. "Your parents would be very proud."

Colwyn's eyes took on a sad expression with the realisation that they would never see her like this, attending her first banquet as a woman and not their little princess.

Further thoughts were interrupted by a knock on the door. It was one of the King's pages, who had arrived to escort her down to the banquet.

The majority of the guests were already seated when Colwyn arrived. However, the page escorted her along the outside of the banquet hall to the royal entrance where King Stuart, Queen Alexandra, Prince Michael, Princess Anne, the young Prince Llywelyn and Bishop Douglas were standing, along with two ladies-in-waiting.

Colwyn dutifully curtsied.

"Why, Colwyn, you look absolutely lovely, doesn't she, Alexandra?" said Stuart.

"Beautiful," Alexandra agreed, but her eyes were sorrowful.

"Thank you," Colwyn said meekly, unused to such glowing compliments.

Stuart glanced around as a door opened and Morgan Bodine entered, looking refreshed after his bath and just a few hours' sleep.

"Ah, Morgan, I was about to send out a search party," Stuart joked.

"Apologies, my Liege. I had a few problems with my attire." Morgan fingered the neck of his jacket, making Stuart smirk, before he bowed respectfully.

Colwyn was acutely aware that she was staring, but she couldn't help it. Bodine was still dressed in black, but at least this was decorated with gold, which accentuated the contours of his broad shoulders and narrow hips. Even his long, leather boots had some simple gold decoration. His dress-sword, also black-hilted and decorated in gold, lay sheathed in a black and gold scabbard. His long, burnished gold hair shone, and, this evening, was loose around his shoulders.

Colwyn felt butterflies in her stomach and her heart missed a beat as she continued to stare.

Chapter Four

Fortunately, the young prince bumped into her, bringing her back to her senses, as he eagerly threw himself at Bodine.

"I have missed you! Where have you been?" the youngster demanded.

"I apologise, my Prince," Bodine said, his voice like velvet to Colwyn's ears. "I had urgent business to attend to for your father."

"Father, you mustn't send him away for so long in future," Llywelyn stated firmly.

"I will do my best. Now," said Stuart, "it's been a few years since you last met, so I believe more formal introductions are required. Morgan, I would like you to meet the Duchess of Invermere, Colwyn Coltrane. Colwyn, this is Duke Morgan Bodine of Rossmere."

"Duke," Colwyn said, inclining her head, slightly.

"Duchess." Morgan took her hand and kissed it. "It pleases me to see you have made a complete recovery. You were gravely ill and we feared for your life."

"I understand I owe my life to you. I am extremely grateful to you and to your battle surgeon, Master Andrew."

They had had almost the exact conversation just a few hours ago, but it seemed the correct thing to play out in front of their royal audience, although Morgan was giving her a totally different look now. There was no mistaking the approval in the grey eyes, and Colwyn felt herself blush and the butterflies flicker again, as their eyes locked.

Looking on, Stuart nodded imperceptibly and smiled to himself. He then risked a sideward glance at Alexandra and sobered, for she was frowning with disdain. Stuart realised he would have to be careful how he engineered this budding romance, as he knew his Queen did not approve of Bodine.

"Come, let us dine before our guests die of starvation," Stuart said jovially and offered his arm to his Queen to lead the way into the banquet.

Bodine, who was still holding Colwyn's hand, pulled himself together, and, placing her hand on his left arm, escorted her through after his liege.

He was attentive to her every need during the meal, and engaged her in casual small talk, attempting to glean if there was any reason for his sudden change in his attitude towards her, but was unable to find any. All he could sense was that she was somewhat guarded, but was enjoying his company, and the evening, very much indeed. There was no fear, just a little apprehension of the situation, gauged with a genuine curiosity to learn more about him. This last fact made the fearless duke somewhat nervous. Oh, he knew his manners and etiquette, but he usually avoided the company of women, especially for conversation, as he had found they never had much in common to discuss. However, for the first time in his life, he found he was attracted—very strongly—to a woman, but had no idea why and it bothered him. He had known Colwyn for most of his life; perhaps that was the reason. She was beautiful, possessing those wonderful green eyes; she was sweet and innocent, but now there was something else about her that was attracting him. Perhaps it was her aura. To him, it was a golden light, almost heavenly and sacred, but it still nagged at him and he vowed to discover what it was, for up until this point, he had always considered that he had a brotherly affection for her, but now he realised his feelings were beginning to change and his thoughts remembered the words that Bronwyn had spoken five years ago, about her welcoming him if he wished to join the family.

Stuart had laid on some entertainment as well, with jesters, jugglers and dancing. Bodine rarely danced, but on this occasion, he made an exception. It would allow him to hold Colwyn's hand, which would enable him to gain access to her inner thoughts. He needed to know.

Stuart's eyebrows rose as Bodine led Colwyn to the floor and he watched with interest as they danced. He frowned slightly and just prevented himself from shaking his head as he recognised what he was doing. Although Bodine

Chapter Four

had taught the King to read the inner mind, he knew he was nowhere near as skilled as the Kadeau Duke. Glancing at his Queen, he sobered sharply. She was watching the pair intently, clearly worried that Bodine might be 'up to no good'.

The Queen favoured Colwyn and had done so since the young Duchess had been a child, probably because, as yet, she had no daughter of her own to dote on. She had high hopes of an arranged marriage for the young woman, but not to Duke Morgan Bodine. The Kadeau was dangerous, and could not be trusted, but no one else appeared to be able to see that. She suspected he had in some way bewitched her husband, son and Prince Michael as well. Now it seemed he was attempting to work his magic on the young Duchess; or perhaps he had already done that back at Belvoir Castle when the poor woman had been so gravely ill. She would speak with Bishop Douglas; perhaps he could perform a religious blessing on Colwyn and rid her of any evil that may have overcome her.

Bodine noticed that although Colwyn was smiling at him, her mind seemed elsewhere, and she kept glancing over at the tables as if looking for someone. Then he realised the reason for her unease.

"He's not here," he whispered to her, as their heads came close together as the steps of the dance dictated.

"My Lord?"

"McDowell. He's not here. Won't be here until the Midsummer festival. I assume that's who you're looking for?"

The relief that came flooding from her mind into his was overwhelming and Bodine nearly made a wrong move in the dance. "Oh, thank goodness for that," she breathed. "My apologies, Morgan," and she beamed a most radiant smile at him. It was from that point on that she truly began to enjoy the evening, and took part in several dances with her handsome companion.

At the end of their fourth dance, Bodine had given up on trying to get to the bottom of his nagging problem and decided that Colwyn had had enough mind-probing and dancing for now. Although she was enjoying herself, he had picked up on a wall within her mind. She wasn't hiding anything from him, it was more a shield to protect herself, but from what he wasn't sure. He began to escort her back to the table, but they were intercepted by a group of the Queen's ladies-in-waiting.

"My dear, we just had to stop you and say how lovely you are looking this evening. This is your first banquet since that terrible affair; the late duke and duchess would be so proud of how you look, don't you think?"

The other ladies joined in, adding their comments, and Bodine suddenly became aware of Colwyn's mood changing. She was smiling politely now, but it was empty and her eyes had taken on a haunted, mournful look. Unfortunately, the noisy crowd of women seemed totally oblivious to the effect their conversation was having, and Bodine felt his temper rising.

Colwyn looked pleadingly at him to help her.

"Ladies, the Duchess thanks you for your kind comments; if you'll pardon us, we really—"

"Oh, but..." and the ladies promptly ignored him and carried on. Morgan wasn't used to this.

Finally, it was Colwyn who spoke out.

"Please, Duke, I need some fresh air." Her radiant mood had collapsed completely and she looked desperate to get out.

Quickly, he took her by the elbow and made the appropriate excuses to the other ladies-in-waiting.

"The Lady Colwyn is feeling a little unwell. I fear the excitement of this evening, may have been too much for her, having only just recovered from her illness," he stated, as he backed away with his charge towards the balcony

Chapter Four

that ran the length of the banquet hall. "I think a little fresh air may be what she needs. Please excuse us."

He guided her out onto the balcony, quietly cursing the inane comments the women had made. Yes, they had been most complimentary, but to have kept going on about Colwyn's parents had clearly distressed her.

The stars were shining brightly and Colwyn stood, staring up at them, gripping the stone wall at the edge of the balcony, her face sad. Bodine said nothing but stood by her side waiting patiently.

"Do you think…" she began, but her voice wavered and Bodine saw her bottom lip tremble. He reached out a hand to touch her shoulder to offer reassurance and suddenly realised what the barrier had been. This was the first time since her terrible ordeal that she had really relaxed. All the pent up grief, anger and despair were poised on the brink, pressing against the wall she had erected. Bodine knew he had to do something, but not here on the balcony, just outside the main banquet hall; it was far too public for a display of such raw emotion, especially for someone of breeding.

Colwyn was gasping, her breathing laboured as she valiantly attempted to keep her emotions under control, but she was losing the battle; the strain of holding it back for so long was too much to take anymore. Forcibly, he placed a hand around her waist and moved her quickly into the left corner of the balcony, where a set of steps led down into the walled rose garden. In the darkness, he found their little arbour and sat, pulling her down beside him.

"Yes, I do," he said, answering her unfinished question.

It was at this point that she collapsed into floods of tears, releasing everything that had been held in check for so long. Gently, Bodine pulled her into his arms and began to rock her, stroking her hair.

Neither of them was sure how long it lasted, but Colwyn was finally emptied of all emotion. Exhausted beyond belief, she was reduced to dry wracking sobs, that slowly became subdued until all Bodine could feel was her trembling body against his. He looked up at the stars himself, wondering if indeed her parents were looking down on them.

Colwyn moved against him, giving a little moan and he looked down again, stroking her hair once more. He hadn't said anything during her emotional outburst, but simply offered her his support. "Shush," he spoke, at last, his voice but a whisper. "It's all right."

"I-I'm sorry," she mumbled almost inaudibly, "for my dis-disgraceful outburst."

"Colwyn, you needed this. Now you will be strong again."

In the darkness, Bodine somehow knew she was looking up at him, and her next words confirmed this as her lips brushed his throat when she spoke. "My Kadeau Lord is the light in my darkness." The words moved him deeply and Bodine moved his head, just as her hand crept up the back of his neck.

Their lips met gently. He could taste the salt of her tears and the sweetness of her lips. They made a heady combination and Colwyn gave a quiet little moan of acquiescence, relaxing totally against him, her lips pliable under his. Bodine may have given the impression of being woman-shy, but he was no novice in the art of love, King Stuart had seen to that. He bestowed several more gentle kisses on her, then drew back a little. He didn't want to stop, but to continue would have been most unknightly; to take advantage of her in her weakened emotional state.

"Colwyn, my apologies, I had no right to take advantage of you just then. Please forgive me."

"There is nothing to forgive, Morgan. You must surely know I have… deep affection for you." Colwyn was glad it was dark so that Bodine would not see the flush of colour that she could feel had come to her cheeks. It was more than affection, but she did not want to admit to it being more until she knew how Bodine really felt about her.

Chapter Four

In response, Bodine kissed her once more and Colwyn felt her heart give yet another flutter.

"We should return to the banquet hall if you are well enough," Bodine finally said, quietly.

"I must look a sight; I would need to bathe my face at least."

"I have to admit, I can't see anything in this light," Bodine confessed, and he was not willing to conjure up some fire-light, in case someone on the balcony saw. "Come, I know what we can do. We'll go back to the balcony and stay in a corner; I'll get a page to bring some wine and water out. It will appear as if we've been on the balcony all the while."

"Yes, court etiquette and all that. I understand."

Carefully, they made their way back to the balcony. Bodine left Colwyn sitting in a quiet corner whilst he discretely went in search of a page, who fetched wine and water, creeping out of a side entrance so that he was not seen.

Colwyn splashed her face with the water and sat quietly as Bodine used the cloth, which the page had hanging over his arm, to pat it dry. Then he bade the page to stay with her and went in search of the Queen.

Bodine knew Alexandra didn't like him, but perhaps by bringing her out to Colwyn, it might show him to be less of a monster than she believed him to be. He approached her and coughed politely.

"Your Majesty, a word, if I may."

Alexandra looked haughtily at him, her dislike clearly evident. However, her court etiquette was impeccable. "Yes, General Bodine?"

Bodine glanced at the ladies-in-waiting who were by her side. Alexandra knew very well that Bodine would not be afraid to talk in front of them unless it was something more serious, and indicated for them to go. He waited until they were out of earshot before speaking again.

"It's about the Lady Colwyn, Your Majesty. I'm afraid some of the ladies-in-waiting got a little carried away with their compliments, mentioning how the late duke and duchess would be so proud of her; it was too much for her to bear, with the excitement of this evening and of her only recently getting her strength back. I know you have a fondness for the Duchess and wondered if you would—"

"Where is she?" Alexandra demanded, her voice full of concern.

"On the balcony; she was feeling a little faint and I thought the fresh air might help. A page is with her."

"Take me to her. Oh, some of my ladies have no brains, no brains at all! The poor child." The Queen glanced at Bodine. "She.... She has not grieved, you know; I am worried about her."

Bodine opened his mouth to speak, then changed his mind and closed it again. It was not for him to say more than was absolutely necessary. Instead, he indicated for the Queen to move to the left corner of the balcony.

Colwyn was sipping some wine as they approached.

"My child," the Queen began, indicating for her to stay where she was. "General Bodine has told me of my foolish ladies' actions. Are you all right?"

"I-I am now, Your Majesty. It was foolish of me to be so affected by—"

"Nonsense! I think you may have overdone things. I think we should get you to bed immediately. Young Mark here can escort you," the Queen said, indicating the page, determined that Bodine would not be involved.

Colwyn, on the other hand, was determined that he should be. She was feeling weak and exhausted after her outpour of emotion. If she were to collapse, young Mark would not be able to cope. She wanted Bodine with her. After standing and taking a couple of steps, the wine goblet she was holding slipped from her fingers and she swooned a little. Bodine immediately leapt forward and caught her before she fell. He went to lift her into his arms, but she protested.

Chapter Four

"Please, Duke, just lend me your arm. I don't want the other guests to know I am unwell."

Bodine nodded and did as she asked. With the Queen at her other side and the page respectfully following behind, they made their way back through the banqueting hall and through into the antechamber. Halfway across the room, she faltered once more.

"I-I'm sorry," she whispered as Bodine swept her up into his arms. "I'm so tired." Her eyes closed and her head lolled against his shoulder.

"We must summon a physician," the Queen stated.

"If you please, Your Majesty, the Duchess is simply exhausted and has overtaxed her strength this evening. I believe a hot toddy would be more beneficial to her," Bodine dared to challenge. "She will feel more stressed if she is subjected to an examination."

"Perhaps you are right. Mark, arrange for a hot toddy to be delivered to the Lady Colwyn's rooms immediately."

Mark bowed quickly and ran off to do as his Queen ordered.

Alexandra then indicated for Bodine to follow her with his charge.

Sarah was beside herself as they swept into the chambers. "Oh, I knew she shouldn't have gone," she muttered half to herself, pulling back the bedclothes so that Bodine could gently lay Colwyn down.

Alexandra could not help but notice the care with which Bodine placed Colwyn on the bed. He then drew back a little and stroked her head tenderly before shifting position so he could remove her slippers.

"It's all right General Bodine, we can manage now, thank you."

Bodine still removed her slippers and placed them at the foot of the bed. As he drew level with the Queen, he stopped and whispered: "I'm not the evil beast you clearly think I am, your Majesty. The Duchess Bronwyn accepted me as a son and asked me to watch over Colwyn; and I will do just that, no matter what you think of me." With that he bobbed a respectful bow and left the room, leaving a perplexed Alexandra behind.

It was late, Bodine had had a hard ride back from Inver; he was tired, and he had a long meeting with the King and his council tomorrow, so he decided to retire for the night. However, the task was interrupted by a soft knock on his door."

"Come," he said quietly.

The door opened and his cousin, Colin McLeod came in, shutting the door behind him.

"Colin!" Bodine smiled a warm greeting.

"Morgan."

The two men embraced a welcome, then stood back.

"I'm sorry to disturb you," Colin said, moving to sit in the chair that Bodine indicated. He paused as his cousin sat opposite him. "I know you've had a long ride, but I felt I needed to speak to you, about Colwyn."

Bodine frowned at him. "You have some… information for me?"

"Not information exactly; more of a… suspicion."

"Suspicion?"

"Colwyn had a… vision, I suppose you'll have to call it. It occurred on our journey here. Morgan, you know when you brought Colwyn to consciousness when she was so seriously ill? Is there any chance… that the two of you could be sharing some kind of residual link?"

"A link?" He was silent for several moments. "What… makes you think we have some kind of link?" he finally asked.

"Morgan, she saw a terrible sight, the first night of our journey here; and so did I."

"Oh my God," Bodine whispered. "Her parents." Now he understood the intensity of the outpouring of emotion earlier that evening and, more importantly, perhaps why he had these increased feelings for her.

Chapter Four

"I'm sorry," McLeod said. "Do you want me to speak to Bishop Douglas, to see if the link can be safely broken?"

"Not yet. I need to analyse this information first. Thank you for notifying me of this; it does… begin to explain some strange feelings I have become aware of since I arrived."

"Well, don't think about it too long. The longer you leave it, the stronger the link is likely become. I'll let you get some sleep; you must be exhausted. Goodnight, Morgan."

"Goodnight Colin…. And thank you."

McLeod left, and Bodine retired for the night, desperate to relax so he could be refreshed for the meeting tomorrow.

His sleep however, was dominated by disturbing dreams of Colwyn and himself. Several times he awoke with a start, drenched in sweat, the rather erotic dream vivid in his memory. Despite the link; could it be that he was falling in love with her? To have dreamt about such intimacy hinted at such, and he remembered how his body had responded to her back in February in Belvoir Castle.

Involvement and marriage was not something he had considered before. As King's Champion and General of the Armies, he honestly had thought it would not be fair or logical to take a wife; besides which, the choice of suitors was limited, with him being Kadeau. Of course the King could always arrange a marriage for him, but he would prefer to make his own choice, and that choice would be someone who loved him regardless of his heritage.

So what of Colwyn? She had the beauty, the brains and, of course, the lands. In fact, a union between Invermere and Rossmere would keep Nigel McDowell under control and strengthen the stability of Devonmere as a whole. Additionally, Colwyn was not afraid of him and had admitted tonight that she felt deep affection, although perhaps it was actually more than that. Initially, Bodine decided he would let nature take its course and see if a romance ensued; he finally admitted to himself that he was not averse to the idea. Yes, that would be safest.

That decided, he attempted to sleep once more, this time allowing his dreams free rein.

ଔ ଓ ଔ ଓ

It was past midday when Colwyn finally awoke. Her eyelids felt heavy, her eyes puffy, and the memory of a vivid dream was annoyingly just out of reach, but she unconsciously knew that Bodine had been in it somewhere. She was sorely tempted to go back to sleep again. Sarah was in agreement with this, but not before she had eaten something.

"I knew you shouldn't have gone; you're still not well."

"Yes, I am; it was simply Lady Constance and her companions, I wasn't ready for…." Her voice trailed off. She didn't want to talk about it yet; the raw emotion was still too close to the surface. She could feel tears prickling at the back of her eyes and, oh dear, what a display she had given Morgan Bodine. Colwyn was thoroughly ashamed about that. She would have to apologise profusely to the Kadeau Duke, but then again, if she hadn't had that outburst, he would not have put his arms around her, rocked her oh, so gently and… kissed her.

Involuntarily, her fingers moved to her lips, as she tried to recapture the moment.

"My Lady?" Sarah asked, seeing her mistress, her eyes closed, her face a mask of concentration as she touched her lips.

Colwyn's eyes flew open and she dropped her hand back onto the bedclothes. "I…I was pondering on what to eat. I really don't feel very hungry at all, Sarah."

In the end, Colwyn grudgingly ate a couple of small pieces of fruit and drank some wine before sleeping for a few more hours. During this time, the

Chapter Four

Queen had paid a visit to see how she was feeling and insisted that Sarah not disturb the young Duchess. The Queen had then left to have words with her ladies-in-waiting and tore them off a strip for being so insensitive; especially as the young Duchess had still not grieved properly.

When Colwyn awoke in the late afternoon, Sarah told her of the Queen's visit. This news warmed Colwyn, and it reassured her to know that she appeared to have an ally so high in the Court of Devonmere. Feeling much better, she vacated her bed, adorned a very informal dress and lounged on a bench on the small balcony to catch the late afternoon sun and do a little embroidery, a blanket wrapped around her to keep the chill of the April day at bay.

It was as she sat there that she heard voices from inside. Recognising the male voice immediately, she quickly pinched her cheeks to encourage some colour into them and straightened her braids. Sarah appeared.

"My Lady, the Duke of Rossmere is here to see you. I've told him that—"

"Please send him through."

Sarah curtsied and did as she was told.

Morgan appeared and Colwyn felt her heart miss a beat. It was no good, she would have to be honest with herself and admit that she was seriously in love with the Kadeau Lord.

"Colwyn." He took her hand and kissed it.

"Morgan, please sit."

Needing no second bidding, he sat beside her. "I stole these from the garden," he admitted, handing her a bunch of spring flowers of every colour that could be found there. "I decided I could get away with taking one of each colour in order to make you a bouquet, without anyone noticing they were missing."

Colwyn laughed delightedly. "They are lovely and they smell divine. Thank you."

"I hope you are feeling better today?" he asked, as his eyes swept over her critically.

"Yes, thank you. Morgan, I am so sorry."

"Sorry?"

"About the disgraceful outburst last night. It was most unladylike and unforgivable. What must you have thought of such a show of emotion? I am so embarrassed and ask that you forgive me."

"Colwyn, my love, there is nothing to forgive. Please do not feel embarrassed; it was obviously needed and a part of the healing process. Let's say no more about it, except that it was an honour that you trusted me enough to witness it." He felt reassured at her apparent lightness of mood.

"Oh, Morgan, I've trusted you all my life, and there is no one I trust more than you."

He smiled kindly at her. "And for that, I feel blessed. Now, if you are recovered enough, I wondered if you'd care to dine with me this evening?"

Her face fell for a moment. "I've been ordered to stay in my rooms tonight but… you could dine with me instead?"

"I would enjoy that immensely. Well, I must go. I've been meeting with the King all day but escaped long enough for this quick visit. I will return this evening Until then…" He kissed her hand once more and took his leave.

Colwyn called for Sarah and told her of her plans for the evening, and asked her to arrange a meal to be delivered to her rooms. Sarah was not pleased but said nothing; she had already been on the receiving end of her Lady's temper and knew that she was her own woman now and no longer a child to be instructed.

For Colwyn, the evening could not come fast enough. She changed clothes and quickly made her way to the stables to treat Archer, repeating

Chapter Four

what she had done before, then returned to her rooms to prepare for her meal with Bodine. She had chosen a cream dress, again with a low neck and tight-fitting sleeves, decorated with gold thread that followed the lines of her body.

Bodine's meeting with the King went on a little longer than planned, as Stuart outlined his plans to his General. For the moment, he had decided he wanted Bodine at Ellesmere until after the Midsummer celebrations and knighting ceremony, mainly to encourage the possible romance that was budding between him and Colwyn. Stuart wanted to be able to make a wedding announcement and thwart McDowell once and for all, though he did not voice this plan to Bodine.

Finally released from his meeting, Bodine went to his rooms, changed, and made his way to Colwyn's rooms. Sarah opened the door and bade him enter, and the duke saw his flowers in a vase on a small table that had been set for the forthcoming meal. The Duchess was nowhere to be seen, so he assumed she was still in her bedchamber.

"Your Grace, would you like some wine?" Sarah asked.

Bodine nodded and Sarah poured him a goblet and handed it to him.

"Thank you, Sarah."

She nodded and poured another goblet in readiness for her mistress.

The door to the bedchamber opened and Colwyn stepped through, her face radiant as she set eyes on Bodine. The duke put his goblet down and went to meet her, his eyes full of admiration at her appearance. Colwyn blushed as his eyes appraised her and she saw in the subdued lighting they had darkened to blue with the desire in them.

"Morgan," she said, her breath catching in her throat.

"Colwyn." He took her hand and brought it to his lips before turning to lead her to the table and place a goblet of wine in her hands. "You look beautiful tonight," he whispered into her hair so Sarah could not hear.

"You are too kind," she replied just as quietly.

"This evening, we shall talk of trivial things and enjoy one another's company. Tomorrow, I shall apprise you of the situation in Inver," Bodine told her.

"Thank you, Morgan."

"Just know, I have left Sir John in charge, so the Duchy is in good hands until you return."

They sat and ate; the wine was free-flowing; they talked of all manner of things that were not related to the Duchy, and afterwards, Colwyn asked if he would like to stay a little longer for a game of tawlbwrdd.

"I would be honoured," Bodine replied, and Colwyn went and retrieved the game from a sideboard. "Do you wish to attack or defend?" he asked, as she returned to the table.

"On this occasion, I will attack, if I may," she replied.

Bodine set up the pieces and they played. He had expected to win easily, as it was a game of pure battle strategy. It was played on a nine-by-nine board, and the two players consisted of an attacker and defender. The defender had a king and eight defenders placed in the centre of the board. The attacker had sixteen men, placed in a pattern partly surrounding the defenders. The object of the game was to get the king to a far corner of the board, whilst the attackers tried to stop them. A piece was removed by being surrounded on three sides by the opposing force.

The game did not go as the duke had planned. Colwyn turned out to be a better player than he had anticipated and put up a very good fight. At one point, he thought he was going to lose, but then, at the very last moment, he spied an opportunity and grabbed it to take the win.

"So, now we know each other's strategies, Colwyn, what do you wager?" Bodine asked lightly.

"My Lord has me at a disadvantage. I have nothing with which to wager and well he knows it!"

Chapter Four

His eyes lit up mischievously. *I will accept a kiss.* He was certain he had only thought it, but Colwyn's next words implied otherwise.

"Sir! You are too bold!" She was blushing and laughing. "But very well, I accept. Come, reset the pieces and no cheating!"

"I have no need to cheat!" he replied, laughing back. What were they both playing at? Bodine decided it had to be the wine.

The second game took longer, but, in the end, Bodine won again.

"I accept defeat," Colwyn finally admitted, though not minding in the least that she had lost. "Does my Lord wish payment?" she whispered so that Sarah would not hear.

"With the greatest of pleasure," Bodine replied in an equally quiet voice.

Colwyn got up from her seat and walked towards the balcony. "Sarah, would you get some fresh wine, please? This jug is dulling my senses and I am losing the game!"

"But, my Lady, I cannot leave you here alone with—"

"Are you questioning the Duke's honour, or mine?" Colwyn's eyes flashed at her maid.

"No, my Lady; I will get you wine." Sarah eyed them both suspiciously before leaving the chamber.

Colwyn turned and stepped away from the balcony, moving into shadows away from any possibility of prying eyes. "Come, sir, claim your prize before my maid returns."

Bodine got to his feet but hesitated. "Colwyn, this is not right."

"We agreed a wager, Morgan." There was almost a plea in her voice. Colwyn also knew it was the wine talking, but she had been on the receiving end of his kisses and wanted to feel that pleasure once more.

He swallowed slowly and walked deliberately towards her, careful to stay away from the windows and the balcony. Colwyn leant back against the wall and lifted her chin to gaze up into his handsome, bearded face, her lips slightly parted.

Bodine noted how her lashes cast long shadows as she blinked slowly, and then she turned on the spell that her green eyes possessed and he succumbed, lowering his head until their lips met, gently, yet firmly. Colwyn surrendered willingly, eagerly. Her arms snaked around his body as the kiss grew more passionate. Within a few moments, he had enfolded her in his arms and almost crushed her against him. He kissed her again and again, then moved to her throat. Colwyn's head leant back further and she squirmed delightedly as his heavy breathing blew gently into her ear, making her groan passionately.

"Oh, Morgan," she gasped breathlessly as the tip of his tongue gently traced a line from the base of her throat to her chin. A hand moved to her breast and squeezed it gently through the material of her dress as her hands played with his hair.

Bodine shuddered as his brain fought to overcome his heart, and, with a jagged gasp, he straightened up, making Colwyn groan in frustration. Holding her at arms' length, he watched as her trembling body drew in deep chest-heaving breaths. Her face was flushed and her lips slightly swollen from the onslaught of passion.

"Morgan," she gasped again, but he shook his head.

"Sarah will be returning shortly," he said with difficulty. He closed his eyes and swallowed hard, forcing his body to calm itself. This reaction to a woman was unprecedented and it shook him to the core. Never, since his teenage years, had he been so out of control, and never had he wanted to possess a woman as much as he wanted to possess her. He backed off towards the small table and sat down, making a pretence of resetting the pieces for another game.

Chapter Four

Colwyn stayed where she was. He was right, of course. They had both just behaved most shamefully, and should Sarah suspect anything when she returned, there would be trouble. She moved back to her original position near the balcony. There, the air was quite cool, so hopefully, her colour would soon return to normal, but her heart she could do nothing about. She was acutely aware of it thumping away in her chest. It was no good, she would have to admit to herself, yet again, that she was madly in love with Morgan Bodine. She also admitted that she had enjoyed what they had just shared, and the fact that her body craved much more.

And so it was in these positions that Sarah found them when she returned with fresh wine.

They played one more game, and, to Colwyn's surprise, she managed to win.

"Well done, Colwyn. That win was justly deserved." He sighed deeply. "I must take my leave of you now, but we will discuss business, as promised, tomorrow. I will call for you after breakfast."

"Very well. Thank you for a lovely evening, Morgan." She turned to Sarah. "Sarah, will you prepare my bedchamber, please? Duke Morgan is leaving."

"Very well, my Lady."

She disappeared into the other room, and Colwyn looked up at her companion. "Until tomorrow then, Morgan." Boldly, her arms snaked around his neck and she pulled his head down to hers to kiss him firmly. He responded, then kissed her throat. "Know, Morgan Bodine, that I love you with all of my heart," she whispered in his ear as she moulded herself to him.

Bodine's body responded at those words, and, for a moment, he was lost as she wove her web around him. He knew now that he wanted her in every way and the recognition of that fact shocked him back to reality. He was breathing hard as he stood back from her, but the look in his eyes made her smile with the knowledge that he did love her in return, even though he had said nothing.

He swallowed hard. "Until tomorrow, my love," he whispered, then he withdrew from the room.

Bodine didn't get much sleep that night; he tossed and turned in his bed as he relived the evening he had spent with Colwyn. Was the residual link the reason why he was so drawn to her? probably, but deep in the recesses of his mind he was enjoying the feeling. That emotional part of his brain he usually kept under tight control; hidden away; scared to let it out because of the danger it put him in; but here in the castle, in the court of King Stuart, he was safe enough to let it have a little freedom. He needed to let it out now and again to keep his sanity, but for some reason, this time, he was having great difficulty in putting it back where it belonged.

CB ʚ CB ʚ

5

Chapter Five

Morgan collected Colwyn the following morning after breakfast. He warned her to wrap up warm, as there had been a sharp frost the previous night, and there was still a chill in the air. He had decided to take her to their arbour in the rose garden to impart his news on Inver and the privacy it offered would be welcome, just in case things became emotional. In addition, because of the chill, he was confident they were not likely to be disturbed.

Sitting next to each other, Bodine explained what he had done and what had been organised at Inver. Servants and staff were now back in the castle; wounded soldiers and knights were well on the mend and Sir John MacKenzie was now overseeing everything.

"We laid the Duke and Duchess to rest in the crypt at the cathedral," Bodine said quietly. "It was all overseen by the bishop."

"Thank you," Colwyn said in a whisper, her voice catching slightly. There were tears in her eyes as she carried on. "How could any human being do that to my mother?"

Bodine looked at her sharply. So his cousin had been right! "How did you—"

"I…I just had…had a vision… Now you'll think me mad," she said.

He turned to face her and took her hands in his. "Colwyn, when did you see this vision?" he asked gently, looking to confirm what McLeod had told him.

She took a deep breath. "Let me see…we left Rossmere on the 1st of March…it was that night, I'm sure of it. Why?"

Bodine's heart missed a beat. That was the day they had arrived at Inver Castle; the day he had found Richard, Bronwyn and the baby…but only he and Sir John had actually seen the bodies at that time. For her to have had that vision meant that she must, indeed, have some kind of link to himself, and the only time that could possibly have happened was when he had brought her round in her fever to allow Andrew to administer the powder, when his mind had received that onslaught of images. Was there a residual link left? It appeared so. Was that why she was affecting him so?

"Morgan, what's wrong?"

"I'm sorry," he said. "I'm sorry you had that vision."

"W-what happened to my brother?" she asked.

"He was laid to rest with your mother, so he is not alone."

She nodded, but couldn't prevent the tears from falling for the baby that had never known life. He put his arms around her then and just held her, offering comfort and they sat for quite a while, not speaking or moving.

Eventually, she dared to speak again. "I don't understand how I came to see that vision. It… it was the worst thing I have ever seen in my life," she finished quietly.

"I'm so sorry," Bodine said softly. "It…it may have been my fault."

Colwyn drew back and looked at him, a puzzled expression on her face. "Your fault? How?"

"I believe… we may have a tenuous link with each other's minds. When you were at Rossmere in February, we desperately needed to get a potion into

Chapter Five

you and the only way we could manage it was for me to bring you to consciousness… I believe the link was established then. I am sorry."

"Truly, we are linked?" Colwyn asked in wonder.

Bodine nodded. "I will have to investigate how to break it. I have never been in this position before."

"Does it…does it have to be broken?" she asked in a whisper.

He looked at her sharply and a few moments passed before he answered her. "No, it doesn't have to be, but…"

"It's not doing any harm, is it?"

"Not directly."

"Then let it be, if you are happy to. It's been in place since February. If it causes you harm, then let it be broken. But, it's nice to know we are connected. Neither of us is alone now."

Bodine absorbed her words, knowing exactly what she meant. He really needed to break it, but the comfort he could detect in her voice at the thought of them having some kind of connection made him waver. "Very well. As I said, I currently have no idea how to break it anyway, so let us see how it goes."

She smiled at him, then sobered and suddenly sat up. "You will think me wicked, Morgan…but I want to avenge them all. I need to do something, but I don't know what. I just know I want my revenge."

"I will avenge them for you, I give you my word."

"That's not enough."

"Colwyn, please don't let your heart be filled with bitterness. You are a beautiful person; don't let it be twisted with hate and the lust for revenge. You are kind and generous and loved. Let me take on that burden, please. I am already tinged with darkness."

"Morgan, there is nothing dark in you; it's just an act. It's not fair for you to take this burden on alone."

"I won't be alone; the King is with me. He has vowed to avenge their deaths also."

"But I still feel I need to do something."

"Then your part will be continuing to learn about your Duchy; to be a just and honest leader when you return. To carry out your duties to the best of your ability."

"My father trained me well, but…he didn't prepare me for having to do it alone."

"You will never be alone. Sir John will be there to help you and so will I."

"But, Morgan," Colwyn was overcome with his continued support and generosity; "you have your own Duchy to govern, and the King's army to command. You can't afford to help me as well."

"I promised your mother I would look after you and that is what I'm going to do. No arguments."

"Thank you." The relief in her voice was obvious; then she spoke again. "I have another problem. What am I going to do about Giles Dernley?" she asked. "He is to be knighted this Midsummer, and I have no idea what I'm supposed to do."

"I will guide you," Bodine replied. "Don't worry, you will do him proud."

"What would I do without you?" she asked suddenly.

He didn't know how to answer that at first, but then said, "You would have the King."

Colwyn sat quietly, absorbing that information.

"Come, let us go inside; it is cold, and you are starting to shiver." The duke stood up and pulled her to her feet.

"I am never cold when you are with me," she replied; turning her spell-weaving eyes on Bodine once again. He placed her right hand on his left arm

Chapter Five

and they slowly walked back but paused at the base of the narrow stairs up to the balcony of the main hall. "Morgan, I don't think I could have survived all this without you. Thank you so much." She pulled his head down to kiss him.

ᛞ ᛞ ᛞ ᛞ

Above in the King's private chambers, Stuart was again near his window when he spied movement below. His General was in the company of Colwyn Coltrane. He had seriously started to think about marriage between the two, but the next action confirmed this as they stopped and kissed quite passionately. He smiled and then turned away suddenly as the Queen entered.

"Pray, what are you smiling about?" she asked Stuart, as he quickly started moving away from the window so she had no opportunity to look outside for herself.

"I've made a decision about Colwyn."

"You're going to betroth her to our son?"

"No." He took a deep breath and then continued. "The Duke of Rossmere."

"Stuart! You can't! Anyone but him, please!"

"The match is perfect. It will stabilise the Kingdom, and the Cantrells will have their Kadeau guardian for the Prince once Colwyn is with child."

"Please find someone else for General Bodine!" she insisted.

"Whom do you suggest?" he asked her. "It can't be just anyone."

"I don't care who you select, as long as it's not Colwyn! She's not to marry him!"

"Suppose she's not averse to the idea?" The King was doing his utmost to hold a calm and civil conversation but could feel his patience waning.

"She's not interested in him."

"And how do you know that, pray tell? Have you even asked her?"

"No; I suspect Bodine may have cast a spell on her—I would not get an honest answer from her if he has imposed his will."

"Oh, for goodness sake!" Stuart exploded, unable to contain his irritation. "Have you so easily forgotten what happened at Invermere the last time we were there? I most certainly have not!"

"I don't know what you're talking about!"

"Colwyn gave Morgan a favour, for one thing."

"He'd bewitched her!"

"Enough!" Stuart ordered. "I am King of Devonmere, and I say that Colwyn will wed Morgan Bodine—and that is final! No argument; do I make myself clear?"

"But—"

"No 'buts'. I have decreed. She will marry the Duke of Rossmere after the knighting ceremony, and I forbid you to interfere, Alexandra. You will not do anything to jeopardise this union. Do you understand what I am saying?" His hazel eyes were ablaze, bringing her up short.

"Yes, husband." Alexandra wisely held her tongue.

"If I hear of any further attempted interference from you, there will be consequences!"

Looking at her face, Stuart could see she was livid, and for a moment, he expected a verbal onslaught, but instead, tight-lipped, she said, "As you decree, Sire," and promptly turned and walked out of the room, leaving a worried King behind.

Concerned, he sent for Bishop Douglas who arrived several minutes later.

"Sire, you sent for me?" he asked.

"Yes. Alexandra is going to be a problem with regard to our plan to unite Rossmere and Invermere. Is there anything… you can do?"

Chapter Five

Douglas pondered for a few moments. "There is something I can do, Sire, but it requires your approval."

"Go on," Stuart said.

"When taking the sacrament at the next Holy Communion, I can… put the suggestion in her mind when I give the blessing, if you will permit it?"

Stuart sighed heavily. He was silent for several seconds. "Will she be able to detect it?"

"No, my Liege."

"Very well, do it," he ordered. "Nothing must stop this union. The Kingdom's safety depends on it." Stuart hated to agree to the action, but knew it had to be done.

"As you wish, Sire."

The King realised his wife and Queen would require careful watching until the union had been completed.

After Alexandra left her husband, she went to her antechamber; summoned a page, told him to find Colwyn Coltrane and to bring her to her immediately.

ଓ ଛ ଓ ଛ

Bodine walked Colwyn back to her rooms. "I will bid you farewell for now," he told her. "I have some errands to run and work to do. Will I see you for dinner tonight?"

"If you wish it, Morgan."

He kissed her hand again. "Until this evening, then," he whispered and left her outside the door to her rooms.

It took the page quite a while to find her, for she had left her rooms almost immediately after arrival, and performed the daily treatment on Dernley's horse, but eventually, he came across her as she was climbing the steps to the keep.

The page bowed. "Pardon me, your Grace, but the Queen requests you join her in her chambers immediately."

"I will be there shortly," Colwyn replied, and the page bowed again and left. *I wonder what she wants?* she thought to herself and then answered her own question. *There's only one way to find out.*

Colwyn went in and removed her cloak, then made her way to the Queen's chambers, where she knocked on the door and received an order to enter.

The Queen looked up as she came through the door. "Come, my child, sit here, by my side."

Colwyn's eyes widened in surprise at the almost motherly fashion in which the Queen was treating her, but obeyed instantly. Somewhat nervously, the Queen took hold of one of her hands.

"Colwyn, you have been of the age at which you can be married for some years now, and although I have tried to keep an eye on you, I feel I have neglected you somewhat, and thus wish to rectify this.

"You are now woman enough to understand what I am about to tell you, and I do not wish you to be afraid. My husband, the King, I fear, has plans for you, and I believe they involve the Duke of Rossmere."

Colwyn's heart missed a beat at these words, and her free hand went to her throat, a gesture which Alexandra mistook for fear.

"My husband is misguided in this; you deserve better than to marry this evil man whom Stuart insists on dealing with. Child, I may be able to help you escape the Duke's clutches."

Colwyn swallowed slowly. Was it possible that His Majesty wanted a union between Invermere and Rossmere? It would of course place a stranglehold on the Duke of Cottesmere. She fought hard to prevent a blush from creeping into her cheeks. Morgan Bodine as her husband? Surely not! But ever since Bodine's return from Inver, the King did seem to be arranging

Chapter Five

for them to spend quite a lot of time together. She thought furiously for the right words that would not make her an enemy of the Queen.

"I-I thank you for your kindness and concern, Your Majesty, but if His Majesty decrees, I am bound to do my duty, and I have my people to think of as well."

"You speak so bravely, Colwyn; but I could not bear to see you go to such a man! If I had a daughter, I would wish she would be like you. The King had been considering you as a wife for our son, Prince Llywelyn, but has now made the decision to betroth you to General Bodine. Please, let me help you; I have friends who could see you safely to the convent at Kinreign in the Mullane Kingdom, far to the east, where you would be safe."

"Your Majesty, what would I be - what would my honour mean if I were to run away? I must obey my King and be honour bound by his decree. If that means a union between Invermere and Rossmere, then so be it."

"I respect your words, but do at least think over what has been said and, most of all, Colwyn, be on your guard against his Kadeau magic; let him not touch you nor taint your mind with his foul ways. Go now, but say nothing of this conversation to anyone."

"Very well, Your Majesty." Colwyn curtsied and exited quickly. As she closed the door behind her, she leant back against it, briefly closed her eyes and gave a large sigh of relief. She didn't want to be the future Queen of Devonmere and was glad that threat had gone. Also, she was not ashamed that she had definite feelings towards Morgan Bodine, but she realised that with his many enemies, any friend within the castle was a valuable asset. It was doubtful that the Queen would believe her anyway and would probably conclude that the duke had already poisoned her mind, and had her under his control. Colwyn hoped it was not too deceitful, but it could well be that her safety may rely solely on the fact that the Queen thought she feared him, and any ally, knowingly or not, was better than none.

She took a deep breath and straightened up, but was not surprised to find herself shaking. Was it excitement, or fear, or uncertainty? Perhaps it was a combination of all three. Deciding she needed to compose herself before she came face-to-face with anyone else, she went and hid in the garden again. The sun was warming the area and she sat quietly in her favourite rose-covered arbour, breathing in the fresh air, and absorbing the sounds of bees hovering around, collecting the sweet nectar of the spring flowers spread amongst the grass, and the birds singing happily. Colwyn closed her eyes and let the sun, filtering through the foliage, caress her pale skin.

"May I sit with you?" a deep voice asked.

Colwyn's eyes flew open and met the intense stare of King Stuart Cantrell.

"Y-Your Majesty," Colwyn stammered, almost throwing herself into a curtsy at his feet.

Stuart smiled kindly, leant forward and lifted her to stand before him.

"Come, sit with me, Colwyn. I wish to talk to you."

Colwyn swallowed a little apprehensively; this was to be her second conversation with the royal household within an hour.

"Sire?" she asked as they sat in the sheltered arbour.

"Colwyn, I made a promise to your father that I would only wed you to a man you loved."

She swallowed again, her heart beginning to thump painfully in her chest.

"Being King carries great responsibility. I have a duty to the Kingdom, to uphold right from wrong, to protect the innocent and to keep the peace. Sometimes the decisions that have to be made are difficult and involve not feelings of the heart, but of things that have to be done to keep the Kingdom stable. Do you understand what I am saying?"

Chapter Five

Colwyn nodded slowly. Her mouth had suddenly gone very dry and she was aware of the colour slowly seeping from her face.

"You're an intelligent young woman, and you know of the underlying tensions within the Kingdom. War is brewing. Duke Nigel McDowell is an ambitious man…" he paused as he saw the colour drain from Colwyn's face completely, and took both her hands in his before continuing. "His ideal plan is to split the Kingdom by forcing a war on Morgan Bodine, thus depriving me of my General and a significant number of my fighting force, leaving me to contend with his supporters. The Duchy of Rossmere lies between Cottesmere and Invermere. Nigel's solution will be to ask for your hand in marriage—no, Colwyn, let me finish," Stuart said quickly as Colwyn began to shake and her eyes widened in horror. "As I said, Nigel's ideal solution will be to ask for your hand in marriage and lead me to believe he will be my loyal ally when I know he is actually after the throne. With Invermere under his control, he gains substantial lands and a powerful army to lay siege to Rossmere from two sides, and then move against the throne. Colwyn, I believe McDowell is on his way here now to ask for your hand."

"N-no… I won't marry him, Sire. I can't; I won't. He murdered my parents! You are my King, it is my duty to obey you, but on this…. I just can't. I'm sorry."

"Colwyn, shush now. I don't want you to marry McDowell; remember once before, I told you he would never have you, and that still stands." He paused again and squeezed her hands reassuringly. "I want to know how you feel about Morgan Bodine."

For a moment, he thought she was going to faint, and then he saw the colour flood into her cheeks and smiled a secret little smile. So, he was right; the kiss he had seen the two exchange was genuine; there was a spark here, but he needed to be sure.

"Colwyn." He fixed his eyes on hers and Colwyn found she was unable to look away. "Tell me what you think of Morgan Bodine."

"I – I don't know what I feel, Sire. I know I like him very much but... I have no experience of being in love. I loved my parents, but what I feel for Morgan is alien to me. He makes me feel strange... I glow... I tingle... I get this peculiar feeling down in my stomach, like butterflies. I'm sad when he's not around and happy when he is."

Stuart blinked, breaking eye contact, happy with the information he had obtained. Colwyn swayed slightly as she came out of her trance-like state.

"H-have I answered your question, Sire? I...I can't seem to remember what I just said."

"You have answered it perfectly, my dear. Thank you for allowing me to speak so frankly with you. Now, enjoy the sunshine and the garden." He leant forward and placed a kiss on her forehead before rising to his feet. "You know," he added thoughtfully, "the Midsummer festivities are approaching, and I feel it will be a time of great celebration." With that comment, he walked briskly away, leaving Colwyn frowning after him.

ଓ ଏ ଓ ଏ

Colwyn was having issues processing everything that had happened so far that morning; the update from Bodine, then the conversations with both the King and Queen. She relived the last two conversations first; her supposed betrothal to Morgan Bodine. The King hadn't actually said that that was his intention; he had only asked her what she thought of him as if to gauge if she had any feelings towards the Kadeau Duke. At least the King had confirmed that McDowell was not in contention and for that she was exceedingly thankful.

Next, she mulled over Morgan's wise words about revenge, but her heart was still broken, and she still felt she wanted to avenge her parents and the

Chapter Five

men who had died protecting them. She would need to be prepared and would need help, but MacKenzie was still in Inver, and likely to be there for several months. There was really only one person who could help her to get fit and ready.

The castle was huge and she was still finding her way around, so, she went in search of a page to get directions to where the squires were likely to be found at this time of day. Having obtained the required information and directions on how to reach the training area, known as the Pell, she made her way there.

The squires were all practising hard. The knighting ceremony was to take place on Midsummer day and they all needed to prove their worthiness. Colwyn spied Dernley and indicated for him to come to her as soon as he was able.

The exercise he was doing finished five minutes later and he went over to the fence. "Lady Colwyn?"

"Giles, I need to speak to you privately."

"We are nearly finished. Just one more exercise. Will you wait here, or shall I come and find you?"

"I'll wait."

He nodded and returned to his exercise partner. Colwyn stayed out of the way and watched as they performed their final drill, then Dernley was free and they walked together in a more quiet area of the castle.

"Giles, I need your help."

"Whatever I can do, you know you can count on me."

"Sir John is away in Inver and likely to be there for the foreseeable future. I need to resume my training."

"Colwyn, I'm but a squire; you need an expert swordsman to instruct you."

"Giles, it's you or no one."

"What about Duke Morgan?"

"Can you honestly see him approving that?"

"No," Dernley answered without hesitation, "he would likely forbid it." He gave a deep sigh. "We would need to do this in secret. Have you still got your sword and armour?"

"Yes, but I've grown since it was made. I believe I need a new set."

"I will…borrow a young squire's equipment. I know where they are kept. Now we need to find a safe place to practice. Are you free for an hour? If so, we could go exploring."

She nodded, and they methodically explored many areas within the castle, looking for a secluded, quiet spot away from people and activities. They were not having much luck and decided to go deeper into the castle. Eventually, they came across an empty room.

"This might work. It has a heavy door, so we shouldn't be heard. It looks like it hasn't been used for a long while. I'll bring the armour and store it down here as well. Colwyn, if we get caught, there could be trouble."

"I will take the blame."

"Do you still remember your warming-up exercises? If so, you can do those in your chambers before we come down here, so we can practice swordplay straight away."

"When can we start?"

"Will you be able to creep out of your rooms at night?"

"Yes. Now that I'm better, Sarah leaves me overnight."

"Very well. Can you be here for midnight?"

"I'll be here."

They retraced their steps and went their separate ways. Colwyn returned to her rooms and opened the chest where her sword was kept. To her, it now seemed small and very light. She would take it with her that night and see what Giles thought.

Chapter Five

Before that, however, was her meal with Bodine. She decided to take the tawlbwrdd game with her, just in case he fancied a rematch after their meal.

Colwyn took a deep breath and knocked softly on the door. A few moments went by and then it was opened by Ioan, Bodine's personal steward.

"Your Grace, please come in."

"Thank you." She entered the room to see a table set for two, with covered tureens already present.

"May I offer you some wine? His Grace will be with you shortly."

"Thank you again."

As Colwyn began to sip her wine, Bodine appeared from the bedchamber and, as usual, her heart missed a beat at the sight of him. He assisted her into her seat at the table, then Ioan served them and refilled their wine goblets before retreating to a respectful distance.

To Bodine, Colwyn seemed a little preoccupied that evening, and in the end, he decided to ask what was wrong.

"Colwyn, is there something troubling you?"

"Yes—no—well, sort of."

"Tell me; perhaps I can help?"

"I'm not sure I should say anything, but the King did not say I could not speak of it…"

"The King?"

She lowered her eyelids, took a deep breath and looked up at him. "The King spoke to me today."

Bodine watched as the colour suddenly flooded into her cheeks and he raised an eyebrow.

"He…he asked me what I thought of you," she whispered. "And… please, you must promise me you will not say a word of this to anyone….the

Queen… the Queen offered to help me escape your clutches by conveying me to the convent at Kinreign."

Bodine swallowed slowly. "What?!"

"She said that originally, His Majesty was considering me as the future Queen of Devonmere, as wife of the Prince, but that he had changed his mind and that I was going to be betrothed to you. I was not supposed to speak of this to anyone."

"I'm not surprised if she is thinking of whisking you away. What did you say in response?"

"I did not want to make an enemy of the Queen, so I told her that I was honour bound to do my duty, and if that meant marrying the Duke of Rossmere, then I must do so. She seemed satisfied with that response, and I am still in favour with her. Oh, Morgan, she hates you so much, it upsets me."

"Do not despair, my love. The King is the important factor in this. I am in his favour; I command his armies. Dare I ask what your thoughts are of the King's plans?"

"Well, he hasn't said that he is going to betroth me; he has just asked what I thought of you."

"It sounds as if he is trying to keep his promise to your father. Tell me, would you…do as he asked?" Bodine asked tentatively.

"Yes," she whispered without hesitation.

"Even though it may make you an enemy of the Queen?"

"Yes," she answered again.

"Oh, my love, you are a rare jewel in the Kingdom," he said as he went to pour more wine and found the jug almost empty.

Colwyn blushed fiercely.

Bodine nodded at Ioan as he lifted the empty jug.

"My Lord, I will be back shortly, I will fetch more wine."

Chapter Five

"Thank you, Ioan."

Colwyn waited until Ioan had left the room, then said, "I need to know what my Lord thinks of the prospect."

Bodine took a deep breath. "I will confess, up until returning from Inver, I had given no thought to marriage. My duties to the King and Devonmere, I felt, would make it unfair to take a wife at this time, plus… my options are limited. I have no wish to marry someone who hates me."

"Then you made me welcome on my return and lifted my heart. I confess I am still unsure, not because I don't have feelings for you, Colwyn, but because of my Kadeau heritage, and whether I would want to inflict that on you."

"Oh, Morgan," she said, getting up and moving towards him. "You have had so much sorrow in your life. Isn't it about time you had some joy?"

They were standing facing one another by now and Bodine couldn't stop himself from grabbing her by the arms and pulling her against him to kiss her hungrily.

"No woman has ever made me feel the way you do," he whispered into her ear, breathing deeply, inhaling the scent of her. "I confess, it…worries me. I feel I have lost some semblance of control over my emotions. Have you bewitched me, Colwyn Coltrane?" he asked, gently nipping her ear.

"Not intentionally, my Lord," she whispered back. "I would never do anything to harm you, or put you in danger, you must know that."

"I know that, my love." He kissed her deeply again, consciously aware that his self-control was slipping, and fought to recover himself, but it was becoming increasingly difficult.

There was a respectful knock on the door, which caused them to break apart. Colwyn returned to her seat, pretending to eat something as Bodine spoke.

"Enter."

It was Ioan returning with the wine. He refilled their goblets and then retreated a respectful distance away again.

"Did you want a re-match tonight?" Colwyn asked. "I brought the tawlbwrdd with me."

Bodine smiled at her. "I can manage one game this evening."

She smiled back. "Ioan," she asked Bodine's steward, "Would you be so kind as to clear some space on the table, please?"

"Of course, your Grace."

The game went on longer than anticipated, and in the end, neither of them could gain enough of an advantage to win the game outright, so they called a truce. Colwyn was conscious of time moving on and reluctantly bade him goodnight after thanking Bodine and Ioan for a lovely evening. The duke insisted on escorting her back to her rooms, where he paused outside and looked carefully up and down the corridor to ensure no one was around, before kissing her goodnight. He clamped down hard on his emotions and as a result, was able to release her from the kiss without too much effort, but it was still hard.

Colwyn watched him walk back down the corridor before entering her chambers, where she dismissed Sarah for the night. She went to her trunk and retrieved her sword before performing warm-up exercises, then made her way to the secret room beneath the castle.

Dernley was waiting for her. He helped her with the aketon and the new hauberk. It did not fit quite right over her breasts, but it was better than nothing. Ideally, she needed to be fitted for a custom-made one, but it would do for now. Dernley inspected her sword and agreed it was now too small and too light, so she tried both of the new ones he had brought with him and selected the shorter of the two. He then corrected her grip and stance and watched her move; then they spent the next hour practising with the heavier wooden swords. Dernley held back, knowing Colwyn was not strong

Chapter Five

enough to withstand anything too heavy, as she was still recovering from her illness.

Breathing heavily, Colwyn asked if Dernley would be available the next night.

"Surely that's too soon," he replied.

"I don't know how long we're going to get away with this, so I have to take every opportunity I have before we are discovered and stopped," she replied, so he relented.

He helped her out of the armour, doused the light and they left the room.

Colwyn's right arm ached the following morning, and she knew she had to hide this fact from everyone, at least until she could think of a reasonable excuse. Fortunately, she managed it, and she managed a further four evenings with Dernley in their secret rendezvous. However, that night, she had shouted at him for holding back and had attacked him with vigour, and he had retaliated more strongly than he intended and knocked her to the floor.

"Colwyn!" He dropped his sword and ran to her. "Wait, don't get up yet. Let me check you over."

"I'm fine, Giles." With his help, she struggled to her feet, doing her best not to show that he had hurt her slightly.

"Are you sure?"

"The only thing that is hurt is my pride," she said.

"You aren't ready for the heavier blows; it's only been five sessions, but you are improving fast. I think we had better finish early tonight. Do you want to carry on tomorrow?"

"Of course."

Back in her room, Colwyn undressed and discovered the bruises. These she would not be able to explain away if Sarah saw them, for they were clearly taking on the pattern of the chainmail. She knew she would have to make sure she was up and at least partially dressed before Sarah arrived.

Colwyn managed it, but she really ached, and she was due to spend some time with Bodine this day. Knowing he was very astute, she realised she would have to be extremely careful.

Later that day, she was sitting in the rose-strewn arbour having now completed just over a week of daily treatment on Archer. She was awaiting Bodine's arrival, flexing her right shoulder carefully, when he suddenly appeared. She immediately stopped what she was doing and stood up to greet him.

"My love, I'm sorry I'm late," he said, and grasped her shoulders to kiss her; he was immediately aware of her tensing and flinching under his fingers. "What's wrong?" he asked, as he released her.

"I... I've been incredibly clumsy this morning. It's very embarrassing," she replied hoping that would be enough of an explanation.

"What did you do?" he continued, as he drew her down to sit beside him on the bench.

"No, I'm not telling you; it's so embarrassing."

"I promise I won't laugh."

She sighed, realising he wasn't going to let her get away without saying any more. "I tripped over the bedclothes and my shoulder hit one of the posts of the bed. Thank goodness it was there, or I'd have fallen flat on my face. As it was, it stopped me, but I struck my shoulder quite hard."

"Let me see," Bodine said concerned.

"No, don't fuss, Morgan. It's just a bit tender. I still don't know how I got my feet entangled in the bedding though."

"Very well, my love."

Colwyn just stopped herself from giving a huge sigh of relief that he wasn't going to pursue the matter further.

"Why were you late?" she asked, managing to change the subject.

Chapter Five

"The King was outlining his plans for the Midsummer festival. There is to be a tournament after the knighting has taken place."

"Will you have to take part?"

"But of course. I am the King's Champion...and I hope I will be your champion again?"

"McDowell will be here, won't he?" Her mind suddenly flashed back five years to the last encounter. "Promise me you'll be careful. Your last meeting was rather...heated."

Bodine smiled ruefully. "I am five years older and wiser now. I know McDowell resorts to dirty tricks when he thinks he is about to lose, so I am prepared. I'm also stronger now, so am confident I can win again, but I am not being arrogant about it. I obtained a lot of information from him when we fought. Do not worry." He touched her shoulder lightly and again saw the flicker of pain cross her face but said nothing.

"Of course you will be my champion again." Her voice still sounded worried.

"Everything will be fine." He reached up and pushed his fingers through her hair, his thumbs lingering on her temples, and it was then, as he brushed her mind, he realised she had lied to him about the way she had sustained her injury. He kept his face neutral, but wondered why she would do so unless she was trying to protect him from something. But what? He would find out.

"I hope so," she said. "You had to miss the pillow fight last time."

"I had to give the other knights a chance to win something," he replied, his lips twisting in a smirk of amusement.

"I have to go; the Queen has requested my presence for this afternoon. Will I see you this evening?"

"Unfortunately not. I too have business, but I will see you tomorrow, my love."

She leant forward and kissed him, then rose reluctantly, and Bodine stood up. "I wish I didn't have to go." Her voice sounded so wistful.

"Perhaps then, soon, you won't have to," he replied softly in her ear.

She smiled, her eyes full of love, and he watched her walk away before sitting down to muse over the reason for the lie. Had someone hurt her and she was afraid to say anything? Surely, she knew by now she could tell him anything; he would protect her. He would get to the bottom of the mystery one way or another.

⊗ ⊗ ⊗ ⊗

Bodine had taken up watch around the corner from where Colwyn's rooms were situated. Even if he had to stand there all night, he would get to the bottom of what was going on.

Then, at a quarter before midnight, her door opened and she looked both ways down the corridor. Seeing it was clear, she slipped out and made her way once again down below the castle to her rendezvous with Dernley. Bodine followed her at a safe distance, and listened outside the room.

"Colwyn!" he heard Dernley exclaim. "Did I do this to you?"

"It doesn't matter, Giles. Come, help me."

"I brought shields with me tonight; you need to be able to defend yourself with one. It's not too heavy, is it?"

"No, I can manage. Are we using the wooden swords or the real ones tonight?"

"Real ones tonight, but only practising moves. Now, are you ready?"

"Ready!"

Bodine heard the clashing of sword against sword, and sword against shield. He decided he couldn't wait any longer and burst into the room.

"Colwyn! Dernley!"

The two opponents froze, then turned guiltily to face Bodine.

Chapter Five

"What is the meaning of this?" His expression was hard as he stared at them.

"Please, Morgan, do not blame Giles. I asked him to help me begin my training again."

"Again?" Bodine came into the room and took the shield and sword from Colwyn. "So, you did not trip over your bedding as you stated."

Colwyn hung her head, shame-faced that she had been caught out. "No, Morgan," she said meekly.

"You lied to me."

"I ask forgiveness for lying to you, but I thought you would not allow me to continue, or approve of this."

"You did not even ask me."

"Would you have said yes?" She dared to look up and saw his masked expression.

"No."

"That's why I didn't ask. I knew you wouldn't approve." Colwyn gave him a defiant look.

Bodine looked long and hard at her, and secretly admired the way she was standing, her chin jutting out in pure rebellion. He turned his attention to Dernley.

"Giles, how could you be a part of this?"

"With respect, Duke, Colwyn and I have fought many battles over the years. Sir John was her tutor, but, as you know, he is in Inver and therefore unable to continue the training. I was the only option, and I can refuse the Duchess nothing."

Bodine considered his words. Finally, he took a deep breath and said, "Giles, return to your room. I will escort Colwyn back to hers."

"Yes, Duke," Dernley said meekly. He nodded respectfully at the duke and Colwyn and left the room.

Bodine returned his attention to Colwyn. "You do not need to do this anymore," he told her.

"Yes, I do. I've been doing this since I was six, Morgan. You can't stop me."

"It's not something a lady should be doing. I must forbid it."

Colwyn snorted, tossing her head like a young, unbroken filly. "And, pray tell, how you plan to stop me?"

"I'm telling you this must stop, and I expect you to obey me."

"Why?" she asked rather rudely, feeling her control slipping.

"Because, to all intents and purposes, I am your elder brother, and you must do as I say."

"Well, I'm telling you…'brother', that's not going to happen. I am going to continue."

Bodine felt his expression hardening at her out-and-out rebellion.

"You have no need to continue," he snapped in a slightly sharper tone than he intended. "I promised your mother I would take care of you."

Colwyn's control shattered and her next words slipped out before she could stop them.

"You obviously can't, because you weren't at Inver when I needed you so desperately, were you?!"

Even though she was furious with him, she immediately regretted what she had just said, as she saw the pain travel across his handsome features for a few seconds before the mask came down once again. Unaware he was doing so, he stepped forward, closer to her, and she drew back, suddenly uncertain, for the first time in her life, of what his next action might be.

Apologising was not something Colwyn was used to doing, but she knew she must make amends for the unjustified, spiteful words she had spoken.

"Oh, Morgan… I… I'm sorry. I didn't mean what I just said."

Chapter Five

"But you are correct," he replied quietly. "I wasn't there when you needed me."

"You have a greater responsibility to the King as General of his Armies. You can't be in two places at once. I… I ask your forgiveness for my harsh words."

He stared into her emerald eyes and wavered in his resolve.

"We really must not argue; we are family." He stroked her hair gently, then motioned for her to turn around in a circle and she did as she was told. "That hauberk does not fit properly. You need to be measured correctly if you wish to wear one, as this one will hamper your movement. And you cannot wear a dress underneath; it will put you at a disadvantage. You will need either hose or breeches. Take up your sword and show me your grip."

Colwyn hesitated for a few moments, not believing what she was hearing, but then did as she was told. Bodine stepped forward and grasped her hand firmly.

"A sword is finely balanced. This one is not right, but it is close. The pommel should balance it perfectly; now, pay attention." He manipulated her fingers and shifted them to the correct position. "You must practise holding the sword thus," he told her. "Now, give the sword to me and take it back, so I can see that you grasp it correctly."

It took her a few attempts, but she finally managed it a number of times in succession. Bodine nodded his approval.

"Tomorrow, we will pay a visit to the blacksmith. If you wish to wear a hauberk, then you must have a correctly fitted one. Your womanly shape means it will have to be specially made. Now, I think that is enough for tonight."

"Morgan," Colwyn began, but he interrupted her.

"Let's remove that hauberk, shall we?" he said, bending down to grasp the bottom of the mail to lift it over her head. Next he unlaced her aketon and removed that as well. "How badly are you bruised?"

"Not too badly, honestly, Morgan."

He ignored her, undid the lacing of her gown and pulled it off her shoulders, inspecting the chainmail-patterned bruising appearing on them. Suddenly shy under his piercing gaze, she clutched the gown tightly against her breasts, as his eyes swept over her.

"What am I going to do with you?" he asked her softly, as his hands caressed her skin.

"What-whatever my Lord wishes," she whispered back, daring to look up into the penetrating grey eyes.

"Colwyn, don't tempt me," he almost pleaded. "I can barely keep control as it is, without you saying things like that." With shaking fingers, he pulled her gown back up over her shoulders and fastened it back up. "Come, it's time you were in bed." He took her hand, doused the candles and led her from the training room and back to her chambers. "Goodnight, my love." He kissed her hand before turning to walk down the corridor.

༄ ༅ ༄ ༅

Colwyn had a restless night. Inappropriate thoughts had filled her mind in the darkness; thoughts a lady of her stature and station should not have. Feeling guilty, she sought out Monsignor McLeod and asked that he hear her confession.

McLeod frowned. He could think of nothing that she could possibly have done to warrant the request, but nevertheless, he motioned her to take a seat within the confessional and he sat in the other side.

"Monsignor, I need forgiveness for I have sinned."

"Go on," McLeod encouraged softly.

Chapter Five

"I... I killed a man; I have wished to take revenge on those who killed my parents, and I... I..." she faltered.

"Speak freely, Colwyn; whatever you say will go no further."

He heard her take a huge gulp and silence reigned for a few minutes. McLeod waited patiently.

"I... have... had... inappropriate thoughts... about a man... I... I want him to..." She could not go on.

McLeod knew exactly who she was talking about—his cousin—and he smiled to himself. The bishop had taken him into his confidence about the situation and the King's plan to try and forge a union between Rossmere and Invermere, and secretly, he had been pleased, and also a little envious. McLeod had loved, just the once, but it was the death of his intended that had made him join the church. His cousin had suffered loss at a very young age and had struggled most of his young life with his heritage and the distrust that came with it. It was amazing that he had turned out to be the kind of man he now was, considering, but the love and care he had received from Richard, and especially Bronwyn Coltrane, had moulded him into that man. Now, it appeared, he may have found love; a love that was more than justly deserved and he was pleased for him.

"Colwyn, as I understand it, you defeated evil when you killed that man. It is the duty of every God-abiding citizen to fight evil, and that is what you did. Regarding your revenge; is it that, or do you wish to avenge your parents? You are young and you are loved; do not let revenge take over your heart; it is not you, no matter how... bitter you may feel at this moment. It is grief that is still talking and you must work through this. As to your feelings for this man; I assume he is single? Do you love him?"

"Yes, Monsignor, he is single and I do love him, with all my heart."

"Then my child, there is nothing wrong with that."

"But—"

"Your thoughts are perfectly natural if you are that much in love. You have not allowed any intimacy. Thinking about it is only natural, but if you are truly concerned…"

McLeod pondered a few moments before issuing penance, if it could be called that, and dismissed her. He watched her go as she left the chapel, and smiled warmly.

The next day, Bodine kept his word and took her to the blacksmiths for a fitting. The blacksmith could not initially believe his ears when the duke made the request, but after a few moments' hesitation, he began his work, taking measurements and making allowances for padding and other garments. He was highly skilled and was confident the fit would be perfect. Next, he asked her to let her right hand lie at her side, then bend it at the elbow, so it was parallel to the ground. He looked at the distance then went along a selection of swords until he found the one that he felt was of the correct length. Handing it to Colwyn, he watched as Bodine made sure she was holding it correctly and then asked her to perform a couple of exercises with it. The blacksmith's eyebrows rose as she skilfully swung it around in a figure of eight, then stopped and balanced it on the edge of her hand, as Bodine had shown her.

The duke nodded in satisfaction and whispered something into the blacksmith's ear. The man nodded.

"It will be done, your Grace."

"Thank you."

"If you come back in four days, it will all be complete." He bowed respectfully.

Bodine nodded and escorted Colwyn outside.

"What would you like to do today?" Bodine asked her.

"Well first, I need to go to the stables to check on Archer, but after that, I don't know; surprise me!"

Chapter Five

"Archer?" he queried.

"Giles's horse. He has a bad leg."

"Very well, we will check Archer and then you can change into your riding leathers," he said affectionately.

☙ ❧ ☙ ❧

6

Chapter Six

Leading up to the Midsummer Celebrations, Stuart had taken every opportunity to ensure Colwyn and Bodine spent their free time in each other's company, much to the displeasure of his Queen. They argued vehemently about it until, in the end, Stuart was forced to take extraordinary steps to ensure Alexandra did not jeopardise his plans and explained the whole situation in detail, that this union was to enhance the stability of the Kingdom.

Alexandra now understood, but still disapproved and pleaded with him to find an alternative suitor, but Stuart would have none of it. In the end, he had turned to Bishop Douglas for help, and the plan had been born to prevent her from interfering further. That was due to be put into action this coming Sunday at Holy Communion, A union between Rossmere and Invermere was perfect, and no one—not even the Queen—was going to interfere; the bishop once more assured Stuart that Alexandra would not speak about it again.

Stuart admitted to feeling rather uneasy about the whole plan, but the stability of the Kingdom, he finally decided, outweighed the cost of forcing the Queen to accept the planned wedding of the duke and duchess.

Colwyn and Bodine took many walks both within the castle rose garden and further afield in the meadows beyond the castle walls.

Chapter Six

Having left the blacksmith's after her fitting, and having performed yet another treatment on Dernley's horse, Colwyn had run to her quarters to change into her riding leathers, and then they had ridden out to the river with a picnic, determined to enjoy the sunshine, food and scenery. Their conversation covered all manner of things and, once again, Morgan was amazed at her intelligence and how she looked at him with love and complete trust in her eyes.

"Morgan, teach me another spell," she pleaded.

He frowned, trying to think of something that would be suitable. "All right…. Let's see if you can hear me…" He closed his eyes and concentrated. *Audite me, Colwyn,* he thought in his mind.

She gasped and a hand went to her head. Bodine opened his eyes.

You can hear me? He questioned in his mind, and she nodded. *Try and speak back to me with your mind. Just think about what you want to say.*

Is this right? her thoughts questioned. *Can you hear me?*

Yes, I can hear you. Well done. You will need to practise this, so you can increase the distance between us.

How far? She queried.

Oh, at least two weeks' travel.

"Two weeks! That's many miles away! I'll never manage that," she said, actually speaking.

Bodine smiled and spoke too. "Remember what I said five years ago? You will need to practise."

"I will do so. Thank you, Morgan. So, basically, you are saying all I have to do is imagine what I want, speak or think it, and it should happen?"

"That usually only works for us Kadeau, but you appear to have some power. The other thing you must learn to do is block. If I, or someone else, were of a mind, we could try and force you to do something against your will."

"Like Duke McDowell tried to do."

"Yes. You must learn to create a mental wall… it doesn't matter what you imagine, as long as it appears impenetrable to you… an actual wall; some kind of barrier. Let's try. I'm going to try and make you do something…build your wall…"

Bodine stared intently at her. Colwyn found herself unconsciously lifting a hand, suddenly deciding to touch her hair, then, as if she realised, her hand froze in mid-air, but she found she couldn't move it down.

"If it helps, think of a thought, like 'stop' or 'no'," Bodine suggested.

Her hand began to shake with the effort, then slowly it started to move downwards; then it stopped again, rose slightly, then went down again.

"That was really very good for your first attempt," Bodine told her.

"You were gentle with me, weren't you?" Colwyn accused him.

Bodine nodded. "Yes, I was. You need to build the strength up gradually. It is possible to cause damage by going in too strongly, and I have no wish to harm you. Again, we will practise. You can even try to make me do something if you wish."

"As if I'm going to achieve that!" Colwyn said, and Bodine smiled; he knew perfectly well that she would never be able to make him do anything he didn't want to do!

"Tell me, is there Kadeau in your pedigree?" the duke asked.

"Not that I am aware of, and I can trace my ancestry back a long way."

"It's not unheard of for humans to have the skills…. The King has powers and he is not Kadeau; it could just be that your mind is unusually focused. Only time will tell, and then we'll know one way or another, but if you say no Kadeau, then we must assume you have a highly disciplined mind."

Chapter Six

She smiled again at those words. Why did men think that women were incapable of such things? She gazed into his blue eyes and sent out a subtle command.

With the sun shining on her long, red chestnut hair, her cheeks flushed with colour and those amazing green eyes, Bodine found he was unable to resist temptation.

Reaching out, he brushed a stray lock of hair from her face. "Have I told you your hair is beautiful?" he asked in a whisper.

Colwyn smiled, dimples appearing in her cheeks. "Only about a hundred times, my Lord," she replied. "And I think I have just made you do something against your will!"

He shook his head. "Oh, my love, I am not acting against my will," he replied, returning her smile, his eyes smouldering.

"Have I ever told you how dangerous your eyes are?"

"Dangerous?" Bodine queried.

"Yes. When you look at me, I can't breathe, and when they go deep blue like they are now, I feel like I'm drowning in them, and it's the most wonderful sensation."

Her lips were slightly parted as if waiting for something and Morgan did not disappoint her. Slowly, he leant towards her and tentatively placed a soft kiss on them, as if asking for permission.

Fire suddenly flared up within Colwyn's body in response to the kiss, and she felt her heart thudding in her chest. Succumbing to the feelings, her body relaxed against his. She couldn't help herself; she wanted the feeling to never stop.

The flames engulfed Bodine, too. He wasn't sure if it was the kiss or her response to it, but she curled her fingers into his hair and relaxed back onto the blanket they were sitting on, drawing him down with her. Bodine kissed her again, this time firmer and longer, and she responded with enthusiasm, succumbing eagerly to his advances.

He smothered her face and throat with kisses. His right hand, which had been resting at her waist, started to move upwards of its own volition. Colwyn unconsciously seemed to know its destination, for she breathed in deeply, which allowed her left breast to make contact with the palm of his hand.

Bodine's fingers automatically squeezed gently and Colwyn moaned her pleasure, encouraging him to continue his assault. Her fingers continued to curl in his golden hair, her thumbs resting at his temple and suddenly a kaleidoscope of sensuous images assaulted both their minds and Bodine was lost. Not knowing he was doing so, he frantically pulled at the lacings on the fitted bodice of the fine leather, so he could kiss the cleft between her breasts. Now, only her thin silk chemise barred his hand from her naked flesh, but not for long. Pulling the material down, his hand encountered the hot firmness of her breast, the nipple hard against his fingers, and then his mouth was there, sucking at the aureole, his tongue rolling around it as she frantically pulled at his clothing, wanting to feel his flesh against hers. His hand moved, grabbing at her skirts so he could touch the silky skin of her thighs.

But it was her desperate groan and her sharp intake of breath as their flesh finally met that brought Bodine back to reality with a jolt.

What on earth had just happened to them? What did he think he was doing, behaving in such a shameful and un-knightly fashion? He jerked his lips from her body and leant back, momentarily mesmerised by the sight of her heaving breasts and the curve of her thighs.

"Morgan?" she questioned in a gasp, her eyes filled with wanton passion.

He blinked and dragged his eyes away from her breasts, then, with shaking fingers pulled her chemise back up and her skirts down to cover her.

Chapter Six

"Forgive me, my love, for my shameful behaviour; but your beauty made me forget myself."

"Morgan..." Her voice was breathless; husky. "I've never felt like this before..." She leant up to plant a kiss on his chest. "It felt so... right... so good. I love you so much." She kissed his chest again. "Am I wicked for feeling this?"

Her lips burnt his skin; her fingers trailed fire up his spine. He wanted her to carry on but knew it had to stop. He couldn't think straight and his mind was still reeling from the explosive assault. Gently, he drew further away and smiled down kindly at her, his usually grey eyes now deep blue with the passion he was feeling.

"No, my pet. You are not wicked, but I have forgotten my manners and the correct protocol." Sitting upright, he carefully pulled her clothing back into place and with shaking fingers, re-tied the lacings on her bodice. It was the last thing he wanted to do. God forgive him, he wanted to make love to her right here, in this meadow by the river, with the sound of the birds around them and the gentle breeze blowing through the willow trees.

There was no denying it now; he wanted her for his own, to be by his side, to bear his children. Forcefully he commanded his manhood to calm itself. He must be patient.

"Come, Colwyn, we should return to the castle." He straightened and refastened his own clothing. "As it is, we have broken court etiquette."

"I don't care. You will think me totally shameless and a harlot, but I enjoyed what we just shared and... I didn't want you to stop." She took a deep breath and looked up at him from under her long lashes. "I'd do anything to have that pleasure again. I can't help myself. I love you."

His resolve almost broke, but somehow he maintained his control. "I cannot deny it. I love you and I want to possess you. I want you by my side and I want to see you with my child within you." He reached out to place a hand on her stomach but stopped himself at the last second. If he touched her, he would be lost and her fierce blush at his over-bold words did nothing to quench his desires.

Bodine drew a ragged breath and stood up, running a hand through his hair. He pulled on his leather gloves before daring to offer assistance to Colwyn, helping her to her feet.

"On our return, I will speak with the King." He dropped to one knee, holding her hand and looked up into those wonderful eyes. "My Lady Colwyn, will you do me the honour of marrying me?"

"Oh, Morgan," she breathed. "It is I who would be honoured." She drew him to his feet, wanting him to kiss her, but instead, he kissed her hand. It was the only way he could manage to maintain his fragile control.

They packed up their picnic and folded the blanket. Bodine assisted Colwyn into the saddle, then mounted his own horse and they rode sedately back to the castle.

To any observer, Bodine appeared the perfect gentleman. He helped Colwyn down from her mount, bowed reverently and politely kissed her hand, before escorting her to the steps that led to her rooms. Colwyn flashed him a beautiful smile as he turned to make his way to the King's chambers.

Bodine requested a formal private audience with his Liege, which Stuart immediately granted, curious to know what was afoot.

Suddenly embarrassed, the duke dropped to one knee, head bowed in respect, making Stuart frown.

"Why so formal, Morgan?" Stuart asked, concerned.

"My Liege, I wish to ask..." he stopped, took a deep breath and started again. "Sire, I am here to request the hand of Colwyn Coltrane, Duchess of Invermere, in marriage and ask that you look favourably on my request." There; he had said it.

Chapter Six

Stuart had heard him, but it took several seconds for it to sink in. He could hardly believe that his plan could be close to fruition.

Bodine dared to glance up at his King. "My Liege?" he questioned, suddenly worried that Stuart might say no. If he did, Bodine didn't know what he'd do.

Stuart smiled warmly at him and held out his hand. "Morgan Bodine, you have my warmest blessings. I am delighted, my friend." He pulled his General to his feet and gave him a fierce hug. "Come, let us celebrate with a drink."

Stuart poured them both a generous goblet of wine and saluted his General before taking a long sip.

"I will make the formal announcement at the Midsummer Banquet. Have you a date in mind?"

"I was thinking sometime in early September, at Belvoir, and later, at Inver Cathedral, a blessing for her subjects."

Stuart nodded. "Nigel McDowell will be attending the Midsummer Banquet, no doubt to ask for Colwyn's hand in marriage. I know this is very un-King-like, but I can't wait to see the look on his face! Now come, we must go to the chapel. I will get James to bless the forthcoming joining." He ordered a page to collect Colwyn and take her to the King's private chapel and another to fetch Bishop James Douglas.

൦൪ ൪൦ ൦൪ ൪൦

My Lady, are you well?" Sarah asked, seeing the colour in her Lady's face.

"I feel wonderful, Sarah!" Colwyn said energetically, stretching in a very un-ladylike manner.

"What's happened?" Sarah demanded as she helped her mistress out of her riding leathers and into a simple day dress. "Something has happened, hasn't it?" But all she got for her persistent questioning was a secretive smile, which alarmed Sarah even more. Her Lady had been out riding with Duke Morgan.... something had to have happened. Something that had delighted her mistress. Wild thoughts immediately sprung into her mind and it frustrated her that Colwyn would say nothing.

Suddenly, there was a knock on the door. Sarah opened it to find a page standing there, requesting that Colwyn accompanying him to the King's private chapel. Colwyn gave her maid a not very apologetic look and followed the page, leaving a fuming Sarah behind.

As Colwyn entered, Stuart, Bodine and the bishop looked up. Bodine immediately came to escort her to the altar.

"Sire." Colwyn bobbed a curtsy and bowed her head respectfully before turning to the bishop, curtsying again and kissing the ring on the Douglas' hand. She straightened and stood with Bodine, facing the King.

"Colwyn, Morgan has asked for your hand in marriage," Stuart began but paused as Colwyn blushed. "I have approved the match and I trust you have no objections?"

"No, Sire, none at all." She dared to glance at Bodine, love clearly evident in her eyes.

"We are here for God to witness Morgan's proclamation of his intentions and for the church's blessing on the forthcoming union."

Bishop Douglas indicated for Bodine and Colwyn to stand at the altar.

Taking Colwyn's hands, Bodine spoke in a deep even-toned voice. "I, Morgan Geraint Rhys Bodine, Duke of Rossmere, do stand here before God and my King to formally ask for the hand of Colwyn Eilwen Anghared Coltrane, Duchess of Invermere, in marriage. I ask for God's blessing on this forthcoming union and ask that my King will also offer his blessing."

"I, Stuart Rhisiart Aiden Eurion Cantrell, King of Devonmere, do approve this forthcoming union and wish you both every happiness," Stuart said solemnly.

Chapter Six

The bishop nodded and placed his left hand on Colwyn's and Bodine's. Raising his right hand, he began a prayer, offering a blessing on the future marriage. Then he indicated for them to kneel to receive the final blessing. Briefly, he touched the top of Bodine's head, then Colwyn's as he spoke the sacred words.

"Amen," everyone said as the blessing finished.

"*The sponsalia per verbade futuro* has been pronounced. You may stand now."

"The formal announcement will be made at the Midsummer Banquet," Stuart told the bishop, who nodded and smiled.

Bodine stood, assisting Colwyn to her feet, and kissed her hand before looking into her eyes, which were filled with delight and desire. There could be no doubt that she did indeed love him and Bodine felt his heart swell with happiness. In fact, the last time he had felt even close to this good, was when the King had proclaimed him General of the Armies.

Colwyn's heart was thudding so hard in her chest, she thought that everyone could hear it. The way Bodine was looking at her was making her feel hot and cold all at the same time and she could hardly breathe. There was a strange feeling in the pit of her stomach and a kind of pleasant ache between her thighs. She decided that if she could be any happier, she would die, it was so intense.

Stuart glanced at James Douglas who gave an almost imperceptible nod. The deed was almost done. The two needed to exchange a token between them, and once the wedding had taken place, and consummation of the marriage had occurred, Nigel McDowell would be thwarted once and for all.

"Morgan, aren't you going to kiss your intended?" he asked his General.

Bodine swallowed slowly, and tentatively kissed his future bride, scared his desire would get the better of him, but with an audience present, it didn't.

Stuart turned and led the way out of the chapel, with James bringing up the rear. As they approached the keep again, Stuart stopped and turned. "I hope you two will enjoy a private meal together tonight in the royal antechamber. I will arrange everything. We will not join you; I need to… ensure that the Queen has fully accepted the situation." His features hardened somewhat at the prospect. The bishop was shortly going to take steps to ensure she would not interfere, but Alexandra would still be livid until the deed was done.

"I think we both understand, Your Majesty," Morgan replied.

Stuart nodded. "Come, take a walk in the rose garden. I know it is one of your favourite spots. Once I have arranged everything, I will send Rhobat, my most trusted squire to you. Enjoy your evening."

Bodine bowed and Colwyn curtsied as the King strode off, then made their way to the rose garden, to stroll amongst the heady spring fragrances there, before sitting in their favourite spot in the hidden arbour.

"Colwyn, my love, are you happy?" he asked her seriously.

"If I were any happier, I would die from it," she answered truthfully. "Can't you hear my heart thudding?"

Bodine shook his head.

"Then surely you can feel it?" she questioned, innocently placing his hand between her breasts and holding it there.

Bodine swallowed very slowly. This was all going to be much more difficult than he had anticipated. Just over three months before they were to be wed; it would require every single ounce of self-control he possessed and this was a shock. Usually unshakable and totally reserved, he found himself suddenly overcome by basic manly urges and unable to take his eyes from where his hand rested between her breasts. Trying to appear calm and collected, he gently pulled his hand away not realising until too late that Colwyn moved closer to him as he did so. The heady aroma of her muddled

Chapter Six

his senses and she willingly yielded to him as he kissed her long and deeply, enfolding her in his arms as if never to let her go. He knew he had to stop, but couldn't. How could she bewitch him so? It was wrong, but it felt so good. His body was aching painfully for her; to possess her in every way.

Thankfully, it was Colwyn who broke the kiss and the embrace. Breathing heavily and flushed from the intensity of it, she managed to whisper breathlessly, "Someone is coming."

It was as good as a drenching of icy cold water and brought Bodine to his senses, but it seriously worried him. It should have been him that sensed someone approaching! His guard was slipping and this simply would not do.

"Your Grace? Your Grace?" a male voice called softly. It was Rhobat, no doubt coming to collect them and take them for their special meal.

Bodine took a very deep, slow breath and stood up, offering a hand to Colwyn. "Here, Rhobat," he said as they appeared from the arbour.

Rhobat bowed courteously and gestured for them to follow him. "Everything has been prepared. I hope it is to your liking. If I may be so bold, I wish to offer my congratulations. The King has taken me into his confidence."

"Thank you, Rhobat, that's very sweet of you," Colwyn said. "It is a shame that not all will take the news joyfully."

Rhobat nodded in understanding. He had heard the rows between the King and Queen regarding Colwyn's future and was at a loss to understand it. Being the King's most trusted squire had meant he had heard and seen many privileged things, and in all his encounters with Morgan Bodine, he had never seen or felt anything that made him feel threatened or frightened of the Kadeau Lord. And by the way the Duchess was looking at the duke, it was clear that she loved him deeply.

Rhobat escorted them to the royal antechamber, where food was laid out on the table. After assisting them into their seats, he poured wine into their goblets, then retreated, leaving them alone to enjoy their meal.

"I'm so excited, I don't think I'll be able to eat much," Colwyn said.

Bodine smiled at her. "We need to set a date for the wedding, my love. I had been thinking of September, but I don't think I can wait that long…" he lowered his voice to the barest of whispers, "…to possess you." He paused as she blushed. "I also think now, there may be danger in waiting that length of time."

"From McDowell, you mean?"

Bodine nodded. "The announcement of our forthcoming marriage will not be enough to stop him, and I fear for your safety until we are truly man and wife."

"Then why don't we set it for the end of June; after the Midsummer Festival?"

"That will give us time to return to Belvoir. If I send word to Edward now, he can have everything prepared for when we arrive."

"I would marry you tomorrow if I could," Colwyn said seriously.

Bodine reached across the table and took her hand. "My love, those words make my heart sing. It is a long time since I can say I've been this happy."

She smiled at him, her eyes extra bright.

They finished their meal, then Bodine said, "On a serious note, I will start to instruct you as to what your role will be in Giles Dernley's knighting, so you can practise and be perfect on the day."

"Thank you, Morgan. It is very important to me that I get it right, both for Giles and for the Duchy."

"You will need to dress Giles in his armour. It is done in a specific order: the hauberk, cuirass, gauntlets, then you kneel down and attach the right

Chapter Six

spur first, followed by the left; then finally, you will gird his sword so it hangs on the right. That's all there is to it, apart from responses you will need to provide to the King. Then Giles will kneel before him and receive the knighthood."

"The most difficult bit will be the hauberk—that's the heaviest part of the armour, but I will manage it."

"You can practice on me. We have a couple of days before the ceremony, so can start tomorrow—after we've collected your new armour from the blacksmith."

"Thank you, Morgan," she said again.

They passed a pleasant evening, and then Bodine escorted her back to her rooms and gave her a parting kiss outside her door.

The following morning, Colwyn was up and out early, accompanied by Sarah. She went into the city to visit the silversmith. In the shop, she explained what she wanted, and stood as the jeweller lifted her hair and cut a length from underneath.

"How long will it take you to make?" she asked him.

"For one to provide such a beautiful gift to someone she loves, I will have it done in three days," he replied. "Your request is very unusual, and I must take care, for it must be perfect. It will be an honour to work on this."

Colwyn smiled her sweetest smile. "Thank you, sir. The clasp must be able to take the weight, you understand."

"It will be strong and firm, yet delicate, you have my assurances."

"I will return in three days. Thank you."

That task completed, she returned to the castle along with Sarah, who was bursting with questions but knew better than to ask what her mistress was up to.

Safely within the castle walls again, Colwyn dismissed Sarah and wandered along to the stables. She wanted to take Archer out, if only for a walk to see how his leg was doing after almost ten days of inactivity. Usually, injuries such as he had sustained meant the horse was no longer fit for work and resulted in it being destroyed, but Archer was responding remarkably well to treatment and she began to suspect that it may only have been a strain.

Archer seemed pleased to see her, and he was in high spirits after the inactivity, but she was firm. "Stop that now," she commanded him, "or you will undo all my good work. You must start slowly and gradually work up to full strength." She removed the bandage and felt the fetlock. The temperature seemed normal, so she untied him and walked him out of the stable, listening to the sound of his hooves on the stone floor of the courtyard.

Smiling in satisfaction, she walked him for a quarter of an hour before returning him to his stall, patting him. Wanting to give Dernley the good news, she wandered along to the Pell to see if anyone was training. Dernley was not there, but she saw Bodine, practicing with his two squires. What really alarmed her was that he was not wearing any armour and was barechested. He was holding a sword in each hand and fighting with both squires at the same time. She stood at a distance, so as not to distract him, and watched his lithe movements. His coordination was exceptional as he manipulated both swords to fend off his attackers and once again, it was obvious to see why he was the best swordsman in the Kingdom. Of course, his squires were nowhere near as skilled as he was, but as he had trained and prepared them, they were of greater skill than the average squire.

Colwyn felt herself squirm with desire as she watched his muscles moving under the tight, lightly tanned skin; knowing she was marrying a man of exquisite physical makeup and beauty; with no excess of flesh visible.

Jonas, the weapons master, suddenly appeared at her side. "The Pell is no place for a woman, let alone a lady," he told her.

Chapter Six

Colwyn bristled indignantly and eyed the sword at his side. "May I?" she asked sweetly.

Jonas frowned as she reached for his sword. It was heavier than she was used to, but she took it nevertheless and stepped back from him, clasping it as Bodine had taught her, and swung it around expertly, trying its weight and balance.

Jonas' mouth dropped open, then he recovered himself. "Feet further apart, my Lady…that's better; straighten that back, yes, that's it; shoulders down slightly." He watched her for another couple of minutes. "Cease," he commanded, and she stopped what she was doing. "Sir John has trained you well, although I see your grip is not his, I assume that is General Bodine?"

"Yes, sir."

"You are lacking strength at the moment. Follow me; although you are not dressed for training."

They walked into one of the training areas. A solid wood stake stood in the ground, bleached white by the sun and age, with an infinite number of sword strikes on its body.

"Let me see you swing at the stake."

Colwyn, relaxing under Jonas' tutelage, started to attack the post with both forward and backward swings.

"Stop tickling it and attack!" he shouted.

Colwyn felt her temper rising.

"Harder! If you can't do it harder, don't bother picking up a sword!"

Furious, Colwyn gave the next swing everything she'd got and saw a small section of wood fly off.

"Now you've got it! Again! Again!"

She kept going but found her arm was beginning to ache.

"Cease. Well done, my Lady. That was much better. I think you have had enough for today."

He held out his hand and Colwyn gave him back his sword, then he saw the expression on her face, and turned to find Bodine striding towards them, silk shirt in his hand, swords in sheaths at his hips.

He ducked under the rail and came up to them. "Colwyn, you should not be here," he said firmly.

Colwyn, her temper still short, let fly. "I'm sick and tired of everyone telling me where I can and can't go; what I can or can't do! I'm here, and I've done some sword practise!" Her eyes were spitting green fire, as she stamped a foot indicating her extreme annoyance, and Bodine could clearly see she was having one of her temper tantrums.

He was aware of his expression hardening. This was a side of her he had not witnessed in person before; only heard about. His eyes flashed a dangerous shade of grey. Disobedience was not something he was used to from his men, and most certainly not from a woman.

Jonas nodded respectfully and made a hasty retreat, sensing the air around him was about to become rather heated. Bodine grabbed Colwyn firmly by an arm, and, whilst she struggled to free herself, dragged her under the rail and away from the Pell until they were out of sight from everybody, in a secluded corner.

"Let go of me!" Colwyn hissed, finally managing to jerk her arm free from his firm grip. "How dare you drag me away like some naughty child!" Her eyes were glittering dangerously, and she was breathing heavily with a mixture of her exercise and indignation at his actions, totally oblivious to the fact that he was still shirtless and standing so very close to her. "You're not my husband or keeper…yet!"

"The Pell is no place for a woman. You will do as you are told," he whispered almost menacingly.

"Try and make me!" she challenged.

Chapter Six

She attempted to walk away, only to find herself held firmly by both arms close against his body. Struggling, she broke free and started to walk away once more, only to find herself grabbed very tightly by an arm and swung around again towards the wall.

"Let me go!" she spat. "I will do what I want, and go where I please when I please!"

He took hold of both of her arms then and shook her. "You will not!" he retorted. "As my wife, I will expect you to do as I say."

Now beyond furious, she managed to free an arm enough to slap his face, shouting, "But I'm not your wife, yet!"

Shocked at her action, steely grey eyes glared at flashing green ones for several seconds, then Colwyn suddenly became aware of Bodine's state of undress, and felt the heat rise in her body at his nearness. She swallowed convulsively at the sight of the muscles of his chest and his biceps as he held her; then something gave, snapped, and the duke slammed her against the wall and kissed her savagely, using his body to hold her there to prevent her from escaping.

She fought him for a few seconds, pressing her hands against his bare chest, and then the fire took hold and she succumbed to the assault, welcoming the ferocious attack that was taking her breath away, making her feel light-headed. She had never felt him so out of control, and subconsciously, it thrilled her; even the sudden awareness of something pressing hard against her belly as he became sexually aroused, excited her.

They briefly came up for air before his lips found her throat. His body was still pressing tightly against her and as his hands moved to rip her bodice, she moaned his name.

"Morgan!"

He froze, his fingers poised on the top of her bodice, against her breasts, and slowly came back to reality. A horrified expression came over his face as he realised what he had been about to do, and the state of his arousal. Bodine gave an exclamation, released her and stepped away, turning his back to her whilst he pulled on his silk shirt, and left it hanging loose until his manhood calmed itself.

After a few minutes of deep, calming breaths, he regained his control and turned back to face her.

"Morgan," she breathed again.

He stared at her, still shaken about what he had been about to do, then shook his head and turned abruptly on a heel and strode off, to get as far away from her as possible.

Colwyn watched him until he disappeared out of sight, then her bottom lip began to tremble and she bit down hard to keep her emotions in check. She had never, ever seen him so out of control, or so angry, and she relived the episode; the savagery within him. If they had been anywhere else, somewhere more private and secluded, would he have continued the assault, she wondered? She had been both thrilled and frightened and her heart was still thumping in her chest. But had they just ruined it all? Was everything they had built going to suddenly come tumbling down? She needed to get back to her rooms to compose herself again.

She walked quickly back into the keep, up the stairs and to her rooms. Sarah was thankfully absent, so she went into the bed-chamber and threw herself down on her bed. The day had started so well—it was only just coming up to lunchtime—and now it was ruined and it was all his fault! She was meant to pick up her armour today; that wasn't going to happen now.

Colwyn didn't eat anything for lunch; she had lost her appetite, and she was still angry. How dare he order her around as if she were a servant! Her rebellious side was still loose, but her anger and frustration made the tears fall. Maintaining that anger was exhausting and eventually, she cried herself to sleep.

Chapter Six

ଔ ଓ ଔ ଓ

Bodine was angry with himself and with Colwyn. Having left her, he had stormed off to his rooms, pulled off his shirt and splashed cold water over his face and chest. He had come so very close to losing control completely and in a dangerously public place, but her anger had goaded him; she had challenged his authority, almost rebelled against him, and what had he done in response? He shuddered at the memory; although, deep down, part of him had enjoyed the sexual feelings the incident had released - the feel of her hands on his naked chest and the way she had aroused him.

Shaking his head, he sat down on a chair; closed his eyes and attempted to calm his mind and practise the disciplines to control his emotions. Several minutes passed and then an aura of peace started to pervade his mind and body. His breathing slowed; calm descended. Several more minutes passed, and he realised he was back in control.

Bodine knew he would have to apologise. He stood up, put his shirt back on, tucking it into his leather breeches, and made his way to the banqueting hall, expecting to see Colwyn there getting some lunch, but she did not appear. He hung around waiting, just in case she came down very late, but then became a little concerned at her absence.

Making a decision, he made his way to her rooms, and knocked on the door. No one appeared to open it. He tried again. Nothing. Now seriously worried, he tried the door and found that it opened. Entering, he found the outer chamber deserted and moved silently towards the bedroom. Carefully, he opened the door and peered in, to see Colwyn apparently asleep on the bed. He knew he had no right to enter her bed-chamber, but he had to apologise and also check to make sure she was all right.

Quietly, he went and sat down on the bed, and gently touched her shoulder. "Colwyn, my love, are you all right?"

She awoke with a start and Bodine felt her stiffen under his hands. He noticed she had been crying.

"Morgan! What are you doing here?" she asked sharply, her body tense, as she prepared for another fight.

"I couldn't find you and I was worried," he answered.

She wiped her hand savagely across her eyes. "I'm all right, thank you." Her voice was still sharp, and he picked up on it immediately.

"I'm sorry," he said. "Forgive me?"

She sat up and stared hard at him, still feeling rebellious.

He took hold of her right hand. She tried to pull it away, but he held onto it tightly.

"Please," he asked softly. "I forgive you."

It was the worst thing he could have said, that he forgave her. The anger, which had started to dissipate, began to rise again.

"You…. forgive me? For what?" she demanded.

"For your rebellion."

"I don't want your forgiveness, and I don't require it either!" she snapped, finally managing to free her hand from his. "I am my own person, and if you can't accept that, then I see no future for us! Just… go away," she said sharply. "Get out of my sight!"

She saw his eyes flash a dangerous shade of grey and was pleased to have provoked him.

He gripped her arms tightly. "Colwyn…"

"Let go of me, Morgan… now!"

She saw the anger rise in his eyes and recognised the fact that he was not used to being spoken to this way; best he get used to it before they were married; she was not necessarily going to be the obedient and submissive little wife he was expecting her to be.

Chapter Six

His hands tightened painfully on her arms, but she refused to let him know he was hurting her. Why was she even doing this? She knew her place, but it was that fact that he took it all for granted. She wanted him to realise that she wasn't going to simply follow his wishes blindly. She had a mind of her own; her own opinions and ideas. He had to accept this, or the marriage was not going to work.

Bodine realised she was challenging his authority; something he wasn't used to. He bit off the retort he had been about to make, suddenly understanding that despite her being a woman, she was, in all but sex, his equal, and she was reminding him of that fact. He also realised that she could be extremely stubborn. If they were going to get anywhere with their relationship there would have to be some give and take on both sides. He closed his eyes and took several breaths, letting them out slowly, to get his emotions in check, because it was obvious that Colwyn had no intention of getting hers under control.

Bodine turned on the charm and the magic of his own eyes, and Colwyn gradually felt her anger subside; however, several minutes went by and still she did not speak, but he saw her expression gradually change; the anger dissipated and a calmness descended.

"Do you forgive me, at least?" he finally dared to ask again.

"Yes," she said eventually. "I…I forgive you." There was another long pause before she spoke again. "I'm sorry too. I lost my temper."

"And what a temper you have!" He smiled at her.

"That was nothing. Be thankful you did not witness what I am like when I really let fly!"

"We must not argue. The Kingdom is depending on us. I would never do anything to intentionally hurt you or cause you pain, you know that."

"I know. But the making up is so much fun," she replied, turning on the full power of those mystical green eyes.

Bodine's breath caught in his throat at her words.

"Were you really going to rip my dress from my body this morning?" she asked in a whisper.

He had the good grace to blush.

Would you like to do it now? Colwyn thought irrationally, remembering what the morning had felt like.

"Colwyn!" Bodine exclaimed.

It was her turn to blush. She now wasn't sure if his exclamation was due to her asking about her dress, or whether it was regarding her unspoken thought.

He stood up abruptly before he lost control again. "We must go and pick up your armour," he said, running a hand through his shoulder-length burnished gold hair, which was already beginning to exhibit its seasonal fair streaks, courtesy of the sun.

She got up from the bed. "Were you really very cross with me, this morning?"

"For a moment, yes. However, I was most surprised that Master Jonas started to instruct you. I expected him to drag you kicking and screaming away from the Pell."

"I think he was taken aback when I took hold of his sword and started whirling it around."

"You almost broke my concentration, and my two squires nearly got through my defences."

"Then you too have learnt something, my Lord. Not to allow yourself to be distracted!"

He paused, and then started to laugh; a rich deep sound.

You should laugh more often, Colwyn thought affectionately.

"Come, my Lady, to the blacksmith's."

Chapter Six

They made their way there and inspected his handiwork. Bodine nodded in satisfaction then inspected the sword, and a smile played around his lips at the inscription inscribed on it; *femina bellator ab Invermere*.

Bodine paid the blacksmith and they left, returning to Colwyn's rooms to try the armour on. It fitted perfectly. He presented the sword to her and she looked at the inscription and blushed. He helped her out of her armour and hung it in her wardrobe.

"Now, it's time to start your training for the knighting ceremony. Are you ready?"

"Yes, Morgan."

"Come then." He led the way to his quarters and to the wardrobe in his bedchamber. "Giles will already be partly dressed in black hose to remind him of death, and the white tunic symbolising purity. You will relieve him of his red cloak and the white belt around his waist." Bodine removed his jacket, reached into his wardrobe and pulled out his aketon which he put on. "Now, let's see if you were paying attention last night. What is the first item you will place on him?"

"The hauberk," Colwyn replied, and retrieved it from the wardrobe on Bodine's instruction. She made sure it was the right way round, gathered it up and helped the duke into it, adjusting it to make sure it fitted correctly. "Now the cuirass," she said, and he nodded. She did up the straps on the left side, then placed it on his shoulders and began to fasten the buckles on the right side.

Bodine looked down at her as she did this, a soft smile on his lips, as she tightened the straps so it fit snugly.

Next, she retrieved his gauntlets, holding the right one out for him to insert his hand into, then the left. Removing his golden spurs from the drawer at the bottom of the wardrobe, she knelt down to fit the right one and then the left one. Getting back to her feet, she fitted his white belt around his waist, very conscious of the fact she was so close to his body as she reached to grasp the other end of the belt, and then did it up.

Finally, she girded his sword, remembering to make sure it hung on the right and draped the red cloak around his shoulders, standing close to him once again as she fastened the clasp, acutely aware that he had stared intently at her the entire time. Tasks completed, she stepped back and surveyed her handiwork.

Bodine stopped looking at her and looked down at himself. Everything appeared to be in the right place; his cuirass glinted in the rays of sunlight that came in through the window, and the spurs threw shadows across the floor. He moved around the bedroom, checking again that everything seemed to be in the right position, and nodded in satisfaction.

"Perfect," he said, and Colwyn smiled. A mischievous glint came into his eyes as he then said, "You can undress me now if you like."

Blushing, she stepped forward and undid the clasp of his cloak, removed it and hung it back up; then, working in reverse, she ungirded his sword, removed the belt, spurs, gauntlets, cuirass and hauberk, before stepping back again.

"You haven't finished," he said softly.

She swallowed and stepped forward again to undo his aketon and slid it off his shoulders, leaving him once again in his silk shirt and leather breeches.

"You will be fine at the ceremony, and will do Giles proud," Bodine said quietly, appraising her before he leant forward and kissed her, as if asking for forgiveness for the argument they had had that morning. "Am I forgiven?" he asked.

"Yes, as long as you forgive me," she replied.

"I will always forgive you, my love. I have no choice; I love you," and he kissed her long and hard, as if trying to prove the point.

ଔ ଓ ଔ ଓ

Chapter Seven

The next Sunday, in the chapel, during the communion, as Alexandra took the sacraments, the bishop's hand seemed to stay slightly longer on her head, but he actually disguised it well by laying his hand for the same length of time on the heads of everyone who took the holy communion. Stuart smiled slightly; *brilliant*, he thought. No one would be any the wiser.

At the end of the service, he glanced at his bishop, who gave the barest of nods; the deed had been done. Stuart mentally crossed himself, asking for forgiveness for what he had ordered his bishop to do.

Two days later, it was Midsummer eve. The knighting ceremony and celebrations would follow the next day. Colwyn was up early and had rushed down to the jeweller to collect the present for Bodine. The craftsmanship was exquisite and she was delighted with the finished object. She just hoped that her intended would love it as much as she did. She would present it to him just before the banquet the following evening, when the King would make the announcement of their betrothal.

As the new Duchess of Invermere, Colwyn had taken over Giles Dernley's sponsorship on the death of her father and was determined to carry out her duties, instructed by the Duke of Rossmere. She had seen Dernley the day before and given him the good news about Archer, and that he could begin some gentle exercise, which somewhat amazed him, as he had been convinced the horse would have to be destroyed. Having told him the news, she then said she would see him the following evening for the vigil.

Bodine was also sponsoring two squires into knighthood and Monsignor Colin McLeod had offered to oversee their bathing and preparation for the night of vigil.

The ritual began with a ceremonial bath the night before the dubbing. All three squires sat in wooden bath tubs. McLeod went to each in turn, starting with Dernley, and asked: "Giles Dernley, are you ready for this water to wash away your former life, so you may begin anew?"

"Yes Father, I am ready," he responded.

McLeod nodded solemnly and poured a large pitcher of water over his head, completing the act of purification. When all three had been re-christened, they donned robes and sat down to be shaved, and a single symbolic lock was cut from their hair. In the olden days, they would have had their entire heads shaved, but this was now deemed an extreme sacrifice, so now only one lock was taken.

Page boys assisted the three men to dress. Black hose were donned first. These were to remind the squires of death. Over this went a new white tunic which symbolised their purity. Next came a magnificent red cloak, denoting nobility and willingness to shed blood for God and the church. The final item of clothing was a white belt, placed around their waists, denoting their chastity.

This completed, the squires picked up their new arms and went to the cathedral to begin their night of vigil. They each placed their arms on the altar steps, along with all the other squires who were to be initiated, before beginning to meditate on the ceremony that was to take place the following day. They could either kneel or stand to relieve aching limbs.

Chapter Seven

Although it was the shortest night of the year, time seemed to pass slowly, so the priests stayed close to give encouragement in case any of them became tempted to sleep.

Bodine accompanied Colwyn to the cathedral so she could offer encouragement to Dernley and also stayed with him, head bowed as he spoke the prayer of initiation:

"Harken, we beseech Thee, O Lord to hear our prayers this night,

And deign to bless us, with the right hand of Thy Majesty,

This sword with which Thy servant desires to be girded,

That it may be a defence of the faith, widows, orphans, the weak, the righteous,

And all thy servants against the scourge of pagans, enemies of Thy church and the Kingdom,

That it may be the terror and dread of all vile-doers,

And that it may be just in both attack and defence, and carry out Thy work,

Amen"

Dernley then spent time contemplating the forthcoming duties and responsibilities of knighthood, before repeating the prayer of initiation once again.

Colwyn stayed with him for two hours, and, satisfied that he was in fact too excited to be tempted to fall asleep, smiled encouragingly at him before returning to her rooms, escorted as always by Bodine. Her place was then taken by Dernley's father, the Duke of Strathmere, who also spent a couple of hours supporting his son.

The initiation ceremony took place the following morning. The cathedral was packed with family members and visitors as the squires' swords and arms were blessed. Once the blessing had been completed, the squires moved to form a row, and their sponsors began to fit their armour. Morgan had checked that Colwyn still remembered what to do. She armed Dernley with his hauberk, cuirass and gauntlets. Then she knelt down to attach his golden spurs, with the right one being attached first. That completed, she stood, refitted the white belt, and girded his sword so that it hung on his right side. Finally, the rich red cloak was placed around his shoulders.

Now formally armed, Dernley moved and knelt before his King, who asked, "Who is thy supporter this day?"

Colwyn stepped forward. "I am the supporter; the Duchess Colwyn Coltrane of Invermere."

"Is thy candidate worthy and free to take the oath and the responsibility of knighthood and all it entails?"

"He is, my Liege."

Stuart nodded and said, "I dub thee Sir Giles Dernley," as he lay the sword first on one shoulder, then the other and then back to the first. "Your sponsor deems you ready for knighthood. Know that to wear the belt and arms of a knight is granting that you will hold the sacred trust of God, the church and your King, and that you are bound to it for life. Arise, Sir Giles Dernley."

Dernley obeyed his King and rose to his feet; bowing deeply, he said, "I will serve thee with honour my Liege," and returned to his place in the line of knights.

The King performed the ceremony on a further twenty-nine knights and then they recited the ten rules of chivalry:

"Thou shalt follow the dictates of moral conscience;

Thou shalt be willing to defend your values;

Thou shalt have respect and pity for all weakness and steadfastness in defending them;

Thou shalt love thy country;

Thou shalt refuse to retreat before the enemy;

Chapter Seven

Thou shalt wage unceasing and merciless war against all that is evil;

Thou shalt obey the orders of those appointed above you, as long as those orders do not conflict with what you know to be just;

Thou shalt show loyalty to truth and your pledged word;

Thou shalt be generous and giving of ones' self;

Thou shalt be champion of the right and good at all times, and at all times oppose the forces of evil."

King Stuart then walked along the line of new knights and delivered the colee, which involved him striking each knight's chest with the flat of his sword. When he had completed this, he returned to his original position on the dais and spoke a final time.

"Let the colee remind you all that knighthood can bring you pain as well as honour. Welcome, knights."

This concluded the ceremony; a prayer was said by Bishop Douglas, followed by a herald, and it was all over until the banquet in the evening.

Colwyn went and gave Dernley a hug, whilst Bodine praised his two new knights. Everyone was now free of other duties and returned to their rooms, but Bodine called Dernley aside.

"Duke?" Dernley asked of him once they were alone.

"How is your father?" Bodine asked.

"He is well, thank you, Duke; you will probably see him this evening at the banquet."

"Call me Morgan."

"Thank you."

"You are fond of Colwyn, aren't you?"

Dernley smiled. "I have been very fond of her ever since we had our first swordfight, as children. I was rather rude about girls and swords, and she challenged me. Since that happened, she has had my heart."

"I am sorry if I have stolen her away from you."

Dernley shook his head. "No, Morgan, you have not stolen her. She only ever thought of me as a brother; nothing more. I am glad she has found love; especially after the happenings of this year."

"Yes. Giles, I know you are a duke-in-waiting, but I would be honoured if you would continue to support Colwyn and myself until you assume your title. If it is acceptable to you, I would pass on my knowledge about ruling a Duchy—unless you would sooner return to your father?"

"Morgan, I would be honoured to stay and accept any advice and guidance you have to offer. I love my father very much, but he is very much a knight of the old order; you are of the new order; things are changing and I need to be able to move with the times."

"Wise words, my young knight. Very well. You will be my companion, and accompany me the majority of the time; attend meetings with me."

"As you wish, Morgan. Thank you."

The two men shook hands to seal their pact.

"Now, off to your rooms to get ready for the banquet!"

༄ ༅ ༄ ༅

The Duchess surveyed her small wardrobe, debating what to wear that evening. The King was going to announce her betrothal, and she wanted to look her very best. She decided on her cream dress with the gold decoration. It would give her the look of purity and innocence that would be appropriate for the announcement. She had the jewellery she had brought with her on the journey from Invermere and pulled out the gold chain and pendant. There was also the gold belt she would wear around the dress and the gold ribbons for her hair. It would be topped by the plain gold band for her head.

Summoning Sarah, she asked her to arrange for a bath. The bruises would be seen by her, but that could not be helped.

Chapter Seven

The tub and hot water were delivered and Sarah assisted her mistress to disrobe.

"My Lady! These bruises!" Sarah exclaimed.

"Don't worry about them," Colwyn ordered as she stepped into the tub and sat down, enjoying the feeling of the hot water soaking her skin. Before washing, she allowed herself to soak for fifteen minutes, which totally relaxed her, , and then she got out, allowing Sarah to wrap her in a towel and rub her down.

"I need to tell you something, Sarah," she told her maid as she sat down at her dressing table, allowing Sarah to comb her hair.

"My Lady?"

"You must promise me you will tell no one." Her voice was firm; even slightly threatening.

"You have my word, my Lady."

"Very well. The King will be announcing my betrothal at the banquet this evening. Sarah, I am to marry Morgan Bodine."

"Oh, Colwyn!" Sarah breathed. "What do you feel about that?"

"I can't imagine being any happier, Sarah! I love Morgan so much, and he loves me."

"If you are happy, then I am happy too, my Lady. In which case, you must look your very best tonight."

Sarah worked long and hard on Colwyn's appearance and was very pleased with the results. "If the duke didn't love you before, he will not be able to resist you tonight," she said proudly. "There will be no one more beautiful than you tonight, my Lady."

Colwyn blushed, which only added to her beauty. "Sarah, you mustn't exaggerate!" she said to cover her embarrassment.

"I'm not exaggerating. Now come, my Lady, let's finish you off. The dress fits to perfection, the belts are in place, as is your jewellery. Your hair shines and the ribbons are in place. You just need your slippers and you are ready. Will you need your cloak?"

"No, I don't think so; it's quite a mild evening."

"Well, it's almost time. Are you going down alone?"

Colwyn didn't get a chance to answer, as there was a knock at the door. Sarah went to investigate and opened it to find Bodine there. She curtsied and invited him in.

"My Lady is almost ready, your Grace."

"Sarah, would you be so kind as to allow me to come through? I have a present for your mistress."

"Of course, your Grace. Please follow me." She led the way through and introduced the visitor.

"Morgan!"

"Colwyn, I have a gift for you, as a token of our forthcoming union, and I wondered if you would do me the honour of wearing it tonight?"

From his pocket, he produced a gold hair comb decorated with precious stones and filigree work.

"Morgan, it's beautiful! Sarah, please can you fit this?"

"Of course, my Lady." She removed the gold ribbons and gold band, brushed Colwyn's hair again, and swept it back, skilfully twisting it, and inserting the comb before replacing the gold band.

"Thank you." Colwyn reached into a drawer and pulled out the gold engraved cloak clasp, complete with precious stones and the length of her hair entwined within. "Morgan, this is for you, as my token."

He took it from her and examined it carefully. "Is this your hair woven in?" he asked incredulously.

"Yes."

"I have never seen work like this before! Thank you, my love. For tonight, I will attach it to my jacket."

Chapter Seven

"Then let me make it secure." Colwyn got up and went to her needle basket, taking out a needle and thread, and secured it to his jacket at the waist, allowing it to act almost like a buckle. "When you have decided which cloak to put it on, I will sew it for you."

Bodine leant forward and kissed her. As the announcement was going to be made in the next couple of hours, he saw no problem in his open display of affection in front of her maid.

"My Lady, after you," he said, bowing respectfully, and followed Colwyn out of the door.

༺ ༻ ༺ ༻

The great hall, already decorated with the banners of all the Duchies in Devonmere, was now also adorned with flowers and greenery on the tables and around the walls. Tapestries had also been cleaned and re-hung.

The head table consisted of King Stuart, with Queen Alexandra to his left, Prince Michael and his wife, Princess Anne. Sitting next to the King was Colwyn, and to her right was Bodine.

The duke glanced at his intended and noticed she seemed relatively at ease, even though McDowell was at the table below, eyeing her constantly. He had been giving their forthcoming wedding serious thought, and was glad they had decided to move the ceremony forward, for two reasons; McDowell was a serious threat to Colwyn until they married and had consummated it and the other was more selfish - he did not trust himself alone in her company any more. He wanted her desperately and felt he would not be able to wait until September before claiming her body; especially as he had become more aware of her as a woman. To his horror, he was now so in tune with her that he could tell when she was ready to conceive. Thus, he had decided to bring it forward to the beginning of July. It was very short notice, but it would be safer; for both of them.

King Stuart leant towards them both and whispered, "I see McDowell is staring quite intently. You are both all right with me making the announcement shortly?"

"Yes, Sire," they both answered.

"Excellent."

He waited a few more minutes, then stood up. A hush descended upon the great hall as everyone waited for their King to speak.

"My Lords, Ladies and Gentlemen. Welcome to Ellesmere Castle. This Midsummer day, we have witnessed the creation of many new knights from the Duchies of Devonmere. This evening, we celebrate their new status, and tonight is the night where any man may ask a favour of me." He paused as he saw McDowell about to rise. "However, before favours are asked, I have an announcement to make. A very happy announcement. The Duke of Rossmere, Morgan Bodine, King's Champion and General of my Armies is to marry in the very near future. His bride-to-be is the Duchess of Invermere, Colwyn Coltrane. Let us drink a toast to their forthcoming union. To Morgan and Colwyn, we wish you every happiness."

Goblets were raised, the toast repeated and everyone drank, except McDowell, who was openly scowling at the couple, and his expression grew harder still as Bodine kissed Colwyn's hand.

Stuart had noticed McDowell's lack of respect and gave thanks that the announcement had been made. He, too, knew that nothing was set in stone until after the wedding night. He decided he would have a word with his General after the banquet and suggest the wedding take place as soon as possible, not knowing that Bodine had already made that decision. The matter was far from over as far as McDowell was concerned.

The actual banquet passed without incident, with all the guests eating their fill, and drinking plenty of wine, which did result in a relaxation of some inhibitions once the after-dinner festivities, like the dancing, started.

Chapter Seven

Bodine had decided he was not going to stay too late, as he needed to make sure he was rested properly for the sword-fighting and the jousting over the next couple of days. He was realistic and did expect to receive some injuries during the competitions. He did not, however, want to leave Colwyn alone in the hall with McDowell around. He did not trust the duke and had seen the scowl on his face at the wedding announcement.

With Bodine's permission, the King escorted Colwyn onto the main floor of the hall and danced with her. Remembering his manners, the duke leant towards the Queen and asked if she too would like to dance, expecting her to refuse, but instead, to his astonishment, she accepted.

As they moved around the hall, the Queen spoke forthrightly to him. "I shall be watching you Duke Morgan, and if I hear of any mistreatment of Duchess Colwyn, I will intervene. Do I make myself clear?"

"Perfectly, Your Majesty," Bodine replied. "I love Colwyn very much, and I just wish you could see and understand that."

"The King has explained the situation to me. I am not happy about it, but I understand the duty to the Kingdom. For the sake of Colwyn, I will do my utmost to treat you with the respect you deserve, Duke, but it will be difficult for me."

"I am grateful that you will try. I know it upsets the Duchess that you do not approve of her wedding to me. She thinks so very much of you."

"And I think very much of her, which is why I am trying to make the effort to be more courteous; but you still have a lot to prove to me."

He nodded respectfully, but a glimmer of hope of his eventual acceptance by the Queen was kindled within his heart.

He danced next with Princess Anne, who offered her congratulations to him, and wished him every happiness, and then, finally, he danced with Colwyn. As it came to an end, he saw McDowell approaching and, as a precaution, he increased the depth of the link he had with his intended, in case McDowell decided to try something to make her turn away from him, and the marriage.

The Cottesmere Duke stopped before them. "Bodine, you will, of course, permit me to dance with your Lady, so I may offer my congratulations on your forthcoming union?" he asked, but the voice was ominous in its tone.

"If my Lady wishes to dance with you, I have no objections. Colwyn, will you dance with Duke Nigel?" He could tell by the link they shared that she did not want to, but her manners made her agree. Also, she could just feel a tendril of warmth and security at the edge of her mind, assuring her that McDowell would not try anything in such a crowded room, and that Bodine was close.

"I will permit one dance," she finally replied, and McDowell took her hand and led her away.

Bodine stood guard the entire time and observed from a distance, maintaining his fragile link to ensure that McDowell did not try any mind control tricks on her.

The dance ended and Colwyn tried to leave her partner, but McDowell had other ideas.

"My dear, why don't we get some fresh air on the balcony and talk awhile."

"No, Duke. I must return to my intended," Colwyn replied firmly.

"But I insist." He attempted to lead her towards the balcony, but she was having none of it and stopped walking. *You will come with me, willingly*, McDowell said into her mind, and was surprised when she did not move. He tried again. *Walk with me!*

She pulled her arm from his grip and backed away. "I am not going anywhere with you, Duke Nigel. You have had your dance, now please, kindly leave me alone." She turned and started to walk away from him.

You will stop!

Chapter Seven

The force of the command in her mind had the desired effect and did make her stop and wince, as a pain shot through her head. She raised a hand to her temple as if to push it away.

Face me!

She faltered as the pain increased, doing her utmost to build a wall whilst she looked desperately for Bodine, whose calming thoughts suddenly flooded her mind, reducing the pain in her head, and then he was there, by her side; his eyes flashing menacingly at McDowell, who glared back at him. For a moment, they squared up opposite each other, neither of them moving, and it looked as though they were going to call one another out, but the Cottesmere Duke wisely held his tongue, backed down and turned away. Bodine slowly relaxed and looked towards the head table to find the King looking at him. He immediately turned his attention to his intended.

"Colwyn, are you all right?" Bodine asked her, his steely gaze softening as he took her elbow and escorted her back towards the table.

"Yes," she replied softly. "He tried to make me go with him."

"I know. But you have a stronger mind than he realises, and I was also keeping guard. If you have no objections, I will take you back to your rooms, as I wish to be fully rested for tomorrow and I do not want to leave you here alone."

"Thank you, Morgan, that would be acceptable. I have no wish to stay here without you by my side."

He smiled at her and escorted her back to her rooms. Pausing outside, his eyes appraised her once more.

"You are truly beautiful, my love," he said softly, taking her in his arms and kissing her passionately. Finally releasing her, he added, "I will see you tomorrow, and I will ensure McDowell pays for his insolence."

"Then, my love, take this, to bring you luck with your task." She reached into a sleeve and brought out her handkerchief, which she tucked into a sleeve of his jacket. "I hope this will help shield you from any evil intent that McDowell has towards you."

"Thank you. The one you gave me five years ago is starting to look rather sorry for itself. Now I have a new token to keep close to my heart."

"You still have it?" Colwyn asked in wonder.

"But of course. It travels everywhere with me;, hence why it is now in such a sorry state."

"Morgan, that is so romantic," she teased gently.

"I keep it with me to remind me, in times of trouble, when I am far away from home, that somewhere, there is someone who loves me," he replied quietly.

They stood for several moments, hands clasped together, then Bodine kissed them, and reluctantly released her.

"Until tomorrow, my pet," he said and turned and walked away.

Colwyn watched him until he disappeared around a corner, then entered her rooms to find Sarah waiting for her. That night, she locked the door for additional security.

ଓ ଔ ଓ ଔ

8

Chapter Eight

As with all tournaments, the area where it was being held was ablaze with colour. Pennants of all the Duchies and participating knights adorned every available hanging space. On top of this were all the highly coloured tents, all with flags or pennants flying on the top. A market had been set up, with traders selling their wares; different sorts of food, ornaments, and trinkets; swords, shields and all manner of other goods, including bolts of material of all kinds, from heavy brocades to fine silks, in all the colours of the rainbow. Music could also be heard; lutes, harps, horns and the sound of voices filled the air.

The tournament got underway the following day with the newly knighted squires taking part in the first part of the swordsmanship tournament. Colwyn was watching with Bodine as Dernley was taking part in it, and she wanted to support him. Bodine was there to keep her company, and also to watch Dernley as well. He was curious about the ability of the young knight, who had affection for his intended. Additionally, he too had a couple of newly knighted squires in this tournament and wanted to see how they fared.

Dernley, and Bodine's new knights made it all the way through, and the final eventually turned out to be between him and Stonewood, the better of Bodine's squires.

The battle was most evenly matched and turned out to be long and arduous for both men. Loyalties were divided. Obviously, Bodine was supporting his man, and Colwyn, of course, was supporting Dernley. Blow after blow struck their shields as they attacked and parried, both moving lithely around the arena.

"They are very evenly matched," Bodine remarked to Colwyn.

"Indeed. I also find it very comforting that our two Duchies have the best new swordsmen in Devonmere," she replied rather smugly.

In the end, stamina turned out to be the key to victory; it was exceedingly close, and, at one point, was almost declared a draw, but at the last second, Dernley made a mistake and Stonewood was victorious.

The spectators were very supportive of both men, and in the end, the King had both of them up on the dais before him, presenting Stonewood with the gold band, and Dernley with some coins. He congratulated both men and encouraged the crowd to cheer them once more.

The duke and duchess congratulated their men, then Colwyn kissed Bodine, wished him luck and went up to the dais. She curtsied and took her place to the right of the King, whilst Bodine disappeared to warm up for the main swordsmanship competition.

"Colwyn, my dear," the King began. "I hope you are well today?"

"Yes, thank you, Your Majesty. And you?"

"Looking forward to this next event. Was there a little trouble with McDowell last night, or was I mistaken?"

"Nothing that warrants your concern, Sire. Duke Morgan took… care of it."

"And how do you think it's going to go today?"

"Morgan will win, Sire, but I believe it will not be a… fair match."

Chapter Eight

"You are remembering the last time they met, are you not? I must admit, I was surprised that you knew and understood the rules of engagement so well."

She smiled. "Sire, you would be surprised at the assortment of information I have stored in my brain."

"Having known your father, I actually wouldn't." He smiled back at her.

"I will admit, knowing Duke Nigel, that Morgan will suffer an injury, but I am hoping that, as he now knows the Duke's love of foul moves, he will successfully inflict a serious injury on him as well." She lowered her voice. "You will think me wicked, Sire, but if I could fight, I too would wish to inflict a serious injury."

Stuart patted her hand. "I understand perfectly," was all he said. "Ah, we are about to begin."

As expected, Bodine despatched the majority of his opponents with ease, hardly breaking into a sweat in the process. McDowell got through almost as easily, and the final was a repeat of the one Colwyn had attended five years ago, back in Inver Castle.

Bodine and McDowell entered the arena and marched to stand at the base of the dais. They bowed respectfully to the royal party above them. Bodine gave Colwyn a warm smile, which she returned. The two opponents then bowed less respectfully at each other and made the final adjustments to their armour. Again, Bodine brought out Colwyn's favour, as he had done the last time, waved it and tucked it away again. The news of the impending marriage had circulated, so most of the spectators knew who it belonged to.

The King smiled also, then indicated for the final match to begin.

"Your wedding may well have been announced, Bodine, but you haven't walked down the aisle yet…a lot can happen between an announcement and the event," McDowell hissed, as they circled around in the arena, sizing one another up.

"Is that a threat, McDowell?" Bodine asked.

"Take it any way you want," came the reply.

"Thank you; in which case, I will take it as a lot of hot air."

McDowell's brown eyes flashed angrily, as once again his taunts failed to have the desired effect on his opponent. Bodine knew the duke was scared about the impending wedding and thus was resorting to every single tactic he could think of to undermine the union. This fight was undoubtedly going to degenerate, with the Duke of Cottesmere breaking the rules of engagement, and Bodine decided that if McDowell started down that route, then he would match him strike for strike.

The Duke of Rossmere adjusted the position of his shield and the fight began. He managed the first series of strikes that drove McDowell backwards. The attack was vicious; Bodine was not in the mood to be charitable or even courteous, wanting to avenge Colwyn after the previous night, when the Cottesmere Duke had tried to force her out onto the balcony by attempting to control her mind.

For a moment, it looked as if it was going to be over before it had even begun, as the relentless attack continued, and the crowd starting murmuring at the intensity of the attack right at the very start. Then McDowell managed to parry and launch his own attack. They were only five minutes into the fight, and already he was beginning to lose his temper. Bodine noted this and expected the rules of engagement to be broken by his opponent any second. He then fooled the duke by performing broken time, which involved a sudden change in tempo of his movements, tricking McDowell into responding at the wrong time, and he followed up with another cutting attack.

McDowell managed to parry again, and physically launched himself at Bodine, resulting in a corps-a-corps - body-to-body physical contact - and the two men wrestled until Bodine managed to push him away and then

Chapter Eight

delivered a blow with his shield. If McDowell insisted on using dirty tactics, then the Duke of Rossmere would make sure he delivered his own in return.

The battle continued; thrusts, attacks, parries, counter-attacks, cuts and feints took place; the speed of the clashing of the blades almost a blur. As he had done five years ago, Bodine drove McDowell back against the rail, expecting a boot to come up and push him back, and he was ready, using his shield to counter-attack, when McDowell hit the ground.

Bodine just about gave him the time to get to his feet before he attacked again, and for the first time, saw the unease in McDowell's eyes as he realised the boy he had fought five years ago was now most definitely a man.

In desperation, McDowell resorted to every dirty trick he knew and the crowd began to boo. Furious, he struck out and his boot landed against Bodine's shield and pushed him back. Bodine came forward again, and McDowell swept a leg round, catching the Rossmere Duke's legs, taking his feet from under him, so he fell backwards onto the ground. McDowell immediately leapt forward and lunged with all his might, just as Bodine recovered his sword arm and thrust upwards as hard as he could.

Both swords found their mark. McDowell staggered backwards from the force of the thrust, failing to bring his shield across to protect him, and felt the blade penetrate through the mail and into his side. He dropped his sword and clutched at the wound.

Bodine got to his feet, ignoring the pain in his own side, and went after him, using his shield to knock him off his feet, then stomped on his right arm and thrust his sword against his throat, purposely just nicking the skin enough to allow a slight trickle of blood to escape the wound.

"Yield, damn you!" Bodine hissed, tempted to break the duke's arm, but somehow managing to refrain from doing so.

"I…I yield," McDowell muttered.

Bodine removed his foot from the duke's arm, and his sword from his throat, grimacing as he sheathed it. McDowell stayed where he was, indicating for his squire to give him a hand to get up.

Up on the dais, Colwyn smiled in satisfaction on seeing that Bodine had won yet again, and that this time, McDowell was injured. However, she knew her intended also had a wound that would need tending. She watched as Bodine straightened up and turned to walk towards the dais. Reaching the bottom, he respectfully saluted and the King indicated for him to come up the stairs.

On reaching the top, he knelt and bowed his head. "Sire," he whispered, as Stuart rose from his seat and placed the gold band on the duke's head.

"Arise, Morgan," the King said softly, and then he addressed the audience. "My Lords, Ladies and honoured guests; I give you our Champion of the Sword; the Duke of Rossmere, Morgan Bodine, King's Champion and General of my Armies!"

The crowd cheered, and Bodine acknowledged their acclaim with a wave of his hand, smiling slightly.

"Well done, Morgan," the King whispered to him. "McDowell may not be fit enough for the joust tomorrow."

"One can but hope," Bodine replied in a low voice.

The King turned to Colwyn. "Colwyn, my dear, take your intended and get his wound seen to."

Colwyn rose from her seat, curtsied and replied, "Yes, Sire, at once."

Bodine indicated for her to precede him down the stairs, then they walked arm in arm away from the arena, back towards the keep and the duke's rooms.

Master Andrew was waiting for them and had already spread his bandages, potions and dressings out in readiness.

Chapter Eight

Colwyn helped him to remove Bodine's armour and padding, and her heart gave a wrench as she saw a grimace go across his face. At least this time, she had had the satisfaction of seeing him inflict a reasonable wound on McDowell, who had to be carried from the arena by his squire and a couple of stewards. With any luck, he would not be fit enough for the jousting tournament the next day.

As Bodine's black silk shirt was removed, the extent of the wound was revealed. Blood was oozing quite badly from an injury along the side of his ribs on the right-hand side. Colwyn had noted the seriousness of the wound and had quietly obtained water for Andrew to carry out his work. However, she found herself staring at her intended. The muscles were more pronounced than they had been five years ago and his lightly bronzed chest had broadened further, which accentuated the narrowness of the hips and powerful thighs. The strangest of feelings centred itself in Colwyn's womanhood as she drank in the sight, making her squirm unconsciously, and the heat rush to her groin. She was also aware of her pulse rate increasing and her breathing becoming heavier as she drank in the sight of him, and for the first time, was fully aware of what her body was asking both of her and him.

Is this what love feels like? she asked herself silently. If so, it was a decidedly heady and breath-taking feeling, leaving her wanting. She knew what the act of sex entailed now and her womanhood constricted at the thought of him possessing her. At that precise moment, she was fighting an almost irresistible urge to reach out and touch his naked chest, with its light dusting of hair; to feel the heat of his skin under her fingers. She made out the faint white line of a scar on his right side, below the new wound, from one he had suffered at the tournament five years ago. Colwyn took a deep breath to steady herself and regain control of her emotions, but it was proving difficult.

The presence of Master Andrew helped in temporarily quenching her desires, and she watched him as he worked, with infinite care, on his Lord.

Somehow, she found her voice. "Morgan, would you like some wine?" she managed to ask, her voice sounding relatively calm and normal.

"Yes, thank you, my love."

Having something to do helped, but her hands were none too steady as she poured him a large goblet, and turned to hand it to him.

"Thank you." Bodine looked at her as he drank the wine, his eyes blue and smouldering as he saw the expression in hers. He knew exactly what she was thinking and he wanted her to touch him; to feel her hands on his skin. The residual link they shared was resonating in his mind, fuelling his desire, and he wished Andrew would hurry up and finish his ministrations.

If his battle surgeon was aware of the charged atmosphere in the room, he gave no indication as he continued with his work.

"Is there no way to pull the wound together and hold it?" Colwyn suddenly asked him. "Can't you sew it, like I sew torn cloth?"

Andrew stopped and considered. "And what would you suggest we sew it with—if we could do that?" he asked her.

"Silk is strong. I have threads and needles."

"Morgan, are you up to us experimenting with this?"

"If it aids healing faster, then yes."

"Very well. Lady Colwyn, go get your needle and threads."

Colwyn literally ran all the way to her rooms, collected the box containing her sewing supplies, and ran all the way back, arriving breathless. She selected a natural-coloured thread, thinking it would be the safest to use as there was no dye in it. Andrew took a length, cut it and soaked it in the water that contained his antiseptic powder. A needle was also left to soak in there for a little while, before being retrieved and threaded with the wet silk.

Chapter Eight

"Morgan, this is going to hurt," Andrew said. "Are you really sure you want to try this?"

"I have the joust tomorrow, I need to be fit. Do it."

"I am thinking; we will need to remove the silk once the wound has knitted, so… I wonder if we should do some kind of single knotted stitch at intervals?" Colwyn said, suddenly feeling uneasy about her suggestion. "Then they can be easily cut and removed."

"That sounds sensible," Andrew replied. "Okay, Morgan, lie down; it will be easier for me to work. Put your arm up above your head, so it's out of the way."

Bodine did as he was instructed, and took a number of deep breaths to prepare himself.

"Colwyn, I need you to be brave and pinch the wound edges a little whilst I pull it together. Can you do that?"

Colwyn swallowed nervously. "Yes, I can do that."

"No," Bodine said. "My squire should do it. It's not something you should be subjected to, Colwyn."

"I can do this," she insisted. "Ioan isn't here, but I am. Please, let me do this for you."

Their eyes locked, and after what seemed like an eternity, Bodine grudgingly nodded.

Andrew picked up the threaded needle and took a deep breath himself. "Here we go," he muttered and nodded at his assistant who gingerly pinched the skin but not completely together so that Andrew could see where the needle was penetrating.

Bodine flinched and sucked in his breath; he could feel the thread being pulled through his skin.

"I have to make sure I do not catch the muscle underneath," Andrew said. "If this works, I think, in future, a curved needle would work better," he nodded in satisfaction as he pulled the silk thread enough for the edges of the wound to be just within touching distance and tied it off, cutting both ends with a sharp knife and letting go of the breath he had been holding.

He worked steadily, and carefully, ensuring he did not catch the underlying muscle. Bodine lay rigid, his gaze fixed on a point on the canopy of the bed above him, biting his lip so as not to make a sound.

Andrew placed five stitches in the wound, and then looked at his handiwork in satisfaction.

"That should do nicely," he said. "Let me just wipe it down with some of this solution to make sure there is no dirt there, and then I'll bind it for added protection."

Morgan sat up again and ten minutes later, they were done.

"How does it feel, Morgan?" Colwyn asked.

"A little uncomfortable, but it doesn't hurt as much as I thought it would." He went to get up but Andrew pushed him back.

"No, stay there and rest. Give it a chance to start working. It's still bleeding slightly."

Bodine nodded and relaxed back.

"Lady Colwyn, thank you for your assistance. I am sorry I had to ask you."

"No, Master Andrew; it was an honour to work with you."

"Are you all right, Colwyn? You're looking a little pale," Bodine asked, seeing her pallor.

"I admit to feeling a little ill, but I'm sure it will pass," she whispered. "I have never touched a wound before."

"You have been exceedingly brave. It is not something a lady of your breeding should be subjected to," Andrew said.

"But I did it," she replied, feeling slightly proud of her achievement. She had not been ill, nor had she swooned and fainted.

Chapter Eight

Master Andrew tidied up his tools, poured another goblet of wine and dissolved another powder in it. Handing it to Bodine with the order to drink it all, he left the two of them alone, taking the hauberk with him to drop off at the blacksmith's. Now that the announcement of their wedding had been made, it was not as scandalous for them to be left together without a chaperone.

Bodine followed Andrew's orders and drank the wine, watching Colwyn as she shifted her sitting position on the bed so she could look at his face.

Giving in to her need to touch him, she reached out a hand and gently drew it across his chest, feeling the tight, warm skin beneath her fingers, fascinated as his nipples hardened under her touch, and felt the heat rise in her groin.

Bodine's eyes darkened with desire as she leant down and kissed him. His hands wrapped around her and crushed her to his chest, kissing her hungrily. They both knew it was wrong, but it felt so good and so right.

The only thing they hadn't bargained for was the fact that Andrew had put a sleeping powder in Bodine's wine, and Colwyn slowly felt him relaxing under her as he succumbed to the drug. His grip on her slackened and his lips were pliable under hers.

Colwyn drew back and looked at him lying so vulnerable beneath her, his chest rising and falling slowly in sleep, his lips slightly parted and a lock of his burnished gold hair falling over his right eye. Gently, she brushed it away, bent and kissed his chest, then carefully rose and pulled a blanket up over him.

She was scared to leave him on his own, so retired to the outer chamber, taking his damaged clothing, her needles and thread with her. She closed the door to his bed chamber and sat on a chair by the table to start work on the repairs as she waited for his squire to return to the room. Bodine had injured

McDowell, but the duke could still be out for revenge, so she would stand guard until relieved.

Ioan arrived about an hour later, surprised to see the Duchess in the room.

"The duke is asleep; Master Andrew gave him a sleeping powder, but I didn't want to leave him alone, unguarded, with McDowell still around," she explained.

"I understand, your Grace," Ioan said.

"I will return this evening to see if the duke is awake and wishes to dine in the hall. Should he wake, please tell him this."

"I will tell him, my Lady."

"Thank you, Ioan."

Colwyn took her repair work, returned to her own rooms to relax for a few hours before dressing for dinner, and found herself reliving the recent experience of assisting Master Andrew. She could not believe that she had actually helped and felt proud that she had managed to get through the ordeal without fainting or being ill.

She finished off her repair work, having a feeling of déjà vu of five years ago, and gave a little smile, shaking her head. Back then, she had been too young to have any sexual feelings towards him, but now, it was completely different, and soon she would be his wife; be at his side; share his bed; bear his children. She blushed at the thought.

Sarah arrived a couple of hours later and helped prepare her mistress for the evening. Finally ready, she picked up Bodine's clothing and returned to his room, knocking on the door.

Ioan opened it and bade her enter. "His Grace is still asleep," he told her.

"Mmmm, Master Andrew must have given him a stronger sleeping draught than I realised," she said. Quietly, she opened the door to his bed chamber and peeked in. Bodine was still lying in the same position as she

Chapter Eight

had left him, the blanket she had placed over him still covering his body. She went in and laid his clothing on a chair, then went to his bedside to check he was okay. Gently, she placed a hand on his forehead, to check he had not developed a temperature, indicating that the wound had become infected, and found it to be normal.

She glanced back at the door briefly, saw Ioan was not in sight, bent down and placed a soft kiss on the duke's lips. He gave a soft moan, smiled and stirred, slowly opening his eyes.

"Oh, I'm sorry, Morgan, I've woken you up," she said softly.

His smile broadened. "It's a nice way to be woken up." He reached for her and gave her another kiss, working across her lips and making her pulse race.

"Did you want to go down to dinner?" she finally managed to ask.

"No, I'd much rather… yes," he finished. He released her, got up from the bed, went to his wardrobe and retrieved a clean shirt, which he quickly put on and tucked into his breeches.

"How does your wound feel?" Colwyn asked him.

"Not too bad, actually. No doubt Andrew will inspect it either later or first thing tomorrow morning. Come, let's go and eat."

McDowell was conspicuous by his absence. Obviously, Bodine had managed to inflict a more serious wound than was first thought and Colwyn was pleased.

The meal went quietly and Bodine decided to go straight back to his room, mainly to make sure he got a good night's sleep for the joust tomorrow. Colwyn went with him; she wanted confirmation that the wound was all right before she retired for the night.

Andrew was waiting for them when they got back. "I assumed you'd be turning in early, so I thought I'd check the wound, and then you can get some sleep."

"Thanks, Andrew. Where do you want me?"

"Sit on the table; it's a bit higher."

Bodine did as he asked, and pulled his shirt off. Andrew undid the bandage and inspected the wound. He asked Colwyn if she would mind bringing some water over, and she, of course, obliged. Once again, the surgeon mixed in his special potion and bathed the wound, wiping away the encrusted blood. It had at least stopped bleeding. Andrew wrapped it up again.

"Looking good, Morgan. I'm pleased with it, and those stitches have certainly helped. I think I may make use of those in the future. Thank you for the suggestion, Colwyn. Now, I suggest you get some sleep."

"Thank you, Andrew. See you in the morning?"

"Yes, I'll want to check on it again before you go jousting. Good night."

He left, and Bodine's steward arrived, but Bodine dismissed him. "It's okay, Ioan, I don't need you tonight. Turn in and I'll see you in the morning."

"Thank you, your Grace." Ioan bowed respectfully and left.

Colwyn busied herself disposing of the bowl of water, then turned to Bodine. "I too will leave and let you rest. I just wanted to make sure the wound was all right."

Bodine stood up and caught her hand, lifting it to his lips. "Thank you for your assistance today," he said softly.

She smiled at him. "I have to make sure my champion and future husband stays well," she replied, capturing his gaze with her large, green eyes.

He kissed her tentatively, then stepped back, letting go of her hand. He was struggling to keep a grip on his emotions. He didn't want her to leave, but she had to so he could rest and be ready for tomorrow. "Your champion and future husband is feeling well; thank you for your concern. I will see you tomorrow."

She smiled at him and backed towards the door. "Until tomorrow," she repeated and left the room.

Chapter Eight

Bodine closed his eyes and took several deep breaths to calm himself. *Not much longer now,* he thought to himself; *no more than sixteen days. I can survive that long...I hope.*

 ⋯

The next day it was overcast, with a slight chill in the air, but by the time the jousting tournament was due to get underway, the sun was breaking through and starting to disperse the clouds, intimating that it was going to be another nice day.

Much to Colwyn's satisfaction, McDowell did not make an appearance at the joust, and, as expected, Morgan made it through to the final. His opponent was the Duke of Stallesmere from the north, but it was over quickly and Bodine maintained his record.

The King pulled him aside and spoke quietly to him after presenting him with his crown.

"Morgan, I need to speak to you with regard to the date you have set for the wedding," Stuart whispered.

"My Liege, I too have been thinking and have decided to bring it forward to the beginning of July. I have already despatched a rider to Rossmere to start preparations. I am planning a trip to Applegarth to visit the horse fair, then we shall return here, before starting our journey home."

Stuart nodded in satisfaction. "Good. I'm glad you've brought it forward. I do not trust McDowell. In fact, I would have liked you to marry before you left, but I know that it would be wrong to deny your people the special day. Make sure you see me before you leave for Rossmere."

"Yes, Sire." Bodine bowed respectfully, before turning, taking Colwyn's hand and leading her from the dais.

9

Chapter Nine

Morgan, Colwyn, Dernley and a small guard arrived at Applegarth, just as the various traders were setting up. They had left very early to allow them to take their time to make sure Dernley's horse managed the journey without injuring his fetlock further. There were a large number of pens containing horses of all shapes and sizes; from knights' destriers, ladies' palfreys, farm horses, ponies for children, and even the gypsies were there with their painted horses.

The choice seemed endless unless a buyer knew exactly what they were looking for. Dernley was looking for a new stallion—a present from his father on his successful knighting. Morgan was looking for a present for Colwyn, although she was unaware of this.

"So many horses!" Colwyn exclaimed. "How do you decide?"

"Well, it helps to come with an idea of what you want," Bodine said, smiling kindly.

"Giles, you are looking for a new destrier?" Colwyn asked.

"Yes."

"Then let's sort Giles out first," Colwyn said, and they made their way to the horse traders who specialised in knights' stallions. They inspected them all and narrowed the choice to three.

"I like the liver chestnut," Colwyn said, stroking his muzzle.

Chapter Nine

"My Lady, be careful! These are stallions," Dernley warned.

"I know, but he's friendly enough. He has good bone and good muscle, but we need to see him move," Colwyn said.

Bodine looked at her in surprise. Was this yet more knowledge she had absorbed? He inspected the chestnut for himself, then looked at the grey and then the bay.

"Either the grey or the chestnut. The choice is yours, Giles."

"Let's see them move," Dernley said.

Bodine indicated to the trader, whose boys moved both of them. There was little to choose between the two, so Giles felt their legs, and Bodine their necks and back.

In the end, the chestnut had the slightly shorter back and Dernley made his decision.

"The chestnut."

Colwyn smiled.

Dernley then started to haggle the price with the trader and was pleasantly surprised when he got the price he wanted to pay; unaware that it was actually due to the fact Bodine was with them. Being a feared Kadeau sometimes had its advantages.

That sorted, Bodine subtly guided Colwyn in the direction of the palfreys to see if there was one she liked. They wandered along, looking at them all. A palomino piqued her interest, as did a very pale grey with a long flowing mane and tail. Bodine was just about to ask the trader if they could have a look at them when there was a commotion behind the tent.

There was a lot of swearing, the sound of a whip and a horse screaming.

Colwyn immediately headed in the direction of the sound.

"My love, wait," Bodine said, taking her arm.

"No. There's a horse in trouble."

"I will investigate."

"No, we will all go," she said and set off, determination written all over her face.

They made their way behind the tents to see a brute of a man beating a horse with a whip in one hand, and holding a knife in the other. The horse, which was tethered, had its teeth bared and was rearing, bucking and kicking.

"Listen you ugly brute! You're nothing but trouble, so you're going to be horse meat!" He raised the knife.

"Stop!" Colwyn shouted. Stop!"

The man turned. "Go away! This is my business!"

"What are you doing?" Colwyn asked, stepping closer.

"Keep away! This horse is vicious, and I'm about to end him."

"No, please wait!"

"I said leave!"

"Do you know whom you are addressing?" Bodine asked him.

"Don't care who you are! This is my horse and I'll do what I please!"

"I'll take him," Colwyn stated, looking at the horse. She had never seen anything like him. He looked black with a white mane and tail, but she suspected he was an extremely dark grey. "How much do you want for him?"

"If you can get near him, you can have him. If you can't, I'm slitting his throat."

"My Lady, no!" Dernley said as she started to step forward.

"Wait here," Colwyn ordered.

"Colwyn…" Bodine began.

"Wait here, both of you."

With her arms down and palms facing upwards, she slowly walked forward.

"Sir, move away from the horse so I can get near," she ordered.

Scowling, he did as he was told, especially as both Bodine and Dernley put their hands on the hilts of their swords.

Chapter Nine

The horse stood, blowing hard, his eyes wide as he glared at his retreating owner, before turning his attention to the stranger who was slowly approaching him. With ears back and teeth bared, he pawed the ground.

Colwyn stopped and started talking in a quiet, soothing voice, and watched as his ears went forwards and backwards several times. There was a lot of head tossing and shaking, then some pawing of the ground, but the teeth were no longer bared. She stepped forward one step at a time, pausing until the horse calmed down. Now almost within touching distance, she took one more step and stood still for a long time, then sat down on the ground and did nothing, staying totally relaxed, waiting for the horse to make the next move.

The horse stood perplexed, not sure what to do. Several minutes passed, then the horse tentatively put his head down and sniffed at her head. Still, Colwyn did not move, but spoke very quietly.

Bodine and Dernley looked on in astonishment as the horse tried to put its head lower, but was prevented from doing so by the tether. Colwyn started to move her hand very slowly, and carefully undid the tether on the bridle, then put her hand down again.

The horse was now free, yet it didn't move, but stood by her, sniffing her, before lowering its head so that its muzzle was almost on the ground. Slowly, Colwyn raised a hand and touched the horse's cheek, just leaving it there. Then, to the onlookers' utter amazement, the horse lay down on his side and placed its head in Colwyn's lap.

Colwyn started to stroke his head and neck and carried on talking to him for another fifteen minutes or so, then the horse lifted his head, and Colwyn moved slowly, and encouraged the horse to get up again.

Both now standing, Colwyn started to stroke the horse, moving along its neck, back and sides, all the time talking to him until she was satisfied that he was now calm and happy. She turned and walked away, back towards

Bodine and Dernley. The horse stood looking at her, then tentatively started to follow her.

There followed some more head tossing as she reached Bodine, but Colwyn simply took his hand and waited until the horse settled down again and with her hand over his, she placed it on the horse's neck. The horse shivered but did not move and Bodine found he was able to stroke the horse without further help from his intended.

Colwyn did the same with Dernley. It took a little longer with him, but eventually, he too was able to stroke the horse.

The horse trader looked on in disbelief, suddenly realising he had made nothing on the beast. He started to step forward and immediately, the horse was on its guard.

"Stay away," Colwyn ordered him. She now began to go over the horse, looking for any faults and found none.

"Colwyn, are you sure about this?" Bodine asked. "This horse is no palfrey. He's big and he's powerful."

"He will be fine," Colwyn said. "Now all I have to do is decide on a name for him."

"How about Storm?" Dernley asked. "His colouring is like the black clouds that bring storms, with the white tops."

"I love that! Storm it shall be, my lad. Now, let's see how you move." She went to take hold of his halter, but Dernley took it from her.

"You need to see him move; let me do it." He talked to the horse encouragingly and started to run away from Colwyn and Bodine. The horse hesitated a moment, then obediently followed him. After running for several yards, Dernley turned and ran the horse parallel to them so they could see his movement from the side, and then brought him back.

"He is sound and moves well," Bodine said. "You're sure you want him?"

Chapter Nine

"Definitely." She looked in his mouth. "He's a youngster, no more than four years old. I want to try something. Hang onto him, Giles." Colwyn lifted her skirts and ran away several yards before stopping and turning to look at them. "Let him go, Giles!" she called. "Storm, here boy! Storm!" She clapped her hands and held them in a welcome. The horse lifted his head and trotted towards her. He stopped in front of her and bowed his head, inviting her to stroke him, and Colwyn obliged.

Bodine walked over to the horse trader and threw him a couple of gold coins. "Thank you for your custom," he said to him and walked away.

They led the horse to where the rest of their mounts were tethered, then went for some refreshments. Colwyn stated she only needed to restock on embroidery threads and she was done. Dernley said he just needed to make a quick visit to one of the other stalls and would meet them back at the horses. He was going to treat Colwyn to some material for her wedding dress, as a thank you for carrying on with his sponsorship to knighthood.

Just over an hour later, everyone had finished with their errands and they started to make their way back to Ellesmere Castle. Dernley was leading his new stallion, and Colwyn—at her insistence—was leading Storm, who now seemed like a totally different horse, trotting and cantering obediently at her side, without putting any strain on the leading rein.

They got back late in the evening. Both Dernley and Colwyn insisted on going to the stables to make sure their new purchases were bedded down for the night and to check that Archer had done no further damage to himself. Tomorrow, Colwyn would get Storm fitted for a saddle, in readiness for their journey to Belvoir.

Bodine had already despatched a messenger to warn Edward and to get him to start preparations for the wedding. He had enclosed instructions and requested they be complete before they arrived back in six days' time.

It was the final day for Bodine and Colwyn at Ellesmere Castle. Sarah had packed things away a few days previously and had left with Master Andrew and a small escort, the material Dernley had purchased safely hidden. The dress would be finished by the time the main party arrived. Colwyn had spent the day with the Queen and the other ladies-in-waiting.

Just as she was about to enter the chamber, she had overheard some rather crude comments regarding her forthcoming wedding night and paused. The married ladies were discussing their various experiences at the hands of their own husbands, and then wondered about Bodine's prowess in the bed-chamber.

"He is devastatingly handsome," she heard Lady Constance say, "I know he's a Kadeau, but I wouldn't mind having him in my bed if Colwyn doesn't want him in hers."

"What nonsense you speak, Constance. Colwyn is besotted with him! Mind you, she could be in for a shock on her wedding night; have you ever seen the General with a woman? It wouldn't surprise me if he was a virgin."

There was laughter and Colwyn bristled indignantly.

"That's rubbish as well, Margaret," another voice said. "You haven't been here as long as I have. The King has made sure the General is no novice, and I've heard he is…well endowed."

"No! Really? Do tell!" the other ladies beseeched, giggling.

Colwyn had heard enough; she decided to warn them she was coming by making some noise, then pushed the door open.

A couple of ladies had the grace to blush, she noticed, but she ignored them, and she went to sit in her usual place by the window.

Grace, the closest person she had to a friend in the room, walked up to her and joined her on the window seat.

"So," Grace whispered. "Are you all prepared for the big day?"

Chapter Nine

"I believe so," Colwyn replied quietly, "although I haven't got my dress yet."

"You're cutting it fine!"

"Well, it wasn't supposed to be until September, but Morgan has brought it forward, due to the threat of Nigel McDowell."

"That must be so frightening."

"Morgan will protect me."

"You love him very much, don't you?"

"Yes, Grace, I do."

"Did he cast a spell on you?"

"What? No, of course not! Why would you think such a thing?" Colwyn suddenly smiled. "I think I may have cast one on him though."

"He's Kadeau. How else would he get a woman to love him?"

"Have you ever spoken to him or spent any time getting to know him?" Colwyn hissed at her so-called friend. "No, of course you haven't! I've known Morgan practically my entire life. He's good, he's kind and very gallant. He is also the King's Champion, my champion and the General of the King's Army. Do you think he cast a spell on the King, his brother, the bishop, and the young Prince?"

"No, of course not."

"Well then! Kadeau have always been in service to the Cantrell family." Colwyn stood up, deciding she didn't want to spend her last day in the company of the ladies-in-waiting if all they were planning on doing was making derogatory remarks about her future husband. She had a sudden urge to call the women out, but ladies did not do such things, so she clenched her fists instead to master her rising anger. She got halfway across the room when the door opened and Queen Alexandra came in.

All the women present dropped into a curtsy.

"Arise," Alexandra said and went to the chair she always sat in. She looked at Colwyn. "Were you going somewhere, Colwyn?"

"I-I... no, Your Majesty," she replied, and reluctantly returned to her seat by the window. As far as she was concerned, the day couldn't end soon enough.

The Queen finally dismissed them all, but called Colwyn back and bade her sit next to her.

"Colwyn, my dear child, you leave here tomorrow to go to your wedding. I shall miss your company, but the King and I are planning to arrive at Rossmere the first week in July; I am not planning on missing the event."

"Thank you, Your Majesty."

"I have something for you, which I hope you will wear on the day." Alexandra passed her a small package carefully wrapped in cloth and tied with ribbon.

"This is so very kind of you; thank you," Colwyn responded.

"Now, I wish to speak to you regarding a very delicate matter. I feel it is my duty to do this, as your mother is sadly no longer with us."

Colwyn swallowed nervously. What on earth was the Queen about to speak to her about?

Alexandra, accepting that the marriage would go ahead and that nothing would now stop it, had decided to reassure Colwyn about the wedding night.

"My dear, I hope you will know the passion of love; but initially, there is a price to pay, and a barbaric ritual that men still insist upon to prove their manliness."

Colwyn was vaguely aware of her eyes widening in a mixture of fear and curiosity.

The Queen smiled reassuringly and took hold of her hand.

"The first time a maiden is taken, it will hurt. How much depends on the skill of her husband, and there will be some bleeding. It is nothing to

Chapter Nine

worry about; the bleeding is proof that your husband has bedded a virgin bride. Then, as tradition dictates, he will take the blooded sheet down to the Great Hall where the rest of the men will be waiting and he will exhibit the sheet as proof of your purity and of his manliness. He will take a drink with the men in celebration and then he will return to your bed. But Colwyn, if your Kadeau Lord is really the man of your dreams, you will know such passion, such excitement. I will pray for you, my dear, that you will."

"Your Majesty…. If… If I may be so bold… is the King the man of your dreams?"

Alexandra smiled at her. "I thought he wasn't; it was an arranged marriage, but my Liege is very skilled. Let me just say he became the man of my dreams."

Colwyn blushed with embarrassment; this type of conversation was not something she was used to, especially with the Queen of Devonmere.

"Thank you for your advice and guidance; it is much appreciated. I admit, I am feeling nervous about what lies ahead."

"That is totally understandable, but I will be there to support you. I am sure the King has had, or will be holding, a similar conversation with General Bodine, although I do know, your future husband is not… a novice in love. That, at least, is a good thing; to have a husband who is experienced for your first time will make it more bearable, as long as he is gentle. Now, you have a long ride ahead of you; I recommend you rest for the remainder of the day, but make sure you eat heartily."

Alexandra stood up and drew Colwyn to her feet. She leant forward and kissed her forehead.

"I wish you a safe journey, and we will see you in a few days."

Colwyn curtsied, and, clutching her gift from the Queen, left the room and returned to her own quarters.

Up in the King's personal rooms, Stuart poured Bodine a generous goblet of his best wine and handed it to him, before sitting down opposite, his own drink in his hand.

"I assume you will be leaving early tomorrow morning, Morgan?" the King asked.

"Yes, Sire."

"You are my Champion and General of my Armies, a loyal and brave knight, and I am grateful to have you by my side. This year began badly, and the loss of Richard Coltrane has most certainly left its mark. But we are now rejoicing and celebrating your forthcoming wedding to Colwyn. You know I wish you every happiness, Morgan. Colwyn is a fine young woman; she has spirit, she is loved by her people, and she will make you a fine wife and hopefully bear you a son.

"I am concerned, however, that this wedding will put even more pressure on you, with two Duchies to govern, along with your responsibilities to Devonmere. You must tell me if there is anything I can do to make life and duty easier; if I am asking too much of you."

"My King, I am honoured to have a position of such high responsibility, and that you think so highly of me. I am young and fit, for which I thank God, and, at the moment, feel able to handle the added responsibilities this marriage will put upon me, but I will defer to your judgement should you feel it necessary to do so."

"Very well. A lot is riding on this marriage; the stability of the Kingdom is of the utmost importance. I confess to being thankful that Colwyn does in fact love you, and that I have not had to arrange this marriage, though I do admit to being a little surprised at the speed it has developed."

"You are not the only one, Sire. I had no intention of getting married yet; it just suddenly… happened. I know Colwyn has always had affection for me, but I thought it was as an elder brother, and that was what I

Chapter Nine

considered our relationship to be. If you had told me last year that I would be marrying her, I would have laughed."

"Well, it is almost upon you. Morgan, I consider you a personal friend, and as such, when we are alone like this, I wish you to call me by my name, rather than as your King."

"Si... Stuart, thank you; this means a lot to me."

"It's the least I can do for you, my friend. I also have a small gift for you." He reached into a pocket and brought out a ring. "I would be honoured if you would consider wearing it at your wedding."

"Stuart, thank you. I will, of course, do as you ask."

"Now, promise me you will be careful on your journey to Rossmere. McDowell has not been seen since he left Ellesmere after the tournament. I deployed scouts soon after he left, but have heard nothing back."

"We will be travelling with a fair contingent of men. Unless McDowell comes at us with a considerable force, we should reach Rossmere safely."

"What horse will Colwyn be riding?"

Bodine smiled. "She has a young stallion now. He's big and powerful, and should be able to handle anything thrown at him."

"A stallion!"

"Yes, she rescued him whilst we were at the horse fair at Applegarth the other day. His owner was about to slit his throat. Colwyn intervened and insisted on saving him. He is actually a fine beast; unusual colouring, but sound. He moves well and has plenty of heart and spirit."

"Colwyn continues to amaze me; from her knowledge of the rules of engagement in sword fighting, and now to horses."

"You may now be aware that she can handle a sword? Sir John MacKenzie has been training her since she was a child, and I have continued her training, as she was determined to carry on whether or not I agreed with her. Stuart, she has a formidable temper, which I have been subjected to just the once—so far—and she informed me that was a mild tantrum; so I would hate to see a full-blown one!"

Stuart began to laugh, a rich hearty sound. "My Champion and General of my Armies, scared to challenge his future wife in case she loses her temper!" He then began to really laugh at the thought. It was infectious, and Bodine joined in too. It did sound totally outrageous; for a man who had won many battles for his King and who was fearless in the field, to back down to his future wife over her training to use a sword.

"You do know that she killed one of the assailants on her way to Ellesmere, before she was taken ill, don't you?"

"What?! I did not know of this! Morgan, perhaps you'd best not make her angry!" Stuart began to laugh again.

"It's not as if I didn't know; her red hair should be enough of a warning."

"I think you are going to have a very interesting married relationship." Stuart then became more serious. "The one favour I would ask of you, though, is a male heir to ensure continued Kadeau support for the Cantrell royal family."

Bodine coloured slightly. "I will do my best, but please, Stuart, forgive me, if a few months pass before she conceives… I would like to… enjoy a relationship with my wife before burdening her with a child."

"Of course, I understand." Stuart reached forward and placed a hand on Bodine's shoulder. "Make sure you get a good night's sleep. Alexandra and I will be at Rossmere in two weeks to enjoy and celebrate your wedding. Be gentle with Colwyn, and you will be rewarded with her love."

Bodine went to say something, then changed his mind.

"What is it, Morgan?"

"I confess, I am glad the date has come forward. I… I am finding it increasingly difficult to show restraint, and Colwyn is not helping matters," he finished quietly.

Chapter Nine

"She is eager, then?" He smiled again. "Enough said. Safe journey tomorrow, my friend."

Stuart stood up, and Bodine did the same. The King embraced him tightly in a brotherly hug, then Bodine took his leave.

※ ※ ※ ※

The duke went to his rooms and picked up a gift he had for Colwyn. It was not a gift in the normal sense of the word, but more a weapon for her protection.

Reaching her rooms, he knocked on the door.

"Enter," he heard a soft voice say.

Opening the door, he saw Colwyn's expression change to one of pleasure as he entered.

"Morgan," she breathed, coming forward to greet him.

"My love," he replied, and kissed her briefly. "I have something I would like you to wear for our forthcoming journey; something that I hope will provide you with additional protection."

She frowned at him. "What is it?"

He produced the item from behind his back. It was a delicately jewelled short knife in a special sheath which obviously strapped to a person's arm.

"Let us quickly try this for size," Bodine said. "It has been designed to enable you to release the knife with the same hand it is strapped to. Let me show you." He took hold of her left arm and put it in the required position, and strapped the sheathed knife on. "It needs to go next to your skin, but this will give you some idea of how it operates. I sincerely hope it will not be needed, but better to be safe than sorry."

He checked it was positioned correctly, made a few adjustments, then nodded in satisfaction.

"It needs to be quite tight. Now, you need to do a sharp movement with your hand; this will cause the hilt of the knife to move forward into your hand, and then you can grasp it with your right and do whatever you need to do. Come, try."

Colwyn did as she was told and the knife moved, just as Bodine said it would.

"Excellent. I will make sure it is fitted properly before we leave in the morning. Until then, I will take my leave."

They kissed passionately before pulling apart.

"Not much longer now, my love," Bodine whispered in her ear, and then he was gone.

10

Chapter Ten

Bodine had only despatched a small guard to accompany Master Andrew and Sarah to Belvoir, as he was convinced they would be allowed to travel in safety as it was Colwyn that McDowell was after; so, he'd kept seventy of his knights to provide an escort for her, along with himself. Unless the Duke of Cottesmere came at them with a substantial number of his army—which was highly doubtful, as he would not want to leave his Duchy undefended—he was positive his men could handle anything that came their way.

They also planned to travel light, to enable them to move quickly should the need arise. Pennants and flags were not going to be on display until they were practically at their destination. Swords and lances were sharpened, shields cleaned and polished.

Speed was of the essence; once they were through the pass, all haste would be made to reach Belvoir as soon as possible.

Both Stuart and Bodine had sent scouts out along the planned journey to look for any signs of trouble. They were highly skilled in reading tracks and would be able to tell whether activity on the trail was recent or not.

The Rossmere party left Ellesmere Castle just after dawn the following morning. Stuart's scouts had reported no sighting of any forces belonging to McDowell or any other unknown parties. Bodine had the remainder of his men with him, to discourage any attack, and had sent his own scouts ahead to scour the route for any form of awaiting danger. They camped that night on some high ground a few miles away from the gorge and resumed their journey just after dawn.

It was a beautiful day for the trip along the river between the High Hills, after which they would turn for Rossmere. However, the travellers were all a little uneasy. The path along the river was narrow, but just wide enough for two wagons to pass. The side rose steeply to their right, and, to their left, dropped steeply again to the river twelve feet or so below them, which was currently running fast following rain that had drained from the high hills a couple of days beforehand. It would not be a good place to get caught in an ambush.

The convoy kept up a reasonable pace as Bodine wanted to be clear of the area before nightfall. He ordered the men to stay alert and sent another couple of scouts ahead to ensure the coast was clear on the immediate route.

"You're worried, aren't you?" Colwyn asked him. "This is a good place for an ambush."

He smiled ruefully at her. "I am blessed," he told her. "Blessed to be having a wife who recognises the possible dangers around her. You would make a good knight."

"Sir John trained me well," she confessed.

"Of that I am certain." He reached out and took her hand, placing it briefly to his lips before releasing it. "I hope that your parents, in heaven, are pleased with our approaching union."

"Mother thought of you as the son she had not yet had." Colwyn's eyes filled with unshed tears.

"Inver always made me feel most welcome. It is like a second home to me. The warmth and love I received will be forever with me. I want you to

Chapter Ten

know, I will do everything in my power to avenge your parent's death and restore Invermere to its former glory."

"Thank you, Morgan."

Dernley was riding rearguard with a couple of other knights, so that fair warning could be given to the main column ahead. The knights frequently looked behind them, checking that the coast remained clear.

Suddenly, riders appeared from nowhere. Dernley whirled his horse around and saw the knights heading straight for them. He galloped forward to catch up with Morgan and Colwyn.

"Morgan! Knights behind us! Gaining fast!"

"Giles, take Colwyn, and make a run for it; take a dozen men with you. We'll hold them off until you get clear of the High Hills," Bodine answered.

"Morgan..." Colwyn began.

"Go, my love, now!" He leant towards her and gave her a parting kiss. "Run! We will catch you up, I promise you."

Not wanting to go, but realising it would be better to follow orders so Bodine could concentrate on the job on hand, she urged Storm forward. He was eager for the run and set off at a thunderous pace, with Dernley and the other twelve knights following in her wake.

Bodine watched them go then rallied his knights to fend off the approaching force. There was very little room in which to manoeuvre, and anyone who got too close to the edge was likely to slip or fall down the steep embankment into the raging river below, which is where a couple of the attackers went, having been knocked off their horses in the fierce fighting.

Ahead, Colwyn's guard had only gone about half a mile when the front scouts came galloping back to them.

"My Lady!" one of them shouted. "Where is General Bodine? A force is approaching from the South!"

"He's fighting an attack from the North!" she replied.

Dernley took charge. "How many?" he asked the scouts.

"At least thirty."

"That means each of us must despatch two, but there will be no one to watch over you, Colwyn.

We'll have to return. Together we may be able to defeat the attack from both sides. Come."

They turned around and galloped back towards the main column. As they got closer, they could hear the sound of the battle. The clash of steel on steel seemed relentless as both sides fought for superiority. Horses whinnied, and cries were heard as blows hit their mark. Bodine's knights were highly trained in all manner of scenarios and held their ground at first, then began beating their opponents back. The surcoats of the attackers were unmarked; they looked very much like the ones he saw at Inver and thus they had no idea who they were actually fighting, but everything still pointed at McDowell. Why else would anyone be here? Bodine's intended marriage to Colwyn threatened no one apart from the ambitious Cottesmere Duke.

Hearing the sound of more hoofbeats, Bodine turned his head and was dismayed to see Colwyn and her guard. He fell back towards them, leaving his knights to continue the battle.

"What are you doing back here?" he asked.

"Another force, Morgan, from the South! We thought it safer to return and combine forces."

Bodine nodded, but his expression was grim. "You did the right thing. Colwyn, stay in the middle so we can protect you!"

The attackers seemed intent on driving Bodine and his knights to the edge of the pass to tip them over and down the steep slope, but the Rossmere knights stood their ground, refusing to move back any further. They rallied, cutting down their opponents; then the force from the South arrived and they were fighting on two fronts.

Chapter Ten

"Morgan!" Dernley shouted. "You must take Colwyn and make a run for it! The wedding must take place; you are both the key!"

"I can't leave you; I must lead!"

"With all due respect, sir, you must leave! We will hold them and catch up with you later. When you get the chance, go! We all understand the situation. For the stability of the Kingdom, you must go!"

Bodine nodded reluctantly and turned to face the southern force. Colwyn drew her sword, ready to repel any opposing knight who tried to grab her or her horse's reins and make a run for it. They battled on; Dernley's mount was driven back towards the edge of the steep slope and he put in a frenzied attack, attempting to gain ground. He spurred his horse, who jumped forward, but two other knights drove him back again, then his horse reared, losing its balance, unseating Dernley, who slithered down the steep slope and into the raging water below; the weight of his armour dragging him below the surface.

"Giles!" Colwyn screamed, seeing him disappear over the edge, to be followed by his horse, who also fell. "No!"

Bodine and half a dozen knights broke through the southern line and were then followed by the others so they were again only fighting on one front. Colwyn, supported on both sides by two others, also made it through.

"Go, my Lord! We will hold them. Take your lady and go!"

Bodine hated to retreat; it was not in his makeup to run away from a fight, but he had a higher responsibility: Colwyn must not be taken at any price. He had to marry her as soon as possible, to protect the Kingdom.

"I will see you at Rossmere!" Bodine shouted. "Colwyn, come!" He glanced at her and saw she was crying. Her childhood friend had plunged to his death down the slope. A new knight, lost already. He would mourn Giles Dernley—another good soul—and avenge his death for Colwyn. The news would be a severe blow to his father, the Duke of Strathmere.

They spurred their horses and galloped along the ledge. Colwyn could hardly see where she was going and was in shock at the loss of her friend. With every passing moment, her hate for McDowell grew and she wished him dead with every fibre of her being.

They put a good distance between themselves and the fight behind them before easing off the pace to let their horses recover.

"Colwyn, are you all right?" Bodine asked, concerned.

She looked at him, her expression sad. "So many deaths," she replied, her voice catching. "It would be better if I were to die, rather than have any more on my hands."

Bodine grabbed the reins of her horse, and pulled them both to a stop. "Don't you ever, say that again!" he ordered, placing a firm hand on her arm. "You are of royal blood, and with that comes duty and responsibility. Often, it's not what we want, but it's what we are born into. It's not an easy life; it's hard and it's cruel sometimes, but we must all play our part." He was silent for a few moments, then said; "I'm sorry about Giles."

Her bottom lip quavered, but she said nothing, so he leant over and kissed her.

"Come, we should make the woods before nightfall, and that should give us cover."

He urged his horse forward at a gentle canter, and Colwyn followed, slightly behind.

Eventually, they emerged out of the High Hills, and the landscape changed to rolling hills with the wood in the distance. They paused a while to rest and water the horses and themselves. Bodine looked back, hoping to see some of his guard appearing, but there was no sign of them. He feared that maybe more of McDowell's men had arrived to support their colleagues, but hoped that it was just that they had taken a little longer than expected to

Chapter Ten

despatch the rogue knights. God help McDowell if he got his hands on him! He'd make the duke pay with his life.

They continued on with their journey, watching the sun as it gradually sank towards the western horizon. They would reach the woods just before dark and be able to find shelter; at least, that's what they thought until they saw mounted figures in the distance.

"I'm sorry, my love," Bodine said to her. "We must fly!" He slapped Storm's rump with a gloved hand and the horse sprung forward, with his own mount following at first, then drawing level. Secretly now, he was pleased that Colwyn had insisted on having the horse, for he was big, and had plenty of stamina and heart. A palfrey would not have stood the pace.

Now into the woods, they wove in and out of the trees, trying to both evade and lose their pursuers. The light was fading fast, which they hoped would help in their quest to avoid capture and detection.

They were not quite sure how many were after them, but Bodine was determined he would hold them at bay if required, until the last breath left his body, as befitting a knight of Devonmere.

Suddenly, they were in a small clearing. He reined in his horse and turned it to face the way they had just come, looking for a sign of his pursuers. Six of them appeared on the edge of the clearing. Colwyn drew her sword in readiness.

"No, my love," Bodine said. "I will take care of this."

"But there are six of them! They won't harm me, but I can harm them! I know you are the best swordsman in Devonmere, but it's still six onto one!"

He smiled reassuringly at her, adjusted his shield, and urged his horse forward.

His assailants paused. They were well aware of Bodine's prowess with a sword. Unbeaten since the age of fourteen, he was known throughout the Kingdom and beyond; there was no better swordsman in existence, but there were six of them; reasonable odds. They too urged their horses further into the clearing.

Colwyn manoeuvred her horse to Bodine's left, so no man could attack him from that side. The knights grinned in amusement behind their helms, then, drawing their swords, formed a circle around them and attacked. Colwyn turned her horse so that her sword arm was now on the outside and she would be able to help defend her future husband.

Bodine despatched the first guard with ease. Another tried to grab the reins of Colwyn's horse, and she slashed out with her sword to see him topple off his horse. Storm then obliged her by rearing slightly and stomping on the helpless knight, crushing his chest. Now there were four.

The duke managed to unseat another from his horse who then tried to attack him from the ground, but Banner lunged into him and Bodine plunged his sword into the guard's neck. Three left.

One of the remaining guards tried to sneak up on Bodine's back, but Colwyn shouted a warning. Banner turned on the spot and the duke despatched him. Two left.

Suddenly, there was the faint sound of something swishing through the air. Bodine lurched forward in the saddle and gave a cry as an arrow hit him in the back of his left shoulder, penetrating both the cuirass and hauberk as if they were made of paper.

"Morgan!" Colwyn screamed, and the remaining knights started to rally round.

"Break the shaft!" Morgan gasped. "Quickly! We will make a run for it!"

Colwyn swallowed, grasped the shaft of the arrow between her hands, took a deep breath and snapped the feathered end off, leaving a short piece sticking out of his shoulder. She could not pull the arrow out as she knew it was barbed, and it would do far much more damage if she did so. It would either need cutting out, or pushing all the way through.

Chapter Ten

"I-I'm sorry!" she cried, as the shaft broke and he gasped at the pain.

"F-follow me!" He spurred his horse and Colwyn followed as another arrow narrowly missed the injured duke.

"No arrows!" a voice was heard to shout, "You'll hit the woman!"

By now, it was almost dark, and the moon was hidden behind the clouds. They went on blindly; deeper into the wood where the trees got thicker still; almost too thick for the horses. The sound of their pursuers started to fade into the distance.

They stumbled across a thicket and forced their way through. It would provide them with some protection.

Bodine turned his horse in the direction they had just come from, raised his right hand and whispered, "*Qui vocat densissima nebula.*"

Immediately, a thick fog began to form around them, making any movement dangerous within the wood. Bodine nodded in satisfaction. No one would find them for now, and this particular fog would linger all night, unless he ordered otherwise.

He gave a soft groan as he managed to slip out of the saddle to the ground, initially landing on his feet, the shield slipping from lifeless fingers. But then he collapsed to his knees, clutching his injured shoulder. Bodine tried without success to get the pain under control. "H-help me out of my armour," he whispered, breathing heavily.

Colwyn dismounted and ran to him, helping him remove his sword belt, the surcoat, and the cuirass. The hauberk was a lot more difficult as she tried to ease what was left of the shaft through it, before getting it over his head. Every time he moved his left arm, the agony left him feeling weak and sick.

The aketon was easier to remove, and then finally the black shirt. Bare-chested, he struggled to his feet, staggered towards a large oak tree and turned so his back was facing it. He took several deep breaths, closed his eyes and steeled himself, then rammed his shoulder back against the trunk. The broken shaft of the arrow connected with the bark of the tree and he cried out as the barbed arrowhead pierced through the front of his shoulder.

"P-pull it out," he whispered to Colwyn. He was breathing heavily and his eyes were screwed shut as he concentrated on staying conscious. "Do it!"

Taking a few deep breaths herself, Colwyn swallowed, grasped the barbed arrowhead and pulled, slowly but firmly. The broken shaft followed through easily.

"T-thank you," he managed to say softly, then sank to his knees, gasping.

Colwyn went to Storm and removed the water bag from the saddle, then returning to Bodine, she lifted her riding leathers and skirt and tore strips off her chemise. It was almost dark in the thicket and she could barely see to carry out what needed to be done, but she knelt by his side to treat his wound.

"Morgan," she whispered, "I can hardly see what I'm doing," she sounded worried.

"Do the best you can," he said softly, his breath catching as the wound throbbed with every beat of his heart.

Colwyn poured some water onto the back and front of his shoulder and used smaller pieces of cloth to wipe the excess water and blood away. She created two dressings, getting Bodine to try and use his right arm to hold the dressing on the front of his shoulder in place whilst she held the back one, then used a long strip to hold them in place. She then wrapped another long piece around in a different way and tied that off, hoping that would suffice until they got to safety.

She helped him to get his shirt on, fetched their cloaks from the back of the saddles and they huddled together under a tree for warmth. Bodine's head lolled against her shoulder as he finally passed out and Colwyn shifted to enfold him in her arms to make him more comfortable and did her best to stay awake overnight, although sleep was the last thing on her mind.

Chapter Ten

Bodine was wounded. If they ran into more of McDowell's men, they wouldn't stand a chance. So she sat, thinking furiously, and wondered. *Focus the mind and you can do anything*, Bodine had told her this five years ago when he had taught her how to conjure the blue flame. Perhaps she could not cure him, but if she could make it a little better; stop the bleeding; she had never attempted anything like this before, but she hoped she might be able to do something. Dernley's horse had recovered from his injury more quickly than anticipated...

Carefully, so as not to disturb her intended, she eased her right hand under his shirt and placed it over the bandaged wound on the front of his shoulder.

Colwyn closed her eyes, took some deep breaths and did her best to clear her mind. Gradually she became aware of a pain in her left shoulder. Her eyes flew open and the pain disappeared. She absorbed this sensation and analysed it briefly, then tried again, this time ignoring it.

"*Corpus curare*," she whispered, frowning in concentration, hoping she was using the appropriate words. She repeated them another couple of times, then became aware of a sensation of pins and needles in her right hand. A pain developed in her left shoulder which then became an agony, causing a sob to escape past her lips, and she was compelled to stop as she felt herself losing consciousness. She forced her eyes open and started to feel a little better. Bodine still did not stir.

☙ ❧ ☙ ❧

Having fallen from his horse when it had reared up, Dernley's hands desperately tried to get a secure grip on any rocks as he tumbled down the steep slope towards the raging river below, but his gauntlets could not get a firm enough hold to stop his descent.

Trying not to succumb to a rising panic, he finally managed to grasp a larger piece of rock that was jutting out slightly more, just before he reached the water. As it was, his legs were partly submerged and the river was doing its best to take him with it. He managed to obtain a further grip and looked up to see his horse slithering down the slope towards him, its legs desperately flailing, as the stallion tried to stop his fall, and Dernley realised he had to move or over half a ton of horse was going to land on top of him.

Desperately, he reached sideward for another handhold but slipped, and suddenly, he was in the river, being swept downstream. His last vision was of his horse slithering over the spot he had just been occupying before he was dragged under by the weight of his armour. Frantically, he struck out, trying to reach the surface as the water buffeted and pummelled him He got slammed into a series of outcrops and felt a rib crack. The impact knocked the wind out of him and unable to prevent a gasp, he breathed in a lungful of water.

Breaking the surface briefly, he coughed and spluttered, and managed to get a little air into his lungs before being dragged under again.

He tried to hold his breath for as long as possible; his lungs were burning, blood pounding in his ears, as he was swept over a rocky cascade and dropped into a relatively calm pool. Fighting hard, he managed to gain a footing and staggered out of the water to collapse onto the narrow, sandy bank, coughing and spluttering in an effort to expel the water from his lungs and get some air into them, all the while gritting his teeth as his cracked rib protested at the violent movement.

Rolling over onto his back, he lay there, chest heaving from the effort, then lifted his head as he heard a whinny. It was his horse, Archer, who found his feet and waded out of the water to join Dernley on the bank. The horse was breathing hard, but shook himself. He had several cuts, one of which was bleeding quite badly and he sent droplets of blood flying through the air

Chapter Ten

as he freed his body of the excess water. Miraculously, he appeared to be standing four square, intimating nothing was broken.

Dernley heaved himself to sit upright and Archer lowered his head and exhaled heavily on the top of his head. He raised a hand and laid it on the horse's cheek to reassure him, before managing to get to his feet.

He carefully checked his horse over, paying particular attention to his legs. Everything seemed to be in order; the cuts were mainly superficial, and Dernley heaved a sigh of relief.

His next decision was about what he should do next. During his fall, his sword had been wrenched out of his hand, so to all intents and purposes, he was defenceless. Having been swept some distance downstream and around a bend, he had no idea if the Rossmere guard had defeated their opponents or not. As far as he was concerned, his duty was to Bodine and Colwyn. They could still be in danger and require further assistance, so he decided to head back to Ellesmere and inform the King of what had happened.

Looking about him, he searched the banking, looking for a place where it was less steep and easier for his horse to ascend. Approximately a hundred yards away, there was an area of banking that had partially collapsed. It was still steep, but not sheer, so he patted Archer, took hold of his reins and started to walk towards it.

Dernley noted Archer was walking a little stiffly, but put that down to him being cut and bruised like he was.

It was hard work struggling up the slope; the ground underfoot was loose and crumbly, but eventually, after a lot of effort, they made it up onto the ledge, where they paused to recover their breath.

Once his heart rate was almost back to normal, he checked Archer over once more, and satisfied all was reasonably well, began to lead him back towards Ellesmere. He needed to make sure the horse was all right, for he was going to ask a great deal of him shortly.

Darkness descended and he realised he could not travel further with a wounded horse; he could finish up causing more damage. The nights were short, so he waited patiently until the dawn started to make an appearance, then mounted and started walking once more, waiting until he was happy that his horse was moving relatively well, considering his ordeal, before breaking into a canter.

Hating to do it, he pushed his horse hard, knowing that time was of the essence. Lathered and exhausted, they arrived back at Ellesmere in the middle of the night. Slithering from the saddle, he patted his trembling horse before ordering the nearest guard to take care of him, then running up the steps to the keep.

Dernley immediately requested to speak with the King and another guard disappeared to obey his order. A number of minutes passed, which he used to pull off his gauntlets and to tidy himself up; then he heard the sound of footsteps and looked up to see the King and a couple of aides approaching.

The young knight took a knee as his sovereign reached him.

"Sir Giles, rise," the King ordered, noting his appearance; the still drying clothes; the cuts and bruises. "What has happened?"

"Sire, we were attacked from two sides on the river path between the High Hills."

"The Duke and Duchess?"

Dernley shook his head. "I don't know, Sire. We persuaded them to make a run for it, whilst we held the attackers at bay. We were still fighting when more arrived; the numbers drove me back to the edge, and I finished up going over and was swept away in the river. I managed to finally get to the bank; my horse also managed to survive, and I thought it best to return here to advise you. As soon as I get another sword and horse, I will make my way back."

Chapter Ten

"You will do no such thing. Get cleaned up, have something to eat and rest. It will take some time to prepare my knights to leave." He turned to one of his aides. "Raise the knights; we leave at dawn. Arrange supplies for a week."

The aide nodded and ran off. Turning to his other aide, he asked, "Do you know where Monsignor McLeod's room is?"

The man nodded.

"Bring him to me. I'll be in the antechamber. Quickly now!" He turned back to Dernley. "Go, Sir Giles, get your wounds attended to; eat and sleep, at least for a few hours."

"Yes, Sire." Dernley bowed, wincing slightly, then turned and left.

The noise of the preparations woke Queen Alexandra. Frowning, she pulled on her dressing gown and went to the window. Below her, people were running about; provisions were being packed; horses saddled. She observed Master Stephen, the King's battle surgeon, checking and packing his medical supplies in his saddlebags and she felt an overwhelming sense of unease. Turning away from the window, she made her way down to the antechamber, knowing that was where she would find the answers to her questions.

Stuart looked up as the door opened. "Alexandra, my apologies; the noise of preparation has disturbed you."

"What's happening?" she asked as she approached him.

"Bodine's party has been attacked."

Alexandra's hand went involuntarily to her throat. "Colwyn—" she began.

The King shook his head. "We don't know," he answered. "General Bodine will protect her with his life, but..." his voice trailed off.

"It's McDowell?"

"It has to be. It can't be anyone else. Try not to worry; we will find them; we must find them. We shall leave at dawn."

"Then I'm coming too!"

"No!"

"Yes! Colwyn is like a daughter to me! I will not wait here like some helpless old woman!" She spun on a heel and left the chamber to return to her rooms to prepare for the journey.

She almost collided with McLeod, who was hurrying to reach the King. He apologised profusely and stepped aside to let her pass before continuing on his journey. Stuart saw him enter and indicated for him to approach. Taking him aside, he whispered, "Monsignor, I need you to see if you can contact Morgan. I fear for his safety." He went on to explain what had happened—as far as they knew—and their preparations to mount a rescue.

McLeod nodded grimly and went to the far end of the room, out of sight, should anyone enter. It appeared as if he were praying, but Stuart knew otherwise.

The Monsignor clasped his hands together, concentrating on clearing his thoughts, and reached out with his mind.

Morgan? Morgan, can you hear me?

He waited patiently. No reply was forthcoming.

Morgan! Answer me!

He could not even sense his cousin. This meant one of two things; he was either unconscious or... he could not bring himself to think of the other possibility... that he was dead.

Morgan! He tried a third time, increasing the intensity of the thought tenfold. Nothing. Seriously worried, he returned to the King's side, shaking his head.

"Nothing?" Stuart asked. "Nothing at all?"

"Nothing at all, my Liege," McLeod confirmed.

Chapter Ten

Stuart's mouth settled into a firm line. "Pray for him, Monsignor; pray hard," he said grimly.

Prince Michael arrived. "Stuart, we will be ready to leave at dawn, as per your orders."

The King nodded. "Thank you, Michael; I just pray we will get there in time…"

ଔ ଽ ଔ ଽ

It had taken longer to defeat the unmarked assailants due to them calling in reinforcements, but the Rossmere Guard had still prevailed in the end. They watched as what was left of the attackers turned and made a run for it. Some of the guard went to pursue, but the Captain stopped them.

"Leave them!" he shouted. "We must find the Duke and Duchess!" He left a small party to take care of the injured and the dead, with instructions to get them to Ellesmere, which was much closer than Belvoir, and then made haste through the pass to emerge onto the plains with the wood visible in the far distance.

They halted on a hill, scanning the horizon for any sign of the duke and his lady, but there was no one in sight. Hoping they had made it past any foes and were safely on their way to Rossmere, they set off in pursuit. Their aim was to catch up with them and escort them to safety, but the light was beginning to fade, and the guard was forced to camp for the night.

The threat of rain was in the air, and the Captain of the Guard was worried about the safety of his Lord. Doubt was lurking in the far recesses of his mind. Maybe they shouldn't have made Bodine and Colwyn leave, but, at the time, it looked as if they were going to be overrun, so it had been the safest and most logical choice at that point in the battle.

In the end, they had been victorious, but at a cost. Several comrades had been wounded—some of them seriously—and a few others had been killed, but it could have been much worse. Rossmere knights were almost the best in Devonmere; the Captain grudgingly admitted that perhaps only the King's Elite Guard were better.

He knew his Lord could manage to fend off six opponents - he had seen him do it, and had been amazed at the duke's skill with a sword - but perhaps his enemies also knew that and had ambushed him with more. He shuddered at the thought. Bodine was a hard taskmaster; he expected a lot from his men, but he was incredibly fair and caring, and none of his men gave a damn that he was Kadeau. Neither did any of them give it a thought, because the duke hardly ever used his magic. The Captain prayed that he had made use of it to stay safe. If it was McDowell behind all this, then the Cottesmere Duke was likely to take the greatest pleasure in torturing Bodine, if he should capture him.

※ ※ ※ ※

The thick fog remained overnight, reducing visibility substantially. Colwyn had finally dozed off in the early hours of the morning, but was awoken by Bodine shifting against her.

His left arm was practically useless, having stiffened up during the night, and even flexing his fingers resulted in a shooting pain in his shoulder.

They drank from Colwyn's water bag, then she helped him back into his armour and checked the saddles and girths on the horses before helping Bodine to mount. Then they cautiously left the safety of the thicket.

With no sun to guide them and no landmarks within the forest, it was almost impossible to know the direction of travel, but Bodine seemed confident about his destination. They moved slowly in an effort to keep the noise they might make to a minimum. Colwyn kept glancing around her, trying to see into the forest, looking out for any of McDowell's men, but no one was visible.

Chapter Ten

Gradually, the trees began to thin as the forest gave way to rolling hills again. Even with the reduced visibility, Bodine seemed to recognise where they were and told Colwyn they were about a day and a half from Belvoir. They increased their speed to an easy canter, and she kept an eye on him, concerned about his wound.

Neither had eaten for almost a day, and they attempted to have some cooked meat whilst cantering, but it did not seem to go down well, so they abandoned that idea, deciding to try again when they finally stopped for a rest.

At least, that had been the plan; however, they found their path blocked at the final pass into Rossmere. Colwyn's heart sank to the bottom of her boots as she surveyed the row of horsemen ahead. Bodine reined in his horse and sat contemplating his next move.

"I'm not leaving you," Colwyn told him before he could say anything.

"But I can delay them and you can make a run for it."

"No! We leave this place together, or not at all! Let's make a run for Inver!"

"'Tis a long way to Inver, my love."

"Then let's head back to Ellesmere. With luck, we may run into the rest of the guard."

"Or we'll run into more of McDowell's men."

Bodine closed his eyes. He was having problems thinking clearly. There were too many of them to fight their way through, and he was severely handicapped. They had two choices; go back, or surrender, and that word did not exist in Bodine's vocabulary.

"Back to Ellesmere and the King!" he decided.

They whirled their horses round and headed back in the direction they had just come from. It took their assailants a few seconds to realise what they were doing, and then they set off in pursuit.

The chase went on for miles, and thankfully, their pursuers did not seem to be gaining, but neither were they losing them. They entered the woods once again and wove at breakneck speed between the trees heading back towards the pass, only to find their way barred as they emerged on the other side of the woods.

Desperately, they changed direction, but the horses were beginning to tire and were lathered with the effort.

"The ruins, up there!" Bodine gasped, and they changed direction again, with McDowell's men in hot pursuit.

Thirty minutes later, they were at the ruins. Quickly, they dismounted and ran for cover, running through a number of corridors and passageways, down steps to a lower level. It was much darker down there and difficult to see anything.

"Colwyn, can you produce fire-light, so we can see where we're going?" Bodine asked, panting.

"Of course." She whispered the required words and the cold blue flame sprang to life in her hand.

They moved cautiously along the corridors, not sure where they were going, only knowing they had to find cover and hide.

They ducked down behind some fallen pillars to get their breath back. Bodine was breathing hard and holding his left shoulder. Even in the dim light, Colwyn could see the colour had drained from his face. She knew he couldn't go on much longer, but he would continue to fight until he could not fight anymore, to keep her safe.

Concerned, she touched his forehead and found it hot and clammy.

"Morgan," she whispered, the worry clearly evident in her voice.

He turned his head and looked at her, his grey eyes filled with pain, his chest heaving.

Chapter Ten

"I'm all right," he gasped, then froze as he heard voices. "Extinguish the light and hold my hand," he whispered, closing his eyes for a few moments as if summoning an inner strength. She did as he asked. "I'm not sure how long I'll be able to do this, but whatever happens, do not make a sound, and don't move." He paused, took hold of her hand, and spoke quietly again. "*Invisibilia me.*"

They sat quietly as the voices grew nearer; then Colwyn somehow managed to stop herself from shrieking as a couple of McDowell's knights drew level. All they had to do was turn, and they would see them.

"I can't see them. You sure they came this way?" one said to the other.

"No, but we have to search every corridor."

"This place is a maze; they could be anywhere down here! There aren't enough of us to cover the area; they could easily slip through."

"Perhaps, but where are they going to go? We've got their horses and they're not going to get far on foot, especially with Bodine having an arrow in him."

"But there's no blood trail; it can't have been that bad a wound."

Bodine gripped Colwyn's hand even tighter, making her wince, as the knight turned in their direction but did not see them. Her mouth dropped open; it was as if they were invisible! She frowned in confusion, but kept quiet and still.

"Come on, let's keep going. The sooner we finish, the sooner we can get out of here."

The two of them walked on. Bodine waited until they disappeared round the next corner, then relaxed.

"They couldn't see us!" Colwyn whispered in wonder. "You made us invisible?"

He nodded, then putting his thumb and finger on the bridge of his nose, as she had seen him do that day in the rose garden when he had arrived at Ellesmere, mumbled, "*Vivifica me.*"

A couple of seconds passed and Bodine seemed to be revitalised.

"Come on," he whispered, getting to his feet.

"You seem stronger," Colwyn said.

"It is merely temporary. If we don't get out of here and find somewhere else to hide soon, it's going to hit me, and I won't be able to protect you until I recover. I try not to use it too often, as it takes a lot out of me." He held out his hand, and Colwyn took it and let him lead her in the opposite direction.

They moved slowly and carefully along the passageway, in near darkness, listening for any sounds; footsteps, voices, metallic clanging. All was quiet apart from the sound of voices, off in the distance, echoing along passages and bouncing off the walls. They cautiously retraced their steps back the way they had come, keeping to the gloomy shadows, that offered the illusion of cover. All seemed deserted, but Bodine knew danger was all around them. Peering round a wall, he saw two knights guarding their horses. In his present state, he was confident he could handle them, so crept closer, hand on the hilt of his sword. He indicated for Colwyn to stay where she was, as he ran the last few yards, unsheathing his sword as he went.

The knights turned, drawing their swords as Bodine reached them. The first one he managed to despatch in one move, the other was far more skilled, and parried his first attack, before launching his own on the injured duke. Realising Bodine was weaker due to his injury, the knight was suddenly brave, and launched a frenzied attack; but the Kadeau was still as dangerous—perhaps even more so.

Dodging a sudden lunge from the guard, Bodine spun round and caught him with his blade, injuring him, but not badly. He was concerned the sound

Chapter Ten

of swords clashing would bring the rest of McDowell's men running. Already, he could feel his strength fading, having over-exerted himself in his weakened state. With one final desperate attack, he managed to kill the other knight.

Colwyn saw the man go down and ran towards Bodine, who was now holding onto the pommel of Banner's saddle, trying to stay on his feet.

"Morgan, I'm here. Mount up."

He nodded weakly, and managed to drag himself up onto his horse. Colwyn quickly mounted Storm, and they turned to make a run for it. As they went through the ruined gate, a knight on top of the wall jumped and knocked Bodine from his horse, and they both hit the ground hard.

Colwyn pulled Storm to a halt and turned him around, urging him to go back. The knight gained his feet first, ran to Bodine, and put his mailed boot on the duke's left shoulder, just as he tried to get to his feet, forcing him back down on the ground and wrenching a groan from him.

Pulling her sword from its sheath, Colwyn gave a cry. The knight turned to face her, and she plunged her sword into his chest, hearing a satisfying grunt as the knight collapsed in a heap on the floor. Banner had returned and stood waiting.

Bodine gritted his teeth and rolled over onto his back. Colwyn literally leapt from her horse and held her hand out to him. Strength almost gone, he grabbed her hand to help him make one final effort to get to his feet and back onto his horse.

It was late afternoon by now, but being June, the days were long and it would be a few more hours before it got dark; somehow they had to evade capture until then. Clouds were gathering and rain was in the air.

Then there was a commotion, and several knights appeared from the ruins.

"Morgan! Get on your horse!" Colwyn almost screamed at him, as she grabbed Storm's reins and remounted.

"Go! Leave me! Go!" he commanded her, as he began to heave himself back into the saddle again.

"No! We leave together or not at all!" she shouted back.

He loved her for it, but she had to go, no matter what happened to him.

Seeing the knights closing fast, he made one final effort and managed to get back into his saddle. Colwyn urged Storm forward and knocked one of them flying, and despatched another with her sword, but as Bodine pulled on the reins to turn his horse, three knights reached him and dragged him back off. Strength gone, he was helpless as they pinned him down on the ground. Colwyn turned her horse to attack the next knight.

"Colwyn! Go!" he managed to shout.

She urged Storm forward, sword in her hand, only to find more knights arriving.

"Please! Obey me, go!" He struggled, but there were just too many of them to fight in his weakened state. The noise attracted the attention of more of their attackers. If she was not to be captured, she had to make a run for it.

With tears in her eyes, she reluctantly started to obey him, but several more knights appeared from different directions, and one grabbed the reins of her horse. Sensing his mistress's distress, Storm reared, his front hooves flailing, lashing out at the knight who had grabbed his reins. The horse broke free and struck him. Colwyn managed to injure another one, before desperately digging her heels into Storm's flanks and he jumped forward and began to gallop away.

"Stop her!" she heard one of them shout.

Risking a glance behind her, she saw two knights had mounted horses and were in hot pursuit. Storm had his second wind now and was flying, but the horses behind were fresher, and slowly started to gain.

Chapter Ten

Realising she wasn't going to outrun them, she reined up and turned to face them, sword in hand. One stopped in front of her; the other swept by, then turned his horse sharply and launched himself from his saddle before she could turn and defend herself and they hit the ground.

Severely winded, Colwyn tried to regain her feet, but the other knight joined his companion and pinned her down. She struggled desperately but was no match for the two men.

"Stop struggling, damn you!" one of them said, as she managed to connect a clenched fist with his jaw.

He hit her in return and she fell back, dazed.

"You'd better hope that doesn't leave a mark," his companion said. "His Grace will have your head if you've hurt her."

"She's like a wild animal. I had to stop her somehow..." He swore as he saw a trace of blood at the corner of her mouth.

"Come on, let's get her back."

They stood up and dragged the still-dazed Colwyn to her feet. One of the guards grabbed her horse's reins and brought him close. The other hoisted her up onto the saddle as if she was a featherweight, then mounted his own steed and took Storm's reins.

"I'll tell you one thing; I wouldn't want to marry her; I'd more than likely finish up with a knife in my back!"

His companion chuckled.

"Guess Duke McDowell better tie her to the bed on his wedding night, or he might get a knife between the ribs; and that'd be such a tragedy!"

They both laughed at that remark.

It took several minutes to return to the ruins. Colwyn saw that Bodine was still pinned down, at the mercy of the three knights who were holding him.

Another came forward and dragged her from her saddle before she could even attempt to dismount.

Struggling, she broke free and ran to Bodine, pushing past the knights to kneel down by his side.

"Morgan!" Her voice was full of anguish, as she reached out and touched his hand.

Barely conscious, somehow he managed to open his eyes and gaze into her concerned green ones, then noted the blood at the corner of her mouth.

"I-I'm s-sorry," he whispered.

She shook her head. "No, don't, don't blame yourself," she replied. "You have—arrgh!" She was cut off mid-sentence as someone grabbed her by the hair and pulled her back.

Bodine forced his eyes to shift their gaze and looked up into the face of a very smug-looking Nigel McDowell. The King's Champion couldn't prevent himself from trying to rise, but McDowell stomped on his left shoulder, causing him to collapse back. Red curtains, hovering at the corner of his vision, threatened to close, but he fought the feeling with what little strength he had left.

"Well, this is a much better situation," McDowell said conversationally, as he ground his foot against Bodine's shoulder, forcing a groan past his lips. The red curtains closed a little further across his eyes and he knew he was losing consciousness.

"Leave him alone!" Colwyn shouted, trying to free her hair from McDowell's grasp without success and struggling violently. She stopped as the Cottesmere Duke tightened his grip.

"My love, do not concern yourself with this Kadeau. Shall we invite him to our wedding?"

"I'm never marrying you, Duke!" Colwyn spat.

Chapter Ten

"Well, in that case, we don't need him. I was going to make him guest of honour, as a wedding present for you." McDowell drew his sword.

"No! Wait!" Colwyn screamed as McDowell placed the sword at Bodine's throat. "If you harm him, I will never marry you!" She was thinking desperately. They needed time; time for a rescue; time to plan; any time; as much time as she could muster; and she would get it for them.

McDowell glanced down at her and smiled. "That's better," he said, re-sheathing his sword and dragging her to her feet. He graciously removed his foot from Bodine's shoulder and gazed down at his unconscious form. Turning to his knights, he ordered, "Bring our guest of honour," before dragging Colwyn away.

Two knights pulled Bodine to his feet but his body remained limp, so between them, they dragged him to his horse and threw him over the saddle.

McDowell, holding Colwyn firmly by an arm, walked her to her horse and indicated for her to mount. Two knights were holding Storm's bridle to make sure she couldn't make a run for it. He glanced up at her face and saw the blood and slightly reddened cheek; his features hardened.

"Who did this to you?" he demanded of her. Colwyn remained quiet.

McDowell turned to face his men.

"Which one of you struck my intended?" His voice had risen slightly.

No one answered.

"If I find out which one of you it was… God help you! I ordered she was not to be harmed!" He turned to her. "My love, are you in pain?"

Colwyn just stared at him as if he were mad, not believing her ears.

"I asked you a question," he said, his voice sounding slightly menacing.

She almost said something exceedingly un-ladylike, but managed to stop herself.

"No," she finally said.

He nodded, briefly touching her knee before turning and walking towards his horse. Colwyn shuddered inwardly.

Once all the knights and McDowell were mounted, they left the ruins and started west towards Cottesmere. They managed to travel for a few more hours and then darkness began to fall, and it was decided to camp for the night.

Bodine was dragged off his horse and, tied securely to a tree, and at that point, it began to drizzle with rain. Colwyn dismounted, grabbed her water bag and went to Bodine. A guard moved to stop her but McDowell shook his head.

She knelt down by her intended. He appeared to be unconscious still, but she gently lifted his head and placed the water bag against his lips, allowing a trickle of the precious liquid to slip down his throat. Bodine coughed and screwed his eyes up at the pain the jarring inflicted; then his eyes slowly opened. His face was pale, and Colwyn knew he had lost a lot of blood. He needed more water and some food. As soon as her captors had some ready, she would ensure Bodine got some.

"Colwyn," his voice was barely a whisper.

"Shush, don't speak, drink," she whispered back, holding the water bag against his lips again.

He gratefully accepted the water offered, then let his head rest against the trunk of the tree.

"Y-you are unharmed?" he asked her.

"Yes," Colwyn confirmed. "I will do my utmost to buy us time to enable our rescuers to find us."

Bodine said nothing; he didn't want to destroy her optimism. Instead, he nodded.

"As soon as the food is ready, I will bring you some. You must eat. And I need to look at your shoulder."

Chapter Ten

He wanted to grab her hand and stop her, but his hands were tied behind his back; he was helpless. "Colwyn, don't worry about me, I'll be all right."

She placed a hand on his cheek and he moved his head to kiss the palm.

Taking a deep breath, she smiled reassuringly at him, stood up and went to speak to McDowell.

"Duke, I want you to untie Morgan. I need to check his shoulder."

McDowell looked over to where Bodine was bound. "He's fine," he responded.

"I do not want a dead guest of honour at my wedding!" she hissed. "You will permit me to attend to his wound… now. And I demand he is fed and treated with respect, as is due his rank."

"You demand?" McDowell's eyes narrowed. "You are in no position to demand anything."

"So, you are a knight under false pretence. You know nothing of honour or duty; and you are afraid of him, even in his weakened state!" she said in a raised voice as she glared at him and refused to back down, even though she expected him to strike her at any second as the anger appeared in his eyes.

"Afraid? Of him?" He laughed, but it was hollow, and Colwyn knew she had hit a nerve.

The next sentence she said loudly to ensure McDowell's men heard every word. "If you are not afraid, then surely, my Lord would not object to him being untied so he can eat and have his wound treated."

She had successfully manipulated him into a corner. If he left Bodine tied up, then it confirmed he was afraid of the Kadeau Duke, even in his present condition, and his men had heard every word of the conversation.

"Very well, you may untie him; but…" he grabbed her by an arm and held it tightly, "…no tricks."

Colwyn heaved a sigh of relief, jerked her arm free from McDowell's grasp and went back to her horse to look in the saddlebags. She found some clean cloth and went back to Bodine. Carefully and slowly, she withdrew the knife at her waist and cut the ropes that bound him to the tree, and then the ones around his wrists.

"Thank you," he said, carefully bringing his arms from behind his back and rubbing his wrists to get the circulation back into his hands.

"Can you stand at all? I need to get all this armour off again to check your shoulder."

"Colwyn, no."

"The bandage has been on too long; it needs changing, or it will fester. Please, Morgan."

There was a long pause, and then he grudgingly nodded his acquiescence.

Using the tree for support and with Colwyn on his right side, he struggled to his feet, alarmed at how weak he really was. He felt the bile rise as his surroundings spun, and he gripped her shoulder tightly, waiting for his equilibrium to settle into some semblance of normality.

As gently as possible, Colwyn removed all of his armour, and carefully eased the aketon off his shoulders. As she feared, it was heavily stained with blood, and the movement had opened the wound again. She had difficulty removing his shirt, but eventually, it was done. She had to do this in such a way as to hide the sheathed knife that he had strapped to his left arm. The meagre bandage on his wound was soaked. Using her knife, she cut it free and poured clean water on the front and back of his shoulder, before tearing her clean chemise into strips, using two to make a padded dressing and using more to tie them in place.

"Do you perchance have a clean shirt in your saddlebag?" she asked him, and he nodded.

She got up, went to his horse and retrieved the item of clothing, then returned and still carefully hiding the small knife, assisted him into it and the rest of his clothing and armour, and helped him sit down again.

Chapter Ten

The drizzle was getting harder and she observed he was shivering slightly, so she went and retrieved a blanket to help keep him dry.

"You are a remarkable woman," Bodine whispered in her ear, as she drew the blanket around him. "I will be honoured to have you as my wife."

She smiled at him, but before she could answer, one of McDowell's knights approached, two plates in his hand.

"Thank you, sir knight," Colwyn said quietly as she took them from him. "Eat, Morgan," she ordered, "or I will force-feed you."

Even in their desperate state, Bodine could not prevent a slight smile appearing on his lips at her words, but he did as he was told, and actually felt a little better having finally managed to get something into his stomach after over twenty-four hours.

Another knight approached with a blanket. "For you, my Lady," he said quietly, and suddenly Colwyn realised that not all of McDowell's men were totally on his side.

"Thank you," she said, smiling slightly at him.

He nodded somewhat nervously and made a hasty retreat.

Colwyn settled herself down next to Bodine and snuggled up to him, to offer him some body warmth. Loss of blood would make him feel colder, even though it was relatively warm despite the drizzle.

McDowell looked over at the two of them and scowled. He was obsessed with being in control of a situation. Bodine would pay with his life, eventually, but he wanted him to witness the marriage of his intended to him, and know he had lost before he had the duke murdered. He was debating whether to humiliate both his future wife and Bodine, by letting the General witness the final consummation that would confirm Colwyn as his; let the Duke hear her cries of passion as he took her, whilst he was helpless to do anything about it, then, McDowell decided, he would kill Bodine himself. That would be a very satisfying outcome of a situation that had existed for over five years. Bodine had humiliated and insulted him for the last time, and now, within a few days, he would pay the ultimate price. He smiled to himself. McDowell decided to be exceedingly generous. Let them enjoy their last few moments together; he would soon have all the time in the world.

By dawn the next morning, the Rossmere Guard were all mounted and on their way towards Belvoir. Two scouts were riding ahead, scouring the ground for hints of trails. All Rossmere horses had special marks on their shoes that left a distinctive impression in the ground. If Bodine had come this way, then they would see those unique tracks.

They came across one set that had come from the wood, heading north towards the ruins of the old monastery; at least, that's what it looked like. The horse had been moving at speed, indicated by the spacing of the tracks, and there were many other hoof prints. The two scouts looked at each other. A chase! Nodding to each other, one of them took off in the direction the tracks were heading, the other back to the Captain of the Guard, to provide him with an update.

Having delivered his message, a fresh scout was despatched. The Captain sent a small detail towards Rossmere; the rest headed north towards the ruins. By now, it was hoped the detail escorting the wounded and dead had reached Ellesmere. Little did they know that Dernley had survived his ordeal in the river, had beaten them there, and the King was already preparing to leave.

The first scout arrived at the ruins just before sunset, under a cloudy sky that finally delivered the rain as a fine drizzle, but there was still sufficient light to see that there were bodies, in the same livery as those who had attacked them, just outside and inside the walled entrance. The site was deserted now so he dismounted and inspected the corpses. He took a deep

Chapter Ten

breath and swallowed nervously, for in the ground were a set of Rossmere hoof prints with dried blood in and around them, slowly becoming damp with the falling drizzle. The tracks were heading towards Cottesmere. He could also see where someone had knelt on the ground, a smaller set of footprints, and where someone had been dragged.

The sound of approaching hooves made the scout get to his feet and draw his sword.

"Darian! It's Niall!" he heard a voice call, and immediately relaxed, as the horse and rider approached.

"I believe his Grace is wounded, but alive. Look here." He showed his companion the evidence on the ground.

Their faces were grim. There was quite a lot of blood and, on closer inspection, a trail of it led away from the ruins, confirming the direction towards Cottesmere.

"When will the guard get here?" Darian asked.

"About noon tomorrow, if they travel hard."

They made camp for the night, discussing a plan of action for the next day.

܀ ܀ ܀ ܀

The next morning was grey and it was still drizzling, which suited Colwyn's mood perfectly. They had at least another three days travelling before they reached Cottesmere. She had been trying to formulate an escape plan for Bodine and herself, but having checked on him that morning, she knew he was not in a fit state to try any form of escape. In fact, it was all he could do to stay in the saddle. By rights, he needed to rest, in a bed; give his shoulder some time to knit, to allow the bleeding to stop. She wished that Master Andrew were there with them, but he would be at Rossmere, expecting their arrival at some point today and totally unaware of what had happened. Colwyn didn't even have any needles and thread that could be used to close the wounds.

They covered a reasonable distance that day, but it was slower than McDowell wanted. Colwyn had purposely done whatever she could think of to slow their progress, from feigning illness and tiredness, to flatly refusing to go faster.

That night, in camp, Colwyn had once again seen to Bodine's wound, and ensured he had received food and water, but she knew he was getting weaker. The constant jarring stopped the wound from knitting at all.

"Is there anything I can do to help you?" she had asked him that evening.

"You must promise me that whatever happens to me, you will not marry McDowell. I will try to protect you from his dark magic, but I know I am getting weaker."

He saw the pained look in her eyes and loved her for it.

"Can you not take energy from me? I would give it freely, you know that."

He shook his head. "I will take nothing from you, even though I know you would give it freely if it would help me; but you will need all the strength you possess to keep McDowell out of your mind. You know he tried a couple of weeks ago. You fought him well; it was your first encounter of what he is capable of, and you were not properly prepared. Now you know what to expect, it should be easier for you to repel his attempt at control, but you must be on your guard constantly. That will take concentration and energy; so, I will not take anything from you that could put you in jeopardy."

Bodine closed his eyes, panting quite heavily, as he leant back against a convenient rock. He could feel the increased pounding of his blood through his veins, as his heart tried to compensate for the loss he had suffered. It was tempting to succumb to the blackness, but that was not in his makeup. He would protect his intended with the last breath of his body. Deep down, he

Chapter Ten

knew the situation was hopeless unless help did arrive; he would summon his strength and try and reach out to his cousin; tell him of their direction of travel; perhaps help was already on the way, but they were only just now overdue. His biggest regret was not having married Colwyn before they left Ellesmere; not to have known her in both body and soul. He forced his eyes open again.

"Colwyn, I want your word that you will not willingly marry McDowell; that you will do everything in your power to resist him. No matter what he does to me! Swear it, on my seal."

"I-I swear, Morgan," she said softly and kissed the ring on his finger that bore the dragon of Rossmere.

He nodded and closed his eyes again, and she bit her bottom lip with worry.

Bodine cleared his mind and attempted to slow his breathing down as he reached out with his mind. *Colin... Colin...*

There was silence for a number of seconds, and then he felt a warmth flood into his mind.

Morgan? I can hardly hear you...

Colin, I haven't much time... McDowell has us... we're heading to Cottesmere. I... am wounded... I don't know how much longer I can hang on... tell the King... it has... been...

Bodine felt himself slipping away from consciousness.

Morgan! McLeod was shouting into his mind, but he didn't have the strength to respond. *Morgan! Hang on! We're coming for you! Morgan....*

Colwyn suddenly stiffened as she felt Bodine go limp beside her. Suddenly terrified, she turned and placed a hand just beneath his nose and felt the slightest warm breath caress her fingers. He was still breathing—just—but she grew very concerned when she saw the rapid pulse at his throat.

Desperate, she gripped his hand and willed her strength into him. *Morgan, please, don't die on me! Take some strength from me, enough to keep living! I can do this for you!*

A few minutes passed, and then she saw his breathing deepen slightly, and closed her eyes in relief. He needed to rest, to stay in one place without movement; how was she going to make that happen? Feign illness? Delay tactics? Anything she could think of.

She hurried to get her cloak and a couple of blankets, then called one of the knights over.

"Please, help me," she said, putting on her best, pleading expression. "I need to get the duke flat on the ground. He is unconscious."

The knight hesitated, then did as she asked. Colwyn placed the folded cloak beneath Bodine's head and covered him with the blankets. McDowell approached, wanting to know what was happening.

"He's dying, damn you!" Colwyn screamed at him, fury written in her beautiful features.

McDowell stood still. He didn't want Bodine to die out here; he wanted him to live to see him lose his bride. They still had two days travelling before they reached Cottesmere. "We will make room for him in the food wagon," he said. "I don't want him to die… yet."

"Is your battle surgeon here?" Colwyn asked.

"No, he's not."

Colwyn's heart fell. It was up to Bodine to fight for his life, but at least in the wagon, he may not suffer as much jarring. She got up and went to the food wagon to inspect it, then went and collected any spare blankets to make as soft a bed as she could for him for tomorrow's journey.

Once again, food was made available, and Colwyn took a large plate with her to feed Bodine. His eyelids flickered as she knelt down by his side.

"Morgan?" Her voice was gentle, yet persuasive.

Chapter Ten

His eyes slowly opened.

"I have some food for you."

He shook his head.

"You can, and you will eat," Colwyn ordered. "You need food to regain your strength. I thought I'd lost you earlier; you were hardly breathing."

His eyes surveyed his immediate surroundings; they were alone, and he whispered, "I-I was making contact with Colin. Help is… on the way."

Colwyn's eyes lit up at this news. "Then you must eat." She helped him sit up, pausing part of the way as she felt him falter; then, satisfied he was comfortable, she practically force-fed him, ensuring Bodine ate the larger amount of the food. The Kadeau Duke had to admit, it did make him feel a little better, but it was wrong. He was supposed to be taking care of his bride, not the other way around.

ઝ ଓ ઝ ଓ

11

Chapter Eleven

As the King and his army were about to leave Ellesmere, the wounded and dead of the Rossmere Guard arrived at the castle.

"My Liege! Rossmere Guard! On the final approach!" a breathless soldier announced as he arrived at a run from the battlements.

"How many?" Stuart demanded.

"Not the full guard, sire… it looks like the wounded and… the dead."

The King delayed his departure until he had received a report from them. He hid his worry well as they reported they had no news of Bodine or Colwyn, but that the rest of the guard were now trailing them and trying to catch up.

Ordering his staff to take care of the wounded and dead, they then left the castle.

The King had split his force and sent one by the Low Road towards Rossmere. This group had both the Queen and Princess Anne in it, and he had made it clear that they were to head straight for Belvoir and make no detours. The other half of the force headed for the narrow pass at the base of the High Hills, making good time. It was overcast, and the threat of rain hung in the air. The tops of the High Hills were obscured by low cloud and it looked like it was already raining on the higher ground.

Chapter Eleven

It was eerily quiet in the gorge, apart from the sound of hooves and the jangling of metal on metal. As they rounded a bend, they beheld the sight of the battle, with several bodies, including one of a dead horse, still lying where they had fallen. Several other horses were just milling around, not sure what to do.

Stuart indicated for them to halt as he surveyed the scene before him. His Captain of the Guard dismounted, and with a couple of other knights, inspected the bodies.

"Any identification on the bodies?"

"None, Sire. They are dressed the same as those we found at Inver."

"Very well. Round up those loose horses; we'll use them to transport the bodies so that the pass remains clear."

A small number of men were left to clear up, whilst the remainder moved on, knowing they were now involved in a rescue mission.

At the far end of the pass, the scouts came forward and examined the ground. It was littered with hoof prints going in several directions. Stuart dispatched two teams, one towards Rossmere, the other north towards the ruins. He had decided if McDowell had indeed captured his General and his bride, they would be heading towards Cottesmere. If his scouts did not find anything, they were to make all haste back to the main group heading for McDowell's stronghold.

They made reasonable progress and decided to camp in the woods. A fine drizzle had started, but the trees offered some protection.

The scouting party that had travelled to the ruins, returned around midnight, reporting there had been some kind of skirmish, for there were four bodies and a blood trail leading away, but they'd lost it in the darkness. There was more than one set of Rossmere hoof prints, two of which were newer and they concluded these belonged to the Rossmere scouts. They had buried the dead before leaving.

Stuart's expression was grim. A blood trail… was it Bodine's? He looked towards the trees and saw McLeod disappearing, and assumed he was going to try and contact his cousin again.

The King simply nodded and ordered the party to get some food and rest, whilst he turned on his heel and followed the Monsignor into the trees. He spotted him a little way in the distance, by a large oak tree; then saw him stagger and lean against the trunk for support. Concerned, he hastened towards him, stopping just short when he heard McLeod gasp.

"Morgan! Morgan! Answer me!" His voice sounded desperate, as he clenched his fists.

Stuart placed a hand on his shoulder, making him jump. "Colin?" he questioned.

McLeod straightened up slowly and turned to face him. It was dark, but not pitch black. The sun did not set completely at this time of year, and the King could see that the priest's face had gone white.

"Tell me," Stuart ordered.

"Morgan is… wounded," McLeod began. "He… he doesn't sound too good. I think he's just lost consciousness; at least I… hope… he's lost consciousness and not…" he couldn't finish the sentence.

"Any clues as to how far behind we are?"

"A day, maybe two. He has confirmed that it is McDowell who has him."

"And Colwyn?"

"I believe she is unharmed. Sire… Morgan really didn't sound good, and has asked me to tell you that… it has been a privilege for him to… have served…" He stopped as he saw the stricken look cross the King's handsome features.

ଔ ଊ ଔ ଊ

Chapter Eleven

They all had a comfortable night, and Bodine did feel a little stronger the following morning, but Colwyn instructed him to play on his weakness, and he was carried and placed in the food wagon.

Colwyn rode Storm behind the wagon, so she could keep an eye on Bodine, who was able to doze for most of the travelling time. Consequently, when they stopped again for the final evening out before reaching Cottesmere, he was feeling a little stronger, although he still decided to play on his injury. Resting in the food wagon was working, and he needed to regain strength to try and protect Colwyn from any mental attack McDowell may try.

Settled again for the evening, Colwyn smiled at her intended. "You have a little more colour in you this evening," she whispered.

"The ride in the wagon has helped a great deal."

"Then we must ensure you ride in it again tomorrow."

Bodine wanted an update from his cousin, so he could formulate a possible plan going forward.

Colin, are you there?

A number of seconds passed.

Morgan, thank God! How are you?

A little better; I rode in the food wagon today, so managed to get some rest. How far away are you?

I believe we're just a day behind you, maybe less. The King has ridden long and hard. Have faith. Where are you?

We arrive in Cottesmere tomorrow. I believe McDowell is planning the wedding for the day after.

We will get there and stop it.

I will do what I can to delay things, as will Colwyn. God's speed, Colin.

Don't do anything stupid, Morgan. We will get to you.

The connection was broken and Bodine sighed.

"Morgan?" Colwyn queried.

"Help is on the way. The King is about a day behind."

"That close? That's good news. I will delay as much as I can."

"Do not antagonise McDowell, my love."

"I will be careful." She looked around, surveying McDowell and the rest of his knights. They all seemed intent on other things, so she leant forward and gently kissed Bodine. "We will win this battle," she whispered.

"You are formidable," Bodine whispered back, grasping her hand and raising to his lips.

"I am inspired by my husband to be," she answered, smiling.

"Be wary of McDowell. No doubt, once we are at Cottesmere, he will try and force his will upon you. I will do what I can, but you must practise building the barriers in your mind."

"I have my knife still hidden," she responded.

"Use it, if you must, to protect yourself."

03 80 03 80

Stuart's party caught up with the Rossmere Guard the following day, just north of the ruins, and they joined forces and continued towards Cottesmere. The Captain of the Guard told the King he still had a scout up ahead, and that they hoped to catch up with him by tomorrow night. They camped for the night, hopeful that tomorrow would bring good news.

The next day, Darian had continued to follow the trail and stopped at the camp the kidnappers had made a day or so before. Evidence of a campfire had been left, as if to tease and show the pursuers they were at least one step behind.

In the campfire, he found traces of burnt cloth, and a remnant that had not perished, heavily stained with blood. He found traces of more blood by a tree, but thankfully no trace of a body. His Lord had to still be alive. He

Chapter Eleven

picked up the evidence and examined it closely. The material was fine and of high quality, and he suspected it was from a woman's chemise: her Grace. Had she attempted to tend his wounds?

Darian re-set and lit the fire. It was dark when he heard the jangle of metal and hoofbeats. Taking a deep breath, he drew his sword in readiness. One man on foot against a group on horseback was not going to be a fair fight, but he stood his ground.

As they got closer, he called out. "Halt! Who goes there?" he shouted firmly.

"The army of King Stuart Cantrell and the Rossmere Guard!" a familiar voice shouted back.

"Giles? Is that you?"

"Yes! Is that Darian?"

"Giles, we saw you go over and assumed you'd been drowned! Approach in safety!"

The hooves and jangling got closer, and then, in the dimness, horses and riders appeared. Darian could just about see the rampant red lion on the King's surcoat, Prince Michael's white unicorn, a Rossmere gold dragon and the griffon of Strathmere, and suddenly, they were all standing in front of the knight.

Darian dropped to a knee as the King approached.

"Sire," he said respectfully.

"Arise, Sir Darian …?"

"I am Sir Darian Forsythe, my Liege. I was scouting ahead for Rossmere's Captain of the Guard."

Stuart signalled for his men to make camp, then dismounted and indicated for Darian to continue his briefing.

"We saw evidence of the battle in the gorge," Stuart informed the knight. "Wounded and dead Rossmere knights arrived at Ellesmere just as we were leaving. Sir Giles managed to drag himself out of the river and get back to the castle to inform us what had happened."

"I found this in the abandoned campfire when I arrived here this evening." He handed over the bloodstained material. "I believe the duke was tied to that tree over there, as there is more blood there, but he must still be alive; there is no body or grave, Sire."

The King nodded solemnly, digesting the information.

As food was prepared, McLeod took himself off again to try and make contact with his cousin, but Bodine beat him to it. The relief was almost overwhelming as he realised he was still alive, and actually sounding a little better, and he returned to the King, looking a little happier.

The two conversed quietly as McLeod updated him on the situation as he understood it. However, they were still two days behind McDowell. They would need to travel harder and faster tomorrow, so Stuart ordered everyone to eat, look after the horses, and rest, as the next few days were going to be very hard going.

The evening passed without incident, and the next day, Bodine was again transported in the wagon.

They arrived late in the evening the following day in the capital of Cottesmere. McDowell escorted Colwyn firmly by an arm into the keep, up a set of tower stairs and into a room, leaving her there and locking the door behind him.

Bodine was dragged from the wagon and down into a dungeon. The knights were not particularly gentle, and jarred his left shoulder as they forced his arm to move more than it was currently able to.

Chapter Eleven

McDowell summoned an old woman who lived in one of the lower rooms in the keep. To all intents and purposes, she was a witch and followed the old Kadeau ways. She arrived a few minutes later.

"You know what I want to know," he said to her. "When will she be ready?"

"I will need to take some blood for the ritual," the old woman replied.

McDowell nodded and unlocked the door again, allowing the woman to precede him.

Colwyn whirled as they entered.

"My dear, we just need to take something from you," McDowell said, approaching her.

Colwyn retreated away from him, until she was against the far wall with nowhere to go.

"Give me your hand."

"No!"

"I said, give me your hand!"

Colwyn put her hands behind her back, and tried to duck past him as he reached her, but he anticipated her move and managed to grab her right arm. He pulled out his knife and sliced her hand, making her cry out in shock, and held it as the old woman pulled a bottle from the pouch slung around her neck and caught a good sample of blood in it.

Satisfied, the old woman put the stopper back in the bottle and left the room. McDowell let go of Colwyn's hand. She immediately grabbed a cloth off the small table and wrapped it around her hand, which had started to throb.

"Thank you for your cooperation," McDowell said, reaching out to touch her face.

Colwyn jerked her head back away from him.

"Soon, you will know what it is liked to be kissed by a real man," he said suggestively. "Perhaps you should have a sample now?"

He stepped forward, pinned her against the wall, and kissed her hard.

There was no love, no tenderness; just an arrogant power. Colwyn fought him with every ounce of strength in her body, and then somehow, managed to bite his lip, drawing blood.

McDowell swore, let her go, stepped back, and struck her, making her cry out and fall, at the force of the blow.

The duke wiped the blood from his lip and glared down at her. "You will learn obedience, my love, or you will receive more of the same," he hissed.

Colwyn shook her head and looked up at him, glad she had inflicted an injury, her expression full of defiance.

"I'm now going to pay a visit to your Champion and make sure he is… comfortable. Would you like me to give him a message from you? How he is treated will rely heavily on your behaviour."

The threat was clear, and Colwyn was aware of the colour leaving her face. Would her action now result in further injury being inflicted on Bodine? She watched McDowell leave the room but stayed where she was on the floor, nursing her bleeding hand.

On his way down to the dungeon, McDowell stopped to see the old woman. "What news do you have for me?" he demanded of her.

"If you will join me, I am about to check."

He watched as she poured the blood into a small bowl that held some animal bones, then added various potions to it, and let it burn on a small fire. Pale blue smoke rose from the bowl and she nodded in satisfaction.

"She is not yet ripe. The colour of the smoke indicates she will be ready in two days. Bed her at that time; she will be with child, and you will have your heir."

"Thank you. That is excellent news."

Chapter Eleven

With that, he turned and left to continue his journey to the dungeons, and to Bodine.

The key turned in the lock and the door opened to admit McDowell into the dungeon. Bodine heaved himself to his feet and faced his adversary. He had sensed Colwyn's pain and revulsion, but she had shielded what had happened to her from him. He did, however, take note of the cut lip the Cottesmere Duke was nursing and wondered if she had inflicted some kind of wound.

"Still alive then, Bodine. You will have pride of place at my wedding the day after tomorrow. I also thought I would do you the honour of letting you witness the consummation afterwards. My new wife will be with child and I will have my heir."

Bodine couldn't stop himself and stepped forward. The two men were around the same height; Bodine perhaps an inch taller. His bearing was more noble; his aura powerful, and it unnerved the Cottesmere Duke.

"I do not like your insolent manner, Bodine," he said to his prisoner.

"I don't care what you don't like, McDowell, you will not touch Colwyn. If you do, I will kill you."

McDowell laughed delightedly. "Oh, I'd like to see you try."

"Is that a challenge?" Bodine retorted.

"Take it how you like," McDowell countered.

Bodine needed no second bidding and before McDowell could even blink, the Kadeau had extracted the knife hidden up the sleeve of his shirt and attacked the Cottesmere Duke.

Adrenaline gave Bodine the strength to make a frenzied attack on his opponent, but he only had one good arm; McDowell had two. Bodine put up a good fight, but he was severely handicapped and still weak from the loss of blood. He had managed to knock McDowell to the floor and pin him down with his body. The knife was raised, but as he attempted to plunge it into his chest, McDowell managed to free an arm and punched Bodine in his left shoulder.

The pain was excruciating but the Kadeau fought on, the knife getting closer to McDowell's chest, until the noise attracted the guards and they dragged the two men apart.

McDowell was livid. "Strip him of his armour!" he shouted, nursing a cut cheek. "You'll wish you were dead by the time I've finished with you, Bodine!" He stormed out of the room, and another couple of guards looked up. "You have my permission to… entertain our guest; but he must be alive for the wedding in two days; do I make myself clear?"

"Yes, your Grace," they responded, their eyes lighting up at the prospect of torturing the Duke of Rossmere.

12

Chapter Twelve

Colwyn was confined to the room at the top of the keep tower, seeing no one apart from at mealtimes. She had tried unsuccessfully to reach out with her mind and contact Bodine, to see how he was faring, and she became concerned at the lack of contact. The delicate tendril of the link was painfully absent from her mind, and, to her, that could mean only one thing; he was shielding her, but from what?

Her blood ran cold as a thought entered her head… they were torturing him; that had to be it. She would demand to see him the next time someone came to her room. McDowell was determined that he was to be the guest of honour at the wedding, so he had to be alive still, but she needed the reassurance that he was.

Her request had fallen on deaf ears when she had made her demand of the guard who brought her breakfast.

McDowell turned up a couple of hours later and presented her with a wedding dress.

"You will wear it."

"I'm not putting it on until I have seen the Duke of Rossmere," she snapped back, eyeing the vivid cut on his cheek.

"You will see him in the cathedral at the ceremony and not before," he answered.

"That's not good enough. I want to see him now! What's been happening?"

"He's has been... entertaining my men," came the cool response.

"You... monster! I want to see him! I demand to see him!"

McDowell advanced on her and struck her sharply.

"How dare you make any demand of me! You will wear that dress for the wedding ceremony!"

"Never!"

"If you don't, I swear to you, you will walk down the aisle naked!"

"I don't care!" she screamed at him.

He grabbed her right hand, making her cry out as he caused it to start bleeding again.

"Very well... if you don't put that dress on, I will slit your lover's throat... slowly, and you will watch him choke on his own blood."

Colwyn was aware of the colour draining from her face.

"Are you going to wear that dress for our wedding ceremony?" McDowell asked her again.

She said nothing.

"Guard!" McDowell shouted.

One of his soldiers appeared in the doorway.

"I want you to go down to the dungeon and—"

"All right!" Colwyn interrupted. "I'll wear it, but you must not touch Morgan. You must promise me you will let him live."

"Very well. He will be waiting in the cathedral when you arrive. Now, I will leave you, as I too must make preparations for our glorious union."

With that, he turned and left, once again locking the door behind him.

Chapter Twelve

Colwyn went to the table to re-wrap her hand, and looked at the dress with hatred, shuddering at the thought of having to prepare for the dreaded wedding.

ಚಿ ಶಿ ಚಿ ಶಿ

Down in the dungeon, the guards had removed Bodine's armour, leaving him in his breeches and silk shirt. The sharp movements had sent waves of pain through his shoulder and he was barely conscious by the time they had finished. Two of them dragged him roughly to his feet and another threw some water in his face to revive him.

The duke coughed as some of the water found its way into his mouth. He grimaced, and, breathing heavily, forced his eyes open, but he couldn't see straight initially, and both the room and his assailants seemed to be spinning in front of him, making him feel nauseous. One of them was talking to him, but he hadn't heard a word, and for his sins, his ribs received a blow from a blunt object which seemed to help clear his vision.

"The great Duke of Rossmere… Morgan Bodine, King's Champion and General of his Armies," one of them said, placing a hand under his chin and lifting his head to take a closer look at the handsome features of his prisoner. "The most feared man in the Kingdom of Devonmere. You don't seem that frightening to me."

His comrades laughed.

Bodine said nothing but simply stared unblinkingly at him, his eyes almost transparent in their challenging, yet regal expression.

The guard stepped back, suddenly unsure. "I don't like the way you're looking at me, Kadeau," he said. His voice shook slightly as he surveyed the intense gaze, and the look on his face gradually lost all expression as Bodine attempted to gain control of his mind.

The guard's eyes dropped, surveying the sword at his side, and slowly, his hand fastened around the hilt and began to remove it from its sheath.

"What are you doing, Thatcher?" One of the men holding Bodine asked. "His Grace said the Kadeau had to be alive for the wedding."

Thatcher did not reply, but brought his sword up in front of the duke and raised his eyes to meet those of his prisoner again. Without warning, the sword suddenly plunged into the chest of the guard on Bodine's left.

Making the most of the opportunity, Bodine wrenched himself free from the other guard's grip, pulling his sword out of the sheath as the wounded man fell, and turned, striking the other one down. Somehow, he forced his left hand to grab the other sword as well.

More guards appeared, and Thatcher, still under his control, rallied round on the new foes.

"What the…" one of the guards muttered, then realised what was happening. "Get Bodine! Knock him out! He's got control of Thatcher!"

Six of them… on any normal day, Bodine could handle six; he had done it before, but today, he only had one good sword arm. He was not going to let that stop him trying for he had one advantage; they couldn't harm him too badly as he had to attend the wedding ceremony.

Attempting to keep control of someone whilst fending off his attackers was something he had never tried before, and he knew he couldn't do it for very long, so he made the most of his unwilling ally to take on three of his opponents whilst he took on the other three.

Bodine tried not to use his left arm at all, and when he did, he tried to make sure his right helped, so the severity of the blows was reduced; however, his wound was bleeding again, and the blood running down his arm, into his hand, was making his grip slip on the hilt of the sword. A well-aimed attack from a guard managed to knock it out of his hand and they started to beat

Chapter Twelve

him back towards the door. It was a possible escape, and he continued to keep them relatively at bay as he stepped back.

It was fierce, but with his unwilling ally to assist, he was holding his own, then, too late, he became aware of a presence creeping up behind him, and as he partially turned to gauge the danger, something hard connected with his head and he fell to the ground. He was just about conscious as he heard McDowell's voice seemingly sounding a long way away.

"You fools! He nearly got the better of all of you! I see I can't trust you to do anything!" The voice sounded exceedingly angry.

Bodine attempted to drag himself onto his hands and knees, ignoring the ringing in his head from the blow. He had just about managed it when a booted foot connected with his ribs once, twice, and the third time, and flipped him over onto his back. Winded, he lay gasping as McDowell leant over and grabbed him by the front of his shirt to lift his head and shoulders off the ground. Bodine struggled to open his eyes, just in time to see a fist approaching, then, thankfully, knew no more.

"Take him back to his cell. I'll send word when I want you to bring him to the cathedral. Make sure he's conscious and can walk."

"Yes, your Grace."

The guards grabbed hold of Bodine and dragged him roughly back to his cell, dumping him on the straw mattress in the corner before leaving and locking the door behind them.

ଓ ଓ ଓ ଓ

The whole ceremony would be a mockery of the church as far as Colwyn was concerned. Bodine had made her promise not to go through with it, no matter what they did to him, but the thought of her being the cause of any pain to the handsome nobleman was seriously making her consider whether to break that promise, even though she was officially engaged to him and had sworn her promise on the seal emblazoned on his ring.

Nigel McDowell had promised her he would spare the Kadeau's life if she co-operated and had left the decision to her. Life or death, what was it to be? It seemed an obvious choice until she remembered the hideous atrocities that had been inflicted on the Kadeau in the past: beaten, crippled, blinded, tortured, branded and worse. Would that be life? If so, Bodine wouldn't want it. Better to be dead than a mere travesty of a man. And what of Giles? The sight of him and his mount falling down the bank into the wild river haunted her mind. Giles, whom she had known practically all her life and who was devoted to her. Colwyn stifled a sob of despair.

No! Nigel McDowell was treacherous and evil! He would twist his promise and make it worthless. He had no real regard for anyone or anything—except his own evil ambitions—and she would not be a part of them.

Dejected, she had reluctantly prepared herself and donned the horrid wedding dress, and now stood, staring out of the narrow window, hoping that help would arrive before it was too late. Was Giles dead? Or had he managed to survive the river and get to Ellesmere? Bodine had said he had made contact with his cousin and that help was on the way. They were supposed to be just a day behind, and yet two days had passed. Only time would tell, and it was running out fast.

The heavy door to her tower prison was unbolted and swung open slowly to admit Nigel McDowell, who walked in arrogantly.

"My dear, you look ravishing! You'll be pleased to know, my bishop has arrived at last; the ceremony can now go ahead. I just have some last-minute errands to run, but the guards will escort you to the cathedral shortly."

Colwyn made no reply or sign to this statement, but continued to stare out of the window.

Chapter Twelve

"When we are wed, our two Duchies will pose a serious threat to Ellesmere. Who knows, you may even be Queen of Devonmere."

Colwyn whirled and faced him. "That is treason! I will have no part in such a plan!"

McDowell strode over, grabbed her roughly by the shoulders and shook her hard.

"As my wife, you'll do as I say!"

"I'll never be your wife!" she spat back at him.

"If you'll not be mine, then you'll not be anybody's! Bodine certainly wouldn't want you after I've finished with you… but there again, I doubt if anyone would want him either, after I've finished with him."

"W-what do you mean?"

"Don't worry your pretty little head about it. Our wedding will take place. I need your lands and your army and I shall have them. You will provide me with an heir, then I shall claim the Duchy of Rossmere. Others shall join me and Stuart will be overthrown." He paused and studied her features for a moment. "Poor Bodine, such a price to pay for loving a woman he cannot have…"

She refused to respond to the taunt, but simply held herself rigid and unyielding, on her guard against him, for the Duke of Cottesmere, although not Kadeau, dabbled in the occult arts and was able to display some considerable powers. Colwyn was not about to let herself fall under a spell that would make her docile and pliable to his will. But his words chilled her to the bone. She would be his wife no matter what words were spoken, and Bodine… She clamped down on her thoughts. All was not lost… yet.

"My bride, you'll come round to my way of thinking." His grip on her altered. Colwyn turned her head aside quickly to prevent him from kissing her. She seriously expected him to force himself upon her, but he laughed instead. "I do like spirit and I can be a patient man; but tonight, my love, I shall have things my way." He pressed against her momentarily, a hand squeezing her breast before drifting down her body to between her thighs to enforce his innuendo, then turned and left, leaving Colwyn flushed with embarrassment and shame.

She barely had time to recover her composure before the door opened again and two guards marched in.

"We have been sent to escort you down to the cathedral, my Lady," one said in a gruff voice.

Colwyn said nothing but simply moved very slowly towards the door, holding herself with dignity and grace. She refused to go kicking and screaming, but she would move at her own pace, and, at the ceremony, would answer each question as Bodine had instructed.

It took a long while to reach the cathedral. Colwyn refused to be hurried, and she hoped that if help was on the way, it had enabled them to get closer.

She paused at the entry to the cathedral and shivered. It was cold, almost damp and dim, reflecting her mood perfectly. She tried to ignore the crowd that had gathered in the pews to witness the wedding, but the sadness welled up. Her heart grew heavier with every step. Briefly, she thought of trying to escape, but there were guards at strategic points all around the nave; she would never get past them all, and, most importantly, she would never leave Bodine alone as a prisoner of the duke. There seemed no way out.

At the altar stood Bishop Malcolm Talbot, complete with colourful vestments that looked incongruous in the sombre surroundings. There were no flowers, no decorations, no rose petals covering the cathedral aisle, and it was drizzling outside. It was as if the sky was weeping at what was about to happen. Nigel McDowell also stood there, resplendent in finery, causing Colwyn to glance down at the gown she was dressed in. The material matched that of his wedding attire.

Chapter Twelve

As she passed the rows of seats, the one or two monks who were present crossed themselves and offered prayers on her behalf.

Her eyes drifted to the left and she almost stopped dead in her tracks, for there stood Bodine, hands bound behind him, with two burly guards, one on either side. As yet, she could not see his face, but the long, burnished gold hair immediately gave him away. He seemed to be standing awkwardly and Colwyn suspected he had been further injured, probably severely beaten and perhaps even tortured.

Forcing herself to keep to the slow, steady pace, she gradually covered the remaining distance until she drew level with Bodine, then she stopped and turned to face him, her green eyes huge and filled with anguish.

"You can see your Lord is not so pretty now, is he? I'm afraid my guards got rather carried away with their work," Nigel stated conversationally.

Yes, Bodine had been severely beaten. His left eye was almost closed, there was a bad cut across the top of his left eyebrow that left a trail of blood down his face and his bottom lip was swollen. There were probably even more injuries hidden under the sodden black silk shirt. He was standing unaided, no doubt on sheer willpower, his grey unfocused eyes staring straight ahead.

Deliberately, Colwyn moved to stand in front of the Kadeau Lord. Her escort went to drag her away, but McDowell signalled them to leave her be.

Gently, she placed a hand on the sodden shirt and felt him shudder slightly under her touch.

"Morgan?" she whispered, trying to reach him.

His eyes slowly focused and lowered to meet hers.

"C-Colwyn," he replied painfully, his breathing ragged. "Re-remember your vow."

It wasn't fair! If only Bodine could help himself, but he'd overtaxed his powers already. He needed help, but there was no one save herself and she...

Colwyn stopped and wondered. Was it possible? She had tried to heal him in that thicket in the woods, but the pain had been overpowering and she'd been forced to stop. Could she have some semblance of power? It was true that Giles's stallion had regained his soundness from an injury that should have left him lame for life, but that had been because she had spent a lot of time tending the horse and gently massaging the tendon, hadn't it? But perhaps it hadn't been torn and only damaged. Doubt riddled her thoughts.

Uncertain, she reached out with her mind, trying to access the extent of Bodine's injuries and was appalled by her discovery; bruises, a couple of broken ribs and the original bad shoulder wound, which she found was bleeding again when she removed her hand from his shirt and found her bandaged palm soaked with blood.

Horrified, she turned to McDowell. "W-what have you done to him?!"

"Nothing compared to what's coming."

"You said you'd let him be!"

"On the contrary, I said I would let him live. I said nothing about the condition he would be in. Now enough; I grow tired of your concern for the Kadeau. Let the ceremony begin."

Colwyn ignored him and returned her attention to Bodine. She placed both hands on his chest and closed her eyes, allowing her mind to drift along, searching for the wounds. His pain assaulted her mind, but this time she was prepared for it and battled on. By comparing unbroken ribs, she saw how they should lie and concentrated on bringing the broken ones into line and repairing the damage. She had never done anything like this before and hoped she would not make things worse.

The power required was far more than she realised and because her eyes were closed, she was not aware of the beginnings of a golden glow around her hands. In the distance, she heard Bodine's breath hiss from between clenched teeth as the first rib began to straighten itself out.

Chapter Twelve

"My Lord!" That was one of the guards. He had a perfect view of the proceedings, unlike McDowell, and realised something was going on. Nigel moved and saw for the first time what was really happening.

His anger got the better of him. Viciously, he pulled Colwyn away, thinking it was Bodine who was performing the magic. Colwyn was favoured by the Queen, who hated Kadeau. This implied his intended bride was human and unable to perform anything like this, and her ancestry gave no indication of Kadeau bloodlines.

The separation was like a physical blow. Bodine cried out in pain and Colwyn screamed and fell to the floor.

McDowell whirled on the barely conscious Bodine. "You vile degenerate! I'll see you burn for this, so help me! Using the woman to save yourself!" He struck out, nearly felling his prisoner, but Bodine refused to fall.

"No, no, please stop!" Colwyn grabbed McDowell's cloak. "I beg you, please!"

McDowell turned and dragged her to her feet. "You will forget this man, I order it! Oh, I shall make sure you can think of only me, my pet!" Roughly, he tried to kiss her and Colwyn struggled desperately.

Bodine couldn't prevent himself from taking a step forward, but a guard prodded him cruelly with the hilt of his sword and he dropped to his knees, gasping in agony.

The other guard grasped his hair and pulled his head back sharply.

"Know thy place, Kadeau!" he spat.

Regaining his composure, McDowell dragged Colwyn to the altar and ordered the bishop to begin the ceremony.

Colwyn glanced over her left shoulder, her emerald eyes huge and bright with tears as she fixed her gaze on her beloved Morgan. Bodine, in turn, fixed her with a stare of his own, deep and unblinking. In her mind, all Colwyn could hear were the words: *'remember your vow'*.

Morgan had all but exhausted his reserves. He knew in his heart that McDowell would wed Colwyn no matter what, but he kept within him that spark of hope.

The bishop's voice quavered as he began the ceremony. Colwyn noticed how it shook. Malcolm Talbot knew this went against every teaching of the church and against every vow made by a knight.

Nigel made his first response. "I do."

The bishop then addressed Colwyn. "Colwyn Eilwen Anghared Coltrane, Duchess of Invermere, wilt thou taketh Nigel, here present, to thy lawful husband according to our Holy Mother, the Church?"

"No!" she replied firmly. "No, I won't. Never!" She glared at the bishop, disdain clearly evident in her eyes, then turned her flaming green eyes on Nigel, whose lips tightened into a thin line.

"Are you quite sure, my love?" he whispered menacingly, at the same time sending a slight nod in the direction of the guards who held Morgan.

Colwyn's fiery gaze turned to one of anguish as she heard Morgan cry out in pain. A sob forced its way past her lips.

Morgan's agonised voice burned into her brain in a last desperate attempt to make her keep her resolve.

Colwyn's hand went to her head in pain and then in a desperate flash of inspiration she used it to full advantage. "N-no-o-o-o!" she screamed and collapsed in a very convincing faint. Time; they so desperately needed time, so she would buy it for them.

"My Lord," Bishop Talbot implored. "We cannot proceed—" He stopped as Nigel fixed him with a wild stare.

"Revive her! Now!" he spat.

The bishop indicated to two monks sitting nearby. Very nervously, they approached the prone figure of Colwyn and attempted to revive her, patting and rubbing her cold hands, but without success.

Chapter Twelve

Nigel grew more impatient with every passing second. "She is pretending!" he screamed and pushed the monks out of the way, so he could reach down and shake her roughly, but she refused to respond. "Get my battle surgeon!"

Colwyn had heard every word but continued to act. It was all valuable time; with every passing second, help could be galloping closer. She heard footfalls and assumed they belonged to the battle surgeon. He would be carrying salts and she would have to revive, for it was too pungent a smell to ignore.

"Donald, my bride has ... fainted. Revive her."

"Yes, my Lord." He knelt down at Colwyn's side and looked at the pale features. He took her hand; it was very cold to the touch. "My Lord.... she—"

"Do it!"

With one hand, Donald gently lifted her head and wafted the evil-smelling salts under her nose. Her reaction was almost instantaneous, making her eyes water and a tickle rise in her throat. Desperately, she clawed at him trying to push the salts away. Satisfied, Donald removed the offending bottle and stoppered it.

Colwyn's eyes opened and she blinked several times to get rid of the stinging sensation caused by the salts.

"Now, my dear, how are you feeling?" Donald's tone was soft, his expression sorrowful. Maybe he did not approve of his master's actions.

"W-what happened?" she asked weakly, secretly proud of her performance.

"It appears you fainted. Come, sit now." He helped her rise to a sitting position and then, after a few minutes, to stand.

"Let the ceremony continue."

"My Lord, your bride has declined—"

"I said continue!"

"Who giveth this woman in marriage?" Talbot asked.

No one moved. Nigel motioned to Donald.

"I-I do," Donald stuttered and attempted to place Colwyn's right hand in the bishop's but found he was having great difficulty, for Colwyn was fighting him every step of the way. It took another guard to hold her hand whilst it was bound to Nigel's.

"Repeat after me," Talbot said. "I, Nigel, take thee, Colwyn…"

"I Nigel, take thee, Colwyn."

"As my lawful wedded wife."

"As my lawful wedded wife." Nigel fixed Colwyn with an intense gaze as he repeated the ancient chant, his eyes glittering brightly, and too late, Colwyn realised what was happening. Bound to him by her right hand, it had given Nigel the continued contact he needed to administer some of his black arts.

Suddenly, her limbs were made of lead and she could not move, but stood placidly waiting. One part of her mind was being instructed to repeat the words, but in a small corner, a very faint voice was whispering '*no*'.

Bishop Talbot knew instantly that something had happened, for Colwyn's expression was blank, and she looked drugged.

"I, Colwyn, take thee, Nigel," prompted Talbot.

Nothing was forthcoming.

Repeat it! A voice boomed in her head.

"I-I-I, C-Colwyn… t-t-take thee…." A word was formed but no sound came. "T-take thee…"

Nigel tried harder, but Bodine was more skilled and used his final reserves to break through.

Colwyn blinked slowly and started again. "I, Colwyn, take thee, Morgan—"

Chapter Twelve

"No!" Nigel wrenched his hand free. "Carry on with the ceremony!"

Colwyn blinked again and came to her senses. By the expression on Nigel's face, she knew she had done something to displease him. What she had done, she did not know, but it didn't matter, because a herald was heard. Someone was approaching.

With renewed vigour, Colwyn prepared herself for the next battle.

"The ring!" Nigel hissed. "Quickly!"

The bishop blessed the ring and attempted to place it on Colwyn's finger, but her fists were clenched hard and he could not get it on. She wriggled, struggled and did everything in her power to prevent that ring from finding its way onto her finger.

Losing all patience, Nigel struck her, turned her around so her back was towards the bishop and twisted her arm up behind her back. Her cry of pain was ignored as Nigel pulled her arm up further, but still her hand remained in a tight fist, blood oozing from under her crude bandage.

"I'll break it!" he hissed. "So help me, I'll break your arm if that's what it takes to get this damn ring on your finger!"

The pain made Colwyn feel physically sick, but now she couldn't unclench her fist even if she wanted to, for the excruciating pain had paralysed her fingers.

Suddenly, there was a loud commotion and mounted horsemen appeared in the cathedral, led by Stuart Cantrell.

"Nigel McDowell, hold!" his voice boomed.

Colwyn lifted her head and looked up the walkway of the cathedral. The sight of Stuart Cantrell astride his huge powerful grey stallion, hand casually resting on a hip, was a welcome sight indeed. His men were streaming down the left and right aisles to surround Nigel's men. The crowds, seated on the benches, cowered and dropped to their knees as the soldiers and knights surrounded them all.

"Surrender, McDowell. There is nowhere to go!"

Nigel altered his hold on Colwyn, a knife appearing at her throat. "I think not, Stuart, not whilst I have a hostage. Keep your men where they are or I'll kill her!"

"Then you will be bereft of a hostage," Stuart retorted.

Colwyn swallowed slowly, trying to unobtrusively release the lady's dagger that was held within the sleeve of her gown, the one that Morgan had given her as a present before their journey had begun. She wondered if it would be worth trying another faint—that, at least, would unbalance him—or, perhaps if he attempted to move, she could 'stumble' and that would result in the same thing.

She shifted her head as best she could to get a glimpse of Morgan. He was still on his knees, held by Nigel's guards, but they were looking very nervous and uncertain, with Stuart's men all around them.

Nigel shifted, pulling Colwyn partly off balance and she took the opportunity to fall in an undignified heap. Nigel tried to hold onto her, but the hand holding the knife at her throat slipped as he tried to maintain his balance, nicking her slightly before it wavered away. Colwyn made sure he lost his balance completely and he too fell, partly on top of her. Desperately, she retrieved the dagger and as Nigel raised himself up to deliver a death thrust with his own knife, Colwyn lunged with her weapon and stabbed him between the ribs on his left side. The thrust had been in an upward motion, and as a result, slipped between his ribs penetrating his lung and heart.

"For Inver! And my parents!" she hissed.

Nigel froze and looked down at her in shock and surprise. Gritting her teeth, Colwyn pulled the dagger out and thrust again, her eyes wide with determination and hatred.

"And that's for Morgan!"

Chapter Twelve

Blood gushed from the first wound, soaking her arm in seconds. Nigel's eyes took on a distant, faraway look, and he slowly toppled over to land in an undignified heap across her.

Calmly, Colwyn managed to pull the dagger out again, cleaned it on Nigel's cloak, then pushed and shoved at him to move him off her body sufficiently so she could wriggle her way free, and stood up. Slowly, she walked away from the altar towards Morgan. By now, Stuart, Michael and Dernley had dismounted and were running down the aisle towards her, but she ignored them and instead, bent over to cut through the bonds that held her intended, before moving to gracefully kneel down in front of him.

"We are saved, Morgan," she whispered.

Slowly, he lifted his head and saw the marks on her face where McDowell had struck her, and a small trickle of blood on her neck from the knife wound. It took every remaining ounce of strength he had left to speak. "I-I am so proud of you, my love; your strength and courage," he just about managed to whisper, then he smiled weakly at her and collapsed onto the stone floor, a pool of blood slowly forming around his shoulder wound.

Stuart threw himself down by her side, shouting for Master Stephen, his battle surgeon. Dernley gently drew Colwyn to her feet and forcibly led her a little distance away. Carefully, he took the dagger from her hand and put it down on a bench, then removed his heavy cloak and wrapped it around her shaking shoulders.

"My Lady, come, sit here."

Her eyes lifted to focus on his face. "Giles? I thought you had… had been killed!"

"They tried, my Lady, but did not succeed. Come, sit down here," he prompted again.

"I... I'm so glad to see you," she breathed, then her eyelids fluttered and she almost fainted, but regained control and clutched Dernley to prevent herself from falling. She sat down heavily as her legs gave way.

Master Stephen, Stuart's battle surgeon, inspected Bodine's wounds, looked at the duke's pallor, and shook his head. "He has lost a great deal of blood, my Liege. I'll do what I can, but I am not hopeful."

The look on Stuart's face stunned Dernley. He had not heard the conversation, but the King's expression said it all.

No! Not after all this. It could not end this way! He strained to hear the conversation.

"You must be able to do something!"

"I need a miracle."

Stuart suddenly looked much older than his years as he stared at Dernley, holding Colwyn in his arms, offering her comfort; then his eyes beheld Colin McLeod, who was making his way forward.

Dernley glanced down at Colwyn, then back at Stuart. Maybe they would get their miracle. Stuart saw Dernley's dawning look and frowned.

"Monsignor McLeod, your assistance, please."

McLeod moved swiftly to his aid, and Stuart followed on his heels. Dernley gently removed himself from Colwyn's side and moved a little distance away.

"Colwyn," he whispered quietly. "Colwyn may be our miracle."

The two of them frowned at him. "What do you mean?"

"Colwyn has some healing powers; I've seen them. Perhaps, if... she were to have help and guidance... it would be enough to save the duke."

There was a long silence.

"Are you saying Colwyn is Kadeau?" Stuart questioned.

"I don't know, my Liege. All I can say is, I have seen her heal."

Chapter Twelve

"Even if she were only able to help him a little, it might be enough to keep him alive," McLeod replied.

"We have to try. Colwyn won't hesitate; she would do anything to save his life."

Stuart glanced back at Bodine, then at Colwyn, took a deep breath and nodded.

"With your permission, Sire," Dernley said and took his leave.

Taking a deep breath, he knelt down in front of Colwyn and took her hands. This was going to be difficult; there was no telling her state of mind after all this, but he had faith. She would be strong enough.

"My Lady Colwyn."

She opened her eyes and looked at him. Dernley noticed how tired and sad she looked, and his heart went out to her for what he was about to ask.

"My Lady," he swallowed nervously and watched a frown appear on her tired features. "My Lady, all is…. not well."

Her eyes widened at the almost terrified look on his face. "What… what is it?" she asked anxiously, suddenly sitting upright and glancing around. She saw Bodine, still laying on the cathedral floor, and the grim faces around him and she wrenched a hand free and clutched the neck of her gown.

"It's General Bodine. He… he has lost a lot of blood, and he is still bleeding; Master Stephen is… fearful. Please, Colwyn, I have seen with my own eyes what you can do; can you help him? Can you save his life?"

"Giles!" she breathed. Her eyes filled with tears, but they did not fall. They really needed Master Andrew, who was more experienced than Stephen, but he wasn't here; he was at Rossmere. "Come, you must help me." Colwyn reached for her dagger and stood up. She took a deep breath and with Dernley still holding one of her hands, strode purposefully over to where Bodine lay, his head now resting on Michael's folded cloak, and knelt down, pulling Dernley down beside her. Stuart and McLeod brought up the rear.

Carefully, she used the dagger to cut away the sodden black shirt and expose his chest. The sight of the purple bruising around his ribs and the bleeding wound made her gasp and swallow, but did not shake her resolve. She could see he was barely breathing; his pallor grey, his lips tinged with blue. They must hurry.

She glanced up at Stuart and McLeod. "I cannot do this alone; I don't have enough experience or power. When I ask, please lay your hands over Giles', as I will need additional strength and support from you." She didn't know how she knew this; it just seemed that she had drawn the knowledge from deep within the recesses of her mind.

They nodded and knelt down, at the ready.

Colwyn took one final breath and placed her left hand gently, yet firmly, on Bodine's broken ribs and her right hand on his shoulder wound, then nodded at Dernley, who placed his hands over hers. She then closed her eyes and frowned in concentration. Her breathing became shallow and almost non-existent. After a few moments, she gave an agonised gasp and gulped a great lungful of air. Dernley heard her cry, but stayed motionless, breathing slowly and deeply, trying to keep his mind totally blank.

Stuart and McLeod watched as a golden glow appeared around Colwyn and Dernley's hands. Their concern rose as Colwyn shuddered in pain and her unshed tears forced themselves out from under her closed eyelids.

Bodine groaned and the others watched in fascination as his and Colwyn's ragged breathing became as one, their soft cries of pain sounding in unison, as one voice. Michael nudged Stuart as he saw the bruises begin to fade from Bodine's chest.

Colwyn sagged slightly and together, she and Morgan gasped, "Colin…"

Chapter Twelve

Needing no second bidding, McLeod quickly placed his hands on Dernley's and closed his eyes. The strangest feeling was coming over him; something was beginning to sap his strength and he realised it was Colwyn who was pulling it from him, through Dernley, to heal his cousin.

"Sire," the request for help was barely audible, but Stuart heard and did as McLeod had done, placing his hands over the priest's and also closing his eyes.

No one was sure how long this went on for, then finally, Colwyn gave a little sigh, and, in a barely audible whisper, managed to say, "It is done." She attempted to move their hands to Bodine's face, but the effort of healing the severe wounds had been too great and she collapsed in a dead faint, falling forward to rest her head on their hands.

It was Michael who moved first and gently pulled her back to rest against his chest. He noted with grave concern that she was deathly white and barely breathing. Slowly, the others opened their eyes and clenched and flexed their hands to rid themselves of the pins and needles before looking in wonder at Bodine's chest. Not a bruise or mark remained to show where he had been wounded and they were aware of their mouths dropping open.

Master Stephen quickly examined both Colwyn and Bodine. "We should make them more comfortable," he said quietly. "Are cots available anywhere?"

A tired Dernley spoke up. "Let's use McDowell's rooms; he no longer requires them. We just need someone to guide us." He studied McDowell's men, but it was Master Donald who spoke up.

"I will show you," he said. "Follow me."

He turned and started to walk back up the aisle.

As Michael got to his feet with Colwyn in his arms and began the long walk down the aisle and out of the cathedral, it seemed to Dernley that she seemed as light and as limp as a child's rag doll.

Stuart would trust no one but himself to carry the unconscious Bodine and followed on his brother's heels, with Dernley, McLeod and Master Stephen close behind.

They travelled in silence and eventually reached the duke's rooms. Donald stopped on the threshold.

"These are the duke's rooms," he said. "There are other bedrooms along this corridor which will be suitable for the Duchess."

Stuart nodded and entered McDowell's rooms, Master Stephen on his heels. McLeod and Dernley accompanied Prince Michael as they followed Donald further down the corridor until they reached another room. The battle surgeon gestured for them to enter, and then bowed and walked away.

The bed was bare but McLeod went hunting and found a couple of heavy blankets. "I think we just need to ensure she is kept warm," he told Michael and Dernley as he carefully covered her with them. "I know it's warm, but I'll see if I can get a fire going as well." He paused.

"I will take my leave of you and return to the King," Michael said softly and left.

"Are you all right, Giles?" McLeod asked.

Dernley's head was bowed. "I will die if Colwyn does not recover," he whispered quietly. "She has my heart. Forgive me, Monsignor, I cannot help it; I love her." He reached out and brushed a stray lock of her chestnut hair away from her face. "I worship the ground she walks on. May God forgive me for loving another man's intended."

McLeod realised that it was exhaustion and raw emotion talking. He knew Dernley worshipped Colwyn; he had seen it from the very first. His heart went out to him, for he knew the pain of loving a woman he could not have. He placed a hand on the young knight's shoulder.

Chapter Twelve

"God forgives you, my son. You have acted knightly in all ways. It is exhaustion speaking. You need rest. Come, help me find wood for the fire and then get some sleep."

Dernley looked up at McLeod and nodded slowly, feeling better for having confessed his feelings to the priest.

Quickly, the pair of them gathered the little firewood that had been long-standing in the pile, and broke up a chair to make more. Using some clothing they found hanging in a wardrobe, they lit a fire in the grate and watched as it took, slowly heating the air in the room. McLeod nodded in satisfaction.

"Why not make yourself comfortable in that chair? You can keep watch over your Lady whilst I see how my cousin fares."

Dernley nodded and made himself comfortable in a corner, where he could watch over Colwyn and gain a little heat from the growing fire. But his eyes quickly grew heavy from the events of the attack, the strenuous journey back for help, the return and the healing, and he dozed off.

McLeod entered what had once been the Duke of Cottesmere's private chambers to see how Bodine was. He noted that Stuart had also got a fire going and that his cousin was comfortable on the huge four-poster bed and covered with blankets.

Stuart looked up as McLeod approached. "Stephen believes Morgan will be fine. He just needs to rest to regain his strength after the blood loss. Would you sit with him? Michael and I must attend to our duties."

"Stuart, you need rest," Michael replied immediately. "I can take care of what needs to be done."

Stuart shook his head. "Thank you, Michael, but I must do this. It must be made clear that any attack on my subjects is nothing short of treason. Punishment must be handed out."

Michael conceded and together they left to deal with Nigel's body and his men.

It was several hours later before Bodine regained consciousness, and night was beginning to fall. He was aware of being warm and comfortable, fully rested and free from any serious aches or pain. Idly, he stretched, sighed and opened his eyes to find himself in strange surroundings, with McLeod leaning over him, a concerned expression on his face.

Suddenly, the memories came flooding back and his hand immediately went to his shoulder, expecting to find swathes and bandages, but there was nothing. Confused, he pushed the blankets off and inspected the wounds, but there was nothing. No bruising, no scar, nothing.

"How are you feeling, cousin?" McLeod asked, smiling.

Bodine sat up sharply, then sank back as the room spun round, totally confused. "On the whole, I…I feel fine, except…" His hands moved to his face, to touch a tender spot where a bruise had formed. "Obviously, I feel a bit bruised, and a little giddy. What happened? How long have I been unconscious? Where am I?" The questions tumbled over one another.

"Slowly; one thing at a time."

"McDowell—"

"Is dead," McLeod replied. "His head has been mounted on the ramparts as a warning to anyone thinking of committing treason in the future. His body has been scattered to the four winds."

"But how? What happened and where's Colwyn? Is she all right? McDowell struck her." Bodine went to get out of bed, but Colin pushed him back.

"She's safely asleep in a room further down the corridor. Giles is keeping a vigil. You need to take things gently; you lost a lot of blood."

"But I have no wounds! Colin, tell me what happened!"

"How much do you remember of the events? I only saw from when we arrived at the cathedral. Nigel was trying to complete a wedding ceremony,

Chapter Twelve

but it seems that Colwyn had thwarted him at every turn. He was trying to force a wedding ring onto her finger when we arrived. I thought he was going to break her arm to get her to unclench her fist."

"To be honest, cousin, I don't remember too much after the beating. I know I forced Colwyn to vow that she would not marry McDowell no matter what happened to me. He tried to gain control of her mind, but I managed to deflect his power, but after that, I don't know what occurred; I was too far gone."

"McDowell had Colwyn hostage, a knife at her throat. It's a little confusing. He stumbled, and I'm sure Colwyn pulled him totally off balance. It's a good thing you gave her that dagger, Morgan. He was about to kill her, and we were all too far away to stop him. She stabbed him; killed him."

"What?!"

"You heard me. I suggest you don't make her angry after you're married!" McLeod joked, trying to lighten the atmosphere before he went onto the miracle.

Bodine gave him a dirty look. "Then what?"

"She went over to you and said something, I don't know what it was, but you smiled and then collapsed."

"'We are saved'. That's what she said. What happened next?"

McLeod took a deep breath. "Stephen took a look at you and said you were going to die. Said we needed a miracle. And we got one."

Bodine looked stunned. "Did..." he swallowed. "Did I die?"

"Not quite. You were saved at the last minute. Morgan.... Colwyn is Kadeau."

"Don't be ridiculous! I've questioned her about her ancestry, and she said there was none. I didn't detect any either, and I'd have sensed that straight away."

"I'm serious."

McLeod went on to explain the 'miracle' and watched as Bodine's mouth dropped open.

"But I should have picked that up! Colin, let's not beat around the bush. I'm a powerful Kadeau; she couldn't have hidden it from me, or James Douglas either, and he would have mentioned it to me if he had known."

"Well, how else do you explain her healing powers? It was pure Kadeau; not the black arts. Not with that golden aura. I felt it flowing through me. She is untrained, but possesses remarkable power."

"I wonder… did our link awaken the Kadeau that may have lain dormant, deep within her? And a healer… I didn't think that was possible… to be able to heal. That makes her very valuable. I would certainly like to learn that."

"What, and put Andrew out of a job?"

"Of course not! But think how useful it would be." Bodine threw the covers back and swung his legs over the bed.

"And where do you think you're going?"

"To see my bride! Where's my shirt?"

"On the fire. Here, I found this for you." McLeod threw him a white one. Bodine scowled at the colour. "Beggars can't be choosers," McLeod retorted, seeing the look.

Bodine sighed and pulled it on, went to stand up, then sat down heavily again, feeling decidedly dizzy.

"Morgan, take it slowly. As I've already told you, you've lost a lot of blood," McLeod chastised. "If you have to get up, move slowly and carefully." He stood up, and assisted Bodine to his feet, holding him steady whilst the duke waited for the room to stop spinning. Taking a deep breath, he straightened up and walked slowly towards the door. He was feeling decidedly weak and queasy, but put that down to the blood loss. As long as he moved carefully, he would be fine. "Where is she?"

Chapter Twelve

"In the next room down to the left."

"Thanks."

Giles Dernley got quickly to his feet as Bodine entered Colwyn's room. "Morgan, I am pleased to see you well."

"Thank you, Giles. Tell me, how fares my Lady Colwyn?"

"She sleeps still."

Bodine saw the look in Dernley's eyes. "You love her too, don't you?" he asked softly.

Dernley flinched guiltily. "Forgive me, Morgan. I can't help it; I've loved her since I was a young page at Inver castle. I apologise; I never confessed to loving her during our previous conversation. Now you know this, I assume you will want me to leave."

"Do you want to leave, Giles?"

"No, my Lord. I would sooner die, but… how can you bear to have another man around who loves your intended wife?"

"I can think of no one more suited, for I know you will defend her with your life. Giles, you are most knightly. I have known, almost from the moment I saw you, that you loved her, but you acted with honour at all times. Why did you think I asked you to stay with us?"

Dernley shrugged. "You are right. I would be trustworthy, for she has never returned my love."

"Oh, but she does love you, Giles. As the brother she never had. And that is a far greater love." Bodine placed a hand on the young knight's shoulder. "And I would be grateful if you would continue as her brother."

Dernley smiled at that. "I would be honoured."

Bodine nodded and slapped him on the back. "Good man. Now, if you don't mind, I'd like to sit with my bride for a little while."

"Of course, my Lord." Dernley bowed briefly and exited.

Once again, Bodine found himself looking down at the pale features of the Duchess of Invermere, as he had all those months ago. Only this time, she was not on the brink of death. He had broken all the rules that night to save her life, both Godly and knightly, but if he hadn't, her healing powers would not have risen to the fore. Kadeau just had to have been in her ancestry; perhaps it was just so far back, that it had been lost in the time of days long gone.

He sat down carefully on the bed and reached out to gently stroke her hair.

"My love, I thank you for saving my life, at least twice over these past few days. McDowell is dead, by your hand; the threat of war has been removed. We can now look forward to our wedding, and the rest of our lives together." He leant over her and gently kissed her lips.

In response, she gave a little moan, and smiled.

"Morgan," she whispered, then opened her eyes.

"And pray tell, how did you know it was me?" he asked in a teasing fashion.

"No one has ever kissed me the way you do," she replied softly. "I would recognise a kiss from you blindfolded."

"Perhaps one day, we will put that to the test!" He kissed her again.

"But I am concerned…. You are not my future husband; are you his twin?"

"Pardon?"

"My intended dresses only in black… you, sir, are in a white shirt!"

Bodine relaxed and laughed softly. "It was the only colour available," he explained.

She ran a hand over his chest. "It looks good on you."

"But it ruins my image," he protested feebly.

It was Colwyn's turn to laugh.

Chapter Twelve

"Your image is safe with me."

The light danced in his grey-blue eyes and he surrendered to the impulse to give her a kiss that took her breath away.

"Tomorrow, we will leave for Belvoir," he whispered in her ear, "and then, you will be mine."

"And I can't wait," she replied, kissing him back. Placing her hands on his face, she held his lips to hers. She wished she could have healed the wounds she saw there, but she was not strong enough yet to complete the task.

Eventually, she ended the kiss, opened her eyes and leant back to look at him. He might be battered and bruised but she was satisfied at what she saw; she smiled.

"What?" he asked.

"Nothing. I am just admiring my exceedingly handsome husband-to-be."

"Even with my cuts and bruises?" he asked.

"Yes."

He smiled, went to kiss her hand, and saw the bandage on it.

"McDowell did this to you?"

"Yes."

"And he struck you at least three times."

"Yes, but how did you know?"

"I sensed it, and I saw the marks on your face."

"I thought I had shielded you from it."

"You almost did, but I think it was more the shock of what he did that caught you unawares and caused your concentration to slip slightly and I managed to sense it."

"I'm sorry, Morgan; you were already suffering, I didn't want you to feel anything else."

Gently, he undid the makeshift bandage she had wrapped around her hand, and studied the wound.

"A knife," he muttered.

"He had an old woman with him, and she collected a sample of my blood. I don't know what she wanted it for."

"Let me try and make it better," Morgan whispered.

"No! You're not strong enough. It's not a serious wound. I might even be able to heal myself in a little while."

He frowned at her.

"I mean it, Morgan. You almost died a few hours ago. I'll be fine, especially now any threat has gone and we can look forward to a life together."

They smiled at one another, love clearly evident in their eyes.

13

Chapter Thirteen

It was a rather emotional reunion. As the King's army rode into Belvoir, they found a reception committee waiting—somewhat anxiously—on the steps.

As King Stuart, Prince Michael, Bodine, Dernley and Colwyn dismounted, Queen Alexandra, Princess Anne, and Sarah ran down the steps to greet them.

The three women looked at the state of Colwyn and immediately started to fuss over her, especially regarding the bruises on her face. The young Duchess felt like crying at their concern, but it was not fitting in such a public place, so she bit her lip and did her best to hang onto Bodine's hand, but they led her away and into the keep.

Master Andrew, who had initially hung back, immediately came to his duke and looked at him critically.

"You look very pale. If I didn't know better, I'd say you had suffered a severe blood loss, but I can't see any evidence of wounds serious enough to cause them; unless they are hidden under your clothes?"

McLeod came over to them.

"Morgan was seriously wounded," he began softly.

"But..." Andrew began.

"Colwyn... saved his life. You may as well know, Master Andrew; she is Kadeau."

"But, I still don't understand. You say she saved his Grace's life; how?"

"She effectively healed him."

"That's not possible!"

"I took part in the process myself, and can swear by all that is holy, that it is true; but it must go no further."

"I understand."

"You are correct, though. Morgan did lose a lot of blood. He needs some hearty meals and rest, so he is fit for his wedding day."

"Don't I get a say in any of this?" Bodine asked.

"No," Andrew replied. "A hearty meal and bed rest. They are my orders as your battle surgeon."

"One thing; where's Edward?"

"Here, my Lord." Edward stepped forward.

"I want to put the wedding back a couple of days until Colwyn's bruises have faded. I can't have my bride walking down the aisle looking black and blue."

"As you wish, your Grace."

"And you can't walk down the aisle looking like that, either!" McLeod retorted.

"Morgan, do you need me to take a look at Colwyn? I see her hand is bandaged as well. Do you want to tell me what happened?"

"To cut a rather long story short, McDowell's men ambushed us from both the north and south in the High Hills; Colwyn and I were forced to make a run for it and were pursued into the woods. We managed to fight most of them off; Colwyn killed at least one, and then an archer caught me with an arrow in my shoulder, so we ran again and found shelter in a thicket. Colwyn helped bind the wound, and the following morning we made a break

Chapter Thirteen

for it, only to find our way blocked on the final turn to Rossmere, so we started to head back, but after emerging from the woods, our way was again blocked, so we turned and made a run for the ruins and hid in there.

"We then attempted to make a run for it again, but by then, I had lost a lot of blood; my left arm was useless and I was knocked off my horse. Colwyn came to my rescue and killed another knight; maybe it was two, but more came, and I ordered her to leave me. She made her escape, but they caught her and brought her back, then McDowell appeared.

"We were taken to Cottesmere. I did try and launch an attack on McDowell, but by then, I was almost spent, and I don't remember much after that until I woke up in a bed."

"We found them both in the cathedral," McLeod continued. "McDowell was trying to complete a marriage ceremony, but Colwyn was fighting him at every step. He had struck her several times, and cut her hand to obtain some of her blood. Colwyn said she didn't know why he wanted it; there was an old witch with him at the time. But… she eventually killed him."

"What?!"

"I'm not sure if that's three or four men she's killed now," Bodine said, thinking about what McLeod had said about not making her angry. "Anyway, it seems I was near death, and she saved me."

"I think I know why he wanted the blood if there was a witch," McLeod said. "I believe it was to ascertain when she would be ready to conceive a child and ensure an heir for Cottesmere. Morgan, you're sure Colwyn is unharmed?"

"Yes, she is untouched; just cut and bruised."

"Enough talking now," Andrew said. "It's time for you to eat and rest, my Lord. Come."

Bodine looked round for Dernley.

"Giles, attend me, I have some errands I'd like you to run."

"Of course, Morgan."

☙ ❧ ☙ ❧

Up in Colwyn's rooms, the Queen had managed to get most of the story from the Duchess, although she left out the part about healing Bodine, and Alexandra was horrified at what she had heard. She listened to how Bodine had attempted to protect her and shield her and realised his actions were now forcing her to reassess how she saw him. He obviously loved Colwyn very much indeed, and had suffered as a consequence. After hearing the story, the Queen immediately insisted that she eat a hearty meal and then go to bed. A hot, soothing bath would be made ready for her that evening when she awoke.

Finally alone, Colwyn permitted herself to shed the tears she had held in check, releasing the stress and strain of the recent ordeal while remembering to shield Bodine from her feelings. He had suffered more than enough because of her, so she would shield him from the guilt she felt.

She eventually fell asleep and slept for several hours, finally being awoken by Sarah to take the promised bath, which soothed her aches and pains and helped to revitalise her.

"I understand his Grace has delayed the wedding by a few days to allow your bruises to fade, my Lady," Sarah told her as she helped her dress.

Colwyn peered into the small mirror and saw a haunted, bruised and cut face staring back at her. She hadn't realised the extent of the damage that McDowell had inflicted.

"I must remember to thank Morgan for putting it back. I can't walk down the aisle looking like this," she said softly.

"Would you like to see your wedding dress?" Sarah asked. "It is all finished."

Colwyn shook her head. "No, not tonight."

Chapter Thirteen

"Just know, it is the most beautiful dress. Sir Giles supplied the material."

"Giles?"

"He said it was his gift to you, for your wedding."

"I must thank him also."

"You will, by wearing it proudly."

There was a soft knock at the door.

"Enter," Colwyn called.

The door opened to admit Bodine.

"Morgan," she breathed.

"My love," he replied, walking towards her. She stood up, and he took her in his arms and kissed her gently. "I came to enquire if you felt up to going down to eat? Or whether you wished to dine alone tonight?"

"I don't mind," she replied sounding a little listless.

Bodine placed his fingers on her temples. *What's wrong, Colwyn?* he asked her.

She shrugged her shoulders. *I guess I'm still getting over our... adventure... for want of a better word. I thought I was going to lose you. I could not have survived that. You are my life.*

And for that, I feel blessed. Do you feel up to going down?

She nodded and smiled tentatively.

"Come then." He held out his hand, took hers and led her from the room.

Some guests had already arrived for the wedding ceremony, so the main banqueting hall was reasonably full. By the looks on their faces, no one had thought the two of them would make an appearance on their first evening safely back at Belvoir. Bodine thought that as Duke of Rossmere, it was his duty to act as host within his own Duchy.

The meal went quietly, and afterwards, a number of guests came up to the couple, tutting and offering their sympathies at seeing Colwyn's bruises.

Bodine decided they both needed an early night, and escorted her back to her room, only to be met by Master Andrew, who was waiting outside the door.

"My lady, I am here to check your hand, and I also have some witch hazel for your bruises."

Bodine led her inside. Sarah fetched water and Master Andrew treated her hand, making her wince as he carefully bathed it with a solution of his antiseptic powder, before bandaging it once more.

"It is healing well, your Grace. Now, let's have a look at these bruises. The witch hazel is very cold, but it should help bring the bruising out and cause them to disperse faster." He issued instructions about how often to use it and how long it should be applied for, then waited outside in the corridor whilst Bodine said good night to his intended.

The duke and battle surgeon walked back to the Kadeau's quarters, where Andrew inspected Bodine's injuries, issued more witch hazel and checked his body for any untreated wounds. Apart from some lingering tenderness around his shoulders and ribs, his Lord appeared unharmed.

"Morgan, do you… do you need to talk about what happened?" Andrew asked quietly as he packed away his medical supplies.

"Not tonight, and maybe not for a few days. I need time to digest what happened on my own. But I will admit, I had never felt so helpless. Thinking back, I should have used more magic, then maybe none of this would have happened."

"Hindsight is a wonderful thing," Andrew agreed. "You mustn't be so hard on yourself."

Bodine shook his head. "I was stupid and I was arrogant," he confessed.

"Then you must learn from your mistakes," Andrew said.

Chapter Thirteen

The duke nodded, and Andrew was struck at how 'human' his Lord was at that moment. The usually confident and calm Bodine looked and sounded uncertain, as he relived the past few days.

"I know you try not to use magic at all," Andrew said softly. "But when the odds are so much against you, no one can blame you, doing what you can to keep the ones you love safe."

"Thank you for your kind words, my friend. I just can't help thinking about what would have happened had McDowell succeeded."

"But he didn't! Between Colwyn and yourself, you won, that's all you need to remember. Now, use this witch hazel and get to bed. I'm still not pleased with your colour, although it is improving. From what I can gather, you were losing blood for at least three or four days. That has just got to have taken a huge toll on you, and you may still feel tired. Go on. Bed. Now!"

Bodine smiled ruefully and nodded, slapping Andrew good-naturedly on the shoulder.

"Good night, Andrew."

14

Chapter Fourteen

Sarah stood back to admire her handiwork. "Stand up, my Lady," she said, "and let me look at you."

Colwyn did as she asked. The white dress was decorated in gold and clung to every curve of her body. The sleeves were long and tight-fitting to the elbows before trailing out, showing off a patterned lining. Around her waist was a double gold belt, and circling her neck was a gold necklace, a present from the Queen. A long veil covered her plaited chestnut hair and was held in place by a gold coronet. On her feet were white leather slippers, also decorated in gold.

"Oh, my Lady, you look beautiful," Sarah said, with tears of joy in her eyes.

Colwyn smiled a radiant smile but was prevented from saying anything as there was a knock at the door, and it opened to admit the King.

The Duchess immediately dropped into a low curtsy as Stuart Cantrell walked up to her and assisted her to her feet again.

"My dear Colwyn, you are looking radiant," he told her.

"Thank you, my Liege."

"Are you ready?"

"Yes, Sire."

Chapter Fourteen

He offered her his left arm, which she took, but for a moment, she looked sad that it wasn't her father who was taking her to the cathedral and to her future husband. They walked sedately along the corridors, down the stairs, and then stepped out of the main castle entrance, down the main steps into the bailey where a carriage was waiting to take them to Belvoir Cathedral.

The carriage was accompanied by Rossmere's Elite Guard, resplendent in their dress uniforms; armour shining; leather gleaming. The procession left the bailey, trotting under the gatehouse to the lower bailey and then under the barbican and across the drawbridge onto the main road into the city and to the cathedral.

People lined the streets, trying to get a glimpse of the bride on the short journey. The carriage stopped at the steps of the cathedral and the door was opened by a page boy. The King got out and assisted Colwyn from the carriage. They walked slowly up the steps and entered the grand building. Rose petals had been strewn on the floor, flowers were everywhere, and as Colwyn glanced down the aisle to the altar, she saw Bodine, also dressed in white. She nearly stopped in her tracks with shock, having never seen him in anything but black until a couple of days ago. Even his ceremonial sword was in a white leather sheath, decorated with gold. His cousin, Colin McLeod, stood at his side.

Bodine turned his head and looked up the aisle, seeing his bride on the arm of his King, and for a moment, his mind drifted back to Stuart's wedding, ten years ago. He had been ten when his Liege had married Alexandra in Ellesmere Cathedral. It had been the grandest of affairs, with not only representatives of the Duchies of Devonmere, but also foreign dignitaries in attendance as well.

The cathedral had been a kaleidoscope of colour, and the sun shining through the huge stain-glassed windows had thrown multi-coloured shadows on the floor.

Bodine was supposed to have been a page boy in the ceremony, but Alexandra was adamant he would not be; so Stuart had him as his ring-bearer, a role he specifically created for the youngster so that he was involved. The King had told him that looking after the rings was a very important role and he had held them proudly on a small cushion for the bishop to take them when they were required.

The duke glanced around the cathedral and at the guests. There were no foreign dignitaries at his wedding, but Belvoir Cathedral was still ablaze with colour; he had ensured there were plenty of colourful blooms dressing the entrance, the aisles and the numerous transepts and chapels. No one would be able to say the wedding was not a beautiful and colourful affair and the flowers also gave the cathedral a very pleasant perfume.

His eyes fastened on Colwyn and Stuart as they slowly walked down the aisle towards him. As they reached the altar, Bodine stepped away from McLeod to stand at her side. The King retreated to stand with Queen Alexandra.

"You are truly beautiful," Bodine whispered in Colwyn's ear.

Bishop Treherne addressed them. "Those present have already confirmed there is no reason why you should not be married. I now ask you, if you know of any?"

"None," Bodine replied.

"There is no reason," Colwyn said softly.

"Very well. We are gathered here to witness the sacrament of marriage – *sarum marriage liturgy*, following the *sponsalia per verbade futuro* that took place at Ellesmere in June."

The ceremony progressed in Latin until it came to the vows.

Bodine spoke first. "I, Morgan Geraint Rhys Bodine, take thee, Colwyn Eilwen Anghared Coltrane to be my wedded wife, 'til death us do part, and thereto I plight thee my troth."

Chapter Fourteen

"I, Colwyn Eilwen Anghared Coltrane, take thee, Morgan Geraint Rhys Bodine, to be my wedded husband, 'til death us do part, and thereto I plight thee my troth."

They then exchanged rings which were placed on the third finger of their right hands, and then the bishop tied their two hands together and gave the blessing. That completed, the bishop then kissed Bodine, who in turn kissed Colwyn.

They both turned to face the congregation.

"You may kiss your bride," Treherne whispered to Bodine, who needed no further bidding, and took Colwyn in his arms to plant a passionate kiss on her pliable lips, before releasing her. She blushed at his open show of intensity of feeling to the people in the cathedral, and then they walked slowly down the aisle towards the exit, where they paused on the steps, acknowledging the crowd for a few minutes, whilst the bells pealed out the news of the union.

Colwyn was presented with a purse of gold coins, and she indicated for the guards to allow the needy to come forward so she could distribute the coins to them. Those who had received the gift bowed and curtsied respectfully.

At the bottom of the cathedral steps, in brand new white leather livery, stood Bodine's stallion, Banner, and Colwyn's spirited Storm, who was fitted with a side-saddle. Both horses had been carefully prepared; washed and brushed until their coats shone like velvet. Sarah was also present, to arrange her Lady's dress and cloak once she was seated.

Having assisted Colwyn to mount, Sarah spread out the white dress and cloak, which lay in stark contrast to the almost black of the horse, and made a beautiful sight. Bodine mounted, and McLeod adjusted his rich cloak to lie evenly on either side, his duke's coronet glinting brightly in the sunlight.

Their horses walked sedately back through the streets towards Belvoir Castle, the honour guard behind.

Arriving in the bailey at the base of the steps to the main keep, Bodine dismounted and helped Colwyn from her horse. He held her tightly against him for a little while.

"Morgan, I almost thought I was marrying someone else," Colwyn teased. "I've never seen you dressed in anything but black until a couple of days ago, and for a moment, I was quite taken aback."

He smiled at her. "Colin said I was not going to be allowed to wear my usual colour, so I had no choice!" He offered her his arm. "Are you happy, my love?"

"Ecstatic," she replied.

He beamed radiantly at her as they mounted the steps, and then paused to exchange another kiss before entering the keep and making their way to the main banqueting hall to greet their guests.

There were gifts set at the tables for all the guests, and, as people arrived, they too bore gifts for the newly wedded couple.

The King and Queen were the first to arrive with their son Prince Llywelyn, along with Prince Michael and his wife Anne. Bodine and Colwyn bowed and curtsied respectfully. Stuart gave the duke a fierce hug and kissed his wife, and, to everyone's utmost surprise, Alexandra kissed Bodine, then hugged and kissed Colwyn, before moving to the head table.

"Congratulations, my boy," a familiar voice said to Bodine, and a smile lit up his handsome features.

"Aunt Meleri!" he exclaimed, as McLeod's mother came forward to kiss and hug him, before taking a step back to look critically at him. Her husband was far more restrained in his congratulations.

"My dearest Morgan," she said softly. "I can sense true happiness and joy within you. I am so pleased for you." She turned her attention to Colwyn,

Chapter Fourteen

embraced her, kissed her cheek and straightened up in surprise. "My dear, I had no idea! A very well-kept secret indeed; Kadeau blood in the Coltrane line! I met your parents on a number of occasions, but never sensed Kadeau in either of them."

"I did not detect it either," Bodine confessed.

She pondered this news. "It was dormant then. Something awoke it."

"I believe it was a link I initiated to save Colwyn's life. I did not know we were linked for a number of weeks."

"Yes, that will have awoken her Kadeau heritage. It has probably been hidden for many generations. My dear, welcome to the family."

"Thank you, Duchess—"

"Oh, call me Aunt Meleri, my dear." She leant forward again. "If you need assistance with your power, please do not hesitate to contact me."

"Aunt Meleri, Colwyn is a healer."

Meleri's eyebrows rose. "There hasn't been a healer for over three hundred years! We will talk later. There is no hurry," she finished, patting Colwyn's hand and moving on.

Gradually, all the guests arrived and were seated, and Bodine and Colwyn were able to take their place at the head table, with the King on one side of them, Alexandra seated next to Bodine, and the Prince on the other, next to Colwyn, then Anne, and McLeod on the end. Alexandra, Colwyn noted, was making a huge effort to be polite to Bodine, and was doing a fine job.

At the first table below the head one were seated the immediate neighbours, which included the Duke of Strathmere and his son, Giles Dernley, and Colwyn smiled warmly at the duke-in-waiting.

Food and wine were free-flowing; dancing followed and eventually, the evening wore on and the time approached for the newlywed couple to disappear for the final act of the marriage, the consummation.

Toasts to the couple were made, and then Stuart, Michael and McLeod led Bodine away, whilst Alexandra and Anne took Colwyn to her room for Sarah to prepare her for the night ahead.

In the duke's private rooms, Ioan had laid out the dressing gown and other clothes in readiness for going to bed. Bodine dismissed him for the night and he found himself facing his King, the Prince and his cousin, and suddenly felt rather shy and uncomfortable.

Michael, sensing his unease, stepped forward and clasped his hand.

"Morgan, congratulations. Anne and I wish you every happiness for the future." He leant forward and whispered, "Everything will be fine; just be yourself." He then stepped back, clasped his shoulder briefly and took his leave.

Bodine swallowed and surveyed his King and cousin.

"We'll wait out here whilst you go change," Stuart said.

He nodded, feeling thankful that, for the next few minutes, he would have some time to himself to calm his nerves, for he was feeling incredibly nervous. The forthcoming night just had to be perfect. The last time he had been this nervous was on his fifteenth birthday. That was a day forever ingrained vividly in his memory; the day when Stuart had presented him with the young Banner for him to train, and the night he had arranged for the black-haired Raven to teach him the art of love.

Raven was the black-haired, blue-eyed young Kadeau woman who had effectively taught him everything he now knew about making love to a woman. He had been so naïve, so gauche, as she had made her advances; transfixed; as still as a statue, until she had aroused him and then she brought him to his first climax. It was something he would never, ever forget.

And then, through the night, he had learnt what pleased him, and drove him over the edge, and discovered how a woman's body worked; the erotic

Chapter Fourteen

areas; how to turn her body in a quivering, burning flame of desire, desperate for him to give her release.

It was also the night he had learnt about the mental link that could be initiated to heighten the pleasure; to feel what his partner was feeling and vice versa. He thought he would die from the sensations it had aroused, it was so potent.

The sense of power was close to overwhelming, as were the collection of sexual positions—and he was still learning.

Now it was his turn to teach Colwyn of the wondrous journey they could share together. He would be forever grateful for the generosity of his King for that night of pleasure, when he had become a man, in the true sense of the word.

Shaking his head, he went through into his bed-chamber, and with trembling fingers, he undressed, before looking at the attire waiting on the bed. In a bold move, he only put on the dressing gown, which reached down to the ground, and donned the matching slippers. Then, taking a deep breath, he turned and re-joined his companions in the outer room.

McLeod went forward and hugged his cousin. "I'll meet you outside Colwyn's rooms," he said, knowing that Stuart wanted to speak to his cousin alone. Bodine smiled gratefully at him and stood waiting whilst McLeod left the room, shutting the door behind him.

Stuart stepped closer and cleared his throat. "Morgan, you have no idea how happy I am for you. At one time, I despaired that you would ever find someone who loved you for who you are, and it turned out to be someone you have known practically your entire life. Who would have guessed it? I could not be happier if I tried. You are my Champion and the General of my Armies; I have asked, and will continue to ask a lot of you, but I also consider you a very close friend; almost a brother.

"Colwyn is a very fortunate young woman to have captured your heart, and you, my friend, are just as fortunate to have found her. I hope you realise, I wanted her to be the next Queen of Devonmere, but I saw that she loves you so very much; I made a promise to her father, that I have been able to honour. Take good care of her, she is a real gem in this Kingdom. Treat her gently and with reverence; you need time to get to know one another properly and, to that end, I want you to spend time with her, rule your two duchies and then return to Devonmere next March."

"Stuart, that's too long away from my duties—"

The King held up his hand. "We are at peace, thanks to both of you; the threat, for the moment, has gone. Enjoy the quiet as long as you can. We both know it won't last, so make the most of it. Now, I think it's time I escorted you to your wife."

He indicated for Bodine to precede him out of the room, and they walked in contemplative silence along the corridors.

The Queen and Princess Anne had escorted Colwyn to her rooms, and they now sat in her day room, ready to offer advice and guidance.

Colwyn was trembling, but she wasn't sure if it was from fear or excitement or a combination of both. She had overheard some of the ladies-in-waiting talking earlier. Some of their conversation had been rather vulgar and crude and had unnerved her somewhat, but Bodine had always been gentle with her: passionate, but gentle. There was no reason to fear that it would change. She had seen the hunger in his eyes; she knew exactly what he wanted of her, for he had boldly told her down by the riverbank just before he had proposed.

"My child, it is perfectly natural to be nervous and apprehensive, and no doubt the ladies-in-waiting have been rather… ungracious and perhaps even tried to shock you. Take no notice of them. You remember our previous

Chapter Fourteen

conversation. Nothing has changed. I pray you will know the passion of true love. Your eyes clearly show your love for your husband."

"Michael and I wish you every happiness, and many years together," Anne said softly, taking her hand. "If, at any time, you feel you need to talk, or wish to ask anything of us, please do not hesitate."

"Thank you, Your Highness. I am overwhelmed by your kindness."

Anne rose, indicating for her to stay where she was and left the room. There were a few moments of awkward silence before Colwyn spoke again.

"Your Majesty, I pray that one day, you will be able to accept that the Duke of Rossmere is not evil. Time and time again he has proved his loyalty to Devonmere and the King. Please, I am speaking of my own free will; he has not bewitched me." Colwyn gave a little smile. "To be truthful, I think it may be that I have bewitched him."

The Queen returned her smile. "It may take me a little time, but for you, my dear Colwyn, I will do my utmost to shed my fear of him. You are still like the daughter I have yet to bear, even though you now be wed to the Kadeau Lord." Alexandra leant forward and kissed Colwyn's cheek. "Now, my child, 'tis nearly the hour and you must be prepared for your husband."

Alexandra rose from her chair, and Colwyn dropped into a curtsy.

"Arise, my child; your handmaiden awaits you." She left the room and Colwyn turned and went into the dressing chamber to sit at her dressing table.

Sarah brushed Colwyn's hair until it shone like a polished chestnut newly prised from its husk. She knew her mistress was nervous for her hands were trembling and she had tried to hide the fact by clasping them together and letting them rest in her lap. Sarah had a reasonably good idea of what was going through her mind; she herself had once been married, albeit briefly, for she had been widowed young and left with a baby who had died. Very soon after, she had entered into the service of the royal household, initially as a wet nurse to the baby Colwyn, and then stayed on as her maid when the Duchess had failed to produce a male heir, or any other child, until just over a year ago, when the announcement had been made that she had finally fallen, and rumours abounded that she carried a son.

"My Lady, it is time," Sarah said softly. "I will fetch your nightgown."

"No, Sarah, I will see to myself. Please leave me."

"But, my Lady…"

"Go, please. I want to spend a few minutes alone."

"Very well, my Lady. I wish you every happiness." Impulsively, she leant down and kissed Colwyn on the cheek. "I will be waiting to take care of you… later," she continued, before running from the room.

The time had come. It seemed she had been waiting an eternity for this moment, ever since his kisses had awakened the passion in her body; and now it was here; her wedding night.

Colwyn took a deep breath and went to the bed-chamber. Scented candles were burning softly, their aroma quite heady. Her eyes fastened on her nightgown, laid out on the bed. Surely, from her brief experience, the idea was to remove clothing, not put it on? In a bold decision, she decided not to wear it, but simply stay in her dressing gown instead, as she was sure Bodine was not going to arrive wearing his full attire. Quickly, Colwyn turned down the bedclothes, picked up the nightgown, and took it through to the dressing room, before returning to the bed-chamber to stand nervously, wringing her hands.

Suddenly, there was a knock on the door that made her jump, even though she had been expecting it.

"Come." Colwyn's voice sounded strained.

The door opened to admit Monsignor Colin McLeod, King Stuart and, of course, her husband.

Chapter Fourteen

McLeod was there to bless the forthcoming union and the King to escort his most trusted General safely to his destination.

Colwyn curtsied as they entered and then stood as Bodine joined her side, where he held her hand as the blessing was read. Colin then moved to the bed and blessed that as well.

"God bless you both," said Stuart Cantrell. He shook Bodine's hand before taking him in a brotherly hug, and then kissed Colwyn on the cheek. "Good night to both of you. Come, Monsignor McLeod."

It was almost a minute after the door closed before either Bodine or Colwyn moved. Still holding hands, Bodine turned to face his bride.

"Nervous?" he asked gently.

"A little," Colwyn admitted.

"My love, know that I will honour you always and never do anything to hurt you. The act of love can be a glorious, wondrous thing and we shall explore it together." He led her to the small table where a flagon of sweet and spicy wine and two goblets waited. He poured wine into both and handed her one, encouraging her to drink it. He hoped it would help to relax her, so she would enjoy the forthcoming experience more.

He had secretly been very selfish; being a Kadeau, he was able to sense when she would be ready to conceive. Her womanly scent changed slightly at that time; he had learnt this whilst spending time with her since he had returned to Ellesmere in April, and he had decided he wanted to enjoy making love to his wife for a while before she fell, so he had delayed the wedding for a few days more, making a valid excuse that he wanted the bruises on her face to fade, and he to regain his strength before she walked down the aisle.

When she had finished her wine, Morgan stepped closer and kissed her gently. Boldly, she loosened the belt on his gown and ran a hand down his chest, parting the heavy fabric as she went.

Surprised at her forwardness, Bodine straightened and looked down at her. Colwyn simply smiled and leant forward to kiss his chest.

After months of waiting for this night, the last thing he wanted to do was rush anything, but it was clear to him that Colwyn was going to be an eager and willing wife; however, she was pure, untouched, and he wanted to make her first experience of love as pleasurable and as memorable as possible.

Her lips caressed him, and Bodine could not stop himself from inhaling sharply as she began to weave her spell around him.

"Tell me how I can please my husband," she whispered huskily, her fingers lightly caressing the dusting of hair on his chest, and brushing across his nipples.

"All in good time, but first, it will be my honour to pleasure you." He pulled at the belt on her gown, causing it to fall open. His eyes widened in surprise and pleasure at seeing her state of undress, then he slipped his hands inside, around her small waist and pulled her against him, kissing her deeply again, before sweeping the gown off her shoulders so that it fell in a heap on the floor behind her. "God, but you are beautiful," he said, stepping back to appraise her naked body.

Colwyn blushed fiercely but proudly stood her ground as Bodine shrugged out of his own gown. Her eyes widened at the sight of his lean, yet firmly muscled form; from the broad shoulders to the narrow hips, the powerful thighs and his partly aroused manhood.

Stepping forward, he swept her up into his arms and strode purposefully towards the bed, where he gently laid her upon it. For several seconds, he made no attempt to join her, but stood, absorbing the sight of her exquisite form. She was breathing quite heavily and he was mesmerised by the rise and fall of her full, firm breasts.

Regaining control of his faculties, he moved to lie down beside her. Leaning upon his left elbow, he bent over and kissed her firmly, whilst his

Chapter Fourteen

right hand glided up her left arm onto her shoulder and down to her left breast, which he squeezed gently, allowing his thumb to delicately brush the nipple erect. Colwyn's right hand moved up his left arm over his shoulder to the back of his neck, to wind her fingers in his hair.

Bodine kissed her throat, and then his lips moved to her breasts. His tongue teased her nipples, then he kissed them. A hand moved down to her stomach, gently teasing her smooth, silky skin, before roaming down her side, over her hips to her legs. With infinite care, he softly teased her inner thighs, encouraging her to open them. His fingers moved in tantalising circles, gradually creeping upwards towards her body, and Colwyn felt a funny feeling in her stomach. Unable to resist, she opened her thighs further.

She suddenly felt flushed and gave a little moan and Morgan's fingers moved upwards a little more; then her back arched and she gave a gasp as his fingers touched her where no man had ever touched. Blood surged through her body as his fingers awakened a fire within her womanhood. Unable to stop herself, she moved her hips, rubbing herself against him. His mouth claimed hers again and her hands clutched at his shoulders, her nails digging into them. Under the kiss, she groaned again and her hips began to move more urgently and eagerly, intensifying the touch of his fingers on her femininity. Morgan released her lips and she began to gasp, her breasts heaving against his chest.

He eased himself over her, allowing his manhood to take the place of his fingers.

"M-Morgan," she gasped. "I – I've never felt like this before," and she groaned, wanting more.

"You are almost ready, my love. I will try not to hurt you." He kissed her again, raised his hips and with one hand, he guided himself, using one firm thrust to penetrate her.

Colwyn cried out as she felt a tearing sensation within.

"Steady, steady," Bodine soothed. "The worst is over." He kissed her hungrily, his hands leaving a trail of fire over her body and she began to moan again. Slowly, he began to move within her. Colwyn gave a sharp intake of breath at the discomfort, but this was slowly replaced by a feeling she had never felt before. She could feel the blood rushing from her head to her stomach and groin. The heat; the feel of Morgan's body on hers, moving against her; it was a heady mixture. A hunger began to grow, the pain being replaced by a growing need and want. Colwyn, unable to keep still any longer, moved her hips against him. Passion was rising fast; she started to gasp, her breathing getting heavier by the second as his firm thrusts claimed her again and again.

Morgan felt her arch against him, moaning desperately. She wanted more but didn't really know or understand what, yet.

Her nails dug into his shoulders; her body was covered in a fine sheen as the heat overtook her.

Morgan wasn't fairing much better; he was fast approaching climax and a groan escaped him as the level stepped up again. Desperately, he gave a final thrust and his seed filled her, its overspill, hot and wet, running down the inside of her thighs.

He felt her go rigid, convulse, a cry on her lips as her first orgasm claimed her. She was light-headed, breathless and she fainted, but her swoon only lasted a few seconds. Colwyn came round to find Morgan's body crushing hers, but it was a glorious feeling. His hard body on hers, muscles supple yet firm. She was no longer a child, but a woman. Her husband had taken her virginity and she was his, forever and always.

"Oh, Morgan," she breathed. "I... I never knew such feelings existed." She was breathing hard as Morgan kissed her lips, her throat and her breasts.

He gently withdrew from her abused body to lie beside her and gather her into his arms, where he stroked and soothed her. Everything had gone

Chapter Fourteen

better than he'd hoped, but he would have to rise shortly. He had one more duty to perform before he could claim her again.

He stayed where he was until the thudding in his chest returned to some semblance of normality. Once his heavy breathing had stopped, he gently disentangled himself from her arms.

"Sarah will be waiting for you. You need to bathe whilst she changes the bedding and I, my love, need this sheet. It's a barbaric custom, but it is still a custom." He rose from the bed, picked up his dressing-gown, put it on and fastened the belt. He then bent down and picked Colwyn's up. Returning to the bed, he held it for her.

Shyly, she rose, wincing as previously unused muscles protested at the abuse they had just received. As she turned to allow the gown to be pulled onto her shoulders, she gave a cry of alarm at the sight of blood on the sheet. Looking down, she saw blood on her thighs.

"Don't be frightened; it's normal for a maiden's first time. It is proof for her husband that she is indeed a maiden."

Reassured at his words, she allowed him to walk her to the door of her adjoining room, opened it and ushered her through. Sarah had returned and was waiting for her. Morgan stopped long enough to kiss her before returning to the bed-chamber to collect the soiled bed sheet, and exiting via the other door where he went to join the men waiting in the banquet hall below, to celebrate the deflowering of his maiden wife.

Sarah came to her lady and led her towards the bathtub of hot water. "My Lady is all right?" she asked tentatively.

Colwyn was trembling, not with shock, but from the passion of the event and of the care and the love with which her husband had possessed her.

"My Lady? Come." She gently undid her gown and removed it, ignoring the blood on the inside of her thighs. "The hot water will soothe you. There is not much blood, my Lady; your husband was gentle."

Still trembling, Colwyn stepped into the hot water and sat down. Sarah gently bathed her mistress, then went to the table and poured a goblet of wine.

"Here, my Lady, drink this. It will calm you. I will be back shortly. I need to replace the bedding."

Colwyn took a large gulp of wine and closed her eyes, letting the hot water soothe her.

There was a lot of noise and joviality coming from the banquet hall as Morgan approached the double doors. A guard saw him approaching and opened one of the doors for him. Everyone turned as he strode into the hall and a hush descended as he strode to the front of the room, towards King Stuart and his brother Michael. He mounted the steps to the raised dais and turned to face the occupants of the hall. The crowd waited expectantly.

With a flourish, he unfolded the sheet and held it up for all the men to see. A huge cheer went up. King Stuart slapped him on the back, and a large goblet of wine was thrust into his hand.

"To the Duke of Rossmere and his beautiful bride. May they be blessed with a happy marriage and many children," said King Stuart.

"The duke and his bride!" everyone chorused, downing their goblets in one go, then cheering loudly, filling their goblets for another toast.

Morgan stayed for another goblet then he was cheered out of the hall as he returned to his bride.

Sarah returned from replacing the bedding and removed the now empty goblet from her lady's hand.

"Oh, Sarah," Colwyn whispered in wonder.

Chapter Fourteen

"My Lady is feeling all right?" Sarah asked, seeing her still trembling.

"Yes, thank you."

"Then let me dry you; you must return to your husband shortly. Come, stand up."

Colwyn did as she was told, stepped out of the tub, and Sarah wrapped a towel around her and led her back to her dressing table to sit down, so she could prepare her for her husband again. Once more, she brushed her hair and sprinkled rose water on it, and dabbed it behind her ears.

"Do you require another goblet of wine, my Lady?"

Colwyn shook her head. "No, Sarah, I'm fine, thank you."

Sarah gently began to dry her off with the towel, then picked up the dressing gown and helped her into it once again.

"Come, my Lady." She led her mistress back into the bedroom and across to the bed. Gently, she undid the gown and removed it, and encouraged her to get back into bed, drawing the covers up around her. She draped the gown over a chair and turned to exit, just as Bodine returned. "Your Grace," Sarah said curtsying.

"Thank you for taking care of Duchess Colwyn, Sarah. You may retire for the night. Your lady will not require your services until the morning."

"As you wish, your Grace." She curtsied again and left the room.

Bodine moved to the table and refilled the goblets with wine. Returning to the bed, he offered one to Colwyn and placed the other on the table beside the bed, before removing his gown. Colwyn absorbed the sight of his lean, muscular body; the broad chest, the narrow hips, tight belly and powerful thighs, and his manhood, at rest. She coloured, thinking of how it had possessed her, and her womanhood constricted as she thought of it possessing her once again.

He slipped between the sheets and picked up his goblet. "My wife," he whispered, his pale blue eyes appraising her, "know that I love you with every fibre of my being."

Colwyn blushed and took a sip of wine before replying. "My husband, you have made me a woman, and I will love you forever."

Bodine slowly drank his wine; there was no hurry as they had the whole night ahead of them still for him to start teaching her of the art of love.

Colwyn was the first to finish her wine. She placed her goblet down and turned to face her husband. Tentatively, she reached out and placed a hand gently on his chest, her fingers teasing the light dusting of hair, and snuggled up to his body. Bodine kissed the top of her head before finishing his wine and disposing of his goblet.

"Morgan," Colwyn started shyly. "Tell me how I can please you."

He kissed her before replying. "Follow my lead," he whispered back, as he trailed a hand lightly up her arm, across her shoulder, and down to her breast, massaging and gently squeezing it, causing the nipple to harden. Colwyn carefully reciprocated the move, watching as her hands initiated a response from his body. His lips moved to her throat leaving a trail of hot kisses that slowly moved down to her breasts, whilst his hand moved down to her belly, gently stroking, teasing, almost tickling, and he felt her skin twitch beneath his fingers. Again, she imitated his movements, to be rewarded by his own response to her mouth and hands.

He took his time, carrying out a detailed exploration of her body, to discover what aroused and inflamed her and, in turn, she began to learn what excited him and brought about the desired response from his body, giving her a sense of power over her husband.

The expression in Bodine's eyes made her gasp as she witnessed them change colour and turn sapphire blue with smouldering passion as her hands and mouth aroused him. He rolled onto his back, dragging her on top of

Chapter Fourteen

him, and gently squeezed her buttocks, making her squirm delightedly against him, then ran his hands up and down her spine. She sat up, sitting astride his hips and looked down into his handsome face, his lips slightly parted; her hands rested lightly on his heaving chest and her fingers teased him briefly before she bent over and kissed him, leaving a trail from his chin, down his throat and chest.

Bodine closed his eyes and revelled in the sensations being aroused within him. Marriage to Colwyn was going to be filled with many erotic nights in the years to come, of that he was sure.

"Am I pleasing my husband?" he heard her ask him in a husky whisper.

He opened his eyes and smiled at her. "More than you could possibly realise…" his voice trailed off as a thought popped into his head. If Colwyn were truly Kadeau… He rolled slightly to deposit her by his side on the bed. "Touch me," he commanded softly. He grasped her hand and laid it upon his partly engorged manhood, then gasped as her fingers gently stroked and teased.

Colwyn was fascinated at how it responded and grew under her caresses, and how Bodine shuddered under her touch. The feeling of power was rather intoxicating. She may have been a novice in the ways of love, but she was a quick learner.

Now on their sides, facing each other, Bodine firmly grasped her thigh and moved it to drape it elegantly over his hip, allowing him to touch her intimately. She moaned under his touch, arousing him more and he rolled again, pinning her beneath him, with her legs wrapped around his hips. Kissing her hungrily, he moved his hands and placed them on her temples, deepening their link. She did the same to him and they were lost in the erotic mental feelings; a kaleidoscope of emotions and sensations even more intense than their first time together, as they felt what each other was feeling.

Climax brought a scream from Colwyn, and a long, guttural groan from Bodine, as they flew over the edge of reason. Several moments passed before Bodine could open his eyes, and when he did, he saw his bride was crying.

"Colwyn, what's wrong?" he asked, suddenly concerned. "Did I hurt you?"

She shook her head, too overcome to speak at first, then managed to gasp, "No, I am unharmed. I just have never… never felt anything like this. It was incredible." She smiled at him and pulled his head down to kiss him with everything she could muster.

Bodine returned the kiss with enthusiasm, then gently moved to lie beside her, pulled the bed coverings up over them both and wrapped her in his arms as they settled down for the night.

The next thing he was aware of was of the sun, just beginning to rise, and a smile crossed his lips. Their wedding day had obviously been more exhausting than he had anticipated! Carefully, he shifted his position, so he could just lie and look at his wife, sleeping peacefully. He found it soothing, and also comforting to have a woman who loved him without reservation; something he thought he would never have. He resisted the urge to reach out and touch her, not wanting to awaken her yet, but content to watch her sleep, a slight smile on her lips.

A little time passed, then Colwyn stirred and opened her eyes to find her husband staring at her, love in his eyes and a soft smile on his lips.

"'Tis early, my love. Go back to sleep," Bodine said in a whisper.

"I felt you staring at me in my sleep," she said, reaching out to touch his face.

He grabbed her hand and kissed her palm, then she continued to caress his features and her eyebrows rose in surprise as she touched his chin.

"I'd forgotten!" she exclaimed.

"What?" he asked, frowning at her.

Chapter Fourteen

"You have a dimple in your chin!"

He gave a broad smile at that, causing two other dimples to appear in his cheeks.

"Do you know how handsome you are?" she asked him.

"Yes; you have told me many times," he laughed. "And I consider myself blessed to be married to the most beautiful woman in the Kingdom."

She blushed, then dragged herself up to be level with him.

"We have our wedding breakfast this morning, and then the day is ours. What do you wish to do today, my love?" Bodine asked her.

"I have never seen your Duchy. Can we ride and view some of it today? Then I take it you will assume your duties and hold court for your subjects tomorrow?"

"If that is what you wish. Rossmere has some beautiful countryside; I will be proud to show it to you."

"Thank you." She smiled and her hands began to caress him.

Their love-making was slow and leisurely and they lay content in one another's arms for a while longer; then Bodine sighed.

"I must leave you and get dressed, but I will return to collect your for our wedding breakfast." He kissed her one final time, and Colwyn watched his lithe movements as he threw back the bedclothes and stood up. He took a couple of steps to a chair, picked up his dressing gown, and slipped it on, covering his exquisite form. She followed his every movement as he walked to the door, paused to look at her one final time, then left.

Several minutes passed and then there was a knock at the door leading to her dressing room. Colwyn pulled the covers up around her.

"Enter."

The door opened to admit Sarah.

"Good morning, your Grace," she said, bobbing a curtsy. She surveyed her mistress and immediately saw the change in her; she was now a woman in every sense of the word, and it showed in her face and new bearing.

"Good morning, Sarah," Colwyn replied as her maid picked up her dressing gown and brought it towards her. "I have a bath waiting for you… I assumed you would want to take one before going down for the wedding breakfast. There is also a present for you, in your day room."

"Thank you, Sarah; I think I am in need of a bath… and a present?" She smiled to herself, mentally reliving the night of passion. The Queen had come close to advising her of how true love could be, but now, having experienced it first hand, she realised how lucky she had been to have had a man like Bodine in her bed, and what a good lover he was. She blushed at the thoughts invading her mind.

Colwyn! Bodine's thoughts suddenly broke into her erotic meanderings. *Please, show some restraint! If you must think of such things, please shield your thoughts when I'm trying to get dressed!*

I am sorry, my love, I couldn't help it!

As she moved to her dressing room, removed her gown and sat down in her bath, Bodine decided to get his own back, and the most erotic vision entered her mind of her writhing beneath him, her body aflame as he touched her, and she gasped. It was so real, she felt her body responding to the imaginary touch of his hands and mouth.

"Are you all right, my Lady?"

Colwyn found she could hardly speak. Closing her eyes only made the vision more intense, and she squirmed in the tub as she felt an orgasm building.

Morgan, please stop! My m-maid is staring at me! Morgan!

Abruptly, the vision ceased, and Colwyn almost groaned in pure frustration at not having reached the orgasm.

Chapter Fourteen

I am sorry, my love; but that is what you do to me, Bodine sent through, and the link softened to a tenuous, but comforting hold.

"My Lady!" Sarah asked again.

Colwyn gulped and opened her eyes.

"I… I'm fine, Sarah, honestly."

"Is the water too hot? You're looking very flushed."

"No, no I'm all right." She concentrated on taking her bath, vowing to take sweet revenge on her husband.

After dressing, she went into her day room to discover a beautiful piece of furniture, obviously from the Far East, by its form and decoration. It was a low couch to lounge on, and Colwyn knew it was a gift as compensation for the loss of her virginity. She smiled secretly as a number of thoughts for its use suddenly popped into her head.

ଔ ଓ ଔ ଓ

15

Chapter Fifteen

Close friends were present for the wedding breakfast. As neither the bride nor the groom had living parents, the King and Queen took their place, along with Prince Michael, Princess Anne, Duke Kenneth Dernley, Giles' father, Giles Dernley and, in a complete break of etiquette, they had also invited Master Andrew, Master Stephen, Ioan, Edward and Sarah.

To everyone's intense relief, the breakfast went well, although Ioan and Sarah were quiet for the majority of the time. Masters Stephen and Andrew exchanged new techniques, and it was then that Andrew mentioned the use of stitches in wounds with cleaned thread. This resulted in the two surgeons excusing themselves to talk more in private.

"Well, I doubt we'll see the two of them for the rest of the day!" Stuart joked, then turned to Bodine. "So, what are your plans for today?"

"Colwyn has requested to see some of the countryside of Rossmere."

"Rossmere is indeed blessed with some beautiful scenery, Colwyn. I hope you enjoy your ride."

"Thank you, Sire. Then tomorrow, if permitted, I will sit with Morgan whilst he holds court."

Stuart nodded. "You will learn a great deal. So, when are you planning to head to Inver?"

Chapter Fifteen

"In a week's time. I think we need to relieve Sir John for a little while at least," Bodine replied. "With Colwyn's permission, I shall despatch a messenger to warn them of our impending arrival, and to prepare Inver cathedral for the blessing."

"Of course, Morgan," Colwyn replied, smiling.

"Come then, my love; time to change into your riding leathers so I can show you my Duchy." Bodine turned to his liege. "With your permission, Sire?"

"Granted, Morgan. I have decided, we will all travel to Inver in a week."

Bodine nodded. "Your company will be most welcome, Sire." He rose from his seat and bowed before assisting Colwyn from hers. She curtsied and they left the hall together.

ॐ ॐ ॐ ॐ

They halted at the top of the rise to take in the vista. Rolling hills and fields of crops lay before them; they had travelled past part of the mere that continued to stretch into the distance for several more miles. Rossmere certainly appeared to be a land blessed with fertile soil and rich grazing lands. The Duke of Rossmere ensured that the land was treated with respect and care, as had been inborn in all Kadeau since the beginning of time.

"Morgan, it's beautiful!" Colwyn exclaimed.

He gave her an easy, relaxed smile. "Thank you. Personally, I think Rossmere has the most beautiful scenery in the Kingdom."

"Not that you're biased, or anything," Colwyn giggled.

Bodine gave her an indignant look, then spoilt it all by grinning. "Well, maybe just a little," he finally confessed. "But can you blame me?"

Colwyn stared off into the distance. On the far horizon, she could just about distinguish cliffs rising, white and gleaming. On her left, also some distance away, she saw that the sky was the most beautiful shade of blue, and knew the sea was somewhere in that direction, for only the sea could give the sky that particular blue colour.

"No," she finally replied, turning her gaze upon him. "The countryside of Rossmere is indeed most beautiful… like its master."

At those words, Bodine moved his horse closer to Colwyn so their thighs touched, and he leant towards her to place a soft kiss on her lips.

She responded by placing a hand on his thigh. "Are you truly happy, Morgan?" she asked quietly. "Despite all we've been through, has it been worth it?"

"How could you even ask that? Of course it has been worth it! Despite the worry and suffering we have endured. You have made me the happiest man alive; your actions have more than proved your love for me, and I hope I have proved my love for you."

Colwyn squeezed his thigh gently as she responded. "You have shown your love for me my entire life, from my earliest memories."

Bodine squeezed her hand, then gathered up his reins and indicated for her to follow him.

They travelled a number of miles and finished up near the edge of a cliff. However, there was no view as a fog had descended.

"Come," Morgan ordered, urging Banner on through the fog.

Colwyn carefully followed him and then gasped in shock. The fog was but a barrier, for once through it, they found themselves above a deserted beach in a small bay, with fine golden sand, backed by a cliff and a narrow path that led down to the shore. Colwyn could not prevent a gasp from escaping at the sight.

"Oh Morgan!" she breathed.

"I'm glad you like it. This is one of my favourite places. I usually come here to be alone if I want to think, or just to admire the beauty. The 'fog' is just a little something to keep everyone else away."

Chapter Fifteen

"I thank you for bringing me here; it's beautiful. Can we stay a little while?"

"If you wish." Bodine urged his horse forward along the narrow path that led down into the bay, and Colwyn urged Storm to follow.

After a little while, they reached the bottom. Colwyn looked around her and saw a small cave in the cliffs at the other side of the bay, which she decided she would explore a little later, but for now, she had a wish to feel the sand and water under her bare feet.

Not waiting for Bodine to assist her, she dismounted and sat on a convenient rock to remove her leather boots. Free from their confines, she placed her feet on the sand and wiggled her toes, smiling like a child. It seemed so long ago since she had done something like this back at Inver.

Bodine dismounted and proceeded to remove his horse's saddle and bridle, before turning to Storm and doing the same. He then gave them both a slap on the rump and they shot off across the sand as if the devil himself were pursuing them.

"Morgan!" Colwyn exclaimed, then relaxed as she saw his lazy smile.

"It's fine. They can't get out of the bay. Let them have some fun." He gave her a quizzical look that made her frown, "Tell me, Colwyn… are you up for some fun of your own?"

Colwyn's eyes widened as she saw the almost roguish expression travel across her husband's face, and a twitch of his lips as he looked at her.

"What do you mean?" she asked nervously. She had never seen this side of him before, and she was uncertain as to what was on his mind.

"Can you swim?" he asked conversationally, as he perched himself on the edge of a convenient rock and began to pull his boots off.

"A little," she replied, watching with increasing nervousness as he began to remove the rest of his clothes. "Morgan… What are you doing? Someone might see!"

"No one will see," he assured her, now wearing only his leather breeches. Colwyn looked up at the cliffs, feeling very insecure.

"You trust me, don't you?" he asked her.

"Yes, but…"

"Well then." He stood up, his lean, powerful physique towering over her as he stood close. Sexuality practically oozed from every pore of his body, and Colwyn gulped in several lungfuls of air as he sent a most erotic thought down the link, of the two of them naked, swimming in the sea.

"Morgan!" she panted, blushing furiously and closed her eyes so she didn't become trapped under his mesmerising gaze. But closing her eyes only made the vision more intense, and she gasped as his arms suddenly snaked around her and crushed her to him, giving her a kiss that took her breath away. Feeling decidedly light-headed, she clung to him as he started unlacing her clothing.

The warm air suddenly caressing her breasts brought her back to reality with a start.

"Morgan… I can't," she stuttered.

"Of course you can, my love," he whispered back as her jacket and top dropped unceremoniously onto the sand, to be quickly followed by the halved skirt, so that all she had left on were her own breeches.

His eyes were literally smouldering as he started on the lacings of her breeches, and she quickly reciprocated his movements and then, they were standing on the beach, naked.

Colwyn was breathing heavily as she absorbed the sight of him. Bodine simply smiled, took her hand and led her to the waters' edge. At that precise moment, Banner and Storm went flying past in the opposite direction, kicking up surf, spray and sand as they went, obviously enjoying their freedom very much.

Chapter Fifteen

The water was a little warmer than Colwyn had been expecting and the two of them were soon hip-deep in the sea. Bodine led her in deeper until she had no option but to swim, which they did for a while, before retreating to slightly shallower waters so they could stand.

Banner chose that moment to come back to his master and gave Bodine a nudge in the back with his head, causing him to stumble forward into Colwyn.

"Sir!" she exclaimed giggling, "You have taught your horse some bad manners!"

"Not intentionally," the duke replied. "But sometimes he tends to get a bit over-enthusiastic!" Banner gave him another nudge in the back then put his head over Bodine's shoulder and snorted softly in Colwyn's face.

Gently, she rubbed his nose and spoke softly to him; then the horse turned and waded back to the shoreline, tail in the air, and suddenly shot off again, Storm in close pursuit. Colwyn laughed as she watched them go.

"They are most certainly enjoying themselves," she said as she looked up into Bodine's handsome face. She wrapped her arms around his neck and rubbed her breasts against his chest as she kissed him, tasting the salt water on his lips.

His hand slithered down her body and he touched her intimately, smiling as she groaned under the assault and moved her hips, causing his manhood to respond favourably.

Her movement against him gradually became more urgent as she grew desperate for release. Bodine grabbed one of her thighs and lifted it so she could wrap her leg around his hip, as she pushed his manhood down between her thighs; then he grasped her firmly by the buttocks and lifted her. She immediately placed both hands on his shoulders and wrapped her other leg around his hip as he slowly impaled her with his shaft. Her head hung back and she moaned breathlessly as she felt him penetrate her deeply.

Colwyn had always considered Bodine to be measured in his actions, no matter what the situation, but today, for the first time, she was seeing another side to him; the impetuous, adventurous side; a side rarely released from within, and she found she was enjoying it. Even now, as he was making love to her in the sea, casting aside all inhibitions as she surrendered her body to his and feeling his firm thrusts as he possessed her, both terrified and excited her as. at any moment, someone might spy them from the cliffs above.

Bodine was well aware of his current carefree attitude. He had never been so happy, and he knew it couldn't last forever, so he had decided for the first few weeks, he would take advantage of this opportunity to live as normal a married life as was possible for a man in his position. At any moment, the King could summon him to go into battle, or quell a rebellion or uprising, which could ultimately lead to injury or even death.

He knew there were many different ways of making love to a woman and he would explore several, if Colwyn were game, and, so far, she seemed willing and eager. Of course, he knew the King expected him to have her with child as soon as possible, but he was purposely delaying that for purely selfish reasons; however, his Liege would be envisaging some form of news that she had either fallen or was shortly to give birth to a child, by the time he returned to Ellesmere next March.

They would have to divide their time between Ellesmere, Rossmere and Invermere, but when the child was due, he wanted her as close as possible, in case of any complications that could arise. He had to keep her safe at all costs.

For now, though, he could no longer think straight as his approaching climax took over his mind and body. They had reached shallower water, and he was now kneeling, thrusting deeper and harder into her body, and she was writhing beneath him, gasping his name as she accepted everything he threw at her; and then he felt her go rigid and scream loudly, her fingernails digging

Chapter Fifteen

deeply into his shoulders as she convulsed in orgasm, and causing him to follow suit.

He felt as though his heart was going to explode from his chest, but also felt totally sated and fulfilled. No prostitute had ever made him feel so complete; not even the highly skilled ones, like Raven, to whom Stuart Cantrell had introduced him, to teach him about the art of sex, and how both a man and woman's body worked during the act.

"Morgan, oh Morgan," Colwyn breathed against his ear, before gently nipping it, making him shudder.

He kissed her throat and held her tightly against him. They just couldn't seem to get enough of each other, but for now, this would suffice. Carefully, he stood up, pulling her to her feet. Sea water cascaded off their bodies, as he slowly led her from the water.

"There is a small waterfall near the cave, should you wish to rinse the salt water off your body," Bodine told her.

"I think I would, thank you."

"Very well."

They paused partway to collect their clothes, then continued to the waterfall, where they both rinsed their bodies before sitting in the sun to dry off.

"You are positively glowing," Bodine told her, as he leant forward and kissed her.

As they were just pulling their boots on, Banner and Storm wandered over to drink from the pool at the base of the waterfall.

Bodine retrieved their bridles and once he had put these on, managed to saddle them; then reluctantly, they left their secret bay and made their way back to Belvoir Castle.

On their return, Bodine spent time with the King, and Colwyn with Queen Alexandra.

My dear," she remarked, as they sat alone in the Queen's chambers, awaiting the arrival of Princess Anne. "I cannot help but notice that married life appears to be most agreeable on you." She then went on to repeat what Bodine had said to her. "You are positively glowing."

"Your Majesty is most kind," Colwyn answered shyly.

"I take it, General Bodine has… been gentle with you."

Colwyn blushed fiercely. Talking about such things was still very much a struggle, even though it had actually been very commonplace at Ellesmere, especially between the ladies-in-waiting, who had taken great delight in describing their sexual exploits.

"Most gentle, Your Majesty. Each time, he has left me… wanting more." She saw Alexandra's eyebrows rise at her comment.

"He is… skilled then."

"I cannot answer that, for he is the only man I have ever known. I have nothing with which to compare. All I can say is that I have never experienced sensations like it when he touches me; my body aches for him, and I believe I am learning what pleases and arouses him."

She stopped, as there was a knock on the door and Anne entered. "I apologise for being late," she said, joining them at the table. "Have I missed anything?"

"Only that our General Bodine appears to be an extremely good lover," said Alexandra.

"So, the rumours were true; he is experienced. Oh my dear; if he is, you have no idea how lucky you are! Perhaps when you are more… relaxed, we can swap notes; it's always good to be inventive where one's husband is concerned," Anne said in a knowing voice.

"Colwyn has actually said very little, but I believe, between the three of us, we have the best husbands in Devonmere!" Alexandra exclaimed.

Chapter Fifteen

"Amen to that," Anne said quietly. "Now, what are our plans for the rest of the week?"

Colwyn explained that she expected to sit with Bodine as he held office at least for part of the remaining days, but if there was anything in particular that their majesties wished to do, then she would try her utmost to make it happen.

Her mother had taught her well; she was an excellent hostess. When she was not performing duties alongside her husband, then she ensured the royal party was well entertained.

At the end of the week; as she lay in the arms of her husband the night before they were due to leave for Invermere, Bodine told her the King was pleased with her, and she glowed with pleasure at this news.

༄ ༅ ༄ ༅

16

Chapter Sixteen

It took just six days to reach Inver, for the weather was fine and warm. Inver's mere was a long crescent, fed by two rivers, and they skirted along part of it as they travelled. The low plains between the rivers contained rich and fertile lands, filled with crops, and the huge wood to the east of the city was green and lush, and carefully managed. Inver was also a major port, and the castle stood at the top of high sheer cliffs above the River Wyvern. Once again, the sound of a herald and of a small army approaching the main street drew people out from inside their homes and those in the marketplace to stop what they were doing and to stare.

The citizens bowed and curtsied as the royal party rode past, and Colwyn heard her people calling her name.

"Lady Colwyn! Praise be to God! Your Grace! God bless you!"

She accepted their welcome and waved at them in acknowledgement, feeling rather choked at their open display of affection.

Bodine, riding by her side, picked up on her increased emotional state and reached out to take her hand. "You are upset, my love?" he asked.

"N-no, Morgan. I am just moved by their affection for me. Having been gone for so long, I thought they may have forgotten about me. Or, perhaps, even thought me dead."

Chapter Sixteen

"They love you," he replied simply, as he raised her hand to his lips and placed a soft kiss on the back of it.

It seemed a lifetime ago since she had last been here; home. As they rode into the castle, she saw Sir John MacKenzie standing at the bottom of the steps to the keep, with William Aulean, Bishop of Inver. Several squires stood to the side, ready to assist when asked, and an honour guard lined the bailey to keep the crowd at a respectful distance.

The royal party dismounted; soldiers and squires took their horses aside. The welcoming committee bowed low as the King and Queen approached.

"Your Majesty," MacKenzie said, kissing the sovereign ring. "Welcome back to Inver." He bowed in turn to the Queen, Prince and Princess; then to the Duke of Rossmere, until Colwyn stood before him. "Your Grace, welcome home." He went to kiss her hand, but instead, Colwyn hugged him tightly.

"Sir John." She sounded very emotional.

MacKenzie held her at arm's length and looked at her. "You look radiant, my Lady. Marriage becomes you."

She smiled at him. "Thank you, Sir John."

MacKenzie straightened up. "Come, you must all be hungry and tired after your journey. Food and drink awaits in the main hall." He gestured for them to precede him up the steps into the keep.

Several minutes later, they were seated in the main hall, taking refreshments. Everything was just as Colwyn remembered apart from the fact that her parents were no longer present, although she could feel their essence. Talk was kept light-hearted, but she was hardly listening; it was proving harder than she realised to step back into normality within her own home. Although she tried to keep her thoughts private, Bodine immediately picked up on the barrier she had erected and guessed what was going through her mind. The last time she had been here, the castle had been under siege and she had been forced to flee for her life, leaving her parents to face death. It had to be rather overwhelming for someone who had known only love and happiness in this place.

Rooms had been allocated to the royal party, and Colwyn found that all her things had been moved to her mother's rooms. She was now the Duchess and it was where she belonged. MacKenzie had been shrewd, though, and had had the room decorated in a similar fashion as her own room had been done, to make her feel more at home.

Bodine, as the new Duke of Inver, had been allocated the duke's old rooms. MacKenzie again had removed all traces of the old duke and redecorated, so that Bodine could create his own new memories of Inver. Everything had been moved from his old rooms to here. Satisfied all was in order, he made his way along to Colwyn's rooms.

Sarah had finished her duties and was just leaving when he arrived. He nodded politely to her and entered Colwyn's rooms. She was not in the day room, so he moved to her inner bed-chamber to pause at the doorway. She was sitting on the bed, a forlorn expression on her face, miles away in another place and perhaps even another time, totally oblivious to his presence.

As he observed her from the doorway, he saw a lone tear slip down her cheek and his heart ached for her. Unable to stay there longer, he moved forward and knelt before her, his love for her clearly showing on his face. Gently, he wiped her tears away, then leant forward and placed a soft kiss on her lips.

"I'm sorry," she apologised quietly, "for my weakness. You must expect better of me."

Bodine shook his head. "Stop that," he ordered. "Your memories will be strong; it will take time for you to adjust. You are strong; you have more than proved that to me and to the King. Take your time."

"Y-you are so understanding, Morgan, and so patient."

Chapter Sixteen

He smiled. "Your feelings are still raw. This is the first time you have been back since February. I know you are hurting, but I will help you through it. You saw the welcome your people gave you; that must give you strength and a warmth to know how they feel. Tomorrow is our wedding blessing, and you will greet as many of the people as you can before beginning your duties. We will go out into the countryside and meet your people outside the city. You have some decisions to make, as our time must be split between here, Rossmere and Ellesmere. You will need to appoint a permanent steward. Sir John has done a fine job so far, but it's whether you wish him to continue in that vein."

"I can think of no one who knows the Duchy better than Sir John. He is getting to the age where he will no longer be able to fulfil his knightly duties, so the position of steward will be perfect for him," Colwyn replied. "I trust him completely."

"A wise decision, my love. He can continue to serve in that capacity for many more years, should you so wish."

"When were you thinking of returning to Rossmere?"

"Not until October or November, before winter really sets in."

She nodded.

"I need to speak to you about another delicate matter," he said, rising to sit beside her on the bed and still holding her hand.

"Morgan?"

"The King will be expecting me to report to him in March with some good news… about an heir." He paused as Colwyn blushed. "So far, I am being selfish and careful. I don't want you with child yet; I want you for myself, but I will be unable to delay the King's wish indefinitely. You must have a say in this next decision, but if you are agreeable, I suggest we have six months to ourselves, and try for a child in February."

Colwyn gulped, suddenly very much afraid of the future. Childbirth was the most dangerous situation for a woman. Death was a possibility, but she was young, strong and fit; all to her advantage.

"February then," she finally said.

"I will ensure you will not be alone. I will see you to Ellesmere well before you are due; the Queen and Princess Anne and the finest midwives will be available, and if permitted, I will be with you."

"I would like it if you could be with me. I feel I can get through anything if you are there."

"Master Andrew is the best battle surgeon. I will have him standing by as well. I will do everything in my power to keep you safe, and deliver our child safely."

He saw her take a large gulp of air.

"Does the prospect… frighten you?" he asked gently.

"Yes," she admitted.

"I understand your fears, really, I do, but I am here and I will do whatever it takes to keep you safe." He moved then, and took her in her arms and held her close. His own mother had been no more than a child when he had been born; Colwyn would be seventeen by the time their child was due; her body would be more mature and capable of coping with the stress of childbirth.

"What if… our first child is a girl?" Colwyn suddenly asked. "Will you be angry?"

"Of course not! Why would you think such a thing? If it is a girl, she will be as beautiful as her mother and who knows… perhaps Queen of Devonmere. If King Stuart had been considering you as Queen, then he may, no doubt, consider our daughter as such."

"Then I must give you a daughter and two sons," Colwyn said quietly. "A future queen, a duke for Rossmere, and a duke for Invermere."

Chapter Sixteen

"Now don't worry about it. God will reward us as he sees fit. What will be, will be. Let us eat, and get an early night, for it is likely to be a long day tomorrow."

ଔ ଚ ଔ ଚ

Sir John MacKenzie had planned hard and in great detail for the wedding blessing. Inver's Elite Guard were resplendent in their dress uniforms, and he had rehearsed the ceremony on a number of occasions to ensure it went perfectly. Horses gleamed, their livery spotless; armour shone. He was pleased. Once again, both Banner and Storm were in their white livery and Bodine and Colwyn dressed in white, as they had been for their wedding. However, this time, they rode together to the cathedral, through the streets lined with people, some of whom threw flower petals.

They dismounted at the base of the steps to the cathedral, ascended the steps together, and then paused at the top to acknowledge the crowds, before entering the grand stone building. Flowers decorated the aisle and flower petals were strewn on the stone floor. Proudly, they walked down the aisle together towards the altar and Bishop Aulean, who stood waiting, in his finest vestments, to perform the blessing.

The ceremony was as long as the original wedding had been, with prayers and songs to celebrate the union. Finally, it was over, and the two once again stood on the top step outside the cathedral. As before, Colwyn issued coins to the needy. She noted how some of the women seemed to want to hold onto her hand a little longer than etiquette required, but she didn't mind. Instead, she smiled and spoke to them.

Finally, it was time to once again mount up and walk back through the streets to the castle. It was quite noisy with all the cheering and calling, and Colwyn was rather overwhelmed with it all. She had been worried that her people might have thought she had deserted them back in February when she had fled Inver, but it seemed that they did understand the reasons behind it and were thankful to have her back. They had accepted her marriage to Bodine, who had been a reasonably frequent visitor and had also been adopted by Colwyn's parents.

Back at the keep, Colwyn paused to make a fuss of Storm and Banner, before squires took them back to the stables, and she and Bodine ascended the steps to the keep. From now on, life would return to a new normality.

In her rooms, Colwyn had just changed out of her wedding attire when there was a knock at the door. Sarah opened it to find Princess Anne standing there.

"Your Highness, please, enter," Sarah said, curtsying deeply.

"Thank you, Sarah. Is your mistress within?"

"Yes, please, this way." Sarah moved into the inner dress chamber.

Colwyn looked up, saw the princess and immediately dropped into a deep curtsy. "Your Royal Highness," she breathed. "How may I serve you?"

"I wish to speak with you privately, if I may?"

"But of course." Colwyn indicated for Sarah to leave and invited Anne to sit. "You wish to ask something?" she queried.

"It is a most delicate matter," Anne started, her hands almost unconsciously moving in a nervous, wringing motion. "You… you have not fallen yet." It was a statement.

"No, I will not be falling until February," Colwyn replied.

"How do you know this?"

"Morgan can… sense my readiness to conceive. At particular times of the month, before we were married, he avoided me, so as to avoid temptation, and the wedding was delayed further not only because of the injuries, but because of…" her voice trailed off in embarrassment at talking of such things.

"Can he really sense when… when you are ready?" Anne persisted.

Chapter Sixteen

"Yes."

The princess bit her lip, took a deep breath and then continued.

"Michael and I have been married for some time, but, as yet, I have failed to fall... having heard that General Bodine can sense... I... I was wondering... do you think he could... do the same for me? Sense when I would be ready?"

Colwyn's eyes widened in surprise. It was the last thing she had expected to hear.

"I... I suppose he could, but I'm not sure... we are... in tune with each other. We share a... bond that makes us able to sense more intently, what the other is feeling."

"Will you ask him for me, please?" Anne sounded almost desperate. "What good am I as a wife to Michael if I cannot conceive?"

"Your Highness—"

"Call me Anne, please."

"Thank you. Anne... there is also such a thing as... being anxious about it. You must be relaxed, and accept what comes, but," she hastily started, "I will ask Morgan. When do you leave? He may need a little time to... detect your readiness."

"I understand. I will endeavour to delay our departure if necessary."

"Do you wish me to summon him now? I can do so."

"Would you?"

"Of course." Colwyn rose and went to the door. Usually, a page or two was lurking in the corridor, and this occasion was no exception. "Owen, please find General Bodine and ask him to come."

"Yes, your Grace." The page immediately went running off to obey his Duchess.

Several minutes passed, and then there was a knock on the door, and Bodine entered.

"My love, what is wrong? I—" he stopped as he saw Anne.

"Morgan, we have a most delicate request to ask of you. Please…" she indicated for him to come close.

Anne stood up.

"Do you wish me to leave, Anne?" Colwyn asked.

"Certainly not! That would be most improper."

Bodine frowned at the pair of them.

"Do you wish me to explain your request?" Colwyn asked.

"No, I… I shall do it." She took a deep breath. "I need your word that this conversation goes no further, General Bodine."

"Of course, your Highness," Bodine replied, frowning even more.

"Very well… Colwyn has told me you are able to sense when… when she is ready to conceive." She paused as she saw Bodine colour slightly. "Could you do that with me?"

The duke opened his mouth and closed it again. He had prepared himself for almost any question, apart from that one. He swallowed, slowly.

"I… er… I believe I would need to establish a link with you to do this. Would you be prepared to accept this?"

Anne swallowed nervously. She looked at Colwyn, who smiled encouragingly.

"May I enquire why are you asking this of me?" Bodine continued.

"I have been married for two years. That is a long time to not have fallen. I… I need to know if it is me; if there is something wrong with me."

Bodine swallowed and nodded. He looked at Colwyn. "My love; are you all right with my creating this link? It will be but temporary."

"I am happy with it if it will help her Highness."

"Very well." He indicated for Anne to sit, and he sat next to her. He flexed his fingers. "I need you to relax, and empty your mind of all thought."

Anne nodded.

Chapter Sixteen

"Close your eyes; breathe slowly and deeply; relax."

Anne obeyed, and after a minute, satisfied with what he observed, Bodine carefully placed his hands at the strategic points on her face, closed his eyes, and concentrated.

A few minutes passed, and Colwyn heard Anne gasp.

"Open your eyes," Bodine ordered. "How do you feel?"

Anne's eyes were wide, as she looked at him. "I… I can sense you, in my head," her voice was but a whisper. "Warm, comforting, the lightest of touches!"

Bodine removed his fingers from her face. "I will need to see you every day. The… window of opportunity is quite narrow… you will need to act quickly when I tell you to."

"I understand."

"I must tell you, you are not ready."

Anne nodded.

"If it is agreeable to you, we will rendezvous here every day, after breakfast, before we begin our daily duties."

"Very well, after breakfast." Anne paused. "Thank you for doing this, Morgan. You have no idea how much it means to me."

He nodded and bowed as Anne rose from her seat and left the room.

"Thank you, Morgan," Colwyn said, and smiled as he shook his head.

"I have been asked to do many strange things whilst in service to the King, but this… this tops them all," he finally said. "Have no fear, my love, I will break the link with Princess Anne once we have succeeded in the task. The link will be easy to sever, as I initiated it."

"Unlike our link, you mean?"

"I would never break our link now; even if I could," he told her as he took her in his arms and kissed her. "You have most certainly bewitched me, my love, and I wouldn't have it any other way."

"As long as it never puts you in danger," she responded.

Colwyn and Bodine held court that morning, listening to requests, pleas, and news from within the Duchy. On the most part, Bodine kept quiet, for this was Colwyn's Duchy and hers to command as she saw fit. He only said anything when she directly asked him, and he was pleased to see that her father had taught her well.

After lunch, the royal party went hunting in the woods and celebrated with a hearty meal on their return.

The next week took on a routine, with Bodine seeing Anne every morning after breakfast, ducal duties and then the entertainment of their guests.

It was on the morning of the eighth day that Bodine detected the change in Anne, a day before they were due to depart for Ellesmere.

"You are ready," Bodine told her that morning. "No more than twenty-four hours. If I may be so bold... I recommend you... entertain your husband today, in your chambers, as often as you feel able to."

Anne blushed fiercely at his words but her eyes seemed alive with hope. "Oh, Morgan, if this works, I shall be in debt to you for the rest of my life."

Bodine shook his head. "No, Anne, you won't. I hope that when I return to Ellesmere in March, I will see a glowing, expectant woman, ready to deliver in April."

"God bless you, Morgan." Boldly, she stepped forward and kissed him. "If this does indeed work, perhaps Alexandra will make use of your services... she so wishes for a daughter." And with those words, she swept out of the room to go in search of her husband.

"Morgan, it is a generous thing you have done for Anne," Colwyn said.

"She is your friend; it was the least I could do."

It was noted that Prince Michael and his wife were conspicuous by their absence that day. Alexandra noticed a little smile on Colwyn's lips and

Chapter Sixteen

frowned. Clearly, the Duchess had knowledge of what was going on, and she was determined to find out what.

After the evening meal, Alexandra summoned Colwyn to her rooms, where Anne was also waiting.

"What's going on?" Alexandra demanded of the two of them.

"Your Majesty?" Colwyn queried.

"Don't play games. Something is going on."

"It is not for me to say," Colwyn replied, looking at Anne.

Alexandra rounded on her sister-in-law. "Anne?"

"It is of a personal nature, my sister," Anne responded.

Anger flashed in the Queen's eyes. Anne saw the look and sighed.

"Very well… You know I have been married for two years and have not fallen. I… I asked General Bodine to help me."

"You did what?!"

"I asked him to tell me exactly when I was ready to conceive."

"But he is Kadeau!"

"Exactly. And… today was the day. Michael and I have been… otherwise engaged." She smiled secretively. "It has been a wonderful day."

"You permitted this?" Alexandra demanded of Colwyn.

"I asked him to help her, Highness."

"You're telling me that… that General Bodine can tell when…"

"Yes. That is why I am not with child yet," Colwyn admitted. "We wish to… enjoy one another for a while."

"I see. Go, leave me, both of you."

The two women curtsied and left the Queen's chambers. Outside, they looked at one another.

"She is not pleased," Colwyn said.

"I know, but I don't care. Oh, Colwyn, I have had a wonderful day, and it is not over yet. Michael has been exceedingly inventive."

"And how do you feel?"

"Happy, relaxed; full of anticipation. It has worked, I just know it has. And I owe it all to your Morgan."

"Anne, don't hex it; I do hope it's worked, but be patient."

Anne gave her a hug and kissed her cheek, but smiled in a knowing way.

The royal party left the following morning and life got back to normal. Colwyn informed MacKenzie that she wanted him to serve as steward in her absence, as there was no one she trusted more. MacKenzie was both surprised and honoured, and vowed to do his best.

With the leaders of the Kingdom no longer on-site, Colwyn began her training again, under the direction of MacKenzie, her husband, and Giles Dernley. In addition, as Bodine had suggested, they went out into the countryside, with a small armed guard, to visit several villages. They held court and listened to complaints, concerns and other comments that the people had. A few women presented Colwyn with flowers and other small gifts, for which she thanked them.

The summer wore on, and autumn approached. Crops were harvested, thanks given at the harvest festival; storage areas were filled with grain. It wouldn't matter if it was a hard winter again, as there was food aplenty for the people if it should be needed.

Colwyn's skill with the sword developed quickly; she was stronger and fitter than she had ever been. Her youthful body made her extremely supple and agile and she was now holding her own against both MacKenzie and Dernley, but her husband was still far more skilled than her. She suspected he was not challenging her hard but was simply defending her easily, and, as a result, she felt she was no longer improving, and it began to irritate her slightly.

Bodine was her trainer this day, and once again, she felt him holding back and accused him of such.

Chapter Sixteen

"My love, I do not wish to harm you," he replied as if that explained everything.

"How can I improve if you don't push me harder?" she retorted.

"Do not be in such a hurry; it is important to maintain the correct posture and technique."

But Colwyn was impatient, and feeling relatively comfortable, stepped up her attack in an effort to make her husband retaliate harder.

Her increased ferocity initially surprised him, but it had the desired effect and he responded in kind. Colwyn suddenly realised that maybe she had made a mistake, but was determined not to back down and fought as hard as she could.

"Colwyn, that's enough!" Bodine said, but she ignored him. "Colwyn!"

Realising she wasn't cooperating, he reluctantly decided to disarm her, to bring the training session to a close. He carried out a particularly complex move that drove her back, then skilfully swept his sword around hers, and basically wrenched it out of her hand. It went flying some distance away from her; she hit the ground, gave a cry and grabbed her right wrist.

Bodine sheathed his sword, immediately went to her and knelt down. "I'm sorry my love, but you needed to stop."

She glared at him. "I could have gone on longer!"

"No, you were going to strain yourself; it was time to stop." He went to help her to her feet, but she pushed him away.

"Leave me! I can manage."

"Let me check your wrist."

"No." She got to her feet, retrieved her sword and walked away, feeling angry.

"Colwyn!" But his calls fell on deaf ears. He ran after her and grabbed her by an arm.

"Let go of me!" she hissed.

"You're angry," he said, stating the obvious.

"What gives you that idea?" she snapped.

"Your eyes are positively blazing." He smiled.

Colwyn was fed up. Her wrist hurt; she ached, was sore and stiffening up, and she was feeling stifled. Bodine had been right but she wasn't about to admit that to him. Wrenching her arm free, she went to walk away once more, but again he stopped her. Anger flashed in her eyes.

"Will you dine with me tonight?" he asked her.

"No."

Bodine's expression hardened. He had plans tonight that involved her.

"Then I will come to you," he responded.

"No… I – I'm tired. I shall retire early."

Bodine realised they were about to have their second argument, and wisely kept silent. Colwyn wrenched herself free from him again and walked away. Through narrowed eyes, he watched her go and took a deep breath to stop himself from losing his temper.

Being close to her, he had become consciously aware that she was ready to conceive. He knew he had told her February, but he had been thinking long and hard, working out where they would be after nine months, and realised he wanted her in Ellesmere when the baby was due. This meant he had to bring the date forward to this month, October, and she was ready, but she was not going to be willing tonight; that much was obvious.

His King was expecting news of a forthcoming birth when he returned to Ellesmere in March. Failure to provide this news was likely to annoy Stuart, and that was something Bodine was loath to do.

He pondered his next move as he walked back to the keep. The harsh reality of the situation was that she was his wife; she had a specific place in the order of things, but he had indulged her, given her more freedom than was usually allowed for a woman and allowed her to do things that a woman

Chapter Sixteen

normally would not do. He had a duty to his king, no matter what he felt for his wife, and she also had a duty to him, the King and the Kingdom of Devonmere.

Colwyn threw her sword belt onto her bed. She was angry. Her husband insisted on treating her as if she were some delicate flower. She realised she was very lucky; many wives had a horrible life; subservient, restricted freedom, little better than slaves. Bodine had allowed her an unusual amount of freedom, and she was using it and more. Most of the ladies-in-waiting had no idea of the type of life she led, and what she had already done in her young life.

But she still felt stifled and overprotected. She wanted a change from the precise, measured attitude of her husband.

Her mind suddenly drifted back to their first argument at the Pell in the castle at Ellesmere. She knew she couldn't stay angry at Bodine for long; she loved him far too much for that, but she remembered the feelings that she had felt; it had both frightened and exhilarated her, and she wondered if she dare rile him to that level again. A game; how far dare she push it, she wondered? And boldly, she decided to try. For a moment, she wondered what was making her act like this, then decided it was her highly rebellious nature that sometimes got the better of her; but there was something on Bodine's mind, and she wondered what it was. Playing the game tonight could be highly dangerous, but also intensely rewarding and she had been an incredibly quick learner these past few months.

Not bothering to send for Sarah, Colwyn divested herself of her armour, washed and got changed. Now she had a decision to make; did she go to Bodine's rooms for a meal, or did she play hard to get? She had already started to put things in motion so she would play hard to get—very hard to get… and find!

Decision made, she changed yet again, this time into her riding leathers and grabbed her sword belt. In the woods was a hunting lodge. Most of the Duchies had one, and Invermere was no exception. It was located in a clearing near a lake, and that was where she had decided to go. She wasn't sure if Bodine knew of its existence, so he would either find her, or he wouldn't, and she planned to disappear for a couple of days. She wrote a note to John MacKenzie, then packed her saddlebags and made her way down to the kitchen for some supplies to see her through. She was more than capable of taking care of herself now, and her experiences these last few months had made her a lot more independent.

Finding a page, she handed him the note with strict instructions to deliver it in the evening, when it would be too late for anyone to come looking for her that night. That done, she went to the stables, saddled Storm, and left the castle. It would take a good couple of hours to reach the lodge, travelling at a good pace, and Storm was clearly up for it, but she waited until she got outside of the city limits before letting him have his head, so as not to attract too much attention.

༺ ༻ ༺ ༻

Bodine was not really surprised when Colwyn failed to arrive; she had said she wouldn't, so he ate alone, and then made his way to her rooms. He knocked on the door and waited. A few seconds passed then Sarah opened it.

"Your Grace?" Sarah asked.

"Sarah, I've come to see Colwyn. Will you let me in?"

Sarah looked totally confused as she stared at him. "She's not here, your Grace... I... I assumed she was dining with you."

Chapter Sixteen

Bodine frowned, suddenly feeling uneasy. "I haven't seen her since this afternoon. Can you take a look around her room and see if there is anything missing?"

"At once, your Grace."

"I'll return shortly; I just need to have a word with Sir John MacKenzie." He turned on a heel and strode down the corridor. He got to the bottom of the stairs, only to find the knight walking towards him, a letter in his hand.

"Your Grace," he said, sounding breathless. "Colwyn has… left the castle."

"What?!" Bodine exclaimed, his eyes suddenly flashing almost transparent.

"A page has delivered this note to me. She has… well, read it for yourself." He handed the paper over to him and watched as the duke's expression hardened.

He crumpled the paper in his fist. "Where is she likely to have gone?" he asked in an even-toned whisper, surprising considering his mood.

MacKenzie took a deep breath as he pondered the question. "Are we sure she's really left, and isn't hiding behind the library, or somewhere else in the castle?"

"Well, there's one way to find out!" He crossed the hallway and ran up the other set of steps, MacKenzie on his heels.

The room behind the library was empty. She wasn't there. Bodine felt his temper shortening again, something he usually managed to keep tightly under control, but Colwyn appeared to have developed the art of making him lose it.

"Sir John?" he questioned.

MacKenzie shook his head. "I can't think of anywhere…" his voice trailed off. "She wouldn't dare have…"

"Have what?" Bodine demanded.

"Left the castle. If she's left the castle, I can only think of one place she could have gone… the hunting lodge in the woods."

"What?!"

MacKenzie kept quiet. He had never seen the duke look as angry as he was looking at that moment. Without another word, Bodine returned to Colwyn's rooms.

"Your Grace, my Lady's riding leathers and saddlebags are missing, as well as some clothes," she told him.

He nodded grimly, ran to his room to grab his sword and his jacket, then headed for the stables.

Storm was missing, and the stable boy told him Colwyn had ridden him out about four hours ago. Night was beginning to fall. Bodine had no idea where the hunting lodge was, but he'd find it. He could have asked MacKenzie, but he didn't want anyone with him when he found her.

After saddling Banner, Bodine rode out of the castle towards the woods. There was a lot of ground to cover, but he did have one trick up his sleeve. He halted and sat quietly, concentrating, then reached out a gossamer thread of thought. After a few minutes, he detected just the merest hint, and headed east, into the woods.

It was dark when he found the lodge, at the edge of a large lake, with a full moon reflecting off it, creating eerily lighted shadows all around. Dismounting a little distance away, he led Banner to the stable and sure enough, there was Storm, happily munching away on some hay. Having made his own horse comfortable, he strode towards the lodge, then carefully peered through a window. As expected, Colwyn was in there, relaxing in a chair in front of a fire. Bodine admitted he was impressed. She was certainly not the helpless lady of breeding like the majority of her sex.

Without any preamble, he unlatched the door and kicked it so hard that it swung back on its hinges and hit the wall with a loud crash, breaking the

Chapter Sixteen

silence, before swinging back towards him. He stopped it easily with a hand as he entered and closed it behind him. The loud noise had the desired effect; she jumped violently and leapt to her feet, her expression a mixture of fright, disbelief and shock at seeing him standing there.

"H-how did you find me?" she finally managed to demand of him.

"Our link," he replied.

She heard the barely contained anger in his voice.

"But I... I blocked you."

"My dear Colwyn," he said in a mocking tone, "you have no idea what I am capable of."

She swallowed nervously and began to think she had made a mistake with this hare-brained scheme of hers, especially as she observed the expression on his face.

"Did you honestly think that I would not be able to find you?"

"No, but I thought it would take longer," she confessed.

He stepped towards her, and she drew her sword, which had been resting on the table. "No closer, Morgan."

His eyebrows rose in surprise. *Really?* he thought.

"And you think that is going to stop me?"

She swallowed slowly and lifted the sword, determination written over her face.

Bodine sighed. "I'd have thought you'd have learnt your lesson this afternoon," he said, pulling off his jacket and drawing his own sword.

Defiantly, she held her head high and slowly moved around the room. She wasn't really sure what her plan was. As she hadn't expected him to find her this quickly, she had changed, and so wasn't really dressed for battle, but that wasn't going to stop her. Of course, she was not going to win, but she had vowed not to make it easy for him.

He toyed with her as she attacked him, easily defending against her. She seemed unwavering in her resolve to keep him at bay, but after fifteen minutes, Bodine grew tired of her game and manoeuvred her back into a corner before she finished up with the point of his sword against her breast.

"Enough," he ordered. "Drop your sword."

Out of the corner of his eye, he saw her grip alter slightly on her weapon, and moved his sword, increasing the pressure on her chest until she winced.

"I said, drop it."

Her grip slackened, and the sword dropped to the floor with a loud crash.

"That's better," he said, but the anger in his voice was still clearly evident.

Colwyn sighed, and as Bodine reached out to take her firmly by an arm, she ducked under him and ran for the stairs. She was slight of build, lithe and fast, and reached the top of the stairs before he had reached the bottom of them.

She darted into the bedroom she had prepared, slammed the door shut and locked it. *There, that should hold you for a while*, she thought, then sobered, realising he was going to be really, really angry; but being a redhead, she dismissed that thought. If he wanted a fight, she'd give him one.

Bodine bounded up the stairs two at a time and tried the door. It didn't budge.

"Colwyn! Colwyn, open this door!" he shouted authoritatively.

"Go away!" came the muffled reply.

"Open the door, before I break it down!"

"No!"

Bodine's expression hardened. He tried one last time. "I am your husband; do as I say and open the door!"

"No! Go away!"

The duke stepped back and kicked it experimentally. As he expected, it held. The door was solid and there was no way it was going to surrender to

Chapter Sixteen

any physical abuse his booted foot could throw at it; so he stopped and cursed silently.

He tried not to use magic at all, as the Kadeau were still feared, but sometimes, he realised, there really was no choice; however, he decided to give Colwyn one last chance.

"Colwyn, I am your husband; you are my wife. I'm giving you one last chance to unlock this door, or you will suffer the consequences."

She would not be able to interpret that last sentence in any other way but a threat, and he hoped she would see sense.

A few minutes passed and there was no sound from the bed-chamber. Bodine sighed. He clasped his hands to clear his mind, took several deep breaths, then stared at the lock of the door and whispered, "*reserare ianuam.*"

There was a click and Bodine reached out and turned the handle. The door opened and he stepped through to find Colwyn getting to her feet, a look of shock and surprise on her face.

"There will be no locked doors between us," he said as he walked towards her.

She backed away from him. Dare she push him? A stupid question; she was a redhead; hot hot-tempered, hot-blooded, and renowned for pushing the boundaries. Colwyn made a dash for the open door, but Bodine waved his hand and it slammed shut.

Horrified, she whirled round and found him mere inches away from her. His arms came up and he trapped her between them, her back against the door. The duke took several deep breaths that were supposed to calm him. The last thing he wanted to do was frighten her, but linked to her as he was, all it did was heighten the smell of her femininity and the fact she was ready.

Being a Kadeau had some disadvantages, and this was one of them. God forgive him, he wanted to rip her dress off her body, but he somehow managed to refrain.

"No, not tonight, Morgan, please," Colwyn said.

"I'm sorry, my love, but I have need of you tonight." His kiss was feather-light and he nuzzled her ear, breathing heavily.

She squirmed and pushed against his chest. "No," she said. "Not tonight."

"I need you… I want you," he whispered back.

"I said no."

"You are my wife," he hissed back.

Colwyn knew she was on dangerous ground, but continued to push.

"I may be your wife, but I have my rights and my own mind." She held her head up defiantly at him, hoping that he would not back down. She pulled herself free of him yet again and walked away.

"Stop!" he ordered and she smiled secretly to herself, carefully keeping her shields intact so he had no idea what she was thinking.

"Make me," she threw back at him and continued towards the other side of the room. She managed to reach the far wall before he caught her. She turned to face him and saw his grey eyes were almost transparent… his temper was rising, just as she hoped.

He tried to kiss her, but she fought him.

"I told you once before, I'll not be the meek little wife if I don't want to, and tonight, I don't want to." Purposely, she breathed hard, straining the material over her breasts.

Bodine held her against the wall with his body and kissed her hard. She struggled against him, pushed him back and slapped him. It had the desired effect. Eyes blazing, he wrenched her gown open, pushed it off her shoulders and ripped her chemise. She continued to fight him, and he dragged her, none too gently, to her bed and threw her down on it. Discarding his shirt, he threw it aside and joined her on the bed, kneeling astride her. She froze as the knife he always carried when travelling, sheathed on his left arm,

Chapter Sixteen

appeared in his hand, and he unceremoniously sliced open her clothing, before discarding the weapon and attacking her body again.

Again, she struggled, acutely aware of his growing arousal as he savagely ravaged her body. They were both breathing heavily when they parted again, and as Bodine knelt up, taking in the sight of her heaving breasts, he noticed the strange, wild look in her eyes and froze, uncertain, until she lifted a hand and placed it on his crotch, squeezing encouragingly, rubbing her hand against his breeches and he unconsciously moved his hips against her. She felt his arousal growing and smiled inwardly as she continued to fondle him.

Bending down, he inflicted bruising kisses, but she didn't care, she was liking this wild side of him; Bodine unleashed was exciting, but she wondered just how far she could really push him before it got too far out of hand. So, she struggled a little more, enjoying the rougher way he was handling her. His hand moved between her thighs, his touch firm and demanding.

Then, totally unexpectedly, he flipped her over onto her front and pulled her onto her knees. This was something new, she thought, as he knelt behind her and pulled her back against his chest. He nuzzled into her neck whilst one hand fondled her breasts and the other touched her intimately. Unable to stop herself, she moaned and fidgeted against him, feeling his manhood hardening rapidly. Within minutes, she was writhing, rubbing herself against his fingers.

He hadn't said a word the entire time. Instead, he released her and used a hand on her neck to push her forward onto her hands and knees before running a hand down her spine, whilst his other fumbled urgently with the lacings of his breeches, and then she felt him nudging for entry. He had never taken her in this position before. Grasping her buttocks, she felt him rub himself against her, and then suddenly, he thrust firmly, deeply, and she gasped at the depth of the penetration. This was a totally different feeling, but something was stirring within, a new sensation as he continued to thrust deeply and she found herself moaning under the onslaught. The thrusts were harder, deeper than she had ever felt before and then she felt him shudder and cry out as he climaxed. As he collapsed onto her, she reached a spasmodic orgasm and fell flat on the bed with his weight on her, but she didn't mind in the slightest.

It took him a few minutes to recover, then he withdrew and rolled onto his side beside her, breathing heavily. She turned her head to face him, a wild glint still in her eyes, and smiled seductively. Bodine frowned at her, slightly suspicious, as she reached out with a hand and ran it seductively over his chest, before moving and dragging herself close to him, so she could kiss him.

He drew his head back, at a total loss to understand her actions, so she kissed his throat instead, and worked her way down his chest.

"What are you playing at?" he finally asked her, as he felt the heat already beginning to rise again within his body. He grabbed her wrist and stopped her hand from moving any further.

She studied him from under her eyelashes. "I wanted my husband out of control. You are always so measured; precise… I was curious to see if I could… anger you… make you… wilder. It worked to some extent."

"You mean you purposely played hard to get; angered me, to…?"

"Yes," she admitted freely.

"You devious…. vixen!" he exclaimed.

"Did you not enjoy it, Morgan?"

"No! I…" his voice trailed off and he stared at her.

"You did enjoy it," she challenged, as she watched the expression on his face change to a mixture of realisation, horror and even shame.

She shifted so she could use her other hand to start teasing him again and he was forced to pin her down so he could attempt to finish the conversation that had been started, but again, she was uncooperative, and in the end, he possessed her again, before removing his boots and breeches, and took her

Chapter Sixteen

again and again, until exhaustion claimed her, and she fell asleep in his arms, sated and satisfied.

They both slept late the following morning, and it was sun streaming through the window that woke Bodine. He jerked awake, slightly disorientated at first, then shifted his gaze, and Colwyn snuggled closer to him, unconsciously moulding her body to his.

Faintly, he heard the birds singing in the trees outside and relaxed again, listening to their song of the approaching winter.

The next thing he was aware of was the heat in his groin as Colwyn caressed his body and awakened him to arousal, encouraging him to possess her once more, and he did, with enthusiasm.

They spent another night of passion in the lodge and returned to Inver the following day to return to their duties.

It was noted that Bodine appeared to have an extra spring in his step on his return to the castle.

Chapter Seventeen

All too soon, November arrived, and it was time to leave for Rossmere. Tearful farewells took place, and they all mounted up and left Inver Castle. The return journey took nine days, due to the shorter days and more harsh weather, but they all arrived safely. Edward was waiting, as he usually did, at the base of the steps and bid them all welcome.

"My Lord, my Lady; welcome home. A letter arrived this morning from Ellesmere. I believe it is from the Princess Anne."

Colwyn idly bit her lip, hoping that it bore good news about Anne's condition. Bodine glanced at her; he had felt the thought in his mind, and smiled gently.

We will soon find out, he sent through the link, as he took her hand and led her into the keep.

"I will bring the letter to your rooms, and we will open it together," he said softly, and they went their separate ways.

The fires were burning warmly in Colwyn's rooms, for which she was thankful, as it had been a cold journey. Sighing, she sat down in a chair at her dressing table, feeling decidedly weary.

"Come, my Lady; let's get you out of your riding clothes and into something more comfortable," Sarah said. "You look tired; perhaps you should take a nap before dinner."

Chapter Seventeen

Colwyn pulled herself together. "No, I'm fine, Sarah." She took a deep breath and stood up again, allowing Sarah to undress her and help her into a more comfortable, but warm dress.

They had just finished when Bodine arrived, carrying the letter from Princess Anne. He handed it to his wife. "You read it," he said simply, pulling up another chair and sitting opposite her.

Colwyn smiled at him and did as he instructed, breaking the seal and unfolding it.

"My dear Morgan and Colwyn

As you are receiving this letter, you no doubt have some idea of what its contents will contain. I cannot thank you enough for helping me whilst at Inver. I am delighted to tell you that I am with child at last. I pray that it is a boy, for Michael's sake, but a healthy baby will be loved most dearly by both of us.

If there is ever anything we can do for you any time in the future, please do not hesitate to ask.

Thank you
Anne"

"I am pleased for them," Bodine said softly. "With luck, we will be at Ellesmere in time for the birth, if you wish it."

"Thank you, Morgan. I think I would like that."

That evening, they had a quiet meal in Bodine's rooms for their first night home. There was much to do, leading up to Christmas, so he had decided to make the most of the calm before the storm, as it were.

Even though it was cold, Colwyn had decided she still wanted to carry on with her training. As she had learnt to her cost, battles did not always wait for nice weather, and she knew she had to learn to fight, no matter the conditions, so she went to the Pell every day, even if it was only for half an hour, and the days developed into a pattern; ducal duties, training, visiting, needlework. At night, she either slept in her own bed with her husband, or in his, enfolded in one another's arms as they slept, or they made love. He was passionate but gentle.

Time slipped by and it was as they approached the middle of December that Colwyn realised something was amiss and she had missed two cycles.

She said nothing to Bodine, but she became a little withdrawn and thoughtful. Sarah noticed the change in her and decided to speak up one morning.

"My Lady, what ails you? You seem quiet and subdued."

Colwyn flashed her a weak, not very convincing smile, and shook her head. "Nothing, Sarah," she finally replied. "I think it's just this miserable weather."

"Are you sure it's nothing else?" Sarah sounded doubtful. Her lady was always full of life.

"No, it's nothing else," she said, as her maid helped her out of bed. She stood up; suddenly feeling queasy, she ran to the garderobe, but nothing happened. The feeling left her and she returned to her bedroom.

"Oh, my Lady," Sarah breathed. "You are with child!"

Colwyn went white; her bottom lip trembled and she burst into tears.

"Now, now," Sarah soothed as she took her in her arms and rocked her gently. "Does his Grace know?"

She shook her head.

"When did you fall?"

"I'm not sure…" Her voice trailed off.

"How many cycles have you missed?"

"Two."

"Mmmm… possibly September or October then. You aren't showing yet."

Chapter Seventeen

Colwyn sat in silence, thinking, and her mind drifted back to the evening in October when Bodine had said he needed her, and forced entry to her room at the hunting lodge. "October," she whispered half to herself. "He said it would be February! He lied to me!"

"Perhaps it was an accident," Sarah replied.

"He's Kadeau; he knows exactly what he's doing." She felt her anger rising.

"He's a man; what can he know of such things?"

"He knows!" Colwyn said vehemently. "He knew I was frightened at the prospect and he lied to me!"

She stood up.

"Help me dress."

Fifteen minutes later, she was ready.

"My Lady, you must eat something; you have your child to consider."

"I'm not hungry!" she snapped and walked out of her rooms to carry out her ducal duties.

Bodine was waiting for her in the antechamber. "My love," he began, "I was about to come and find you. I sense you are… out of sorts this morning."

"I'm fine," she replied, doing her best to keep her voice normal and failing slightly.

He gave her a long hard stare, but in the end, took her hand, and they went into the main chamber to listen to the various queries, questions and requests.

The morning wore on, and Colwyn began to lose interest. This was not intentional, but she was having problems concentrating and she now wished she had taken breakfast as Sarah had advised.

Finally, they were finished, and she knew she had to eat something soon, as she was beginning to feel light-headed. She took a deep breath, hoping the large lungful of air would make the growing feeling of weakness go away.

Bodine stood up and held out his hand to her. She hesitated, then took it, as he assisted her to her feet.

What's wrong? He queried in her mind.

Nothing, she retorted.

That isn't the truth.

In response, she erected a wall, as solid as she knew how, as they walked towards the antechamber. As they left the room, she started to look for a place to sit for a few moments; her sense of reality was deserting her and she began to feel decidedly faint.

"Colwyn!"

They stopped walking and she glared at him for several seconds, then he saw her expression change; it became vacant; her eyelids fluttered several times, and she crumpled.

Bodine managed to catch her before she hit the floor, and swept her up into his arms, shouting for a page, a squire, anyone within earshot.

Dernley was the first to arrive from the antechamber and skidded to a halt at the sight before him.

"Morgan! What's happened?"

"Find Master Andrew, quickly! Tell him to come to the Duchess's rooms."

"Yes, Morgan." He turned and ran.

The duke strode purposely along the corridors, up the stairs to her rooms, and kicked the door, which was partly ajar. It flew back on its hinges, making Sarah jump and turn, and her hand went to her throat as she saw him come in, carrying Colwyn's limp body.

"Your Grace!" she exclaimed, and ran through to the bed-chamber to pull back the blankets on the bed.

He laid her down gently and touched her cheek.

"How was Colwyn feeling this morning, Sarah?" he asked.

Chapter Seventeen

"She seemed quiet and subdued," Sarah replied, "She ran to the garderobe to be ill, but she wasn't."

A few seconds passed, then realisation dawned. "She is with child," he whispered in awe.

"Pardon me, your Grace, if I am speaking out of turn, but she was very angry and upset; she… she said you lied to her; that it was supposed to be February."

The duke looked at her, guilt in his eyes. "Yes, it was supposed to be then but… she seemed so scared about the prospect, and I re-examined the timeline and realised it had to be sooner. As much as I would have liked the child to be born here, the best midwives are at Ellesmere, so I brought it forward to October. Was she…very angry?"

"Yes, my Lord."

He nodded but got no further, as Master Andrew arrived on the scene with Giles at his side.

"My Lord, Giles said that the Lady Colwyn had fainted." He leant over her seeing the almost waxen complexion.

"Andrew, she is carrying my child."

The battle surgeon's face registered surprise then he broke into a smile. Beside him, Dernley initially looked shocked, then he pulled himself together. He still found it difficult to accept that Colwyn was a woman, and married; not the little girl he had grown up with.

"Congratulations, your Grace, but if this is so, then you need a physician, not me. I'm but a humble battle surgeon."

"I'm not letting a physician near her. I want you to look after her."

"But I—"

"I will trust no other until she is delivered into the hands of Ellesmere's midwives."

Andrew swallowed, and nodded slowly. "Thank you, my Lord. I will do my best, as always." He sat on the edge of the bed, his bag of medical supplies by his side. Then he placed a hand on her forehead before moving it to place fingers on the pulse at her throat. Next, he undid her jacket and loosened her clothing, and placed his ear against her chest, listening to her heart. Finally, he gently felt her abdomen and nodded.

Satisfied, he reached into his bag for his faithful bottle of salts, unstoppered them, and wafted them gently under her nose.

Colwyn unconsciously turned her head away from the pungent smell, but Andrew simply moved the bottle. She moaned and turned her head in the other direction, and a hand came up to push the offending article away. Her eyelids flickered, and slowly, she opened them, to see four concerned faces peering at her.

Satisfied, Andrew put the cork back in the bottle, put it back in his bag, then rose from the bed and pulled several blankets up over her slender form.

"Sarah, you must keep her warm, and feed her rich broth. Ensure it has meat and blood in it, as well as a good mixture of vegetables."

Bodine took his place, sitting by her side on the bed, and took her hand. "My love, how are you feeling?"

"What happened?" she asked in a whisper, ignoring his question.

"You fainted," Andrew answered. "Tell me, Colwyn, how far along are you?"

Colour returned to her face at his question. "Around eleven weeks," she finally admitted and dared to glance at her husband, albeit briefly, conscious of his thumb, gently stroking the back of her hand. She looked up at him again and saw the expression in his eyes. How could she remain mad at him when he looked at her with such love and concern?

"Can we get you anything?" Dernley dared to ask.

"I... I would like something to eat. I missed breakfast."

Chapter Seventeen

"Aha," Andrew said. "You must not miss your meals, your Grace. It is important for you to eat regularly and well now, to give your child the best chance of survival. If you feel tired, then you must rest."

"You're not confining me to my bed, are you?"

"Goodness, no," Andrew replied. "But you must not overdo things. You are a Lady-in-Waiting, in the true sense of the word."

Sarah quietly left the room to arrange for food to be brought up, then returned to her mistress's side, assisting her to sit up, and placing pillows and cushions behind her to make her comfortable. Dernley and Master Andrew left, and Bodine gave Sarah a look that indicated for her to leave the room so he could talk to his wife alone. He waited until she had left and shut the door before looking back at Colwyn.

"Are you not talking to me?" he asked softly.

She stared at him, meeting his gaze. "I am angry with you."

"Sarah said that you feel I lied to you."

"You did! You said we would not try for a child until February. You knew I was nervous about it, and yet you came looking for me at the lodge in October and… and I fell."

"Wait one moment; you were the one who instigated the game that night! You pushed me almost beyond total control because that's what you wanted," Bodine countered.

"But you knew I was ready; you didn't have to come that night. You were determined."

"I knew you were nervous about it and was worried that it could affect the outcome. I also re-evaluated the timeline and realised that if the baby was to be born at Ellesmere, where the best midwives are, I needed to bring it forward. I did not tell you because I wanted you to be relaxed, and enjoy our love-making, as you normally do." He reached out to take her hand again. "Will you forgive me?"

Colwyn stayed silent.

"The child is a product of our love for one another. I am sorry I wasn't completely honest with you, but I didn't want to frighten you; please believe that is true. I love you with all my heart."

"We were supposed to be completely honest with each other in this relationship. I feel like you have deceived me. I'm sorry, Morgan, but I will have to learn to trust you again. Now, please go."

"Colwyn…"

"Go!" She pulled her hand free from his and looked away.

"Colwyn…" he tried again.

"Get out!"

He drew back as if she had struck him. She did not want to listen to his excuses; she was still angry. He took a deep breath and stood up. Reluctantly, he would give her the space she needed. When she was ready, he would be there and, without another word, he turned and left.

Colwyn watched him leave, and as the door shut behind him, she felt her resolve leave her, and she cursed her weakness as the tears began to fall.

18

Chapter Eighteen

A week went by and the only time Colwyn had seen Bodine was during their ducal duties in the main chamber. Regardless of how she felt about the way he had treated her, her sense of duty would not let her shirk her responsibilities to the duchy, even though it was the Duke of Rossmere's stronghold. However, she would not let him touch her, or help her; nor would she meet his eyes, for she knew if she did, she would forgive him instantly, and she was not yet ready to do so.

Bodine suffered in silence. He yearned to touch her, to hold her in his arms, to kiss her and make love to her. As her husband, he knew he was within his rights to do all those things, but he also knew that would destroy their relationship totally and, grudgingly, he admitted it was his actions, lack of honesty and failure to talk openly that had led to the current situation. Five months on and their marriage was teetering on the edge of a precipice.

Colwyn found the nights the worst to bear. It was lonely and emotionally cold without him next to her to keep her warm, especially now it was winter. She ached for him but did her best to be stubborn and not give in to how she felt.

On the tenth day, she dared to glance at him when he was not aware of her doing so, and noticed a hardness about his mouth that had not been there before, and a sadness in his eyes when he had swept the room, and she found herself wavering.

A movement in the corner of her eye caught her attention, and she saw Dernley looking at her with such a sad expression that she felt tears forming. She faced the front again and blinked them away, realising that he knew all was not right with her relationship with her husband.

The main chamber emptied; their duty was done once again for the day and as he had done every single time, Bodine held out his hand, ever hopeful that Colwyn would finally yield and allow them to start rebuilding their relationship.

As always, it seemed as if an eternity passed, and as he was about to lower his hand and step back, she tentatively raised hers. His pale eyes flashed hopefully. Somehow, he stopped himself from grabbing at it like a drowning man floundering around in the water, trying to prevent himself from sinking below the surface, and gently took it. He dared to kiss the back of it and waited until she had risen from the chair before placing her hand on his left arm to lead her towards the antechamber.

"My love, may I escort you to your rooms?" he asked, sounding hopeful.

Colwyn could feel the carefully controlled emotion of hope trickle through their link and dared to search his expressive face. How could she stay mad at him for so long?

"Yes, Morgan," she finally replied, and saw a smile light up his face; but she wondered where her knight was. Her Morgan was sure, confident, master of his domain, and she desperately wanted him back. Colwyn had the good grace to admit that she was the cause and that he was in fact desperately in love with her; as much as she was in love with him.

She purposely walked slowly back to her room, and Bodine adjusted his stride to match hers. They walked in silence all the way. At the door to her room, he paused and dared to speak.

Chapter Eighteen

"Will you join me for dinner this evening?"

She considered his question for a few moments and decided to surrender. The pregnancy was wearing, even in these early stages, and she was feeling tired.

"Yes, I will join you."

The smile he gave her lit up his face and Colwyn felt her heart miss a beat. He brought her hand to his lips, deciding not to try and kiss her invitingly full lips as he wanted to. *Later. Be patient*, he told himself. Bridges needed to be built.

"You look tired; will you rest?"

"I will have something to eat and then take a nap, so I am refreshed for this evening."

"Until tonight then, my love."

Reluctantly, he let go of her hand, turned, and slowly walked away. Colwyn watched him until he disappeared out of sight round a corner before entering her rooms.

Sarah had food ready and waiting for her, and breathed a sigh of relief as she saw the slight smile on her mistress's face. The rift was healing.

ଔ ଓ ଔ ଓ

That evening, Ioan admitted her to Bodine's rooms and was attentive during the meal, ensuring their goblets remained full, and empty plates cleared away. Finally, though, they had finished. Both of them were thinking exactly the same thing. *What will happen next?*

The duke dismissed his squire for the evening and poured Colwyn a fresh goblet of wine. The silence in the room was almost painfully deafening, and finally, Bodine could stand it no more.

"How are you feeling?" he asked gently.

"On the whole, I am feeling well," she replied.

"I sense a 'but' in there somewhere," he prompted.

"I have to take a nap in the afternoon to get me through the rest of the day," she confessed.

"Are you suffering in the mornings?"

"A little, but Sarah gives me hot water to drink and that seems to do the trick."

He fidgeted in his chair, then reached across the table to take her hand.

"I am truly sorry for lying to you, Colwyn. I was thinking only of you. You seemed so frightened at the prospect of falling, I… I was worried that you wouldn't fall, and I didn't want to fail the King."

She stared hard at him, understanding why he had done it, but still angry that he had not discussed the situation with her. Finally, she spoke.

"You must promise me that you will never deceive me again, Morgan. I may be just a woman, and your wife, but I won't stand for it, going forward. If you do anything like that again, our marriage will be over."

She saw his eyes flash, that she dare to speak to him so; that he wasn't used to being talked to that way; that he was lord and master; but he held his tongue, and after what seemed like aeons, he nodded but did not speak. Colwyn decided that wasn't good enough. She wanted his word.

"Swear it, on your seal," she insisted.

There was a lengthy pause before he gave a large sigh. He didn't want to fight; was she really being so unreasonable?

He touched the ring on his right hand. "I swear it," he finally said.

At those words, Colwyn let go of the breath she suddenly realised she had been holding. Now it was time to repair the rift, but she was feeling weary.

"Thank you for your company this evening," she said, rising from her chair. "I am tired. If you will excuse me, I will return to my rooms."

"I had hoped you would stay," he replied stiffly.

Chapter Eighteen

"I am tired, Morgan."

"Then stay, and just let me hold you." He knew he was pushing, but he needed her to remain.

She looked at the hopeful, yet pleading expression on his face and knew she could not deny him. She was desperate for him to enfold her in his arms, but was determined not to make it too easy for him.

He was standing now, in front of her, holding both of her hands. She tilted her head to look up at his face and his expression melted the ice that had surrounded her heart these past ten days.

His kiss was feather-light and she succumbed, leaning towards him as it gradually deepened. How she had missed his kisses and his touch on her body. He let go of her hands and they immediately snaked around him. Bodine was determined to take her breath away with the growing intensity of the kiss and he succeeded, as he felt her legs buckle. Immediately, he swept her up into his arms and walked through into the bed-chamber, where he put her back on her feet and proceeded to slowly undress her.

"Morgan," she protested, "I...I can't."

"I understand," he soothed. "Just sleep with me, in my arms, that's all I ask."

Her feeble denial died on her lips as he kissed her again, at the same time, sweeping her chemise off her shoulders to lie in a heap on the floor. He stepped back and appraised her body, noticing the beginning of a swell of her belly, indicating the existence of the growing life within her. Suddenly overcome, he reached out and placed a hand on her stomach, feeling the slight curve beneath his fingers, then knelt before her, and gently placed a kiss there, making Colwyn blush.

Unable to resist, she ran her fingers through his burnished gold hair, hugged him as he got back to his feet, then slowly unlaced his shirt and helped him out of it. She ran her hands over his chest, over the light dusting of hair there, and smiled as he closed his eyes and took a deep breath, clearly absorbing the feel of her hands on him.

Confidently, she loosened the lacings on his breeches and eased them off over his hips. Bodine completed the task, removing them, along with his boots, before pulling back the bedsheets, lifting her into his arms once again, and depositing her gently on the bed. He joined her and pulled the covers back over them to keep the chill out, then settled her into his arms, content to just hold her, but Colwyn found she wanted more than to just to be held in his arms. Slowly, she ran a hand down his body and heard his sharp intake of breath as she rested it on his manhood. She shifted her head so she could look up into his face. The pale eyes looked at her intently and his hand moved to rest on her breast, squeezing softly.

They caressed and kissed one another, but it wasn't enough; they hungered for each other, but Bodine was uncertain; he did not wish to harm the child she carried, but she seemed insistent.

"If we are careful, Morgan…please." Her hold on him became firmer and he felt himself responding favourably as she aroused him.

Carefully, he touched her intimately, hoping that would suffice, but instead, she moved to sit astride his hips.

"Colwyn, I really don't think we should… the child…" His breath caught in his throat as she sheathed him within her.

Their love-making was slow and sensuous; Bodine was careful how he moved and handled her that night, and, finally spent, they enfolded themselves in one another's arms.

"I love you, so much," Colwyn said, finally speaking at last.

He laid his hand back on the slight swell of her belly. "Soon, we will be complete; but you must take things carefully."

"Morgan, I am not sick, I am carrying our child."

Chapter Eighteen

"The most precious thing of our union. He will be the Prince's protector, and replace me as General of the Armies."

"But… but what if it's a girl?"

"Then she will be Queen, and still a protector of the crown."

He kissed her tenderly, then gradually they relaxed into sleep, dreaming of the future that awaited them.

☙ ❦ ☙ ❦ ❦

Character Map

Master Andrew	Battle surgeon to Morgan Bodine
William Aulean	Bishop of Inver
Morgan Bodine	Duke of Rossmere, King's Champion and General of the Armies. A Kadeau with magical powers.
Anne Cantrell	Princess and wife of Michael
Alexandra Cantrell	Queen of Devonmere, wife of Stuart, mother of Prince Llewellyn
Llewellyn Cantrell	Prince and heir to Devonmere, son of Stuart and Alexandra
Michael Cantrell	Prince of Devonmere, brother to Stuart
Stuart Cantrell	King of Devonmere, husband of Alexandra, father of Prince Llewellyn
Bronwyn Coltrane	Duchess of Invermere, wife of Richard, mother of Colwyn
Colwyn Coltrane	Daughter of Richard and Bronwyn
Richard Coltrane	Duke of Invermere, husband of Bronwyn, father of Colwyn and one of the most trusted Dukes of Devonmere
Giles Dernley	Son of Kenneth Dernley, Duke of Strathmere, currently a squire
Kenneth Dernley	Duke of Strathmere, father of Giles
Master Donald	Battle Surgeon to Nigel McDowell
James Douglas	Bishop of Ellesmere and King's Confessor. Also a Kadeau
Edward	Steward to Morgan Bodine, responsible for the smooth running of the Rossmere estate during the Duke's absence
Sir Darian Forsythe	A knight in the Rossmere army
Ioan	Personal steward to Morgan Bodine
Sir John MacKenzie	Master of Arms for the Duchy of Invermere, in service to Richard Coltrane
Nigel McDowell	Duke of Cottesmere, who dabbles in the black arts
Colin McLeod	A Monsignor in the church, cousin of Morgan Bodine and also a Kadeau.
Mereli McLeod	Mother of Colin, Aunt to Morgan Bodine. Kadeau
Sarah	Colwyn Coltrane's personal handmaiden

Chapter Eighteen

Master Stephen	Stuart Cantrell's Battle Surgeon
Malcolm Talbot	Bishop of Cottesmere
Oliver Treherne	Bishop of Rossmere
Rhobat	King Stuart's most trusted squire

Bibliography

Books which provided the source material for some of the knightly ceremonies:

- C Mill, *History of Chivalry* (London, 1841)
- W.C. Meller, *A Knight's Life in Days of Chivalry* (London, 1924)
- Richard Barber, *The Knight and Chivalry* (Longmans, 1970)
- Julek Heller & Deirdre Headon, *Knights* (Bellew & Higton, 1982)